Praise for *Mahu: A Hawai...*

"Plakcy deftly keeps up the tension of the hunt for the killer and the exoneration of Kimo, who is suspended from the force. In addition, Plakcy weaves in the emotions of Kimo's relation with his family, as they all, including Kimo, come to terms with reality and find the courage to love."
—*Lavender*

"*Māhū* is a tale told with old-fashioned, square-jawed masculine values. [The book] also knows to not take itself too seriously, as it maintains a kind of simple, eager energy all throughout that harkens back to this literary genre's dime-store, detective serial comic origins."
—AfterElton

"The author has a keen appreciation of the pleasures of the island, especially the joys of surfing. He has an even keener appreciation for the many cultures that make up Hawai'i. The novel explores the strength of familial ties, in particular different kinds of relationships between fathers and sons. For a variety of reasons, then, the book can be recommended to a wide audience."
—*Reviewing the Evidence*

"*Māhū* shows a great deal of knowledge, in the author's part, about Hawai'ian people, language and culture. [The] combination of personal drama and exciting mystery—not to mention the Hawai'ian setting—makes *Māhū* such an original and interesting novel."
—*The Book Nook*

"A wonderful debut for this first mystery . . . skillfully intermixed with Kimo's self-discovery is a tightly constructed crime novel."
—*Spinetingler*

"In this carefully paced mystery, Plakcy manages something most mystery writers struggle for years to achieve—he knows his hero inside out. He's a character you can care about, a character you can root for."
—*GayWebMonkey*

Other Books by Neil S. Plakcy

Mahu Surfer
Mahu Fire
Mahu Vice (2009)

Paws and Reflect: Exploring a Special Bond Between Man and Dog
(co-authored with Sharon Sakson)

MAHU

A Hawai'ian Mystery

NEIL S. PLAKCY

ALYSON*books*

© 2005, 2009 by Neil S. Plakcy

Manufactured in the United States of America

This trade paperback is published by Alyson Books,
245 West 17th Street, New York, NY 10011

Distribution in the United Kingdom by Turnaround Publisher Services Ltd.
Unit 3, Olympia Trading Estate, Coburg Road, Wood Green
London N22 6TZ England

FIRST ALYSON BOOKS EDITION: 2009

FIRST EDITION BY HARRINGTON PARK PRESS: 2005

09 10 11 12 13 14 15 16 17 18 a 10 9 8 7 6 5 4 3 2 1

ISBN 1-59350-082-3

ISBN-13 978-1-59350-082-5

(Previously published with ISBN 1-56023-533-0 by Harrington Park Press)

Library of Congress Cataloging-in-Publication data are on file.

Cover design by Victor Mingovits

PREFACE TO THE NEW EDITION

When I first started writing about a surfer named Kimo Kanapa'aka back in 1992, I had no idea that the character would take such a hold of my imagination. I have now written nearly twenty stories, both mysteries and erotica, about his adventures, and I'm currently working on the fifth novel in the series.

Along the way, I've tried to understand Kimo's appeal—both to me, and to the many readers who have written and emailed. I think the secret is that he's a guy who's trying to do the right thing, even when it's difficult. Sometimes he succeeds, and sometimes he makes a mistake and tries to learn from it.

After I finished the final draft of *Māhū* and sent it off to my publisher, I couldn't stop thinking about Kimo. Like him, I came out of the closet somewhat later in life, and I realized that the process didn't stop the first time I told another person that I was gay. I thought it would be interesting to put Kimo through those same steps—first kiss, first date, first gay friends, first real boyfriend, and so on.

At the same time, I have tried to find cases for him to solve that force him to confront these issues, and to accept his place in the larger gay community. As a college professor, I feel it's important to be a role model to my students, and I've given Kimo that same desire. He's not just a cop, he's a gay cop, and that extra designation carries a lot of responsibility, both to himself, the GLBT community, and his employers, the City and County of Honolulu.

I am delighted that Alyson has chosen to reissue *Māhū*, and hope that this new edition will serve as an introduction to Kimo for new readers. Thanks to Dale Cunningham, Anthony LaSasso, Paul Florez, and all the folks at Alyson who have made this possible. Thanks also to Jay Quinn and Greg Herren, my original editors at Haworth Press, who gave Kimo his first chance to shine.

ACKNOWLEDGMENTS

This book is for Marc, my love and my inspiration, and for the dogs who give us so much unconditional love: Sam, and in memory of Pierre, Charlie, and sweet Mr. Gus.

Thanks to Steve Greenberg, Pam Reinhardt, and Vicki Hendricks, my earliest readers, and to my mother, Shirley Plakcy, for all her love and support. Jim Hall, my MFA thesis advisor, read a very early draft of this book and convinced me I had to know more about Kimo before I could proceed. Lynne Barrett, Les Standiford, and John Dufresne are great instructors at Florida International University's creative writing program, who provide instruction, mentoring, and friendship in equal doses.

Thanks to Caren and Tom Neile and Ginny and David Wells, for all the encouragement, advice, and editing over the years, as well as to all my FIU classmates and friends. Thanks also to Dan Jaffe, who gave Kimo his first literary exposure in *Blithe House Quarterly*. Other faithful friends and readers were David Beaty, Karen Blomain, Jessie Dolch, Lynne DuVivier, Jill Freeman, Sally Huxley, Christine Kling, Kathy Lawrence, Eileen Matluck, Stewart O'Nan, Barbara Parker, Ginny Rorby, Sharon Sakson, and Andrew Schulz.

Thanks to Maury Blitz and Morena Carvalho for help with the *Māhū* logo. Robert Phillips introduced me to the range of authors writing mysteries with gay detectives, for which I am quite grateful. Al "Woody" Wood checked my surfer terminology. Finally, thanks to Mr. Norman Haider, my tenth-grade English teacher at Charles Boehm Senior High, who first showed me how rewarding writing could be, and to all the other teachers who encouraged me.

Chapter 1

THE EXCHANGE WAS SET for six o'clock, under the arbor that ran between the zoo and the old aquatic stadium where Duke Kahanamoku swam for his records. By that time, as the sun was beginning its nightly drop into the darkening sea, there were still enough strollers and fishermen to provide cover, but not enough people to make the place crowded. I was dressed like a moke, a Hawai'ian criminal, in a grubby T-shirt from a surfing contest I'd lost years before, a pair of low-slung shorts, and worn tennis shoes. I had a tattered backpack slung over one shoulder, and inside it were stacks of twenties and fifties that had been treated with fluorescent powder. I hadn't shaved for two days, and when an elderly couple wearing matching aloha shirts gave me a wide berth on the sidewalk along Kalākaua Avenue, I knew the look was complete.

Tourists were packing up on the beach, toting their blankets and suntan lotion back toward the motels and time shares on the mauka, or mountain, side of Kalākaua. Japanese businessmen were stopping in at the chic boutiques, using their strong yen to buy European designer goods for neglected families back home. And somewhere in the distance I heard the rattle of an ipu gourd and the pound of a pahu hula, a sharkskin drum. That meant a hotel or bar was starting its hula happy hour for the Midwesterners among us, a chance for Grandpa to get up and dance the hula with a pretty wahine while Grandma trained the videocam on him for the folks back home, and everybody got brightly colored drinks with little umbrellas.

Across the street, I saw my partner, Akoni, a beefy Hawai'ian who went through the academy with me. We were an odd-couple pair, me tall and slim, Akoni short and stout. He had more pure Hawai'ian blood in him, and darker skin. My father was half Hawai'ian and half haole, or white, so even with a deep tan I was still fairer than Akoni. He wore a double-extra-large aloha shirt in a bright pink and red pattern, shorts, and tennis sneakers, and he looked like one of those guys at the beach who rent out the surfboards. He looked pointedly at his watch. I nodded slightly and crossed the street diagonally at Kapahulu, past the lovely Hawai'ian-style Denny's, with its second-floor porch overlooking the beach, where you can get papaya with your Grand Slam breakfast.

I followed the shoreline under the big spreading banyan tree, walking along the beach called Queen's Surf, which ran alongside Kapiolani Park. There was a volleyball net on the beach, and then a breakwater, and then the beach got really narrow.

That narrow section was the gay beach. About a dozen guys were on the sand there, even though the tide was coming in, bringing with it scattered leaves and seaweed. There were fat guys and fit guys, guys wearing everything from the briefest of thongs to double extra-large swim trunks. Another ten or fifteen guys sat on the grass and benches, one group on towels under a palm tree. A guy with both nipples pierced winked at me and I quickly looked offshore, where a snorkeler swam toward Diamond Head, as if he was heading to the same rendezvous I was. Beyond him a range of sailboats and fishing boats cruised the glowing water.

A kid on a skateboard zoomed past, then stopped nearly in front of me to practice a jump, which he missed. I was jittery and I wanted to yell at him, flash my badge and give him the kind of scare he'd given me, but I held back. I headed along the narrow walkway behind the zoo, trying to concentrate on the shallow blue-green water, think only about the barnacle-encrusted pipe that rests on the sea floor and stretches out toward the horizon, bringing in deep, pure water for the aquarium behind me. But it didn't work; I kept thinking of the bust.

Akoni was behind me. One of the fishermen along the shore, Lou See, was a member of the SWAT team, and he had a .357 Magnum in a shoulder holster under his baggy shirt, and a second in his creel. Evan Gonsalves, who was our link to the state's import cops, was at the end of the path, waiting to monitor my conversation on a radio. I knew Evan carried a five-shot Smith & Wesson .38 Undercover, with a two-inch barrel. The two young lovers leaning against a tree were beat cops from the Waikīkī station, Lidia Portuondo and Alvy Greenberg, and I wondered idly if they were enjoying this assignment. I think they were both carrying Smith & Wesson .38s, too.

I walked along behind the aquarium, where the pavement has been patched roughly. A single guard dog barked among the refrigeration equipment, which was poorly camouflaged behind a cluster of succulent hinahina plants with scattered white flowers. The low susurrus of the surf ebbed and flowed through my consciousness, and I breathed deeply, smelling salt air, car exhaust, and the low, sweet perfume of coconut tanning oil.

The week before, a source had told me about a shipment of heroin coming in from Mexico, a kind they call black tar. It was cruder than the heroin produced in Asia and sold on the streets for up to $100 per quarter gram. It was smoked rather than injected, and that made it easier to get into, especially for teenagers. I was about to buy a pound of the stuff, with a street value of $150,000. If I didn't screw anything up.

I got to the front of the stadium, by the big stucco gates sealed off with chain-link fence, and waited. I looked up at the gates, thirty feet high, with Ionic pilasters and THE WAR MEMORIAL written on a lintel above. On either side of the Hawai'i state seal above that were a pair of eagles, only the one on the Diamond Head side had lost his head, just a metal rod sticking up out of his neck. On the fence, signs said NO TRESPASSING and DANGER: FALLING ROCKS. I looked through the fence out at the pool and the ocean beyond, waves breaking on the deep blue water, the dying sun glinting off the crests of the surf.

A battered blue pickup stopped at the curb, and two Mexicans got out. When I met them at a seedy bar down near Fort DeRussy, they presented themselves to me as college kids on vacation, doing a favor for the boy's uncle. The boy, Pedro, had said it was a way to finance the trip. His girlfriend's name was Luz Maria, and she was the one I didn't trust. There was something cold about her mouth, a determination that was a little scary. I had the feeling she was along to keep Pedro in line.

As I started walking toward them, across the faded brown concrete worn down by sun and time, I heard a phone ring and saw Luz Maria open up a cell phone. She spoke for just a moment, then turned to Pedro and said something. They both turned and ran for the truck.

"Shit, something's gone wrong," I heard Evan say through my earpiece. Cops erupted from their hiding places and began to chase the Mexican, dodging mothers with strollers and tourists in aloha shirts so new they still had the original creases. I saw Luz Maria take the briefcase from Pedro and toss it in a high, sailing arc. It landed on the rail surrounding the truck bed, teetered there for an instant, and fell into the bed. Almost simultaneously, the driver of the truck floored the engine and it squealed off down Diamond Head Road.

I was the closest, and I tackled Luz Maria just seconds after she threw away the briefcase. We scuffled, each of us struggling to get a purchase on the other. For those few minutes, everything moved in slow motion. I felt the sinews in her biceps, smelled her earthy scent, an accumulation of a day or two's sweat. I heard the crackle of a radio behind me and the noise of running footsteps.

I hadn't been that close to a woman in a long time. She twisted and turned under me, grinding her pelvis and breasts against me, simultaneously trying to get my gun and to knee me in the crotch. I outweighed her by fifty pounds and I was on top, but she was strong and lithe.

Then Akoni was there, wrestling her arms behind her back and into a pair of cuffs. I picked up her gun, a small .45, then stood up. I was still charged, feeling nothing but the rush of blood, the electric tension in my fingertips. I knew I'd feel the effects of that tackle the next day. I shook my arms out and did a couple of deep knee bends.

Evan had Pedro flat on the ground with his foot in the small of the college boy's back, and Lidia and Alvy were running along Diamond Head Road, trying to get a plate ID on the pickup. Lou See was already radioing in for the paddy wagon.

Lidia and Alvy returned, empty-handed, and took over custody of the two Mexicans. "Shit, what went wrong?" I asked, as Akoni, Evan, Lou, and I sat down at one of the picnic tables.

"Looked like the woman got a tip-off at the last minute," Lou said. "You saw her on the phone."

"Can we subpoena the phone records?" Evan asked. "Find out who called her?"

I shook my head. "Not without some supporting evidence," I said. "Peggy's not going to be pleased about this one."

Peggy Kaneahe, Assistant DA, was waiting for us at the main station downtown. I had a long history with her—we'd been high school sweethearts, and then broken up after our first year away at college. While I'd come back to Honolulu after four years in California, it had taken her longer, and she'd only returned about six months ago, to take her current job. We'd started dating again, very casually, hadn't even gone to bed yet. As she'd put it, "In my job all I meet are cops and criminals. And if I'm going to date a cop it might as well be one I already know."

There was an edgy tension between us even at the best of times, as though she was just waiting for me to hurt her again, and that night we hardly talked except for the bare details of the failed bust. A couple of the guys decided to go to a cop hangout on

Kuhio Avenue, a few blocks mauka from the beach, and I went along. Peggy declined to join us. In Honolulu, we don't use north, east, south, and west. We say something is *mauka,* meaning toward the mountains, or *makai,* meaning toward the sea. That's roughly north and south. West is *ewa,* pronounced like Eva Gabor, after a town beyond the airport. The other direction, toward Diamond Head, we simply call Diamond Head.

I spent some time talking to Evan Gonsalves over the blare of rock and roll from the bar's speakers. It was nice there, under a thatched roof, with a cool trade wind fluttering the paper flyers on the table. Around us, couples cuddled in the shadows, and single men prowled the edges of the dance floor or stood idly around the well-lit bar.

"How's Terri?" I asked Evan. Seven years before, he had married Teresa Clark, whose grandfather had founded Clark's, the biggest department store chain in the islands. Nobody had been more surprised than I was. Terri and I had been friends in high school, but I'd always thought I was out of her league as boyfriend material. When she married a cop, the son of a Portuguese fisherman, I'd joined the crowd in wondering why.

Evan winced. "She worries a lot. You know." He leaned over closer to me, his beery breath in my face. "Sometimes, I wonder what more I can do for her. She deserves a hell of a lot more than I can give her."

Evan was a nice guy. He was handsome and well built, with wavy black hair and intense eyes; he spoke well, and he was clearly on his way up in the police hierarchy. Like everybody else, I'd expected Terri to marry better, somebody with a mainland education and a lot of money. But so far, they'd seemed very happy, with a five-year-old boy they both doted on.

I didn't know what to say. Fortunately, at that point Akoni came over to say good-bye, to head back to his pretty little wife, and so Evan realized it was time for him to go too. A couple of the other single cops and I remained well after midnight, getting progressively drunker as we trolled for wahines.

At least that was what I told myself I was doing. I had a reputation in the department as a love 'em and leave 'em type, because I never seemed to settle down with a girl. It was trendy to pass such problems off as fear of commitment, and Akoni regularly got on my case about growing up and accepting my responsibilities. But I knew the problem went much deeper than that.

By 2 a.m. the cops who were still there had paired off with wahines, except for me. I wasn't interested in a wahine, and I was tired of lying to myself that I was. I hadn't really been in danger that day, but I could have been, and every time I sidestepped trouble I wondered, what if today had been my day? Was I ready to die? Had I lived my life the way I wanted to?

I was more than a little drunk, and horny too, and generally disgusted with myself. On the job, I was pretty fearless. I trusted my instincts, my weapons, and my backup. I went out and did what I had to do. In my personal life, it was a lot harder.

I dropped some money on the table for my beers, waved goodnight, and walked out into the cool velvety darkness. It had turned breezy, and clouds scudded across the canvas of the sky. I saw the crescent moon reflected in the darkened window of a shop that sold thousand-dollar Hawai'ian shirts to Japanese tourists.

Unconsciously I found myself heading for the Rod and Reel Club. It was only a few blocks away, almost on my way home. There had been a couple of incidents of gay bashing outside the club in recent weeks, and I tried to tell myself I was just being a good neighborhood cop, checking out the scene and protecting the population. Right.

From the outside I could hear the thump of a bass line, and when the door opened and a couple of guys spilled out, their arms around each other, I heard the blast of rock and roll. I stood around outside for a couple of minutes, debating whether I should go in or not, and then said to myself, *Shit, Kimo, don't be such a wimp,* and walked inside.

The Rod and Reel Club was decorated like one of those old fishing lodges, wooden paneling and stuffed yellowfin tuna and amberjack on the walls. It had a very masculine feel, but on the walls where you'd expect to see pictures of guys with their fish, there were photos of guys in drag, guys kissing, guys dancing on tables in colored jockstraps.

My heart was pounding harder than it had that evening out behind the zoo. I walked up to the bar and ordered another beer, then found a piece of wall I could lean up against. The bar was partly enclosed and partly open air. From where I stood, under the roof, I could look out to the patio and see long strands of white lights hanging from the high trees. A big-screen TV in the corner was playing the videos that went with the music on the loudspeakers. At that moment they were showing Bob Seger's "Old Time Rock and Roll," probably just so we could see Tom Cruise dancing in his underpants.

I didn't know what I was doing there. I was too scared of AIDS, and of facing the truth about myself, to pick anybody up. Maybe it was some kind of practice run for actually having a life, forcing myself to look in the mirror often enough so that someday I'd be able to look without hating myself. I had known I was attracted to guys since I was about twelve or thirteen, but except for some experimentation I had managed to ignore it. I'd created a personality for myself as a stud, forcing myself to go out night after night, dating and bedding women, hoping the next one would be the one who could change me.

One of the last women I dated was a Minnesota high school phys ed teacher in her mid-twenties, on spring break with a couple of college friends. There wasn't an ounce of fat on her, and she was very athletic in bed, too. It scared me how much I was attracted to her biceps and strong calves. I found myself fantasizing she was a man, and we had the best sex I'd ever had with a woman. It scared the hell out of me.

As my eyes got accustomed to the darkness I started checking out the other guys. The bar was halfway between the dance floor and the patio. About a dozen guys were dancing to the pounding beat, and there were another dozen or so clustered around the bar. A few mixed couples, and a few groups of guys, were seated in the plastic chairs out on the patio.

I took my Longboard Lager and made a slow circuit of the bar and patio area. A gray-haired guy, in his sixties maybe, cruised the room counterclockwise to me, and I had to look away every time we passed. A cute guy in a rugby shirt was leaning up against a palm tree, but he never seemed to look my way. It was easy to find excuses not to talk to anyone. No one seemed able to make eye contact with anyone else, and none of the guys who stood alone appealed to me. One was too thin, another too fat. I couldn't talk to the guy in lime-green bell-bottoms and tank top because he looked too faggy. The two beefy guys in muscle shirts looked too mean, and too caught up in each other anyway.

At the side of the bar was a long hallway. The first two doors I saw were clearly marked KĀNE, for men, and WAHINE, for women. There were other doors, though, farther down the hall, and every now and then someone would come or go down the hallway, and I didn't want to know what was going on back there. Or rather, I did want to know, desperately, but I wouldn't let myself admit it. I found a place by the patio wall where I could see what was going on in the bar, on the patio, and down the hallway. I cradled my beer like it was my only friend, and watched, and waited. A really buffed guy in a tank top kept going up and down the hall, and two Japanese guys holding hands went back there and disappeared.

About half of the guys standing around the bar wore their hair just a little too short or their mustaches a little too trimmed, but others looked like guys you'd see on the street. I started to feel more like there was a chance I might fit in here someday. Of course, it was kind of sad seeing all these guys who couldn't connect with each other, and striving on my part just to get to that level, where I was comfortable enough with myself and my sexuality to stand around in a room full of gay men and not feel desperately awkward.

I was almost through my second lager when a guy came up to me. I was still dressed in my moke outfit, still hadn't shaved. He was tall and thin, gawky as a giraffe, his head shaved so that only a blond stubble remained. He almost passed me, then leaned up close to my ear and whispered, "I like it rough." His tongue grazed the outside of my ear.

I shivered and pushed away. Suddenly I knew I had to get out. If I didn't, I'd do something, I wasn't sure what. I might follow the giraffe into a back room, or punch his lights out, or tear off my clothes and jump up onto a table and dance. I dropped my empty bottle on a table and nearly ran for the door.

Outside, I stood next to a lamppost, gulping moist warm air. A wave of traffic passed on Kuhio Avenue, and a guy in a Miata with the top down cut off a Ford Explorer to make a sharp left. The Ford blasted his horn. My heart was racing again and my hands were shaking. The door to the club opened, and the giraffe stepped outside. I caught his eye, shook my head, and walked around the corner. I found a place in the shadows and slumped against the wall, facing the back door of the club.

The giraffe didn't follow, and I was grateful. It was nearly three, and I was due on the second watch at eight in the morning. If I went home now, I could sleep for a couple of hours and then get out onto the surf by first light. Just me, my board, and the ocean, and I could feel better. I knew I could.

I was almost ready to start home when I heard the sound of somebody dragging something down the alley. I thought it was a manager dragging a trash can out to the street, until I rounded the corner and saw a man bent down low. When he reached the shelter of a kiawe tree by the street, he turned and ran back up the alley.

I heard a car door open and then slam closed, and then a black Jeep Cherokee swung out of the alley behind the club, fishtailing a bit as the driver made his turn. I figured the driver was probably running away from somebody he'd met at the bar. I knew how he felt.

Then I saw the body.

I looked up, making the connection between the dragging sound and the hurried driver, but it was too late; the car had already made the turn onto Kuhio and was gone. I was kicking myself for my slow reactions as I leaned over the guy. Even in the dark, I could see the blood already pooling beneath his head. I felt his neck for a pulse and couldn't get one. "Shit," I said out loud.

I wasn't carrying my cell phone, so I had to jog to the corner, looking for a pay phone. There wasn't one. I went two blocks before I could find one that worked. I dialed 911, and covered the mouthpiece of the phone with my T-shirt. "I want to report a murder," I said, mumbling but trying to get the words out. "Behind the Rod and Reel Club on Kuhio Avenue."

The operator asked, "May I have your name, sir?"

I wanted to go back to the guy in the alley. I didn't want him to be alone. And I knew that as the first officer on the scene I ought to investigate, secure the area. Most crimes are solved within the first twenty-four hours, and I'd been given a golden opportunity to be in at the start of the investigation.

But I didn't want to explain what I was doing back there, long after I'd left my buddies. I spent my time looking for the truth behind other people's lives, but I wasn't prepared to look so closely at my own. After all, despite whatever had happened in my past, I was dating a woman. I was still trying. So despite everything I knew I ought to do, I hung up the phone.

A light breeze swept through the trash along the side of the street. I pulled off my T-shirt and used it to wipe the sweat from my forehead. I started to jog for home, hoping the breeze could blow away my sins.

Chapter 2

KUHIO AVENUE WAS NEARLY DESERTED, as I ran home, just a skinny black guy on the other side of the street going in my direction, and an old woman swathed in layers waddling along on a side street. The air was hot and humid, heavy with the scent of motor oil and crushed plumeria blossoms. The light breeze died as I ran past darkened store windows and lonely hotel lobbies.

All the events of the evening seemed to catch up to me by the time I got to Lil'uokalani Avenue and the exterior stairs to my apartment. From the moment we put the sting in action, I'd been running on adrenaline, and it finally ran out. Sweat dripped off my forehead and my heart was racing, as much from exertion as from my own fear and panic. I knew it wasn't right to leave the body there, and yet I knew I couldn't stay. I careened into the decorative railing, palm trees encased in a cage of wrought iron, and used it to pull myself upstairs. With a shaking hand, I unlocked my door and stumbled inside.

I pulled off the rest of my clothes and stepped into the shower. Just before I turned the water on, my hand brushed my face and I found it was wet. As the hot water started to pound, I realized it wasn't sweat; I'd been crying.

I couldn't sleep. I felt as guilty as if I'd killed the guy myself. What kind of cop was I? By hearing that guy drag the body out to the street and not staying around to report what I'd seen to the officer who responded, I'd made myself into an accessory to a homicide. I was as bad as every crappy witness I'd ever interviewed. No,

I didn't see the license number of the car. I couldn't give more than a general description of the guy I'd seen dragging the body. It all happened so fast, officer. There was nothing I could do.

I paced around my little studio apartment until just before dawn, waiting for dispatch to call me, trying to convince myself I should call in. Akoni and I are not the only homicide detectives currently assigned to District 6, Waikīkī, but in a departmental experiment on community policing, the two of us had been assigned to work out of the Waikīkī, substation on Kalākaua. Other detectives, including ones from the other units, work out of the main headquarters. I guessed maybe dispatch was handing the call to detectives from downtown, so finally I said, "The hell with this," and put on my bathing suit. I grabbed my board and walked out to Lili'uokalani Avenue, which leads directly to Kuhio Beach Park, where I surf.

I am renewed, reborn, and revitalized every time I step into the salty water. With my board under me, balanced on a wave, surrounded by sea spray and blue skies, I am finally complete. It's a moment of rare transcendence, a chance to rise up out of the scum and bitterness and shame I find on the streets. It's the only way I can keep being a cop.

The sun hadn't come up over the Ko'olau Mountains by the time I waded into the water, and the surf was cool, but there was a halo of light over the rocky crests beyond the city that promised day was not far behind. The waves were small, and it wasn't hard to set outside. I lay on the board, dangling my right hand in the water, trying to get a feel for the surf.

I can take a while like that, falling into the rhythm of the waves. That morning it took even longer than usual. I couldn't seem to empty my mind of the image of that guy, lying in the alley, or of the shame I felt at leaving him there. Finally, though, I relaxed at least a little, and then saw a good wave building. I paddled fast to catch it, then stood up on the board just as a ray of light rose beyond the top of the Ko'olau, stabbing me in the eye. The nose of the board pearled, or dipped below the wave, and I wiped out, tumbling into the water. The wave washed over me, dragging my board toward the shore, and the leash that kept me tied to the board dragged me forward with it.

The dunking and the swim toward shore revitalized me. The sets were good, and I caught a couple of powerful waves. Before I knew it, it was daylight and time for me to get back home. Sure enough, when I got home I found a message to call dispatch. I called in before I stepped into the shower again. "Homicide reported at two-fifty-eight a.m. in the alley behind the Rod and Reel Club on Kuhio Avenue," the dispatcher told me. "Detective Hapaʻele is en route."

That was Akoni. I jumped through the shower and came out running, and about twenty minutes later I was next to Akoni in the alley, a narrow strip of often-patched pavement that ran between Kuhio and Kalākaua Avenues. It looked even more desolate in the full light of day than it had in the middle of the night.

On the Diamond Head side the alley backed up against the blank rear wall of a budget restaurant, and on the ewa side sat the Rod and Reel Club's back door. At the Kuhio Avenue end, a couple of the high trees inside the Rod and Reel's patio hung out over the alley, but the rest of it was open to harsh sun. Small dumpsters were scattered at intervals, behind other back doors, and coupons for some tourist restaurant skittered in the wind. The walls that faced into the alley had been painted different colors, and some looked like they hadn't been painted in years. It was a back side of Waikīkī most tourists don't see.

"You missed him," Akoni said sadly. "I finally had to let the body boys take him away, because nobody knew where the hell you were."

"You know where I was," I said. I nodded toward the ocean. The sun had cleared the tops of the mountains and was shining brightly on the tourists, the orange-vested guys working on the street, the Japanese men in suits, and the little girls in plaid uniforms on their way to school.

"Jesus, what time did you get to bed last night?"

"Tell me what I missed."

We started walking down the alley. "Apparent gay bashing," Akoni said. "Somebody called in a dead body about three this morning. Uniforms on the scene found a John Doe, underneath the kiawe tree over there. The night shift was swamped with a gang-banger scene downtown, so nobody could get here to investigate until dispatch finally called an hour ago."

"So no detectives interviewed anybody last night?"

Akoni shood his head. It made me feel worse, knowing that if I'd stuck around I could have started a canvas, interviewed guys at the bar, the bartender, people passing by.

The ME speculated that the cause of death was blunt trauma to the cranial region. Not hard to do with a big chunk taken out of the side of the guy's head." No ID. No jewelry except a thick gold chain around the victim's neck that was probably too bloody to get off."

My stomach was doing flip-flops. I needed a cup of coffee bad. Saunders, a beefy haole uniformed cop with sandy hair and a bushy mustache, was standing under the tree, trying to look busy, so Akoni and I got him to get us some coffee from the malasada shop across the street. These little shops were springing up all over the islands, serving a kind of Portuguese doughnut, usually alongside pretty decent coffee.

"I figure the guy left the club late last night, ran into some bad dudes, and they tried to knock him for a loop. They knocked a little too hard and the guy bought it."

"Think they stole his ID?"

"Maybe. Maybe he was afraid to carry anything." He leered a little. "Thought he might get lucky—didn't want to risk getting rolled."

I nodded toward the club. "They ID there?"

"We can ask, once they open." He looked at me. "You know I'm not going in there alone."

"Oh good. Can we hold hands when we go in?"

"One of these days I'm going to hurt you," he said.

The two techs were already searching the alley, while a uniform stood guard at each end, blocking access. They'd strung yellow crime scene tape along both ends and I could see one of the uniforms arguing with a driver in a delivery truck. "Maybe we'll get lucky and one of the techs will find his wallet," I said. "Maybe the bad guys just took the cash and left the ID somewhere. Why don't you see if a uniform can check out the trash cans along both of the avenues for a couple of blocks in either direction?"

While Akoni got on the radio, I walked up and down the narrow pavement with my hands behind my back, looking slowly and carefully at everything. There was a clear trail of blood from a spot at the back end of the alley up to where the body had been found. I followed it, then walked back to where I'd seen the Cherokee the night before.

Akoni had already taken notes, but I got out my pad and pen and starting taking my own. It was getting hot, so I stood in the shade of the high trees and drew a rough sketch of the alley first, including the back door of the club, the position of the body, and, in a cryptic note only I could understand, the direction the Cherokee had traveled.

Saunders returned with coffee and a malasada, and I kept writing while I ate and drank, leaning up against the side wall of the club. It was 7 a.m., and the street was already busy. Delivery trucks pulling up at the back of the Kuhio Mall, joggers out for their morning runs, elderly mama-sans scurrying home from night jobs. There was a mass of gray cloud cover over the Ko'olau, but a stiff trade wind coming in off the ocean kept it away from Waikīkī. It was going to be a great day for the beach, a tourist office poster kind of day, full of thong bikinis, surfboards, and palm trees swaying in a gentle breeze. Oh, and murder, too.

I wrote down everything I could remember from the time the giraffe followed me out of the club until the time I left the alley to find a phone. Then I started taking notes on what I saw around me. It's a rule you have to pound into your head when you graduate from the beat to detective—write everything down. Even if it doesn't seem important, write it down. You'll forget it otherwise, and then it's bound to be the one thing you need to know, or the first thing the DA asks when he's putting together his case.

On my first case as a detective, I neglected to write down whether the window in the victim's bedroom was open or closed, and we nearly lost the case over whether the perp could have escaped that way. Fortunately a witness came through who remembered seeing the curtains flying through the open window, and I got off the hook. Since then I've written everything down. I sniff the air, listen for ambient sounds, feel the textures of things. Even stuff that seems ordinary, that you take for granted, like garbage cans in an alley, I write down. You never know when you're going to find out it wasn't trash day that day, and that valuable evidence was in the garbage.

I finally ran out of things to write. While the crime scene techs finished up their search, I walked over to Akoni and stood with him at the end of the alley, drinking another cup of coffee. "He look like a tourist?" I asked.

"He no had ID, Kimo. How I gonna tell he tourist?"

When Akoni gets angry he lapses into pidgin, the Hawai'ian dialect we were all suckled on. "Red skin from sunburn," I said. "A new T-shirt that says 'I heart Waikīkī. Flip-flops fresh from Woolworth. One of those cheap shell leis they give you when you tour the aloha shirt factory. You know the signs just as well as I do, Akoni. Why you so bull-headed this morning?"

In the distance we heard the protesting squeal of hydraulic brakes, and somewhere nearby a truck was backing up and beeping. "You know what time they called me? Five a.m. I didn't get home 'til after midnight. I was going to sleep late this morning. Maybe call in late for my shift. Maybe do a little dirty with Mealoha. Instead I roll out of bed at five, and nobody knows where the hell you are."

"I'm sorry, all right? I'll make it up to you. Someday you get Mealoha ready for some afternoon delight, and I'll cover for you."

He was still grumpy, but I could see that idea had some appeal to him. "So what you think? Tourist? Malihini? Kama'āina?" A malihini is a newcomer to the islands, one step above tourist. A kama'āina, literally "child of the land," is a native or longtime resident, like Akoni or me.

He thought. "Chinese. Mid to late forties. Expensive suit, fancy shoes. No way to tell if he's a tourist or not."

"Good start," I said. I wiped a bead of perspiration off my forehead. "Maybe he was out to dinner, had a couple of drinks, didn't know what kind of place he was going into. Somebody might have seen him as easy prey. Remember, the other bashings here have been big fights, half a dozen guys on each side."

"You can't just take the easy way out, call him a faggot? You haven't even seen him."

"That's right. I haven't seen him," I said, and the lie made me wince a little. I hoped Akoni would just think it was the sun streaming in through the branches of the high trees. "That's why I don't have any preconceived ideas. Just because the guy was found behind a gay bar doesn't make it a gay bashing."

Akoni looked at his notes. "Spider tattoo between thumb and forefinger of his right hand indicates possible tong connection."

"Tong connection," I said. "Interesting. Wonder who owns this place." I wiped my forehead again. It was going to be a bad day if it wasn't even eight o'clock and I was sweating already.

We saw the techs begin to pack up their gear and walked over to them. They'd picked up a few things but nothing looked that relevant. Larry Solas, the head tech, said, "Trail of blood leads back to that back door there. Seems pretty clear he got whacked just outside the door, then dragged out to the street. There's a lot of crap out here, but not much of it seems relevant. We're done."

I looked at Akoni and he shrugged. It wasn't practical to leave the alley blocked off all day; there was already a line of trucks waiting to make deliveries. A clutch of drivers stood together on a shady corner across Kuhio Avenue, drinking coffee and grumbling about us. We pulled the crime scene tape down, though we isolated the small corner where the body had been found with cones and more tape.

Dispatch was busy with a massive accident on the H1 at the Pali Highway exit, and we had to wait a few minutes for the radio chatter to subside before we could convey our status. We let Saunders and the other uniforms go.

The drivers went back to their trucks and gunned their engines, and Akoni and I headed back to the station. The Waikīkī substation on Kalākaua Avenue is right in the heart of Waikīkī, and ordinarily we would have walked back. But Akoni had driven in from home direct to the club, and his car, a Ford Taurus, was illegally parked down the block. It took us just as much time to drive to the garage where he parks as walking would have taken, between the slow lights and the even slower tourists. Waikīkī is a small place, roughly one and a half miles long and a half-mile wide, and close to 25,000 people live here. Of course, there are also 34,000 hotel and condo rooms, which are occupied close to 85 percent year-round. That means an average of 65,000 extra people crammed in on any given day. No wonder traffic's so bad.

We got into the office just after nine and started filling out the paperwork. Akoni called Mealoha and apologized again, then covered his mouth and whispered something to her. I snickered, just on general principles, and he glared at me. Sitting at my desk, which faced out toward Kalākaua Avenue, filling out forms, I could almost forget I had any personal involvement in this case. Almost.

Kalākaua was swarming with tourists on their way to the beach. Honeymooners holding hands, elderly people walking with slow, arthritic gaits, busloads of Japanese tourists carrying Gucci shopping bags and talking fast. In the middle of them all were people handing out flyers for time-shares and restaurants with early bird specials. I called the medical examiner's office on Iwilei Road, near the Dole cannery, and found that the autopsy was slated for two o'clock. "Just after lunch," I said to Alice Kanamura, the receptionist there. "You guys schedule them deliberately like that?"

"We got lots of sickness bags, you need," Alice said. "I'll put one aside with your name on it."

She was laughing merrily when she hung up. I guess you get your laughs where you can when you work for the coroner.

There were no witnesses to interview yet. Dispatch faxed us a transcript of the call I'd made, which did us no good. The 911 operators have a computer-assisted dispatch system now, which transmits emergency information direct to the radio dispatcher. The computer shows the address any 911 call is made from, along with the phone number and subscriber name. That way, in case somebody's in trouble and can only dial the number, the police have a way to trace the call.

On a whim, I dialed Motor Vehicles on my computer and checked registrations for a black Jeep Cherokee. There were thousands. I quickly disconnected when I saw Akoni coming over to my desk.

"We got nothing on this case, you know." he said. "Nothing."

"We'll have more this afternoon," I said. "Let's get the reports finished on yesterday before we get buried in this one."

We spent the rest of the morning writing our reports on the failed drug bust. Neither Pedro nor Luz Maria were registered at the colleges they pretended to attend, and Luz Maria had a drug-related rap sheet as long as her sleek black ponytail. We didn't find any priors on Pedro, but that could have meant he'd been more careful, or maybe he'd given us a false ID. They'd been held downtown overnight and released when there was no physical evidence to tie them to any crime.

At 12:30 we walked up the block for a lunch of saimin, Japanese noodles in a broth flavored with chicken or beef. "Good choice, brah," Akoni said as he slurped his from a paper bowl. "Easy going down, easy coming back up if the autopsy a bad one."

The noodle shop was tucked into a corner of a building on a

side street just makai of Kuhio Avenue, and we stayed back against the building to take advantage of the meager shade.

The sun was high in the sky and the shadows of the palm trees were nearly symmetrical around their bases. There was a light trade wind, though, so out of the direct sun the temperature wasn't too bad. Around us swirled the constant parade of tourists, beachgoers, and store workers who make up the daily population of Waikīkī, including a tall Hawai'ian guy in a red feathered cape and traditional curved headdress, passing out flyers for Hawai'ian heritage jewelry. A rainbow covey of tiny kids, each wearing construction-paper name tags and holding hands in pairs and threes, passed us on their way to the IMAX theater, chirping and laughing.

"You want to go back to your place for your truck or take my car?" Akoni asked. Detectives drive their own cars in Honolulu, though we get an allowance from the department to help subsidize the cost. The department has to approve our choice of vehicles, and requires certain minimum standards—size of engine, ability to install a radio, and so on. My truck was a hand-me-down from my father, and its black paint was pitted with dings and dents and the effects of salt water. The back windshield was cluttered with surf decals and the back end sagged a little, but I could carry as many surfers and their boards as I wanted, and it was comfortable and didn't cost much to run.

Something about Akoni's comment stung me, and it took me a minute to register why. I wondered how long I would associate going back to my apartment with running away from my troubles. I said, "We can take yours."

Chapter 3

DETECTIVES WITNESS AUTOPSIES for a couple of reasons. Often evidence, such as bullets embedded in a victim, is removed during the autopsy and transferred to police custody. The detective's presence makes the chain of possession simpler. Going to the autopsy yourself means you find out the results much quicker than if you had to wait for the formal report. Most important, if you go to the autopsy and force yourself to pay attention, you may find out information you didn't even know you needed.

At the autopsy of an elderly woman who had been strangled while visiting Honolulu on vacation, the medical examiner, Doc Takayama, had mentioned she showed signs of high blood pressure and undoubtedly had taken medication to control it. I wrote that down, and later that day, going through her hotel room one last time, I'd looked for her medication. Hadn't found it.

A check with her son on the mainland, and her doctor, revealed that she took Prinivil, a blood pressure regulator, and wouldn't spend a night without it. I filed that information under "unsolved mysteries" until a couple of days later when an elderly man showed up at the station asking questions about her. He wanted to know how to contact her next of kin about money she owed him. I was suspicious enough of him to get a search warrant and, surprisingly, found her Prinivil in his medicine cabinet. He admitted romancing her, and finally killing her.

Akoni and I took Ala Wai Boulevard to the ewa end of Waikīkī, then connected to Ala Moana Boulevard, which took us past the mall and finally connected to Nimitz Highway, sliding us into the flow of traffic along the edge of downtown. Past the Aloha Tower Marketplace and Chinatown, over Nuʻuanu Stream, and into the more industrial district that surrounds the airport. The medical examiner's office is on Iwilei Road, just off Nimitz, in a two-story concrete building with a slight roof overhang. The paint on the building is peeling and the landscaping is overgrown—after all, the dead don't vote. The building is between the Salvation Army and a homeless center—something I always thought was an ironic comment, but maybe was intended as an object lesson to those less fortunate. You never know what the city fathers are really thinking, after all.

We pulled into the small parking area in the center of the building, and walked through the glass block entrance, where Alice Kanamura greeted us with a renewed offer of sickness bags. "I'll get back to you on that," I said. "Doc ready for us?"

She buzzed him. "He'll be right down." Doc Takayama is the medical examiner for Honolulu City and County, though he looks barely old enough to have graduated medical school. He was a kind of whiz kid, graduated in record time from the U of H, and he told me once he went into pathology because he didn't have to worry if the patients would trust him. He came into the vestibule to meet us, patting down the pockets of his white coat for his tape recorder.

"Good, I'm glad you're here. We can get started."

We followed him up the stairs to a white-tiled room where we all put on surgical scrubs, paper booties over our shoes, and paper shower caps. You can't be too careful today, especially with an unidentified corpse. The scent of formaldehyde and death wafted around us, but Doc Takayama was oblivious to it.

We walked beyond the white room into another, where the body was laid out on a metal table, ready for the medical-legal autopsy. That's a special kind of exam, ordered by the authorities in the case of deaths that may have legal implications. Suspicious deaths, like murders and suicides, or unexpected sudden deaths without clear causes.

Doc's assistant, Marilyn Tseng, was taking photographs. On the wall beyond us, against lights, were a set of X-rays of the guy's head. From where I stood, I could see a bloody matted place on the back side of the head, where he'd been hit. I hadn't seen that the night before—it was the side that had rested against the ground.

The guy looked paler than he had the last time I'd seen him. Then it was probably only an hour or less after he'd been killed, and the skin on his face had been waxy and blue-gray. His lips and his nails had seemed pale in the limited light available to me then. He was still pale, though where the blood had settled at the back of his neck I could see a lot of postmortem lividity.

"The body is that of an Asian male approximately forty-five years of age," Doc began narrating into his tape recorder. "Black hair and brown eyes. The body shows signs of good nourishment and care, is seventy inches long, and weighs one hundred sixty-five pounds. Death was pronounced at three-twenty-five this morning by an emergency medical technician. Preliminary finding, based on initial examination of the body and X-rays of the skull, is that death occurred due to blunt trauma of the head."

He clicked off the recorder. "Take a good look before we undress him, boys."

Akoni and I looked. It wasn't so bad yet, before they cut him open. He could have been sleeping, except for his pale color and that matted wound on his head.

"It's clear he was killed up by the door to the office," Doc said. "The techs found blood spattered around him for as much as a meter. Head wounds are real bleeders."

Doc Takayama dictated a few more things about the general condition of the body and then Marilyn turned the lights off and began surveying the corpse with some kind of black-light device. That went on for a while, as she and Doc took fibers off the guy with tweezers, rolling him over to do his back as well. They'd be examined, and then matched against the fibers found in the alley.

Finally, Doc was content. Marilyn turned the lights back on and started cutting off the guy's clothes. "From the condition of the body and the head wound, I'd say he was killed almost immediately before he was found," Doc said.

Marilyn continued putting the pieces of the guy's clothes into larger plastic bags, labeling everything carefully. He was wearing a heavy gold chain around his neck, expensive shoes, and good-quality clothing. He would be missed, eventually, and then we would know who he was. That was the first step in figuring out who killed him.

We stood and watched as Doc and Marilyn worked. The only identifying mark on the body was the spidery tattoo on his right hand, and we knew that meant he was somehow connected with a tong. They'd already taken dental X-rays, which we could use to confirm identity if we couldn't find someone who knew him. "Any news from missing persons?" Doc asked as he worked.

I shook my head. "You know the drill. No one is really missing unless he's been missing twenty-four hours."

Doc fingerprinted the guy, rolling the tips carefully across the pad just as we'd been taught to do with live subjects, and put aside the prints. We'd run them through our computer, and with luck we'd find a match, because based on the tattoo he was likely involved in something illicit. There are also a few reasons why law-abiding citizens have their prints on file; for example, some states require fingerprinting for licensing, and once in a while you'll find a match with a real estate broker or stock dealer.

Doc carefully examined the guy's fingernails and hands, looking for any signs he might have grappled with his assailant. Often examiners can find microscopic elements under the fingernails that could lead to the killer, but in this case it was pretty obvious to all of us that the guy had been hit from behind and hadn't had a chance to fight. Doc made a detailed record of the condition of the body, noting a small mole on the chin and a tiny scar on the left ring finger. It made me wonder if the guy had been married, because I've seen men who wear wedding rings get them caught on something and cause cuts.

The lights went out again for a while as Marilyn shone a light all over the guy's body. "Since he was dragged down the alley, we may get lucky and find some fingerprints on him," Doc said. "This scope helps us find them."

Akoni nudged me. "How you holding up, man?"

"Okay. You?"

"I've felt better."

When we turned back, they were lifting prints from his skin. "Not much luck," Doc said. "We might get a good one from his hand. And there's a nice clean one up by his neck. Somebody taking his pulse, probably."

Marilyn turned the lights back on. Something was bothering me, but I couldn't put my finger on it. I chalked it up to my general discomfort level. While Doc and Marilyn made the Y-incision down the guy's body, Akoni and I stepped back. I had seen this before and it wasn't pretty. Since the guy had died of a head trauma, I didn't think there was much his insides could tell us, and I didn't really want to lose my saimin if I could help it. Akoni was already looking pretty pale.

Doc cut the poor guy open and removed his internal organs, weighing them and remarking on them. "Too much fatty foods," he said at one point. "That can kill you."

Akoni and I looked at each other. I waited until the sound of the saw had stopped before I turned back. That's always the worst part to me, cutting off the top of the head and removing the brain. "You want to see the blood vessels?" Doc asked.

"We'll take your word for it, Doc," I said.

"Death definitely occurred as a result of blunt trauma to the head. Almost instantaneous. Probably no more than an hour before he was found. Maybe even less."

Doc promised to fax over a final report within twenty-four hours. We collected our evidence and went down to the car.

"Well, I can't say we know much more than we knew when we went in there," I said. "He confirmed what we thought, though."

"That still doesn't give us much of a place to start," Akoni said.

"Well, we've got a guy with tong connections, and he was killed outside a gay bar. Tongs own any of those bars, you know?"

Akoni shook his head. "No clue." I handed the evidence bag to him so I could fish out my keys, and the zipper lock popped open, the guy's gold neck chain spilling out. Akoni reached for it. "Hey, careful, we don't want your fingerprints on it, too," I said.

Then it hit me. Fingerprints. There was a clean print on the guy's neck, where somebody had tried to take his pulse. Suddenly it felt like I hadn't eaten in days, a big hollow place in my stomach. I knew whose fingerprint it was. Mine.

Chapter 4

WE PARKED AKONI'S CAR and walked back toward the station. On the way, we passed the Makai Market, the food court. The time I had been avoiding couldn't be put off any more. I knew I needed to tell Akoni everything. He deserved it; after all, it was his investigation too. "You want a coffee?" I asked. "I could use one."

I chose a table for us at the edge of the traffic, private enough so no one would overhear us. The food court is shaped like an L, with one end open to the covered parking lot. Little birds fly in, swoop around the rafters, and peck for crumbs on the tile floor. As in much of Hawai'i, there's a strong contrast between light and shadow—it's bright in the area under the skylight, but dark in the corners. I wanted to be in the dark.

We sat down with our coffees. Akoni put cream and sugar in his. I just stirred mine for a while until it cooled off. With Akoni, it had always been an us-versus-them thing, and we were the good guys, the mainstream, the keepers of the peace and the representatives of the population at large. I was about to cross over from us to them, and I wasn't sure how he was going to take it.

"I did something bad, Akoni," I said. "I need you to stand by me, all right? But if you can't, then tell me. Just tell me straight out so I know what I have to do."

Akoni looked at me. "You're my partner, man, my friend. What did you do?"

"I checked the guy for a pulse. It's my fingerprint they're going to find on his neck. They're going to run the prints through the computer, and that one is going to match mine, and everybody is going to wonder how the hell my fingerprint got on a corpse I didn't see until the autopsy."

Akoni put his coffee cup down. "Start at the beginning of the story, Kimo," he said. "Tell me what you did."

I sat there for a minute, my coffee cooling in my hands, trying to decide how much I had to tell. I had an urge to go back to the beginning, to tell him about the first time I had sexual thoughts about another guy. Through all the years of denying it, trying to be a big stud with a string of girlfriends. How else could he understand how I'd ended up at the Rod and Reel Club that night, how I'd stumbled out into the alley and seen some guy drag a dead body to the street. How I'd run away, and how much that act shamed me.

"Last night I stayed at the bar until about one," I said. "Alvy was still there, and maybe a couple of the guys from the fifth squad. But I didn't go home." I took a deep breath. "I went to the Rod and Reel."

Akoni was looking at me. A couple of sparrows pecked around under the table next to us, and in the background I could hear upbeat jazzy Muzak that was directly at odds with how I felt. "I had a couple of beers there and a guy tried to pick me up. I walked outside. I was just heading toward the alley when I saw this guy dragging something toward the street. It was dark, so I didn't see what it was, and I didn't think anything of it. Then he ran back up the alley, jumped into a black Cherokee, and peeled out. I didn't even see if he was alone or if there was someone else driving."

I tried to pick up my coffee cup, but my hand was shaking. "I kept walking down the street, and I saw that what the guy had been dragging was a man's body. I leaned down and took his pulse. He was dead. I started looking for a phone, and I had to go two blocks down on Kuhio to find one. I called it in to 911 but I hung up when they asked who I was." I lowered my head and looked down at the table. "Then I went home."

"Jesus, Kimo."

I waited for him to say something else. He just said, "Jesus," again and shook his head.

"You goddamned motherfucker!" A loud thud immediately followed that, and both of us turned toward the sound, which caused a momentary stop to the bustle of the Makai Market. A young guy with long, scraggly blond hair and a brownish blond goatee was screaming at another loser across an overturned table from him. "Why the fuck'd you do that, man?" the blond guy screamed again. "Why'd you fucking do that?"

"She was fucking there, man," the other loser said. He was about the same build, drug-thin, and disheveled. Akoni and I both looked around for security, but like a pay phone when you've just gotten an emergency beep, they were nowhere in sight. "She fucking wanted it, anyway."

The two guys started pushing and shoving each other, and the crowd backed away, giving them a clear circle. I looked at Akoni and he looked at me, and we both stood up.

He took the blond and I took his friend, and we strong-armed them out of the market in different directions. I talked low and calm to my loser as I walked him to the parking lot, though my heart was racing. "You just gotta take it outside, man," I said. "You got a beef with your buddy, you just take it outside, you work out your differences, and nobody gets hurt, all right?"

"I knew she was his girlfriend, but, fuck shit, man, a stiff prick has no conscience, right?"

"All depends on your definition of friendship," I said. I released his arms when we got to the parking lot. Because of the configuration of the mall, I knew Akoni and his friend were around the corner, out of harm's way for now. I watched the guy stumble down to the bus stop, and it seemed the harm had gone out of him.

I met Akoni back at the table where we'd been sitting. A couple of cleaners had materialized from the shadows and righted the chairs and tables, and the conversational buzz had returned. We sat back down.

"Now let's get back to you," Akoni said. "What the hell were you doing at the Rod and Reel Club at two o'clock in the morning?" He crumpled his coffee cup and I could see he was mad. I knew him inside and out. He'd wanted to punch the blond guy, but he hadn't, and his anger had to go somewhere. It was all mixed up with me, the blond guy and his friend, and having to get up so early in the morning for a murder case. "Were you tailing somebody again? We've been through this before, Kimo—the Allen case. I told you I can't have a partner who goes off on his own, tailing people and doing stuff without telling me . . ."

"I wasn't tailing anybody, Akoni."

He stopped talking. It took him a minute, then he said, "Then tell me what the hell you were doing at a gay bar at two a.m., drinking beers and talking to a guy who tried to pick you up."

"I didn't talk to him," I said. "He stuck his tongue in my ear and I walked away."

"He stuck his . . ." Akoni was almost speechless, stuttering. "He stuck his tongue in your ear and you walked away. Jesus Christ, why didn't you clock the guy!"

"I guess he was just trying to be friendly."

Akoni put his left hand over his face and shook his head. When he put his hand down, his face was dead serious. "Brah, you in a heap of trouble. And I don't know what to do. Man, I thought I knew you. But I can see I don't know dick about you."

I couldn't help it. I started to laugh. "It's a figure of speech, man," Akoni said. "Jesus, Kimo, you got to take this seriously."

"Akoni, if I wasn't laughing, I'd be crying. I mean it, man. You have no idea how broken up about this I've been. I mean, leaving that guy in the alley, it was the hardest thing I ever did. I thought I could walk away. I wouldn't have to admit what I'd been doing."

My throat suddenly got dry but I knew I had to keep going. "I thought I'd never have to sit here and tell you I'm gay."

"Oh, man. What do you got to be gay for? You were always such a stud, Kimo."

"I was trying to avoid the truth. But now my fingerprint's on that dead guy's neck and I've got to explain why."

There was a moment when the noise in the Makai Market died away and I could hear the birds chirping. In the background I heard a blender making some frothy drink, the sizzle of meat on a grill. The sun must have come out from behind a cloud, because suddenly the center of the food court was flooded with a much brighter light. I didn't exactly feel good, but there was a weight off my chest, something that had been keeping me from breathing. And that was okay.

"You know you could get fried for this," Akoni said after a while. "Being gay is one thing. But you witnessed a homicide and you walked away." He shook his head. "That's a hard rap to walk out of."

"I didn't witness a homicide." Two elderly Chinese women came over and sat down at the table next to us, and I lowered my voice. "I saw a guy drag something down the alley, and it wasn't until the Cherokee was gone that I realized that something was a body. I checked the guy's pulse, and when I couldn't get one I called for help. And I walked away. I know I did wrong. But I didn't do anything an ordinary citizen wouldn't have. Hell, I did more than your average Joe."

"You're a cop, Kimo. You have a different standard to live up to."

I didn't know what to say. He was right. The two women next to us began gossiping in Chinese, their voices high and chattery. I think life is like some kind of ongoing movie. Sometimes you play a minor character, sitting back, commenting on the action around you. Then sometimes, you have to step forward, take the starring role. This was one of those times. I was moving out of the background, up to center stage.

We sat there for a while, not talking. Finally Akoni said, "When we get back to the station, you run the guy's prints and the print Doc pulled off his neck through the computer. I don't want to know about it."

"I can't put you in that position."

"What position?" Akoni said. "What position is that? We don't do everything together. You question some people, I question some people. You fill out some reports, I fill out others. We work together. You run those prints through. Who knows, maybe that one from the neck is smudged. You never know with prints."

"I can't wreck evidence. That would make it even worse."

"You stupid?" he asked. "Did I say you should smudge the print? No. Did I say you should destroy evidence or lie about anything? No. Put it in your goddamn report. The fingerprint on the victim's neck matches the index finger of Detective Kanapa'aka. If that's the finger you used. Leave it there. Who's going to challenge it? You're the detective on the case. End of story."

"I had to tell you," I said.

He looked at me. "No, you didn't." Then he stood up. "Come on, let's get back to the station."

Chapter 5

THE PRINT FROM THE GUY'S THROAT was a clear match. Detective Kimo Kanapaʻaka, Waikīkī Station. More important, though, was the match to the dead guy's prints. We now had a name to go with our stiff: Thomas Pang. He had a couple of minor arrests in the past, nothing for the past few years. He was suspected of tong activity, but nothing was ever proven.

I dutifully made notes for the case file, then turned back to the computer and punched in a few keys. After a minute, a list began scrolling down the screen.

Tommy Pang had a long record, from possession of illegal weapons to armed robbery. It was clear he had been a low-level jack-of-all-trades for one of the tongs, the kind of guy who takes the rap for whatever goes down. But he had served remarkably little jail time given all his time in court. He'd often been acquitted, or charges had been dropped, and the few times he'd actually been convicted, he had paid fines or served at most a few months behind bars.

I pulled up Tommy Pang's address, then looked at the clock. It was just after three. "You want to take a ride up to Maunalani Heights with me, break the news to the widow?"

Akoni shrugged. "Can't let you out of my sight," he said. "Only this time, you drive."

Tommy Pang had lived pretty nicely, on a ridge overlooking Diamond Head, Black Point, and the Pacific Ocean. We stopped at a wrought-iron fence, and I identified myself through a speaker phone.

The gate buzzed and we drove up a curving driveway to a sprawling one-story house, part ranch and part Chinese pagoda, with a blue tile roof curved up at the ends.

A very beautiful woman opened the door as we drove up and stepped out. She was about forty-five, perfectly dressed and made up, with a kind of China-doll beauty that made her seem like she belonged in a magazine. On her best days, when she is dressed up for a party or special event, it's the look my mother strives for. On this woman, however, it appeared effortless.

"I am Genevieve Pang," she said, extending a tiny, manicured hand to me. I introduced myself, and Akoni, and then the two of us stood there with Tommy Pang's widow, rocking a little back and forth, neither of us knowing quite what to say.

She smiled. "You don't have to be shy, Detective. You can tell me. Have you arrested my husband again?"

The air around us was still, and I heard the chirping of birds and a slight rustle in the underbrush. The driveway and yard were as perfectly manicured as the woman before us, the gravel raked, the bushes carefully pruned.

"I'm afraid not," I said. "Your husband was killed late last night, outside a bar in Waikīkī. We'd like to talk to you about him, if you think you can."

Genevieve Pang didn't look surprised. Rather, her face hardened a little, like this was something she'd expected for a long time. "Of course," she said quietly. "Please come inside."

She turned and led us into the house. We sat in a formal living room, on elaborately carved mahogany chairs, in front of a Japanese lacquered screen that probably belonged in a museum. There was a display of Javanese puppets on a mahogany table, and on the wall above it was a collection of what looked like Balinese masks. The room was elegant and tasteful, much like Genevieve Pang herself. I found it hard to imagine the man whose body we'd seen on the autopsy table, the man with that long record, there in that house. "When was the last time you saw your husband?" I asked.

"Let me tell you about our house, detective," she said. "You are in the south wing now. That's my part of the house. My bedroom is behind us. To your left is the kitchen, and beyond there the family room. On the other side of the family room is my husband's part." She smiled. "He has his privacy there. If he wishes to have company for the evening, he can do so." Her smile hardened again. "I don't have to know about it."

"Do you know that your husband was here last night?" Akoni asked.

"We are not total strangers, Detective," she said, turning to him. "We had dinner together last night at a restaurant on Waikīkī. Then he brought me home and went on to what he said was a business meeting. I don't know if that was correct. I was reading until midnight, and if he had come home before then I would have heard his car come through the gate." She looked at me. "You may have heard, when you drove through, that the mechanism needs oiling. My bedroom window faces in that direction. I hear it often. I suppose now I can have it repaired."

"Do you know anyone who might have had reason to kill your husband?" I asked.

Genevieve Pang laughed lightly. "I am sure there are many people who wanted to kill Tommy," she said. "But he was careful to keep his business dealings secret from me, and I was careful not to pry. You see, in many respects I am a good Chinese wife."

"I'm sorry to have to ask this, ma'am, but it's routine," I said. "Do you know if Mr. Pang had a will?"

"We made wills a long time ago, detective. If my husband hasn't changed his, then I inherit everything. I can have his attorney call you, if you'd like."

"That would be good of you," I said. "Is there anyone you would like us to call for you? Children, a sister or a brother?"

"I have a son, Derek. But I will call him myself."

"May we have his number?" I asked. "Perhaps he knows more about his father's business."

Genevieve Pang laughed. "My husband was even more careful with Derek than he was with me," she said. "He was determined that Derek would have all the advantages he did not have, that Derek would become a respectable person. He is going to run an art gallery, as soon as he gets himself organized." She smiled. "He just graduated from Yale in May."

"We'd still like to talk to him," Akoni said.

She looked at her watch. "You can probably reach him now," she said. "He has a friend staying with him, from college. They are both such lazy boys, late sleepers. Not like my husband and me. Derek is different from his parents in many ways. Very American." Then she straightened her back in a mocking kind of way. "Very Yale," she said. "But then, it's what we wanted for him, isn't it? To be American?"

I didn't know what to say. After a minute, Akoni said, very gently, "Your son's phone number?"

"Of course, Detective." She took a pen and a pad from the gilt-covered stand by the phone and wrote the number down, then stood. "My husband's . . . remains?"

"The medical examiner's office will release the body," I said. "If you contact a funeral home they'll take care of the arrangements for you."

With Genevieve Pang's permission, we searched Tommy's part of the house, but he was very meticulous, and we could find nothing that indicated any illegal dealings, and certainly nothing that gave anyone a motive for murder.

She thanked us again and stood on the front step of the house until we had driven out the gates. I heard them squeal as they closed.

From his cell phone, Akoni dialed the number Genevieve Pang had given us, but got her son's answering machine. He left a message.

Akoni was quiet for a minute, as I negotiated the entrance to the Lunalilo Freeway. Finally he said, "It's just after four. They have a happy hour at that bar?"

"The Rod and Reel? I think so."

"Fortunately our shift is over. I could definitely use a beer."

"I'll second that emotion. You're sure you want to go there?"

He frowned at me. "Don't think we really have a choice. We've got to find out who owns the bar, what Tommy Pang was doing there."

I parked back at my apartment, and we walked the couple of blocks to the club. It was funny, but I felt none of the tense expectation I'd felt the night before. Now it was just business, just me and my partner going into a bar to ask some questions. Yeah, right.

The Rod and Reel was a different place in the afternoon. Liquid sunlight dropped down through the trees overhead, and mixed couples, tourists, and guys in tank tops sat at the plastic tables in small groups. The testosterone level seemed to have dropped about a thousand percent, and no restless, horny guys circled the room. The back bar, where they showed the videos, was closed.

Akoni and I sat down at a clean table right underneath a big overhead fan that moved the warm air around.

It was a typical Waikīkī happy hour. Keola Beamer was playing on a stereo behind the bar, and around us people compared sunburns and drank fruity frozen drinks. When the waiter brought our beers, I showed him my badge and asked, "Do you work the late shift here, too?"

He said, "Sometimes. Why?"

I held out a picture of Tommy Pang. "Recognize this man?"

"Sure. He owns the place. Mr. Pang."

I nodded. "He here last night?"

"He comes by almost every night. I think he was here last night. But not at closing. Fred and I had to close up ourselves."

"Fred the bartender?"

The waiter nodded. "Look, I got customers. Can I take care of them?"

"Sure."

The waiter walked away. "That was easy," Akoni said.

"Too easy. You wait here. I'm gonna talk to Fred." Akoni looked distinctly uncomfortable, and the idea that a guy his size would worry about anything made me laugh. "Don't worry. Anybody comes over to talk to you, you just tell them you're my bitch."

"Keep it up—you'll see what a bitch feels like," Akoni said, but he sat back in his chair and picked up his beer.

I carried mine with me to the bar. It took a couple of minutes for Fred to finish with a gaggle of pretty young boys at the far end of the bar, but eventually he came over to me. Up close, he was older than he looked from far away, the kind of guy who spent too much time in the sun when he was younger and too much time in the gym now. I showed him my badge and said, "Tell me about Mr. Pang."

He shrugged. "What do you want to know?"

"Anybody ever threaten him?"

Fred laughed. "No, my guess is that Mr. Pang does all the threatening." He leaned close to me. "What's this all about? He in trouble? I've seen his tattoo."

"Yeah? You know what it means?"

"Tong," Fred said. "He's some kind of gangster. But he only comes out here for a minute at a time—he doesn't particularly like our clientele. And I only go back to his office to lock up the receipts for the night."

"You do that last night?"

"Sure, just like always." A lightbulb seemed to go on over Fred's head. "Say, there were a lot of police out there last night, when I was closing up. You have anything to do with that?"

"They were out there because your Mr. Pang's body was out there."

"Shit," Fred said. "He's dead?"

I nodded. "You have any idea who might have wanted him dead?"

Fred shook his head. "Not a clue. I said maybe five words to the guy on a daily basis, usually just a greeting." He grabbed a rag and started wiping down the bar. "So who's gonna take over here?" he asked. "Not that peckerwood kid of his?"

"Peckerwood?" I asked. "That some kind of tree?"

"Where I come from it means jerk," Fred said. "That pretty much sums up Derek."

"So Derek comes around here?"

"With his boyfriend. Usually when his dad's not here."

I started taking notes. "Got a description?"

"Derek's a kid, just out of college. Chinese, about five-seven, hundred fifty pounds soaking wet. Black hair down to his shoulders. Sometimes when he wears it pulled back into a ponytail, he looks like a gangster. Beautiful clothes—silk shirts, linen pants. Italian shoes. Guy has a thing for Italian shoes. Skinny. Moves like a dancer. Cute butt."

I raised my eyebrows at him. "So we get him in a lineup, we gotta turn him around so you can see his butt?"

Fred smirked. "You asked, I told."

"Know the boyfriend's name?"

"Wayne Gallagher. Six four, I think. Maybe two-fifty, maybe a little more or less. Hard to judge at that size. Curly hair, kind of halfway between blond and brown, cut just to the neck. He's much looser than Derek. You know, sometimes he does the Ralph Lauren Polo look, oxford cloth button-down shirts and khakis, but sometimes he wears big aloha shirts and tight jeans. Caucasian, in case the name didn't tell you that. Big hands, big feet. Dick the size of a beer can."

I put my pen down. "I'm not even going to ask how you know."

Fred held up his hand. "I was pissing next to the guy one night. Course I had to look."

"Course. Anything else?"

Fred shrugged again, and the party of boy toys called for him.

"One last thing," I said. "Anybody else work back in the office there?"

"Arleen," he said. "Secretary." He looked at his watch. "She's still there, at least another few minutes."

I let him go and went back to Akoni, where I told him almost everything I'd heard, leaving out the part about Derek's butt and his boyfriend's dick.

I drained the last of my beer. "You want to head back and say hello to this Arleen?"

"Why not," Akoni said. "Though I got to tell you, if Arleen's a guy in drag, you do all the talking."

Chapter 6

THE ROD AND REEL CLUB occupied a square at the corner of Kuhio Avenue Street. A group of tall trees sat at the corner, behind a wooden fence, and shaded a large open patio. The bar itself wrapped around the patio as an L, with one side facing Kuhio and the other Laniu. Roll-down grilles sealed off the bar area from the patio when the club was closed.

An alley ran parallel to Kuhio Avenue; it was narrow but cars often parallel-parked back there. The waiter pointed down the hallway where I'd seen guys coming and going the night before and said there was a door back there that led to the office, but it was locked, and we'd have to go out to Laniu and then up the alley to the first door on the left.

At the entrance to the alley I stopped. "I heard the guy dragging the body as I was standing in the shadows over there, by the patio entrance." I remembered the giraffe following me out the door, making eye contact with him and shaking my head. "He'd just dumped the body over there, by that kiawe tree, when I came around the corner. I saw him run up to the Cherokee, which was parallel-parked up there, facing this way. He jumped in, and zoomed down the alley toward me."

"Where were you standing then?"

I pointed to the left about ten feet. "Under those trees over there. It wasn't until the Cherokee had passed that I walked over to the kiawe and saw Tommy Pang's body."

We walked down the alley to the office door, and I buzzed the intercom.

"Who is it?" a woman's voice said.

We identified ourselves, and the door buzzed. We walked right into an open reception area, where a young Japanese woman stood behind a desk. The room was slightly dingy and not very attractive— nothing on the walls, the furniture older, kind of crappy. A little boy, about five, sat on the floor in the corner, coloring. On the desk a little name plate read Arleen Nakamura. "Can I help you?"

"Are you Arleen?" I asked.

"Uh-huh. What's this about?"

I told her Tommy Pang had been killed, and she said, "Oh, wow. I wondered why he wasn't answering his cell phone, why he didn't call me."

"What's your job here?"

"I'm Mr. Pang's personal assistant. I answer the phones, order the supplies, you know, that kind of thing." She sat down in her chair and motioned me to her visitor's chair. Akoni leaned up against the wall.

"What kind of business did Mr. Pang do besides run the bar?"

She held her hands out, palms up, in a gesture of defeat. "I have no idea," she said. "Nobody ever comes by. It's like totally boring, but my little boy goes to school around the corner, and I can bring him over here when he's done." She motioned to the boy in the corner, still absorbed in his coloring book. "So mostly I surf the Internet and talk on the phone."

Just then the phone rang and she answered it. I noticed she just said hello. Then she quickly switched into Japanese. It was her mother, so that was probably a natural kind of thing, but I always think it's rude to switch languages in front of someone. Makes it sound like you want to hide something.

Because my family is so mixed up, I don't look too much like anything, so she probably figured I didn't speak Japanese. But then, she didn't know that my mother's maiden name was Kitamura. I couldn't help listening in, though my Japanese is a little rusty and I missed some nuances. She sounded almost gleeful in explaining that Tommy was dead, which I thought was ghoulish. After a couple of minutes she switched back to English and said, "Listen, Mom, I have to go. The cops are still here. I'll call you later."

She smiled at me as she hung up. "My mother."

She toyed with the rings on her fingers, and I noticed there was no wedding band, though there was a picture of her with her little boy in a silver frame on her desk. At first I'd thought she was barely twenty-one, but looking closer I saw the fine lines that had started around her mouth and eyes, and refined my estimate upward at least five years.

"Kind of strange to have a secretary when there's no business going on," I said.

"Oh, he was doing business. Faxes and phone calls and deliveries, but he never let me see anything. The fax is in there—" she motioned to his office. "And he always locks it when he leaves."

"Was it locked this morning?"

"Yup. And before you ask, I don't have the key, so you'll need a locksmith."

"How about that other office?" Akoni motioned to the open door.

"We used to have a bar manager, but he quit a couple of weeks ago and moved back to the mainland. I was supposed to put an ad in, but Mr. Pang's son told me not to. I think he wanted the job for his boyfriend."

"Tell us about them," I said. "The son's name is Derek, right?"

"Yeah. He's a pretty nice guy. He's opening an art gallery, so I've been helping him with paperwork, like licenses and stuff." She leaned over to me, lowered her voice. "I don't think his father knows he's gay."

Suddenly she sat back. "Guess I don't have to whisper that anymore."

"How about the boyfriend? What's his name?"

"Wayne. I don't know him that well. He's only come by a couple of times. He's really big, though. Doesn't look gay at all."

I wondered if Arleen thought I looked gay, but I didn't say anything. "Mr. Pang didn't have a watch, wallet, or keys on him when he was found," Akoni said, stepping into the breach. "Did he usually?"

"Oh, yeah, he had this gold Rolex, and a thick gold and diamond bracelet, and a diamond pinky ring. He told me once he was born in April. It was his birthstone, the diamond."

Akoni took notes. "And he always carried a wallet, a money clip, and a key ring," Arleen continued. "Oh yeah, and his Palm Pilot."

"Really," I said. "You know what kind of stuff he kept on there?"

"Not a clue." The phone rang, and Arleen said, "Mom, I'll talk to you tonight, okay? The police are still here."

"I don't want to hold you up much longer," I said, looking at the clock. It was almost five, beyond the end of our shift, and I figured Arleen would be closing up soon anyway. "We'll have to get a locksmith in and come back tomorrow."

"Don't you need a search warrant?"

"Not if we have the approval of the person in control of the office," I said. "That would be you, right?" She nodded. "And you want to do what you can to help us find out who killed Mr. Pang, don't you?"

"Sure." She thought for a minute. "I come in around nine, after I drop my son off at school. Then I go out at two thirty to pick him up and get some lunch, but I'm usually back by three."

Akoni and I walked out into the alley. "I'll call the locksmith first thing tomorrow," I said. "That's about all we can do. You think the same person who bashed him in the head stole his jewelry?"

"Awful big coincidence if it wasn't," Akoni said. "You see any jewelry first time you see him?"

I tried to remember but couldn't.

"How long you think the body was alone?"

"Ten, maybe fifteen minutes."

"Enough time for somebody to see him, think he's drunk, and roll him." Akoni shook his head.

I didn't think it was possible for me to feel worse about what I'd done, but ways just seemed to keep cropping up.

I didn't feel like going home yet, so I got my truck, put an old Springsteen tape on, and just started to drive. I ended up way up the Pali Highway, driving fast and singing along with Bruce. I wanted to wipe everything out of my brain, give it a chance to cool down. I kept thinking about my confession to Akoni at the mall, trying to figure out what it meant for my future. It seemed like it had happened so long before, but it had really only been hours.

Eventually I pulled off at a switchback that gave me a view of the city and the Pacific below and got out of the truck. It was almost dusk and Waikīkī glowed against the dark ocean. It seemed to me like some fantastic golden city, the place where all my dreams could come true, if only they didn't shut me out of it.

There was a rustling in the brush across the road from me, and somewhere an owl hooted. I stood there for a while longer, people in cars passing on their way home to their families, me just standing there outside the city, wondering.

I didn't realize how exhausted I was until I pulled up in front of my apartment building. Then it hit me, and I barely made it up the stairs and into bed before I fell into a deep, dreamless sleep.

Chapter 7

I WOKE EARLY the next morning, surfed for an hour, and was at my desk at eight o'clock. Akoni came in a few minutes later and said, "Let's take a walk." As we left, we passed a tourist wahine in a skimpy G-string bikini who was complaining about having her wallet stolen on the beach.

"The bad guys get an early start, miss," I heard the desk sergeant telling her. "You've got to watch out all the time."

Good advice, I thought. Outside, the morning air was fresh and bright. You could see tiny bits of dust and sand dancing in the shafts of sunlight coming from over the top of the Ko'olau Mountains. We got coffee from a little hole-in-the-wall souvenir place on the mauka side of Kalākaua Avenue and walked along the beach.

"Here's the way I see it," Akoni said finally. "You did two things wrong. You failed to report a crime under your badge number and notify your lieutenant, and you failed to secure the scene of a crime. Neither of those is enough to lose your badge."

He took a sip of coffee. I didn't say anything.

"You don't have to say anything else. Nothing to anybody. Not the business about being in the Rod and Reel Club, or the guy who stuck his tongue in your ear. If you feel you want to tell somebody something, you say you had a lot to drink, you went for a long walk, you stumbled onto the body, the guy in the Jeep. You were pretty drunk, confused."

"I did drink a lot, first when I was out with the guys, then at the Rod and Reel."

"Cops and drinking, they go together. It's a long tradition. Guys can handle that. The department can handle that. This other thing, you're blazing new territory. You want to take your chances?"

"You're telling me to lie."

Akoni crushed his empty cup and pitched it into a trashcan. "I have never told you to lie about anything and I never will," he said. "You know me better than that. But you're no virgin, Kimo. You know the way the world works. Sometimes you have to put some spin on the truth to make things come out the way they should."

I thought about it. It was true. Many times, we'd known who the bad guy was, and we'd eliminated confusing evidence from our reports. Or we'd bluffed our way to confessions, pretending we knew more than we did. It was just something you did. But those situations weren't about me. Somehow I'd always applied a higher standard to my personal life.

"You want to tell the truth?" Akoni said. "The way I see it, you've been lying for years, never telling anybody you were really a fag. What about all those girls you took home? You tell them the truth?"

There was a sour taste in my mouth. I said, "No."

"So why start now, when the truth can ruin you?"

"Because I owe it to Tommy Pang," I said, before I could think about what I was saying. The conviction built inside me. "That poor jerk is dead and I did wrong by him. In the past, when we've adjusted the truth, it was because we were trying to be faithful to the dead, to do right by them. This is the opposite."

"Tommy Pang was a two-bit crook who never did anything nice for anybody," Akoni said. "Nothing would probably give him more pleasure than to feel like his death caused a cop to lose his job. You come out with this, they'll reassign you to a desk downtown, or put you on leave. You won't be able to do a thing for Tommy Pang, or for any other vic we ever find." He paused. "You won't be able to do a thing to feel better."

He was right. It would be the end of my career. Not right away. I'd ride a desk for a while, and then there'd be a hearing, and eventually I'd turn in my badge. Maybe they'd ask for it; maybe I'd just do it in the end out of frustration. "So I write up what you said. What then?"

"We keep it between ourselves for now. If we never find the bad guys, it goes into the cold case file. If we do, and we take the case to the DA, we see what he has to say."

"You could get fried over this yourself, you know. You don't have to be a part of my troubles."

"You're my partner." He started walking. "Come on, let's get back to work."

When we got back to the station, an elderly Chinese lady was at the front desk complaining about kids making noise in her building, and a couple of tourists were reporting a purse snatching. I called the number Genevieve Pang had given us for her son and left a message that it was important he call me at the station. Then I called the locksmith, who arranged to meet us at the alley behind the Rod and Reel Club, and Akoni and I walked over there together.

Arleen opened the door and ushered us into the reception area. She was so tiny, barely five feet, and next to me and Akoni she looked like an elf, or maybe some kind of Japanese pixie. She even bounced on the balls of her feet when she walked. As the locksmith got to work on the door, I said to her, "You're sure this is okay, giving us this permission?"

"Well, when I was little, my mom always told me if I was lost, to go ask a policeman. So if you can't trust the cops, who can you trust?" She smiled goofily.

The locksmith popped the door to Tommy's private office easily, and we walked in. The room was as sparse as the rest of the office, just a big leather chair and a desk, and two chairs across from them. A big computer sat on the desktop, but unfortunately it was password protected and Arleen didn't know the password.

"What's that?" Akoni asked, pointing to a little contraption on the desk next to the computer.

"The docking station for his Palm," Arleen said. "You want to find out everything about Mr. Pang, you find the Palm." She bit her lip, thought for a second. "But I think he backed everything up onto the computer, too. If you can find somebody to break into that file, you'll know where he went, who he saw, all that stuff."

We looked through the desk but there was nothing to find. Tommy Pang had held his cards close to his vest.

Before we left, we looked carefully at the outer door, to make sure no one could have broken in. There was a police lock on it, a rounded metal bar about three feet long, maybe two inches in diameter. It slipped into a catch on the door and then slid in a semi-circular track set into the floor. It was designed so that you could open the door just enough to pass something through, but wouldn't open wide enough to let a person in.

"So nobody broke in," I said. "Hey, Arleen, how do you get in if this lock's on?"

"That door there goes through to the bar," she said, pointing. "Usually Mr. Pang sets the police lock before he leaves, and goes out through the bar. I come in that way."

I nodded. There didn't seem to be anything else to look at, so we left. "It's going to be days before we can get some computer guy out of downtown," Akoni said, as we walked down the alley.

"You know my friend Harry? He can break into any computer— I know, he's bragged about it enough, no matter how much I tell him it's a crime. Maybe I can get him to come back with us."

"I don't like involving civilians in a case."

"We hire experts all the time," I said, stepping aside to let a pair of nuns pass. "It's either that or wait for the department to send us somebody, after the trail is cold."

"Won't get us much, but if it pleases you." We didn't talk much on the way back to the station; when we stall on a case it gets us both down. "I'm heading over to see what the FBI knows about Tommy Pang," Akoni said, when we came to the garage where he parked his car.

"I can go with you."

Akoni planted his feet and looked off toward Diamond Head, not at me. "I need to do this on my own."

There are times when we go off and investigate on our own. Usually it's when we have so many leads that we can't afford to waste time together. That wasn't the case now. "Why?"

He shuffled his feet. I added, "Don't stonewall on me, Akoni. Tell me what's up."

He opened the door to the garage stairwell. Before he went in, though, he said, "I've done as much for you as I can, Kimo. Now I gotta look out for me."

"What?" I asked, but he'd already gone inside.

I didn't know what to think anymore. Was he in a bad mood? Was he separating himself from me in case I took a fall? It only took me a few minutes to get back to the station, but all the way I kept wondering what freight train Akoni saw heading my way. It was easy to believe it was something going wrong with the case, but it was also quite possibly something else. Akoni had always criticized my bullheadedness, the way I have to see something through once I've started it. It's a trait that frightens me sometimes.

Back at the station, I sat at the computer, pulling up names of every person known to be part of a tong, and then got on the phone, calling detectives and snitches to see who might have had it in for Tommy Pang. Printouts piled up on my desk, I got a backache, and my garbage can filled with crumpled coffee cups. There were no rumors of tong wars, and nobody had a special grudge against Tommy Pang. As a matter of fact, he was a relatively small player, not even catching much notice among the big boys.

When Akoni still had not returned by lunch, I left for the records office in Honolulu Hale, our city hall, an impressive stone building with a pseudo-Spanish motif—narrow windows, turrets, the whole nine yards. You walk through a short lobby and into a central courtyard with a high ceiling. Straight ahead are the city council chambers, but the records office is tucked away in a corner in the back. I stood in line and checked out the microfiche I needed, then took it to one of the readers.

I was interested to find out if Tommy Pang really owned the club, or if perhaps he was a front man for some larger group. I slid the fiche into the machine and navigated to the appropriate section, where I discovered that the Rod and Reel Club was owned by Hui 812.

Hui is a common Chinese term for a kind of holding company. It was what I expected; if you're going to own a gay bar, you probably don't want to make it easy to find out who you are. I pulled the fiche out and got back in line.

By the fourth fiche, I was annoyed and intrigued. I started taking notes and drawing lines on my pad from one company to the next. It took me all afternoon. I went back and forth between the records library and the tax office, showing my badge and asking questions. Finally I found a name, hidden under layers of bureaucracy and red tape. The eventual owner of the Rod and Reel Club, once I went back through level upon level, was Tommy Pang. No other name showed up anywhere.

By the time I got back to the station, Akoni had returned. The FBI had nothing, he said. No open investigations involving Tommy Pang, no rumors of tong wars, nothing. I told him what I'd found.

"Doesn't get us any farther, does it?" he said. "What now?"

"We wait for Derek to call us back, or we call him again tomorrow. Then we start questioning Tommy's business associates. Anybody with known tong affiliations. See if this is business-related."

He frowned. "You think it could be anything else?"

"You heard Mrs. Pang. He had 'company' sometimes. Maybe the company had a jealous husband or boyfriend."

"I hate this part of a case," he said. "Too many ways to go, no real leads. Just lots of legwork." He started packing up his stuff.

"Listen, Akoni, you want to get a beer? We could strategize."

"I gotta get home."

"Look, I think we ought to talk."

He stood up. "We got nothing to talk about. I'll see you tomorrow."

He walked out, and the door shut behind him with a bang.

Chapter 8

I SAT AT MY DESK for a while, until Alvy Greenberg, one of the uniforms who'd been with us on the drug bust, came in and said, "Hey, Kimo."

Alvy was about five years younger than I was, and a surfer, too. We'd met when I'd just come back from the north shore, when I was in the academy, and because he was maybe interested in becoming a cop we'd talked, off and on, about my experiences there. At the time he'd been a waiter, taking a couple of classes at UH, trying to decide, as I had, if he was good enough to make a career out of surfing.

He wasn't, either, and just before I made detective he'd entered the academy. I guess I had been kind of a mentor to him, advising him on how to deal with problems that came up, surfing with him now and then. Once in a while on a holiday weekend we'd throw our boards into my truck and drive up to the north shore, just to keep our hands in.

"Hey, Alvy." He was the kind of guy who looked older than he was, the one you always sent in to buy the beer when you were still illegal. About five seven, thin, already balding rapidly at twenty-seven, and incredibly ambitious. You can't take the detective's exam until you've had three years on the beat, and most officers wait another year or two beyond that. Alvy had taken the exam right after his third anniversary, just a couple of weeks ago. He was still waiting for the results, but we'd already talked about where he might be posted. He didn't want to leave Waikīkī, but he was tactful enough to realize that unless they expanded our staff, he'd have to wait for me or Akoni to leave. So we'd talked about District 1, which covers most of downtown and is administered out of the main headquarters on South Beretania Street. Lots of government and corporate offices, and Chinatown to provide work, and the chance to be at headquarters and make contacts.

Or maybe District 2, Central Oʻahu, which also included a lot of military installations. It wasn't as glamorous, but he'd get a lot of experience. I was also pushing for District 5, Kalihi, which included the airport, and I agreed with him that the other districts, Pearl City, Waipahu, Windward Oʻahu, and East Honolulu, wouldn't be very interesting, and wouldn't give him the opportunities for advancement he was lookng for.

He walked over and sat on the edge of Akoni's desk. "That was some bust yesterday, huh?"

"You can't win every time," I said. "Sometimes things just go wrong."

"I heard you got another case already."

He was an eager guy, handsome in a way, red hair you might almost call auburn, blue eyes. He was a little too skinny to be a great surfer—he didn't have enough weight to master the really big waves, but he made up for it with endurance.

If you want to be a good surfer, I mean a really good one, you have to work at it. You have to be totally focused on making yourself the best surfer you can be. You spend hours out on the water, learning to anticipate the waves, practicing your moves. You have to understand a little about physics, a little about oceanography, a little about wind speed and ground swells. Surfing has to be what you live for.

I thought I could live for surfing when I was twenty-two, crashing on the floor of somebody's house on the north shore, surfing Haleiwa from dawn to dusk and talking surfing the rest of the time. Nobody screwed around too much up there—we were too focused, and at the end of the day, too tired. So I could ignore the part of my brain that was always scared, always holding my secret.

Then I came in fifth in the Pipeline Spring Championships. By March, the great winter waves on the north shore have died down a little, and the best surfers have gone to chase waves elsewhere on the globe. So I wasn't facing top competition, but still, it was the best I'd ever done. I was riding high, thinking I was finally reaching my potential. Most surfers start when they're fifteen or sixteen, peak in their early twenties, and lose the competitive edge by thirty. I was twenty-three, and at the top of my form.

A bunch of the guys took me out drinking that night, buying me beers and shots until they closed the bar and dawn started to streak the dark sky over the north shore. I was in no condition to drive home, so my buddy Dario dragged me over to his place to crash. He was staying at a one-room cottage north of Haleiwa, right on the sand. I remember wanting to lay down right there on the beach, I was so wasted.

The next thing I remember is waking up in Dario's bed, naked, with his mouth on my left nipple. He bit and sucked at both nipples until they were hard and sore, and then licked a trail down my stomach to my crotch, where he gave me a blow job.

Then I must have passed out again, because when I woke again it was almost noon and there was a note on the refrigerator from Dario. "You're a champ, Kimo," it read. "I'm on the water."

I felt paralyzed. My mouth was dry and my head pounded, and my body was sore in unaccustomed places. When I looked in the mirror I saw my nipples were raw and red, and I had a hickey on the side of my neck. I knew then that I had made the best showing I would ever make in a competition. It would only get harder to keep holding back my desire for men, and the effort I had to put to that task would take away from what I had left for surfing.

So I left. I hitched back to the place where I was staying, packed up, and went home. After hanging around my parents' house for a while, I entered the police academy, the most macho thing I could think to do. I thought if anything could save me from being gay, being a cop would be it.

Alvy and I talked for a while, and eventually I felt better. If Akoni couldn't deal with me, that was his problem. Alvy went back to the locker room to change out of his uniform, and I walked home.

A couple of hours of daylight were left when I got home, so I went surfing. It felt good to empty my mind of all my troubles—my sexuality, the danger I might face if I came out as a gay cop, the dead ends in Tommy Pang's murder case.

On my way home, I stopped at a little grocery just across Lili'uokalani from my apartment and picked up some shrimp, mushrooms, and red and green peppers to grill on my little barbecue. It's a tiny, dark little store, and from the outside you'd think it was nothing more than a place for cigarettes and beer. But the owners, an elderly Chinese couple, take a fierce pride in the quality of the produce, and it's better than any grocery I know in Honolulu. The clerk is a surfer, and he lets me run up a tab when I don't have cash with me. "How were the waves?" he asked as he rang me up.

"I got a couple of good ones. Not many, though."

"Yeah, it's been slow."

He was a skinny blond dude, long stringy hair, and tiny silver rings in his right ear, his nose, and his left eyebrow. He was wearing a tank top and as he reached for a bag his shirt shifted a little and I noticed he'd gotten his nipple pierced, too. To avoid looking at him anymore, I turned a bit and scanned the store. "Hey, throw these in too, will you?" I asked, spotting a bag of chocolate-covered Oreos and putting them on the counter.

"Eating healthy, dude," he said, with a smirk. "These are killer, by the way. I keep a bag behind the counter and scarf them for energy sometimes."

Back outside, the sun was setting through the low motels and high-rise towers, turning the sky a range of pastels from yellow to blue. It was a peaceful time of day, and I started to feel like someday

I might get my life back in order again, and that in the end all the uproar might just be worth it.

I skewered the shrimp and veggies and grilled them, and put them on a plate over rice. With a Rhino Chaser, it was a perfect supper, and then I sat back with a Sue Grafton mystery until I was yawning more than I was reading. I could do this, I thought, as I crawled into bed, under the Hawai'ian quilt my haole grandmother had pieced together in the first days after she'd married my grandfather, when she was struggling to fit into life as Mrs. Keali'i Kanapa'aka. I could make a nice life for myself, by myself, without the complications of romance or sex. But then, as sleep overcame me and I snuggled up next to my pillow and I missed having someone next to me, I doubted my own resolve.

Chapter 9

THE NEXT MORNING, Akoni and I spent the first hour of our shift catching up on paperwork. By nine o'clock I was ready to get back to Tommy Pang's murder. "I'm tired of giving Derek time to grieve," I said. I picked up the phone and dialed Derek's number, and was rewarded by a sleepy voice in my ear.

I introduced myself and asked if I was speaking to Derek Pang. "Derek can't really speak to anyone now," the voice said. "He's very upset."

"Mr. Gallagher, I know Mr. Pang is upset, and I sympathize with him, but we're investigating a murder. I'm sure he'll recognize it's very important to catch whoever killed his father. We need to talk to you both as soon as possible. How soon could you see us?"

He tried to put me off but I wouldn't give up. Finally he said, "Give us an hour?"

I agreed to meet them at their apartment at ten o'clock. Akoni printed out a list of known tong members we could ask Derek about, and then we sat and brainstormed on a bunch of questions as well. At nine thirty we headed ewa from Waikīkī, hitting a lot of traffic on Ala Moana Boulevard. The address Wayne had given me was for a pair of luxury high-rise condominiums in Kakaʻako, an industrial neighborhood across from the port of Honolulu, out past the Kewalo basin, with its assemblage of small boats.

Kakaʻako was in the middle of a transformation. The condo tower where Wayne and Derek lived dominated the neighborhood; on one side was Restaurant Row, a collection of twenty-some restaurants and a multiplex cinema, but on the other side was a derelict empty lot. Low warehouses and parking lots were all around. We parked at a meter on a side street and walked up to the condo, where we checked in with the doorman, then rode the elevator to the twentieth floor.

Gallagher answered the door. He was about six four, broad-shouldered, with sandy hair and a mustache. He probably weighed 260, which was about thirty pounds too much for a man with his build. He was barefoot, wearing a black silk kimono embroidered with red dragons. His eyes were still sleepy and he hadn't shaved or combed his hair yet. I thought he was incredibly sexy.

The thought jolted me and made me tongue-tied for a minute. Akoni introduced us and Gallagher led us into the living room, a large, white room with a white marble floor. There was a black leather sofa along one wall, and a big entertainment center with a large-screen TV and a fancy stereo system. Sliding glass doors led to a half-round balcony overlooking Waikīkī, Diamond Head, and a vast expanse of Pacific Ocean. What dominated the room, though, was the art.

All four walls were hung with paintings. Some large, splashy colorful flowers, a couple of Jackson Pollock spatters, even a small impressionist-style piece in a heavy gilded frame. There were Chinese watercolors and what looked like South American primitives, as well as a large Hawai'ian quilt on one wall that even I could tell was quite valuable.

The art wasn't confined to the walls, either. In one corner stood a brightly painted wooden chair, with a collection of wooden animals painted in clashing colors around its base. A small pedestal held a glass-topped box with a few pieces of what looked like museum-quality early Hawai'ian artifacts. It was like walking into a gallery. "I'll get Derek," Gallagher said. "He's resting."

"Perhaps we could talk to you first," I said, regaining my voice.

"Sure." He sat down on a black leather recliner catty-corner to the sofa and motioned to us. "Have a seat."

His arms and calves were lightly dusted with sandy blond hair.

When he sat, the kimono fell away from his right thigh and I could almost see down to his crotch.

Get hold of yourself, I thought. "Let's start chronologically," I said. "Where were you Tuesday night, the night Tommy was murdered?"

"We were at the club for a while, the Rod and Reel Club. Derek was trying to convince his father to make me the manager." He preened a little. "I've been working in bars and clubs for years. Worked my way through Yale as a bouncer, bartender, and assistant manager."

"Around what time was that?"

Wayne had to think for a minute. It was almost like he was running through his story and making sure he got the details straight. "I guess around midnight. Yeah, had to be around then, because we went off to another club after that."

"Anyone else in the office when you were there?"

"Some guy who worked for Mr. Pang came over for a meeting. I don't know his name. Mr. Pang had a lot of other businesses besides the club. He was an important guy."

"Did he know about you and Derek?"

"You mean did he know we like to suck each other's dicks?" He sat back in his chair and folded his arms in front of him. "We never talked about it. If he wanted to ignore it, then that was his business."

"You and Derek knew each other in college?"

"Doesn't your friend ever talk?" He looked at Akoni. "What are you, the strong, silent type?"

Akoni said, "I'll talk when I have something to say."

Gallagher turned back to me. The lapel of his robe had fallen open, exposing one pink nipple surrounded by dark blond hair. "We met sophomore year. We both lived in East Asia House. It's a dorm, but they have special programs, Japanese culture, Pacific Rim cooking, world politics, that kind of thing. I was always interested in the Orient—my father was a businessman, and we lived in Japan for a year when I was a kid."

I nodded. "You moved out here a couple of months ago, right?"

He shifted position, closing his robe, tucking his right leg under him. "Derek had to get settled, see what things were like out here, before I could come out. He hadn't really been home much since he went away to college." He laughed. "He didn't even know his dad owned a gay bar. Can you believe it?"

"Do you recognize any of these names?" I handed Wayne the list we'd made up of known tong members.

Wayne shifted around a little in his chair and the black silk rode up on his thigh again. I was getting pretty annoyed at myself for noticing so much about him, but somehow I couldn't help it. He read through the list, pausing once or twice. Finally he looked up and shook his head. "None of them ring a bell. Mr. Pang really wanted Derek to go legit, you know. He didn't want to tell Derek about anything he did that was shady at all. I mean, we only knew about the bar because the office is in back there."

He handed the list back to me. I looked down at my notes. "How about this 'guy who worked for' Mr. Pang? Do you have any idea who he was, what he was doing at the bar on Tuesday night?"

"I don't know what made me think so, but I always thought the guy was a cop. Not in a uniform, but he kind of carried himself that way."

"You ever been arrested?" Akoni asked.

"So you do talk," Wayne said. "I know cops. Every bar I ever worked in, we had to call the cops now and then."

"You didn't answer the question."

"I don't like your tone," Wayne said. "And I don't think I want to answer that."

"What was it?" Akoni asked. "You get caught sucking some guy off in the bus station? Maybe in a men's room at Yale?" Akoni put a particular emphasis on the college name.

I could see Wayne was starting to get worked up, so I jumped in. "Look, that's not important," I said. "You said you went to another club after the Rod and Reel. Where'd you go?"

He was clearly making it up. "A bar out near the Aloha Bowl."

"That far out?" I asked.

"It's a gay club, the Boardwalk. An after-hours kind of place." He paused. "If Derek and I want to hang out, we can't exactly do it at the bar his dad owns. Some dumb queen would have ratted us out in a heartbeat."

"You see anybody you know at this place, the Boardwalk?"

He shook his head. "It's pretty dark in there. We got a couple of beers and sat in the corner. I guess maybe we were there an hour or two."

I was willing to bet no one at the bar could ID either of them.

Derek emerged from the bedroom then, looking freshly showered, wearing black linen pants and a white T-shirt, his short black hair slicked back. He was about five seven, 150 pounds. Behind wire-framed aviator glasses, his eyes were red. "You look like shit," he said to Wayne. "That's the way you come out and talk to people?"

"I didn't have time," Wayne said, with a little whining edge to his voice. "You were in the bathroom."

"That's never stopped you before." He motioned to the bedroom with his thumb. "Put some clothes on."

"I want to stay here with you."

"That's all right, Mr. Gallagher." Akoni and I stood up to shake hands with Derek. "We won't be too hard on him."

Wayne tried to give Derek a look but Derek wasn't having any of it. So Wayne got up, tightened his kimono, and strutted back to the bedroom. I have to admit I was a little sorry to see him go, and I hoped nobody noticed the way I watched his ass as he left.

Chapter 10

"DID HE OFFER YOU ANYTHING, Detectives?" Derek asked after we'd introduced ourselves. "Coffee? Juice? Sometimes the man has no manners." Without waiting for an answer from us, he continued, "I'm making cappuccino. You want?"

We agreed. He led us over to the kitchen, and Akoni and I sat at a round glass table with a white marble gargoyle at its base as Derek Pang started making cappuccino. While the coffee brewed, Derek busied himself getting out mugs, spoons, even a little shaker of toppings like you see in fancy coffee shops. His movements were quick and delicate, and I was reminded of someone describing a homosexual as "light in his shoes."

That description really worked for Derek. He could have been a ballet dancer, perhaps, with the kind of china-doll looks I saw in some of my aunts and girl cousins on my mother's side. It's a fragility and femininity that many men, obviously including Wayne Gallagher, found attractive.

I started asking Derek the same questions we'd asked Wayne.

"We left the club around midnight on Tuesday," he said. He stuck a metal pitcher filled with milk under the frothing arm of the cappuccino maker. He had to talk louder over the noise of the steam frothing the milk. "I wanted my father to make Wayne the manager. So we were hanging around the Rod and Reel a lot, trying to show that Wayne knew the business."

He poured the cappuccino, and I took a sip of mine. It was

good. "Wayne mentioned an associate of your father's was there that night, too. Did you know him?"

Derek looked into his mug, holding it with both hands. It took him a long time to answer. "How much do you know about my father?" he asked, finally.

"A lot," I said. "He had a pretty extensive record."

"Growing up, I never knew what my father did. Or I knew, but I didn't, you know what I mean?"

I nodded.

"He owned a bunch of legitimate businesses, you know. The bar's just one. Once I came back from college, he promised that if I worked with him for a while, he would help me set up my own gallery."

"My father wanted me to work with him," I said. "He's a contractor, and I spent most of my summers on crews on his projects. When it came time to choose, I became a cop instead."

"Then you know what it's like. It's worse when your father's a crook, Detective. You always try to keep your head turned so you won't see what's going on. I know the guy who was with him was a cop, but I didn't want to know any more than that."

"You're sure?" Akoni asked.

Derek nodded. "I'm sure it's not unheard of," he said dryly. "For gangsters to have cops on their payroll. And make no mistake, my father was a gangster. I don't know what he did, exactly, what put the food on our table or paid my tuition to Yale, but it wasn't pretty."

I kept worrying that Wayne would come out and join us, so I hurried on. "The night your father was murdered, you left around midnight, you said. Where did you go after that?"

He thought, and for a minute I thought they had worked their stories out in advance. "We went for a drive." He looked down at his mug briefly and said, "We went up to a bar called the Board-walk, and we, well, made out for a while." He looked up at me again. "Kind of crappy, isn't it? My dad's getting killed and I'm off getting laid."

Gallagher came in then and pouted because Derek hadn't made him a cappuccino too. "I didn't know whether you'd eaten or not," Derek said. There wasn't a chair at the table for him, so Gallagher stood awkwardly against the counter, dressed now in white shorts and an emerald-green polo shirt that was a little too tight for him. He reminded me of my brother Haoa, big and beefy, but even clothed there was a sexuality to him that I found very attractive.

"This associate of your father's, the man you think was a cop," Akoni said. "Do you think you could recognize him again?"

"I think so," Derek said. "He came around a couple of times. My father gave him something that night, in a box." He thought for a minute. "I remember thinking it was funny. It was a little box, kind of long and narrow, like you'd put a necklace or a bracelet in, and I thought it was a funny gift for my father to give him."

I finished the last of my cappuccino and handed the mug to Derek, who stood up and took all three mugs to the sink.

"Can you clean up, Wayne?" he asked. "We're going back into the living room." As he passed by, Wayne's hand passed over Derek's chest and I was sure he tweaked Derek's nipple.

"How about his associates, from his other businesses?" I asked Derek, when we were sitting in the living room again. "Are there any you might have met sometime?"

He thought about it for a while. In the kitchen I heard Wayne banging pots and pans and generally reminding us he was around and mad that he hadn't been asked to join us. "There's one man I met a couple of times," he said finally. "An old man, a little stooped over. He said to call him Uncle Chin."

I felt an electric jolt run through my body. My father's closest friend, a man I considered my own godfather, was a gangster of sorts, retired by then. I had always called him Uncle Chin.

"Did you feel that this Uncle Chin was a gangster like your father?" Akoni asked.

Derek nodded. "I mean, I got the feeling he was some kind of Godfather, you know? An old guy who didn't really do much but everybody kind of looked up to him. It was almost like, I don't know, I was presented to him. It was all very formal."

I was lost in thought, but Akoni and I had talked about Uncle Chin in the past, so he kept the interview going. "Do you have other family?"

"My father was an only child, but he had a lot of cousins," Derek said. "They're all still back in China. My mother was a bar girl in Hong Kong when my father met her. She's never told me about any family at all." He must have noticed the look on our faces, because he said, "Does that surprise you? The very proper and respectable Genevieve Pang was a bar girl in Hong Kong? It's amazing how we can reinvent ourselves, isn't it?"

"How about your father's other businesses?" I asked. "Do you know anything about them? Who runs them, what they do, that kind of thing?"

He shook his head. "He wouldn't tell me anything. I knew, but I didn't know, you understand?"

"I understand," I said.

There wasn't much else we could ask. Derek looked over the list of tong members too, but didn't recognize any of the names. Wayne finished in the kitchen and came into the living room, and the four of us talked for another couple of minutes. They both walked us to the front door. "You'll let me know if you discover anything about my father's murder?" Derek asked, and we both agreed.

≈

"MAYBE WE NEED to think about the murder weapon," I said. I thought back to the autopsy. "Doc's best guess was something like a lead bar or pipe."

"Where the hell do you get one of those in Waikīkī?"

Something was nagging at the back of my brain. I'd seen a bar like that only recently. Where had it been? Suddenly I remembered. "We are really lousy detectives," I said. "Come on. If I'm wrong, I'm buying you dinner."

"Duke's Canoe Club," Akoni said. "I've been wanting to go there."

We grabbed sandwiches at a fast-food place and ate in the car. We made a quick stop at the station so I could pick up an extra-large evidence bag, and we were at the Rod and Reel Club just after one. Arleen buzzed us in. "Hey, guys, what's up?" she asked.

"My partner here's had an inspiration," Akoni said, as I walked around behind the door and kneeled to the floor. "But he's been keeping me in the dark."

I looked closely at the police lock, a long steel bar that rotated in a groove on the floor. No matter how well someone had tried to clean it up, I could still spot a couple of flecks of blood on it. "Our weapon," I said, pointing it out to Akoni.

"Ick," Arleen said. "I've been touching that bar since Tuesday."

We carried the bar back to my truck, and then drove it over to the evidence lab at the main police headquarters. We have a pretty modern lab down there, in the special investigations section on the B1 level, along with a little minimuseum of how far crime detection equipment has come. They have old scientific equipment like a centrifuge, a spectroscope, and a compound microscope. Also an old ultraviolet lamp and an ancient fingerprint camera, and photos of old evidence types.

In the document lab, they analyze stuff like typewriters, documents, footprints, and tire treads, as well as fingerprints. One of my favorite signs is down there, on the wall outside. It reads, THE ABSENCE OF EVIDENCE IS NOT EVIDENCE OF ABSENCE.

"So we've got our weapon," Akoni said as we walked down the hallway from the document lab to the elevator. "You got a couple of suspects up your sleeve, too?"

The hallway is lined with windows into the other labs, like the drug lab, and serology, where they do the blood analysis. The firearms lab has a chart with actual bullets on it for matching purposes, and a one-lane firing range for firing tests. There are eyewash and safety shower signs all over.

"You want everything, don't you?" We both agreed the week had been a long, stressful one, and we'd feel better about tackling the idea of suspects on Monday. Akoni dropped me back in front of my building, and as I was climbing up to my apartment, my cell phone rang.

The number belonged to Harry Ho, my oldest friend. Harry had just come back to Honolulu a few weeks before, after a protracted stretch on the mainland, which involved several degrees from MIT and a few patents registered in his name. From what I understood, he'd made enough money that he could afford to tinker with his inventions, and at the same time he'd taken an adjunct teaching job at UH.

In high school, Harry and I had sneaked off as often as we could to surf. We'd ride the city bus down to Kuhio Beach park with our bathing suits on under our school clothes. We stored our boards with the guy who ran the surfboard concession at the Beach Princess hotel, and we'd ditch our clothes on the sand and surf until dark. I don't know when he managed to do his homework—I rarely did mine. But he graduated at the top of our class at Punahou and dragged me along behind him somehow.

I went to college at UC San Diego because I could surf there, and Harry went to MIT. We kept in touch—I sent him photos of me surfing, with snotty captions, and he wrote regularly to tell me what an asshole I was. Now that he was back, he was mad to surf again, even though he's terrible. I'm not much good anymore, though, so I don't mind going out with him.

Harry's brain isn't like mine. He can do lots of things at once and never seems to be shorting any one of them. If he'd been able to get the education he wanted at UH, or somewhere else near a beach, he could have gotten a lot higher than fifth place in a regional tournament in the off season. But we're over thirty now, and he missed that peak when he could have been great, and even with all those degrees and the money and the patents, he regrets it. Since I have my regrets, too, I humor him.

"Hey, brah, how's life?" he asked.

"I'd say it pretty much sucks." I had no intention of telling Harry why life was sucking at the moment, beyond Tommy Pang's corpse at the county morgue. I'd stepped out on that limb once already and found it pretty damn shaky.

"Sounds like you need some attitude adjustment. What do you say you meet me at the Canoe Club bar in twenty minutes and we work on some wahine action?"

I took a deep breath. "I could use a beer, but maybe someplace quieter. Can you handle that?"

"I am the master of handling," Harry said. "How about the Gordon Biersch at the Aloha Tower?"

"I'm there. You just can't see me yet."

I picked up a second wind as I drove back downtown. I parked on the pier and walked over to the Aloha Tower Marketplace. The tower was the tallest building in the islands when it was built in 1926, and on "Boat Days," when the cruise ships left Honolulu, it was the place to be to watch the ships go out, kind of like that scene at the start of *The Love Boat* when the horn sounds and everybody gathers on all the decks to wave and throw streamers. Now there are clusters of clever shops selling island handicrafts, postcards and magnets of island girls (and boys) in thong bikinis, and jars of pohā jam and coconut syrup.

The Gordon Biersch brewpub is at the far end of the marketplace, just a stone planter filled with orange, red, and purple bougainvillea and a short piece of tarmac separating you from Honolulu Harbor. I walked through the indoor bar and the restaurant, looking for Harry. As I came back out into the fierce afternoon sun I saw him at the outdoor bar, where he'd just gotten a beer. Fortunately, he'd ditched his habitual pocket protector full of mechanical pencils, but, God bless the guy, he still looked like a geek. He's thin, Chinese, about five-feet six, with his black hair cut like somebody put a bowl on his head and snipped. As you'd expect from someone who looks the way he does, he's a genius; as you would not expect, he's also very good with people and able to charm the pants off any wahine he sets his sights on.

He raised his wheat-logo mug to me and headed off to snag us a table, not an easy task in a bar crowded with happy-hour beer drinkers. He was successful, though, as he seems to be in everything he tries, and by the time I had my glass of marzen, a German wheat beer they specialize in, he was sitting at a table at the very edge of the patio. Just beyond us a tanker was coming in through the narrow channel, silhouetted against the setting sun. A few clouds were massed over the Waianae Mountains, but otherwise it was a glorious, clear, golden afternoon. Then why did I feel so bad?

"It sounded like you wanted to talk," Harry said, motioning to our relative obscurity.

"I do," I said, sitting down. "How's it going?"

"It goes. I'm remembering how to sense the waves. It's something I'd forgotten, you know? I know all the physics, but I forgot how you just have to sit there and feel the water."

I nodded. "You settling in all right at the university?"

"I've got a couple of smart students," he said. "Better than I expected. But enough crap. What's wrong?"

I shifted uneasily in my seat. A young Japanese couple just beyond us on the pavement stood by one of the yellow bollards and kissed, and then a fat tourist in a garish aloha shirt offered to take their picture. I realized again I would never go on a honeymoon, never mug for the camera with a pretty wahine on my arm, never build up memories to share with my children and grandchildren. I had an urge to spill everything to Harry, but I'd done that with Akoni already and look where it got me.

"Just a case," I said. "Listen, maybe Monday morning you can give us a hand. We got a computer with a password we don't know, and a missing Palm Pilot that maybe was backed up onto the hard drive. You know anything about that?"

"You have to ask?" Harry put his hand over his heart. "I'm hurt. Of course I know about that. They haven't made a password yet I can't break."

We made a time to meet at the station Monday, and then I directed the conversation back to surfing, and Harry went along with it. We ordered some food, and by the time we staggered away I was feeling almost good again. I'd been thinking for a while that I was being the good friend to Harry, helping him get adjusted to life in Hawai'i again, going surfing with him while he flailed his way back to proficiency. But it was clear he was doing something for me, too.

Chapter 11

THE NEXT MORNING was Saturday, and I spent most of it surfing, riding my bicycle, and trying not to think about Tommy Pang or any revelations that his death might bring up about me. I was only partially successful.

Sunday morning I drove over to my brother Haoa's house for a big family luau. My oldest brother, Lui, was the general manager of the island's best TV station (at least in my opinion), and Haoa, my second brother, owned a landscaping business. Haoa lived in a big house, lavishly landscaped, in St. Louis Heights, the same neighborhood where we all grew up, but much higher up on the hill than my parents.

Lui and Haoa always competed for attention when we were kids, and that rivalry still continued. Each wanted to make more money than the other, have a nicer house, smarter children, prettier wife. Neither ever scored a particular advantage in this game of one-upmanship; every time one did something, the other aped him or tried to top him. Last summer Lui sent his son Jeffrey to Japan for a summer exchange program; this summer Haoa sent his daughter Ashley to England. Lui put a pool in at his house; Haoa a pool and a hot tub. It's an accelerating spiral I refuse to get sucked into.

Of course they were much closer to each other than they were to me, or than I was to them. There were only two years between them, while there were eight years between me and Lui, six between me and Haoa. In childhood, the only thing they joined forces on was picking on me. As an adult, though, I was reconciled to them and loved them as much as any brother could. I would always be the "kid brother," the baby of the family, and just as my relations with my father had improved as I'd matured, my friendships with my brothers had grown and deepened as well.

It was scary to think that I might lose that closeness to them if I told them I was gay. Haoa was the more macho of the two, big, heavyset, and blustering, looking more Hawai'ian than anyone else in the family. He often made fag jokes, in fact, jokes about almost every ethnic group, even Japanese, and I had often seen our mother wince at those jokes, since she is half Japanese and knew the prejudices her parents went through during World War II.

Lui's eyes were more oval, and he was the shortest of the three of us, barely topping six feet. He was shrewd, with our father's business sense, but doubled. He was also fiercely competitive, not just with Haoa and me but with the world at large, always seeking to assert his primacy as first boy.

I pulled up outside Haoa's house and parked at the curb. Already I could hear my nieces and nephews in the backyard, and a stereo playing Keola Beamer's *Wooden Boat* CD. "Mama going fishing, Papa going fishing, rocking in a wooden boat," he sang as I walked up the path. "We're rocking in a wooden boat, several generations old, we'll be going on forever, rocking in a wooden boat."

Everybody wanted hugging and kissing. Haoa wrapped me in a big hug, his breath already a little beery. "Welcome, little brother," he said. He stepped back. "What, no pretty wahine with you? You must be getting old, slowing down."

"Must be," I said. Another big hug from Lui, and little kids stampeding around wanting hugs from Uncle Kimo. We took lots of pictures out in the backyard, under the tecoma tree, where its fallen petals had produced a pink carpet laid over the lush green lawn. My favorite was a picture of me reclining on the lawn with all my nieces and nephews crawling over me, from Jeffrey and Ashley, who were twelve, down to the little babies barely out of diapers.

We played the Makaha Sons on the stereo, along with Hapa,

Keali'i Reichel, and Israel Kamakawiwo'ole. The day before, Haoa and his landscaping crew had dug the imu in one corner of the yard, and the luscious scent of roasting pig floated out into the surrounding hills.

When I was a kid, we had luaus at our house now and then, usually to celebrate something. The best one was for Haoa's graduation from Punahou. He had been a big football star there, and all his friends came for the luau. My father and brothers and I were up early in the morning, digging the imu. My mother kept saying, "Make it bigger. Lots of mouths to feed today." We had every kind of food imaginable. Chicken long rice, poi, shark-fin soup, sweet and sour spareribs, Portuguese sausage and beans. And desserts, pineapple like crazy, ten different types of crack seed, malasadas, mango ice cream. I thought we would have leftovers for days, but those football players ate everything in sight. At the end of the night, I remember my parents sighing happily, glad that it had gone so well, and equally glad that it was all over.

Haoa's luau was not as fancy; after all, this baby was the fourth. Still, the people kept streaming in. Old family friends, distant cousins, neighbors, clients of Haoa's landscaping business, potential clients he wanted to show off for. My father and his cronies held court on the screened porch, a bunch of old men smoking cigars and telling stories from thirty years ago.

My father has been building houses in Honolulu since before I was born, and building friendships, too, across communities. His father, a full Hawai'ian, was trained by missionaries, learned to read and write English, and became a teacher at the Kamehameha School. My grandmother was haole, a schoolteacher from Montana who came to the islands to teach, fell in love, and never left. My father grew up in Honolulu, and his parents encouraged him to make friends everywhere. As a boy, he had pākē, or Chinese, friends, as well as friendships with the leading scions of the haole community. He began college at UH, but World War II intervened, and he served in Europe in a unit comprising many island boys.

The result is that my father knows almost everybody in Honolulu, in both licit and illicit sectors. One of his best friends is Uncle Chin, a tall, stately man who always has an air of ineffable sadness, even when bouncing his dozens of honorary grandchildren around him. In part that stems from a paralyzed nerve in his face that causes the left side of his lip to droop a bit, giving him a faintly perplexed look. Uncle Chin is not really active in his tong any more, at least not according to police records. But police records aren't always up to date.

I tried to stay out of trouble during the luau, preferring to play uncle with my nieces and nephews and second cousins. At one point, though, I went up to the bar to get another beer and ran into Peggy Kaneahe.

We always sat next to each other in school, Kanapa'aka and Kaneahe. When we were sixteen I took her to the junior prom at Punahou, and she was the first girl I ever kissed. We dated for almost three years, through high school graduation and our first year away at college. She was the first girl I had sex with, in her pink bedroom, one Saturday afternoon when her parents were at a christening on the north shore. I broke up with her right after coming home from my first year in San Diego.

I had never known anyone who was gay until I went to college. Then, on my first day at UC, right after my parents left, I met a guy down the hall who was tall and thin and very effeminate. A lot of the jocks on the floor used to tease Ted, write fake love notes on the message board on his door, steal his towel from the shower room, that kind of thing. I remember once he walked down the hallway, stark naked, his hair dripping wet, making eye contact with every guy who lined up to watch. I got a hard-on when he looked at me.

One night in the spring I got drunk and was sitting on my bed with the door to my room open when Ted walked by. I don't remember what I said to him, why he came into my room, but I know that after a while he got up, very deliberately, and locked the door. Then he stood in front of me, without speaking, and unbuttoned his shirt. He unbuckled his belt, unzipped his pants, and dropped them to the floor, then shucked off his shirt and tossed it next to his pants.

I remember being stunned that he didn't wear any underwear. Then he came over to me.

By the time I got home that summer, I was totally confused. But I knew that dating Peggy hadn't cured me of my interest in men, so somehow that meant I had to stop seeing her. I didn't have a reason to give her, and I don't think she ever understood.

Peggy accepted her drink from the bartender.

"Hello, Kimo," she said. We kissed briefly, like friends.

"You look great," I said. She wore a pink polo shirt and a navy skirt, and her hair, which was usually pulled up on her head, now hung free to her shoulders.

"I'm sorry I've been so busy," she said. "And I can't even stay long today, because that jogger hit-and-run is coming up before Judge Lap tomorrow and I've still got pages of discovery to go over."

"Your parents look good," I said. I nodded toward them, a nicely dressed couple who had always been friendly toward me.

"You're lucky you have brothers," she said. "My parents are still waiting for me to give them grandchildren." She made a face. "Peggy, when you gonna find nice boy, have keikis for us to play with?"

"I still get that. Parents have no shame when it comes to grand-children."

We talked for a while longer, walking around the party together. I wondered how I was going to tell Peggy that I was gay, that I'd been fooling her as much as I'd been fooling myself. I hoped that we had so much history that it didn't matter that there weren't any sparks between us anymore, that we were really just friends. At least, I told myself it didn't matter.

Chapter 12

MONDAY MORNING I was up at first light and on the waves at Kuhio Beach. By the time I made it to the station I was feeling almost myself again. Akoni arrived a few minutes after I did, and I said, as he arrived, "Hey, brah, how was your weekend?"

He pulled a chair up next to me and said in a low voice, "Look, Kimo, I don't want to know about your personal life. I don't want to know what kind of magazines you got stashed under your mattress, who blows in your ear, and who you grab your ankles for. All right?"

All my good spirits evaporated. Although the weekend had helped me put aside some of the problems of the week before, it obviously hadn't worked that way for Akoni. "You want another partner? You want me to put in for a transfer? I will."

"I don't know who you are anymore."

"Well, here's a news flash, buddy," I said, as I turned to my computer. "I'm not sure I do either."

We were scheduled to meet Harry back at the Rod and Reel Club at eleven. At about ten of, I asked Akoni if he wanted to come with me. "You handle it," he said. "I don't know any of that computer stuff anyway."

Harry and I met up in the alley behind the bar. Arleen was on the phone with her mother, as usual. I introduced Harry as "my computer expert" and she waved us into Tommy's office.

Harry sat right down at Tommy's computer and turned it on. "Let's see what he's got here." He'd asked me to prepare some basic information about Tommy for him—his birthday, his wife's name and birthday, and their anniversary; Derek's name and birthday. He did some typing and after a couple of unhappy sounds, the computer started whirring to life.

"Easy as pie," he said, as the Windows warm-up screen appeared. "That's not to say some of the files aren't encrypted, too. We'll have to see."

Most computerese was gibberish to me. The computers we use at the station are very simple, and pretty user-friendly. You move a cursor around, click on items on lists, type in what you want to search for, that kind of thing.

Around noon Arleen came in. "It's almost lunchtime," she said. "My boy's on a half-day today, so I've got to go pick him up."

"I wish I had a kid," Harry said, shocking the hell out of me. "How old is he?"

"He's five," she said. "You want to see a picture?"

Harry nodded. She opened her wallet and pulled out one of those studio pictures, the kid posed on a carpet with a teddy bear. "Cute," Harry said. "What's his name?"

"Brandon." She had a couple more pictures, which she showed us. I looked at them politely, Harry with more interest. "He's why I have this job, you know. I'm not some kind of criminal or anything. I just need to work, and this way I get to see my son as much as I can."

"Cool," Harry said.

"I actually have an associate's degree in computer science," she said shyly, making eye contact with Harry. Once again I was amazed at his ability to attract women. It was almost like I wasn't there, this thing that was going on between them. "But I make more here than I could as a junior programmer somewhere, and the hours are better."

Arleen gave us a menu for a local deli before she left, and we ordered take-out. Harry sat back down at the keyboard and I wandered around the office, looking for anything we might have overlooked. But I guess there just wasn't much to find, and I'd been over every inch by the time the delivery boy came. I paid him, tipped him, and took the sandwiches into Tommy's office.

"Find anything interesting?"

"Nothing much. But I still have to crack into his Palm backup software."

Just then we heard the door open. Arleen had that same cute little boy with her who I'd seen before, with coal-black hair in a crew cut, wearing blue and white striped overalls with a pattern of trains across the bib. He looked hapa haole, or half white, his eyes a little too round to be fully Japanese.

She smiled shyly, and introduced Brandon to Harry. I felt like drumming my fingers on Tommy's desk, hurrying them along, but I caught myself. It was like this transformation was going on inside me—I'd never been an "us versus them" kind of guy, maybe because my family's such a melting pot that I never felt like there was a group I didn't have at least one relative in.

But being gay was different. Every time I heard the word *fag*, I felt my body go tense. I was starting to look at straight couples together and get mad, because they had something I didn't. I was about to start calling people with kids "breeders." And all within less than a week. Kind of took my breath away.

It took Harry a little longer to break into the Palm Pilot software than it had to get past the computer's password, but eventually he was able to sync up the Palm to a copy of Microsoft Outlook on Tommy's computer, and export the calendar and address book. "This won't be completely up to date," Harry said, as the PC whirred and clanked. "I mean, if you're expecting to see he had a meeting Tuesday night, it might not be there. This is only current up to the last time he hot-synced to the computer."

"I love it when you talk geek to me. What does that mean in English?"

"It means that he carried the Palm around with him and made entries directly into it," Harry said. "Adding people to his address book, putting in appointments, making notes. But in order to get that stuff into this file"—he pointed at the icon on the screen—he had to perform this function they call a hot sync. You drop the Palm into the cradle, press a couple of buttons, and everything copies."

We discovered that the last time Tommy had done a hot sync had been a week before. "So nothing on his calendar for last Tuesday," I said.

"But you wanted some names and numbers," Harry said. He clicked over to the address book. "Voila."

We printed out his address book, which was unfortunately quite sparse. A few names and numbers I thought the FBI might like, but very little in the way of personal contacts.

We finished up after that, but it took a couple of minutes to get Harry past Arleen's desk. Brandon was fascinated with his glasses, pointing again and again to his own reflection and laughing. Harry found all this very cute, though I got tired of it fast. I love my nieces and nephews, but I think they've gotten more interesting as they've started to have interesting things to say—usually around nine or ten. Harry promised to send Arleen some information on classes at UH, too, even volunteering to get together with her and help her polish her programming skills.

I finally got Harry outside. The trade winds had died, and Waikīkī sat under a dark gloomy cloud. As we got out to Kuhio Avenue, a guy in a red Porsche with vanity plates DR DR veered in front of a huge black Lincoln Navigator, and the Navigator almost crunched his very expensive bumper. There were times when I really wanted to drive a black and white again.

"You up for a little wahine action tonight?" Harry asked. "Canoe Club bar?"

I don't know how it came out. I certainly hadn't been planning to say it. I said, "Harry, I'm gay," as we turned makai toward Kalākaua. "No more wahine action for me. I'm not lying anymore."

"I wondered when you were going to figure it out," Harry said. "Good for you."

"You mean you knew?"

I looked over at him, and he nodded. "I wasn't a hundred percent sure, but I had an idea. I mean, you could never stick with a woman for more than a week or so."

"There was Peggy in high school. That was three years. Although I have to say I'm not quite sure what I'm doing dating her again."

"High school was different. None of us knew what was going on back then." He paused. "So what made up your mind?"

"It wasn't really one thing. I don't know why, all summer long, I've been noticing things I never noticed before. Porno magazines in a bookstore window. Two guys holding hands at midnight on the beach. Then I came here."

I told him about that night, from the failed drug bust down to finding Tommy Pang's body in the alley. "It doesn't matter to me; you know that," Harry said. "You're my friend and I hope you'll always be my friend, no matter who you decide to sleep with."

I didn't know what to say. I felt elated, and also a little scared and weird, like my secret was out. I'd told Akoni, of course, but the circumstances and his reaction had been so different. Harry put his hand on my shoulder. "Mahalo," I said. "I'll call you. Maybe we'll surf tomorrow."

"Just not at six a.m., okay?" he asked. "I need my beauty sleep." Then he smiled. "Plus, now you're not going to know if I'm alone or not."

I nodded and smiled, and he crossed the street, heading back toward his apartment.

On the way back to the station I ran into Alvy Greenberg on patrol, under the trees behind the Royal Hawai'ian Shopping Center. It was cool back there, nicely landscaped, quiet. We stood in the shaded lobby of the shopping center, surrounded by the hushed voices of serious shoppers and the occasional small child racing around the courtyard. We talked for a couple of minutes, mostly me expressing my frustration at how few leads we had on Tommy Pang's murder. "I'm sure you'll figure it out," he said. "If you want my honest opinion, I think you're the best detective we've got on the force."

"Mahalo, brah. I appreciate the vote of confidence, even if I don't feel like I deserve it most of the time."

I walked past the open air market, full of T-shirts, plastic leis, and coconuts you could send home like postcards. A parrot called out, "Hey, pretty baby," over and over again. There was a lazy flow of tourists from one stall to the next, but nobody seemed to be buying much.

Back at the station, I checked out all the people in Tommy Pang's address book. Akoni was out tracking down his own leads, and I only spoke to him long enough to determine that we'd start talking to the people in the book together the next day.

As I left the station, I passed an elderly Japanese woman, dirty and dressed in rags, sitting on the curb shouting obscenities. Alvy Greenberg was on his way to roust her, and I nodded as we passed each other.

I took my time walking home. At Kuhio Avenue and Lili'uokalani Avenue, a good-looking guy passed me, heading toward the beach. He had a surfer's physique, like mine—shoulders built up from paddling, well-defined pecs, a dusting of blond hair down the center of his chest. His legs were long and his calves and thighs well-muscled. He was wearing a skimpy bikini that didn't cover much, and as we made eye contact I experienced a sudden pang of horniness. Our eyes met for a moment, but both of us kept on walking. I couldn't help turning to stare at him; though I forced myself to look away eventually, I watched his butt go halfway down the block before he blended in with the rest of the crowd. And then I knew what Akoni was worried about, and it scared the hell out of me.

My life had become my latest case. Like a bulldog, I was going to keep gnawing at my personal problems until I had worked them out. I knew then that I couldn't keep my sexuality a secret forever, and that revealing it would rip open my life and hurt many people around me.

I knew my parents loved me, but I also knew my father's bad temper and remembered the frequent disparaging comments he'd made about māhūs when I was growing up. And though my brothers loved me, too, they had teased me mercilessly when we were kids. Suppose they chose to shut me out now?

I'd always appreciated my sense of being rooted in Honolulu. Landmarks in town had personal meaning to me, and my parents' network of friends and distant relatives was all around. Now that I was an adult, I often ran into distant cousins and Punahou classmates at the grocery, on the beach, or on street corners downtown. What if I was shut out of that community, shunned? What if I didn't belong in my own home anymore?

A storm was coming. Akoni had just felt the winds a little sooner and was scrambling to get under cover.

Chapter 13

WHEN I GOT inside my apartment, the red light was blinking on my answering machine. I thought it would be my mother, with some follow-up to the party of the day before, and I just didn't feel like talking to anyone. There was still a couple of hours of daylight left, and I thought I might go for a swim. I hit the play button on the machine as I started to strip down.

It wasn't my mother. A different female voice said, "Hi, Kimo, it's Terri Gonsalves." I dropped my shirt on the bed and stopped, listening. There was a pause before she went on. "I really need to talk to you, Kimo. Can you call me, please? Maybe we can meet." She left her number. "It's important, Kimo. Please call me tonight, if you can. Evan is working late." She paused again. "I'm counting on you." Then the line went dead.

I looked at my watch. It was almost six, and Terri answered on the first ring, as if she'd been sitting by the phone waiting for me to call. "I'm sorry to bother you, Kimo. I know you're probably busy."

"Never too busy for you, Terri. You know that. What's wrong?"

"I'm worried about Evan. There's something wrong with him— the way he's been acting. It's not like him. Do you think you could come over tonight? I can explain it."

"Sure. When?"

"Danny's playing at a friend's house, and he'll be home any minute for dinner. Do you think maybe eight o'clock? By then he'll be asleep and we can talk. Evan won't be home until midnight at least."

I agreed to go out to Terri's house on the Wailupe peninsula at eight. I finished stripping down and put on a bathing suit, and headed for the beach to get in a quick swim before dinner. I told myself I was just looking to cool down after the long, hot day, to refresh myself by contact with the ocean. But maybe I was hoping to run into the guy in the skimpy bikini, too.

Not that I would say anything to him, even if I saw him. As I walked to the beach, I wondered when I would stop running, when I'd make a move toward another guy the way the giraffe had moved on me at the Rod and Reel Club. I doubted I'd ever be blowing in a stranger's ear, but I'd always been comfortable walking up to unescorted wahines, saying hello and trying to start a conversation. If it worked, it worked. If the girl snubbed me, I'd move on. It was just a matter of transferring that attitude to guys.

It had to be different, though. When you walked up to a girl, there was a big chance she wouldn't like you, that she'd be engaged or dating someone, or just not interested. But chances were she'd be heterosexual and wouldn't be offended.

Unfortunately, the chances were that most guys on Kuhio Beach were heterosexual, too, and they'd be pissed off by any kind of overture, and ready to punch me out. Which left me at kind of a loss. The only men I can generally peg as gay are the faggy ones, and they don't do it for me. The way I figure it is, if I was attracted to someone feminine, I'd stay with girls, and my life would be a lot easier. Unfortunately, the kind of guys who appeal to me are masculine, athletic, all male. I supposed there might have been a few of them at the Rod and Reel Club, and that eventually I'd have to make my way back there.

Once I got to the ocean, though, I stopped thinking. I swam out beyond the breakers, where the surfers waited, and then swam parallel to the shore down toward the old marine stadium. I did a couple of trips like that, back and forth, until my legs and arms started to feel like jelly. Then I floated for a little while, looking up at the crisp blue sky dotted with a few lazy clouds. As it started to get dark I realized I had to get in, to grab a quick dinner and drive out the Kalaniana'ole Highway to Terri's house in Wailupe.

I found my towel on the beach and started drying off. While the towel was over my head, someone said, "You're not surfing tonight."

I looked up. It was the guy I'd seen on Lili'uokalani, sitting up on a beach towel a couple of feet away. I realized I'd probably seen him on the beach a couple of times, but hadn't taken much notice of him, thinking he was a tourist. But now, after my reaction to him back in the street, I got nervous, feeling like there was a big empty place at the bottom of my throat. "No, I surfed this morning," I said, trying to sound casual, but sure my voice was squeaking. "I just wanted to do a little swimming tonight."

He nodded. "I swim every day, but I haven't gotten up the nerve to try surfing yet."

"You should try it. It's fun," I said, trying to keep the towel around my swimsuit to avoid any embarrassing revelations. "People around here are pretty friendly about giving advice." I paused. "I could give you a couple of pointers sometime, if you want."

"That'd be great." He stood up and walked over to me, with his hand outstretched. "I'm Tim, Tim Ryan. I just moved to Waikīkī a couple of months ago."

I gave up holding the towel and shook his hand. I told him my name and asked what he did. Fortunately my interest in him wasn't too evident, and I could relax a little.

"I'm an attorney," he said. "It's boring."

I laughed. "Not from my perspective. I'm a cop."

"Really?"

We talked for a couple more minutes, and then I caught a glimpse of his watch. "Jesus, it's late. I've gotta run. Maybe I'll see you around this weekend. I can give you that surfing lesson."

"I'll look forward to it." He looked directly into my eyes and smiled, and I felt a shiver run down my back. I smiled myself, a goofy kind of grin. We shook hands again, and I picked up my towel and headed down Lili'uokalani toward my apartment.

He was a nice guy, I thought, as I walked. This was a perfectly innocent conversation. I'd never been sex-mad, like some of my friends in high school and college, imagining that every time a woman talked to me it was because she wanted me. I hoped I wouldn't change now. Tim Ryan was probably just a good guy who was interested in making some friends and learning to surf. Of course, there was the way he looked at me and smiled. I realized then he must have noticed me watching him earlier that evening.

I'd been around the sex wars long enough to know what that kind of smile meant. It was funny to realize it meant the same thing from a woman or a man, but I knew then that I was going to sleep with Tim Ryan, and for the first time in my life I thought, *that's okay.* It's like I was giving myself permission to be who I was, and that felt good.

I had barely enough time to microwave myself a couple of frozen burritos and jump into my clothes before I had to leave for Terri's. When she and Evan got married, her parents gave them a honeymoon in Europe and the down payment for this house, a four-bedroom ranch on the makai side of the Kalaniana'ole Highway. On the mauka side of the highway, the Wiliwilinui Ridge is very steep, but it opens out to a flat plain and a little peninsula that sticks out into the Pacific. It's a dramatic vista, the stony mountains coming almost to the water's edge, with Koko Head in the distance.

The neighborhood, full of ranch-style homes with broad lawns, is protected from the busy highway by a yellow brick wall. If you don't look up at the mountains or the towering palm trees, you could be anywhere in suburbia—sidewalks, basketball hoops in driveways, lots of boats on trailers. Terri's house isn't on the water, but Wailupe Beach Park is right next door. There's a nice lawn, and a semicircle driveway, and a row of tall coconut palms. When I drove up it was dark and the neighborhood was quiet. I could see a light on in the front window.

Terri heard me pull up on the gravel driveway and came to the front door. She looked even prettier than she had in high school.

She was still slim, and her brown hair was cut in the same page boy she'd had since she was a teenager. Back then, when I didn't understand the feelings I had for guys, I wanted to marry Terri Clark. She was smart and funny, along with being beautiful, and we used to pass each other notes in algebra class.

Then we went to college, and I realized the gulf between us. Terri's family was rich, while my father was a small-time contractor who'd have been delighted to get the contract to remodel one department in one Clark's store. I went to Punahou on scholarship, while Terri's family paid full freight and donated money whenever the school came calling. My parents wanted me to go to UH but I convinced them I had to go to the mainland, and I ended up at UC San Diego, majoring in surfing. At least, that's what I spent most of my time doing. I actually majored in English because the classes were often in the late afternoon and I could surf in the morning if the conditions were right.

I came to understand, when I saw Terri at home during those college years, that she was out of my league. She came back to Hawai'i with her degree, summa cum laude, but without a husband, and started working in the Clark's at Ala Moana, standing behind a counter in the perfume department. She told the other girls it was just a funny coincidence that her last name was Clark.

After six months behind the perfume counter Terri joined the management training program, and when there was a burglary at the Ala Moana store she was assigned to deal with the police. That's when she met Evan Gonsalves, and no one was more surprised than I was when they announced their engagement.

In the years since then I'd seen her occasionally, more so after I gave up on being a professional surfer and came back to Waikīkī. I went to the christening for her son, Danny, and the regular Christmas party she and Evan held every year. We talked about Punahou a little, and she always asked who I was dating.

"Thank you so much for coming," she said, as I walked up to the front door. I kissed her cheek and she took my hand. I followed her into the graceful living room, decorated with her family's antiques. The room was dominated by a mahogany sideboard that had been brought to the islands by her missionary great-grandfather, and it was filled with fragile Chinese export porcelain. But her couch, covered in a floral fabric, was overstuffed, and a child's plastic train sat on the highly polished coffee table, so the room wasn't as oppressive as it could have been.

She gave me a splash of single-malt scotch over ice in a crystal glass, and we made some small talk. Finally I said, "So tell me what's wrong."

"You have to understand something," she said, facing me. "I love Evan. I wish I could convince him that I love him for himself, that he doesn't have to constantly fight to keep up with my family. But I can't."

"What do you mean, keep up with your family?"

"Buying things." She held out her wrist to me, to show me a thick gold bracelet set with tiny emeralds. "Yesterday was my birthday. This is what he gave me."

"It's beautiful."

"I took it to a jeweler on Fort Street and had it appraised today. He told me it was worth five thousand dollars."

"Wow."

"Evan doesn't make that kind of money," she said. "I know." She waved her hand around to encompass the living room, the house. "He'd kill me for telling you, but we don't live on his income. I have a trust fund, and even though Evan hates it, we use that money to pay most of our bills."

"Maybe he's been saving his money. You know, putting away a little each week so that he could buy you something special."

"I don't want money from him, or expensive jewelry. I can't convince him of that." She paused. "Besides, his paycheck gets deposited automatically. It goes into our joint checking account, and he never makes big withdrawals."

"He could be doing private security work somewhere. Maybe

sometime when he says he's working late, he's actually on duty for somebody else."

She shook her head. "I know him. And I don't mean to say that I'm checking up on him, but sometimes I have to call him when he's working late, and he's at his desk."

"So where do you think he got the money for the bracelet?"

She put her hand to her mouth and looked away. A minute later she looked back. "I don't know, I think maybe . . . I think maybe he's taking bribes."

I sat back. "Whoa, Terri, that's a serious accusation to make. Evan could lose his job just over the scandal. Do you have any evidence—I mean, beyond the bracelet?"

She shook her head. "I was hoping you could help me find out. Unofficially, of course. Then I could confront him and make him stop."

"This is a bad idea, Terri. Remember, I'm a cop too. If I find evidence of a crime, I'm morally obligated to report it. That would mean I'd be snitching on a fellow cop, which is one of the worst things a cop can do."

"I didn't realize it would put you in such a bad position."

"If you have suspicions about Evan, you need to talk to him about them."

"I can't, not without evidence," she said. "What if I'm wrong? What if there's a logical explanation for this?" She waved the bracelet at me again.

I drank the last of my scotch and she offered me another. While she fixed it, I tried to think about what she should do. When she handed the glass back to me, I said, "I'm no expert on relationships between husbands and wives, but it seems to me you guys need to talk to each other more. You have to find some way to tell him you don't want the bracelet and get him to take it back."

"It's not just the bracelet. It's a lot of little things. We'll go to dinner, and Evan will insist on an expensive restaurant. Then he'll pay the bill in cash. Or he'll bring me flowers from a fancy store and I'll never see the bill. He's getting extra money from some-where, and I'm so scared I don't know what to do about it."

She started to cry a little, dabbing at her eyes with a tissue.

"I can't do anything for you, Terri. Officially or unofficially. It's not unheard of for cops to be on the take. Evan's a prime candi-date, living like this on his salary. It's got to make him feel bad. You don't want to have to move out to a duplex in 'Aiea just to be able to live on a cop's salary, not when you don't have to. But let's face it, you're accustomed to living well, and Evan is going to do what-ever he can to make you happy. If he thinks you want a richer hus-band, he'll try to make himself that person."

"Mommy?"

We were both startled. We turned simultaneously and saw Danny standing at the edge of the living room in his pajamas. "Can I have a glass of water?"

"Of course, darling." She stuffed the tissue in the pocket of her dress and stood up. "You remember Uncle Kimo, don't you?"

Danny nodded. I usually got out to Terri and Evan's every cou-ple of months, and Danny and I always spent a little time hanging out. Like my nieces and nephews, and most of the island kids, he was mad for pogs—paper disks that originally came from milk bot-tles, but now were given out by every island business as a promo-tional tool. Kids loved to flip them, trading them back and forth based on how they landed.

"I'll let myself out," I said. "I wish I could do more for you."

"I understand."

I stood in the velvety darkness of her driveway for a minute before getting into my truck. Looking out toward the ocean, I could see the vast compass of stars. There was a slight scent of jasmine and new-cut grass in the air, and I could hear distant traffic and the slight rus-tle of a lizard in the underbrush.

There are always days like this, but that doesn't make them any easier. I couldn't help Tommy Pang, and I couldn't help Terri

Gonsalves or her husband Evan, a nice guy who had probably already started down the wrong road. Hell, who was I kidding? I couldn't even face my own demons, no less help someone else with hers.

I got into my truck and drove back to Waikīkī.

Chapter 14

TUESDAY MORNING, lieutenant Yumuri called Akoni and me both into his office. He's full Japanese, only about five seven, and all business. "Where are we on this murder?" he asked.

We gave him the rundown, walking through everything we had done, the interviews, the tong research, the discovery of the murder weapon. We told him our plan to start tracking down the people in Tommy's address book that day.

"You've done all that, but you don't have any suspects?" he asked. "Go back to investigation one-oh-one, gentlemen. Who benefits from the crime?"

Akoni and I looked at each other. I said, "The wife inherits everything. But I'll bet the son and his boyfriend take over the Rod and Reel Club."

"Boyfriend?" Yumuri asked. "Figures. The guy was found behind a fag bar, after all. Those queens are always mixing it up, sticking bottles up their boyfriends' butts, clawing each other with their fingernails." He made a limp-wristed gesture.

Yumuri had been a homophobe as long as I'd worked for him, but it hadn't bothered me before. I didn't say anything, and I didn't dare look at Akoni either.

Yumuri thought for a minute. "You're doing good," he said, finally. "Wrap it up as soon as you can. Murders are bad for tourism, you know. If we let this go, I'll have every hotel manager on Waikīkī on my back."

Akoni and I went back to our desks. "Let's take a look at that address book," he said, and I pulled out the printouts. There were records on a couple of businesses Tommy owned besides the Rod and Reel Club, including a lingerie shop in Chinatown that we were pretty sure was a front for prostitution. Live models would stroll around the store in their underwear, and for a fee you could take one into a back room and examine the merchandise more closely. Vice had closed the place down once or twice, but they hadn't been able to make any charges stick.

He also owned a pack-and-ship place that specialized in sending goods to and from mainland China. They did a big business in relocation of ancestral bones, and it seemed like it was all legit. Chinese have a big thing for ancestor worship, and it's important that the graves of their dead relatives be maintained properly, that the right prayers are said and the right offerings made. As Chinese émigrés become successful and settle in the United States, one of the things they do is arrange for the remains of their ancestors to be brought to the United States for reinterment where they can visit more frequently and don't have to depend on a Communist government that might interfere with their observances.

"I'd say these two places give us a good head start," Akoni said. "Which one you want to start with?"

We decided to do some more research before calling anybody. I gave him the lingerie shop and took the pack and ship for myself, and we spent the time until lunch on the phone, finding out as much information as we could on Tommy Pang's business life. Akoni made an appointment for us to go out to the lingerie shop and interview the manager, so we decided to get lunch in Chinatown. We found a parking space on Pauahi Street, named for one of the royal families of Hawai'i, and ended up eating at a place on North King across the street from the lingerie shop, called Sally's.

"They have nice stuff over that place across the street?" Akoni asked the waiter as he delivered our kung pao chicken. "I need a present for my wife."

The waiter leered. "Very nice stuff." He made curving motions with his hands. "You like very much."

"Me, I'm not married," I said to the waiter. "They have pretty girls that work there? Maybe I can get one to go out with me."

He shook his head. "They no go out." Then he broke into a wide grin. "They have rooms in back, no need go anywhere else. You like," he said, nodding. "You like very much."

The waiter went back into the kitchen and Akoni looked at me. "You're still interested in girls?"

I gave him a look. "And you're really going to buy something there for Mealoha?"

"I might," he said defensively, and turned his attention to his chicken.

When I was a kid, I remember Chinatown was a lively neighborhood, full of colorful groceries, lei shops, and dark little restaurants and bars. Now, though, it's pretty dismal. The streets are dirty, with old soda cans, shriveled dog turds, and shreds of newspaper rustling in the wind. Most of the storefronts are shuttered and many are scrawled with graffiti, and there's nothing much Chinese about it.

There are still a bunch of lei stores on South Beretania and Maunakea Streets but they're tiny rooms with folding shutters or rolling grills, and the leis are all behind glass refrigerator cases. You can walk past and only smell car exhaust and fried oil, not a single flower. North King is the only street with any life on it—groceries with tubs spilling out to the street, stacked with garlic, ginger, hard-boiled eggs, and packages of dried mushrooms, noodles, and soy sauce.

We paid our bill and crossed the street, past a stand with row upon row of leis made of orchids, velvety orange 'ilima flowers, and fragrant maile leaves intertwined with tiny white pikake blossoms. Behind the counter, an elderly grandmother sat stringing even more. Chattering teenagers and haole tourists crowded around the booth, debating the merits of different leis and bargaining for better prices.

Through the window of the lingerie store, we saw three elegant young Chinese women and one Filipina strolling around inside in lacy undergarments, periodically stopping to strike poses for the half-dozen male customers. We walked in, and a soft, musical bell rang. No one paid any attention to us.

Each of the girls was wearing more than you'd see on any public beach, particularly since the invention of the thong, but their effect was totally sexy, from their high-heeled shoes up to their expert makeup and hair. And each had a flawless body. "If you see something you like, just ask," a girl in a red lace teddy said, brushing past Akoni. He turned almost as red as her outfit.

"Where do we find Norma Ching?" I asked the girl.

"She's in the back."

Akoni and I steered our way past tables of panties, racks of bras, and waterfalls of see-through nighties to a desk in the back where an improbably elderly Chinese woman sat behind an elaborate French renaissance desk.

She looked tiny, barely four feet, and wore a bright blue silk cheongsam. Her gray hair was as elegantly coiffed as any of the girls', and her skin was hardly wrinkled. Even so, I guessed she had to be at least eighty. "Mrs. Ching?" Akoni asked.

"You must be the detectives," she said. "Please sit down."

She motioned us to two tiny embroidered chairs across from her desk, and Akoni and I perched on them like embarrassed elephants. "We're interested in anything you can tell us about Tommy Pang," Akoni said.

"That man, what a flirt!" she said, with a light, musical laugh. She had almost no accent and her voice was high and girlish. "He used to come around once a week or so to meet the girls and examine our merchandise. He was very interested in quality control."

I'll bet he was, I thought. "Did he ever bring anyone with him?"

"Oh, yes, often," she said. "He often brought business colleagues here to show them our facilities."

Akoni took out a pad and pen. "Can you give us any names?"

Norma Ching looked horrified. "Our business is very confidential." She leaned toward us. "Sometimes, you must understand, our clients are making purchases they would not want revealed to their wives."

"We understand," I said. "And we're not interested in anything that goes on here, or in connecting anyone to this facility. We're trying to find out who killed Tommy Pang. And in order to do that we need to talk to people who knew him." I smiled at her. "We won't find it necessary to reveal how we were able to secure these names."

"Let me see." She opened a box filled with index cards and flipped through for a minute or two. "Melvin Ah Wong," she said. "Dong Shi-Dao. Those are two associates he brought here occasionally."

"Melvin Ah Wong runs his shipping agency," Akoni said. "I don't know Dong Shi-Dao."

"Anyone else?"

"Others were usually businessmen visiting from other cities. Sometimes Hong Kong, sometimes Manila. Once or twice Japan, Singapore." She paused. "You might also want to speak with Treasure Chen. She used to work here."

I nodded. "A special friend of Tommy's?"

"You could call her that," Norma Ching said. "She worked here once. Mr. Pang took a liking to her. They became good friends. She now works at a restaurant in the Ward Center, the Lobster Garden. She is the hostess."

That was about it. I knew Akoni wanted to check out the merchandise, but was too embarrassed to say so, so I said, "May we look around for a few minutes?"

"Of course," she said, smiling. Akoni almost blushed, but he looked happy. He got up and walked back to the front of the store.

As I was going, she said, "We have some gentleman's items in the corner there."

So she knew. That was interesting. I wondered if, now that I had acknowledged my sexuality to myself, there was some change in my body language that enabled an astute observer to see. On an impulse, I turned back and asked, "Did Tommy Pang ever bring his son here?"

"Once. As you can imagine, he was not particularly interested. Although it was at his suggestion that we included the section to which I referred you."

"Ah," I said.

"Do you know if the ownership of this store passes to him?" she asked.

"I don't know. You know, of course, Mr. Pang was married." She nodded. "It's possible that either Mrs. Pang or Derek will contact you."

"I will look forward to it."

I walked over to the gentleman's section, as she had called it. They had a nice selection of extremely skimpy men's thongs, as well as athletic supporters in a wide range of colors and styles. I had never realized you could buy a gold lamé jockstrap, and wondered under what circumstances it would be appropriate. You could buy an improbable-looking triangular patch that would cover your privates, but I couldn't figure out what made it stay on. There was a lot to learn about my new life, I decided. A lot.

Chapter 15

THE CHINATOWN AIR was filled with the scent of ginger, frying fish, and something rotten coming from Nu'uanu Stream, just down the block. The offices of U.S. China Ship, Inc., were sandwiched between the dirty windows of the Floating Palace restaurant, long since closed, and Hin Shee Dook dry cleaning, which may have been open at some time during the day, and then again may not have been open since statehood. The front windows of each store, like all those around, bore legends in both English and Chinese.

Inside the pack and ship, there were racks of Chinese greeting cards, and displays of the different-sized boxes you could purchase, as well as packing materials such as tape, twine, and Styrofoam peanuts. Melvin Ah Wong was in his mid-fifties with thinning hair and a wool vest. An air conditioner hummed somewhere in the back of the store, but it was still hot and stuffy inside, and I couldn't understand how he could dress so heavily. He stood behind the counter making change for a bent old man with one prominent tooth. As the man shuffled away, Akoni and I stepped up.

Akoni showed his ID and introduced us. We established quickly that Tommy was the owner of the store, and a personal friend of Melvin's, but that he was not involved in the business. "How about his son, Derek?" I asked.

Melvin Ah Wong nodded. "Yes, Derek comes by once, sometimes twice a week."

"For what? To look at the books?"

Ah Wong looked offended. "I have full responsibility for running this business. They don't look at my books at all."

"Then why does he come here so often?"

Melvin Ah Wong looked around. "We should go in the back. Where we can be private." He opened the hinged countertop and we followed him past a huge hopper full of peanuts and stacks of flattened boxes. "Jimmy!" he said as we turned a corner.

A teenage boy was sitting at a desk in front of us, doing what looked like his homework. Though he was Chinese, he had a shock of bright yellow hair that stood straight up, like a Mohawk, and the rest of his head was shaved. He was about sixteen, thin, and effeminate. "Go watch the desk," Melvin said.

Jimmy slouched off to the front and Melvin closed the door behind the three of us. "Derek and Wayne come here to ship packages," he said. "They do everything themselves. Weigh, wrap, fill out customs forms."

"Do you know what's in those packages?"

He shook his head vehemently. "No! I don't know. I don't want to know."

"But you suspect they're doing something illicit."

"Who am I to suspect? Maybe they're just very careful. Perhaps these are important things of great personal value. They don't trust anyone else to handle them."

"Or they're smuggling something."

Melvin shrugged. "I don't know."

"How about other friends of Tommy Pang's? You know any of them?"

"Dong Shi-Dao," he said. "He's a friend. And then Chin Suk, he's like Tommy's mentor, I guess you could call it. Knew Tommy's family in China."

There was Uncle Chin again. It was clear I was going to have to talk to him about Tommy at some point. It wasn't something I looked forward to. Since I became a cop, I'd managed to maintain a good relationship with Uncle Chin by keeping my professional life and my personal life separate—though it appeared that concept had flown out the window the night I went to the Rod and Reel Club. "Anybody else?"

"Tommy didn't have many friends."

"How about enemies?"

Melvin's eyes narrowed. "I don't know what you mean."

Akoni said, "Sure you do. Anybody who disliked Tommy enough to kill him."

You could see the wheels turning in Melvin Ah Wong's head. He was trying to say something without incriminating himself. "We know Tommy Pang was a criminal," I said. "And I don't care what you know or don't know about his businesses. I just want to know if he mentioned any particular rivalries to you, anybody he cheated, anybody who might want him dead."

That didn't seem to make the connection for Melvin. He was still thinking. I had a flash of inspiration. "How about cops? Any cops who might have been working for Tommy on the side, who might have a grudge against him?"

That hit the jackpot. Melvin smiled. "Tommy often had reason to become friendly with police officers. Because of the work he did, he sometimes needed both business and personal security. And," he paused, again searching for delicacy, "occasionally he may have skirted the law and needed an officer to look the other way."

Now we're getting somewhere, I thought. "Names, Melvin. We want to know who these cops were."

His face fell. "He never told me. I know most of the officers he dealt with were Chinese. There was at least one haole, I know, with a Portguese name. Tommy was particularly pleased to have recruited him. Apparently the man had financial problems, and was in a particular position to do Tommy good. I don't remember the name—I only heard it once—but I remember it was Portugese."

"Great," Akoni said. "A haole cop with a Portuguese name. There must be hundreds of those."

Melvin Ah Wong could tell us nothing more, though he did give us an address and phone number for Dong Shi-Dao, who he said worked in import-export. He said he couldn't be more specific. We walked back through the storeroom with him. "Can I get a soda, Dad?" Jimmy asked.

Melvin frowned. "All right, but come right back. You still have homework."

Jimmy walked out of the store with us, and hesitated for a moment, waiting to see which way we turned. Then he followed us.

"Give me a few minutes," I whispered to Akoni. "Go on ahead a little."

He picked up his pace and I slowed down. In a minute Jimmy Ah Wong was walking next to me. "Where do you go to school?" I asked.

"Honolulu Christian," he said, naming a Chinatown private school not far away.

"Good school. I was in a speech and debate club when I was at Punahou, and we used to compete against them."

He nodded. We came to a little convenience store across the street from Nu'uanu Stream. "I think I need a soda, too," I said. "Hot day."

We went inside and got Cokes. There was a tiny park alongside the water and I said, "Want to go over there?"

"Sure."

The smell of something rotten was stronger right there by the river, but when the trade wind blew it didn't bother me too much. We sat down on a picnic bench under a big kiawe tree. There was a clutch of old men behind us, gabbing in Chinese, but they couldn't hear anything we said. "If you have something to tell me, you can," I said.

He looked down at the picnic table. "I'm ashamed."

"Hey, when I was your age I was ashamed all the time," I said. "Ashamed and scared. Matter of fact, I still am. I'm just more accustomed to it."

He didn't speak. "You know something about Tommy Pang's murder?" I asked gently. "Was your father involved?"

He looked up fast. "No, nothing to do with my father."

Then I knew. "Derek and Wayne, right? They got friendly with you, didn't they?"

A tear was trickling down his left cheek but he made no move to wipe it away. I could see that I'd moved too quickly. "So what's with the hair?" I asked, flicking a couple of fingers at his yellow coxcomb. "Pretty radical. I bet your dad's not too pleased."

He didn't say anything. "You like music?" I asked. "Don't tell me you're a punker. Sex Pistols and all that retro eighties music." I drummed my fists against the picnic table and howled, "I wanna kill you and put lots of goo in my hair and talk in a funny British accent."

The clutch of Chinese men looked up in alarm, then went back to their conversation. Jimmy finally smiled. "It was just something to do," he said. "Piss my dad off. You know."

"I know all about it. I was the youngest of three boys. I practically had to dance on the dinner table to get anybody to pay attention to me."

"I never had to do that." The tension seemed to have left his shoulders, and I thought I could try again. "You were going to tell me about Derek and Wayne."

I could tell he made a decision then, just to get it off his chest, and I knew that though that would be painful, it would be good for him in the long run. "Just Wayne," he said, almost whispering. "He said we could never tell Derek."

"It's really hard to be a teenager and like other guys," I said as casually as I could. "I remember when I was about sixteen, I was scared shitless of taking a shower after gym, afraid I'd get a hard-on in the shower and the other guys would tease me."

"He was nice to me," Jimmy said, and he was really crying now. "Nobody else was ever nice to me like that."

"Did you have sex with him?"

He nodded and looked down at the table. His shoulders were shaking, and I put an arm around him. "It's all right, Jimmy. You didn't do anything wrong. Wayne was the one who was wrong. It's not right for an adult to take advantage of a kid."

It made me want to nail something on Wayne Gallagher, but I couldn't do it in a way that would hurt Jimmy Ah Wong even more than he'd already been hurt. That's child abuse in my book, taking advantage of somebody young and scared. "Don't worry," I said. "I'll make sure he can't hurt you anymore."

We sat there for a few minutes, Jimmy resting against my shoulder, that improbable coxcomb of yellow hair in my face. It made me think about community policing, about how our job, at its heart, is to be out there among the citizens, protecting them from anyone who wants to harm them, in any way. I'd thought for a while, while I was at the academy, about going to work in the school system, riding around in a patrol car protecting kids from drug dealers and child molesters and people who speed through school zones. Kind of like a Hawai'ian J. D. Salinger, out there catching the kids in case they should fall.

Jimmy seemed to regain his composure and sat up. I was about to get up and go meet Akoni when Jimmy said, "He had me do stuff."

"I know. It's all right."

"Not that kind of stuff," he said, wiping a hand across his face. "I mean, that stuff, too, but other stuff. My father's a notary public, he has a seal he stamps on papers to testify that they're legitimate. He keeps it in his drawer."

I pulled out a pad and started to make notes. "Wayne would come by sometimes when he knew my father was out with Mr. Pang, that I would be there by myself. He'd bring these papers, and he'd make me get the seal out and stamp them, and then sign my father's name."

"Anything else?"

"Sometimes we got forms back from Customs about things they shipped, Derek and Wayne. I'd get the mail and keep them back from my father, give them to Wayne to handle. Sometimes he had me sign my father's name to those too."

He had stopped crying by then, but there were still shiny places on his face that glistened in the hot afternoon sun. I had him go over as many dates as he could, remembering when Wayne had come to the store and what he'd had Jimmy do. "I don't want my dad to get in trouble because of me," he said when he'd finished. "I never should have done it."

"Here's a sad fact of life, Jimmy," I said, sitting back on the bench. "Men will do almost anything for sex. Believe me, I've done a lot of stuff myself I'm not proud of. But sometimes you get so— sad and horny and I don't know what—and all you want is somebody to be nice to you, to hold you. You do whatever you have to do to get that."

"You're really nice."

"And I'm way too old for you," I said. "You know there's a center for gay teens on Waikīkī , don't you?"

"I could never go there," he said, registering something like shock.

I nodded. "You could. And you should. There are people there, counselors, who can help you figure out everything you're feeling."

"What's going to happen to my dad?"

"We're not investigating anything other than who killed Tommy Pang," I said. "If your dad didn't kill him, you don't have anything to worry about."

He looked at his watch. "I better get back. He looks at my homework every day. If I don't finish by supper he gets really mad."

He stood up. "Thanks," he said. Then he turned and headed back to the store.

As he walked away, Akoni pulled the Taurus up next to me. "Man, it's hot today," he said when I got in. "Must be ninety degrees. Days like today, you get a trade wind and it still doesn't do any real good."

I leaned my face down to the air conditioning vent and felt the cold air blast me. My polo shirt was soaked under the arms, and I could feel the tiny drops of sweat sliding down my back, but at least the cold Coke had done my throat a world of good.

As we drove back to the station, I told him what Jimmy had said. "So Derek and Wayne were much more involved in Tommy's businesses than either of them let on," Akoni said finally. He looked over at me. "What about the kid? He gonna be all right?"

"I told him to go to the center in Waikīkī. Who knows, maybe it won't take him another twenty or thirty years to figure it all out."

Akoni nodded but didn't say anything for a while.

Chapter 16

WE WENT BACK to the station and worked for a while, and around six we headed for the Ward Warehouse, a complex of shops between downtown and Waikīkī. It's a mini-mall, two long lines of stores facing each other on two levels with parking in the middle. To me, it's one of the least attractive shopping centers around—it looks like a child's play set, girders bolted together, corrugated metal sheets painted clashing colors. The Lobster Garden is a touristy Chinese restaurant on the upper level.

The very sexy Chinese girl behind the podium wore an incongruous happy-face name tag attached to the shoulder of her tight red cheongsam that read, "Hi, I'm Treasure." We showed her our ID and asked if we could talk to her.

"Here?"

"You could get us a table, and then come over when you get a break," Akoni said.

"All right. Follow me."

The centerpiece of the restaurant was a huge fish tank filled with live lobsters, their claws tightly banded together. Grandma and Grandpa from Des Moines could walk up to the tank with their waiter and decide which of the spiny creatures crawling around on the bottom of the tank would become that night's dinner. It was a festive place, decorated with framed Chinese calligraphy and red paper lanterns, and it was lively, full of tourist families resting after a day's trek to Pearl Harbor, the Kodak Hula Show, or Hilo Hattie's aloha shirt factory.

Treasure seated us at a four-top in the back corner, where we could talk relatively undisturbed. "At six-thirty the second hostess comes on duty," she said. "When she gets here I can take a few minutes break, but not much, because we get a big rush by seven."

We ordered cashew chicken and shrimp in lobster sauce. "So you think we made any progress today?" I asked, after the waiter left.

Akoni shrugged. "Hard to say. We learned a lot about Tommy's businesses, but not much about why anybody would want to kill him."

"There's that stuff going on at the pack and ship. Those boxes Wayne and Derek bring over. There could be something there."

The waiter was back with big steaming bowls of wonton soup, and we dug in. We had just finished when I saw Treasure Chen approaching us.

Treasure came up to sit with us, and I couldn't help noticing Akoni's appreciative glance at her narrow waist and tight butt. It was interesting, though, that she made no impression on me beyond an aesthetic one. "I guess this is about Tommy," she said.

"You knew him?"

She nodded. "I was his mistress for the past six months or so." She paused. "That is, until he dumped me for that Mexican bitch."

"Excuse me?"

"The night he was killed, I worked until ten, and he picked me up here. We went out to a club for a couple of hours, and that's when he told me he was seeing another woman. Had been seeing her for a month or more by then. We had some words, and then I left him. Took a cab home. I don't know where he went from there—probably to see her."

"Do you know her name?" Akoni asked. "Anything about her?"

"He said her name was Luz Maria," she said, running her right hand through her sleek black hair, cut bluntly so that it just brushed her shoulders. "She's a Mexican woman he met through some business deal. I don't know anything more about her."

Akoni and I looked at each other.

She looked directly at me. "I didn't want to know anything about his business. I know he owned Sally's, that's the place I was working when he met me, and he owned a couple of other things, but he didn't talk about business with me and I didn't ask him."

"You worked at Sally's?" I asked.

"She's my auntie, Norma. I didn't do anything but model. I'd worked there for a couple of months when I met Tommy, and he helped me get this job."

"Do you know what he did after he left you?" Akoni asked.

"He got a call while we were at the club, on his cell phone. I don't know who it was, but it was somebody he was going to meet back at his office."

I made a note of that. We had to get hold of the records on Tommy's cell phone. "Do you have any idea who it might have been?" I asked. "From the tone of his voice, from anything he said? Was it a friend, a business colleague?"

"I was pretty angry," she said. "I mean, we were in the middle of this big dramatic scene, he's telling me he's fallen in love with someone else, and his cell phone rings."

I looked at Akoni. "Anything else you want to ask?"

He shook his head. Treasure looked at her watch. "I have to get back," she said, and stood up.

I handed her my card and said, "If you think of anything else, will you call?"

She took the card and nodded. "I did love him, you know. I mean, he was very good to me, up until that night, and lots of people thought he was really hard, but he had a good side. I don't know what I'm going to do without him."

She turned and walked away fast, dodging a party of six with two babies, and two busboys carrying infant seats behind them. The waiter was right on Treasure's heels with our dinners. We started to eat. "That Luz Maria's got to be the same one from the black tar bust," I said.

"Got to be. That would mean Tommy was behind the drug deal. You think she was mad that things didn't go as planned, maybe blamed Tommy?"

It was my turn to shrug. "It's a possibility. Maybe this Dong Shi-Dao will know something useful."

Akoni was about to answer me when the restaurant erupted into song. It was someone's birthday at the next table, and we had to wait while the waiters sang a Chinese-accented "Happy Birthday" to him.

"We'll put him at the top of our list tomorrow," Akoni said. He bent over his teacup, and I couldn't help noticing the way his black hair stood up in stiff bristles at the top of his head, falling into spiky bangs on his forehead. Funny, I thought, you can work with somebody for years and never really look at him.

I thought about the way Norma had been able to look at me and see who I was, see something others hadn't seen, or at least that I'd tried to hide for years. I wondered what Akoni was hiding, and if it would change my opinion of him.

I picked up my fortune cookie and cracked it open. None of the numbers looked particularly lucky to me, but then I wasn't feeling very lucky. I flipped it over to read the fortune. "Your future will be very interesting," it said.

I read it out loud to Akoni. "I'll bet." His read, "You are talented in many fields." He said, "Be nice if investigation was one of them," and threw it in the ashtray.

≈

THE NEXT MORNING, I called Harry at six. "Hey, brah, you want surf the morning glass?"

"Shit, Kimo, what time is it?"

"Come on. I'll meet you at the park in fifteen minutes."

"Asshole," he said, and hung up. But he was there, rubbing the sleep from his eyes. The sky was gray and street lights were still on, and the water was cold when I first stepped into it. But I felt connected, and peaceful. Happy, almost.

We didn't speak much, just paddled out beyond the waves and then surfed back in, and passed at least an hour that way. By then the sun was up and I was feeling great. There was a little tightness in my thighs and my lower back, but it was a good feeling, reminding me I had muscles. I watched Harry off and on, saw that he was starting to gain his confidence again. It reminded me of the endless hours we'd spent as kids at that very beach, surfing waves that had seemed so much bigger then. Energy seemed to flow back and forth between us, rising up out of the salty water and the trade winds.

We walked back through the streets of Waikīkī together when we were finished. We passed a man with a bulldog on a leash. The dog was wearing a flowered hat, and two Japanese women stopped to take its picture.

An elderly woman wearing headphones and towing a shopping cart stopped in front of us, in the middle of the sidewalk, and began to do a little dance. "Waikīkī," Harry said. "You gotta love it."

I picked up coffee for myself and Akoni on the way into the station, and we arrived at the same time. "Just to let you know, I've got a doctor's appointment at nine," Akoni said. "You'll have to keep things together here for an hour or so."

"How about we try for an appointment with Dong Shi-Dao?" I said, picking up the phone. Just to show that luck comes when you don't particularly need it, I got through to him right away and scheduled a meeting for eleven a.m.

I called Peggy and left a message for her, letting her know we were going to need a subpoena for Tommy Pang's cell phone records. Akoni left a little later, and I got caught up in a bunch of Internet articles on tongs, not noticing the clock until it was almost too late. I had just enough time to make it to Dong Shi-Dao's office downtown. I sprinted home for my truck, racing past eager families on their way to and from the beach. It was a nice day, and sprinkled among the commuters on the drive downtown were bunches of tourists, driving rented convertibles with the top down or strolling along Fort Street gawking at the high-rise office buildings. I could almost hear them commenting how our business district looks just like home, only with palm trees.

My favorite thing is when mainland tourists ask dumb questions, such as if I ever get over to the States, or if we accept all the regular U.S. coins, or wonder if they have to dial any special telephone codes to call back home.

I parked in a garage and cut across King Street to Smith, where the office was, in a small one-story building sandwiched between high-rises. A nice trade wind was coming off the ocean, and the sky was a deep blue dotted with small white clouds. I had a moment of real longing, wanting to chuck this case and go back to the beach. Then I ran into Akoni.

Just as we met, I saw a woman come out of Dong Shi-Dao's office. She looked both ways, then set off in the direction opposite us.

"She looks familiar, doesn't she?" I asked. Akoni and I walked a little faster, trying to catch up to her.

"We've seen her before," he agreed.

She stopped at the corner of Smith and Hotel to let a bus pass, and turned her profile toward us. "I know," I said, stopping short. "It's Luz Maria."

Chapter 17

WITHOUT ANY COMMUNICATION between us, we both took off after her, but she was already a block away, heading mauka on Smith Street. We got stuck at a traffic light, and by the time we got across she had disappeared in a crowd of tourists.

We split up and circled the block in opposite directions, but neither of us could pick her up again. "She was Tommy's mistress," I said. "You think maybe now she's moved over to his friend?"

"We'll find out," Akoni said as we headed back to Dong Shi-Dao's office, where we entered a small reception area, painted white with a few simple watercolors on the wall. A very attractive Vietnamese woman in her early twenties was sitting behind a small desk typing from a handwritten page. She looked up as we came in.

We explained our business, and she got up from her desk and knocked at a door behind her. Then she opened the door, stuck her head in and announced us. "Please come in," she said, turning back to us. "Would you like coffee? Tea?"

We both declined. Dong Shi-Dao was a Vietnamese man in his mid-forties, wearing a khaki-colored Armani suit and a black turtleneck. He stood up to shake our hands. His grip was solid and firm and his voice carried echoes of some kind of untraceable accent. "Let me say I want to do everything I can to help you solve this terrible crime. Tommy Pang was a dear friend of mine. I was horrified to hear that he had been murdered."

"How did you know Tommy?" I asked, as Akoni and I sat down

in chairs across from Dong's broad mahogany desk. The office was decorated with classic Chinese antiques, Persian rugs, and exquisite calligraphy. It was hard to imagine Tommy Pang in these surroundings.

"We met in Hong Kong," Dong said. "My family left Vietnam shortly before the Communist takeover and relocated there. Tommy was already a successful businessman. We were introduced and did some business together, and gradually became friends. In nineteen eighty-four his father sent for him and Tommy moved here. We continued to do business together across the Pacific until I relocated my family here. I could not consider staying in Hong Kong under Communist rule."

"When you say business," Akoni asked, "can you be more specific? What kind of business do you do?"

"I am a trader. I find someone who wants something, and then find someone who has it. Sometimes I match them up and collect a fee; sometimes I buy the needed good and then resell it."

"Do you know anyone who might have had a reason to kill Tommy?"

He shook his head emphatically. "No one at all. He was respected in the community and loved by his family."

"Did he ever express any anxiety to you?" I asked. "Any business deals that might not be going right, any person he had problems with?"

Dong steepled his hands and looked down at them for a minute, then looked up at us. "How can I put this diplomatically?" he asked, not really expecting an answer. "Tommy was a good businessman. To be good, sometimes you have to be strong. Other people can see that as hardness. There were people Tommy dealt with who were not happy with the outcome of their dealings. But that happens to any businessman from time to time. I don't know of anyone who felt strongly enough against him to kill him."

I looked at Akoni. It was obvious we weren't going to get much more out of Dong Shi-Dao. As we stood, though, I said, "By the way, I think I saw someone I knew coming out of your office as we were coming in. A young woman."

Dong stood with us. "Ah, yes, a friend of Tommy's. She was looking for financial backing for a business enterprise. Sadly, I was unable to help her."

"That young woman was arrested in a drug deal in Waikīkī," I said. "She and an accomplice were about to sell me a pound of heroin before someone warned them off. I know she was Tommy's mistress, as well. Was he her backer?"

Dong tried to look horrified. "I don't know anything about this."

"We may be back with more questions," I said. I handed him my card, which he took as if it was contaminated. "If you think of anything else you want to tell us, about Tommy or his mistress or a pound of Mexican heroin, you'll know where to find us."

Dong closed his office door sharply behind us. "You think he was telling the truth?" I asked, as we walked toward the garage where we had both parked.

"About what?"

I shrugged. "Anything."

"I think he probably doesn't know who killed Tommy," Akoni said. "And that means we're no closer to figuring it out either."

"If Luz Maria was Tommy's mistress, then he was behind the drug deal. I wonder if Dong was in it with them."

"You think he might have shot Tommy to take over the business?"

"I don't know," I said as we reached the garage. "There are a lot of pieces floating around and most of them don't seem to fit together yet."

Akoni and I met up again at the station, where we ate lunch at our desks, takeout sandwiches from the deli across Kalākaua Avenue, and tracked Luz Maria through the system. She and Pedro had been processed at the main station, but without any evidence, no charges had been filed. I checked my city directory for the address they'd both given, and—big surprise—it didn't exist.

"I think we need to sit down and go over what we've found," I said, leaning back in my chair.

"Agreed."

"According to their accounts, Derek Pang and Wayne Gallagher were with Tommy Pang at the Rod and Reel Club around midnight."

"Wait a minute," Akoni said. "What time did Treasure Chen say she left Tommy?"

I looked at my notes. "She just says she met him at ten, when she got off her shift, and they were together for a couple of hours. That could put him back at the club at midnight."

"All right. Go on."

"Derek and Wayne say Tommy met with a cop. If that's true, then the meeting was probably related to the deal that failed."

"Maybe this mystery cop is the one who tipped off Luz Maria and Pedro, and Tommy was showing his appreciation."

A light bulb clicked on. "Derek said he saw his father give this cop a jewelry box, the kind you'd put a bracelet or a necklace in. That could have been the thanks."

Something else was rattling around in my brain about a jewelry box, but I couldn't pin it down. Finally I gave up. "Derek and Wayne say when they left, the cop and Tommy were together. They went to the Boardwalk bar and made out for a while."

Akoni reached for his coffee cup, found it was empty, and got up to refill it.

I said, "We have to see if we can find the cop Tommy was with."

"If there was a cop, and not just the two fags blowing smoke up our asses." He looked at me. "You're not going to get pissed off if I use the word *fag*, are you?"

"Did I ever get pissed off before? I don't want you to change anything because of me. That's what being partners is about. I accept you, you accept me."

"Deal," he said. He took a long drink of his coffee. "So you believe that there really is a cop somewhere in this story."

"Too many independent sources," I said. "Melvin Ah Wong says Tommy had Chinese cops, and a haole cop with a Portuguese name, on his payroll. Derek and Wayne say there was a cop at the office that night. If it walks like a duck and quacks like a duck, it's a duck."

"Quack, quack."

"Going on," I said. "Tommy Pang was bashed in the back of the head between one thirty and two thirty, by person or persons unknown. The event undoubtedly took place in the back alley behind the Rod and Reel Club, adjacent to the door to Tommy's office."

"And our suspects would be . . . ?"

I started ticking them off on my fingers. "Derek Pang. Wayne Gallagher. They alibi each other, but their alibis are weak. Treasure Chen, Luz Maria, and Genevieve Pang. He'd just broken up with Treasure; she could be lying to us. Maybe they actually broke up at the office, and she got mad and whacked him."

Akoni shook his head. "I checked her out. Didn't have the upper body strength."

"So she has a brother. I'm leaving her on the list. Maybe he and Luz Maria argued over the drug deal that didn't work and she killed him." I looked at Akoni. "You check out her upper body?"

"She could do it. But Genevieve Pang couldn't."

"Genevieve Pang could have hired someone. Final suspect is the mystery cop. We need to do something to try to track him down."

The station was particularly busy, with a pack of skateboarders in receiving. They all seemed to have streaked hair, baggy clothes, and body piercings, and they all wanted to talk at once. The desk sergeant was having a hard time keeping them in line.

"That's a needle in a haystack, Kimo. We got thousands of cops on the force."

The desk sergeant was yelling at the skateboarders by then and

Akoni had to move closer to my desk so he could hear me. "Yeah, but not everyone has information Tommy can use," I said. "You think we can look up Tommy's past beefs, maybe find somebody he might have crossed paths with?"

"Still a needle in a haystack." Akoni was not convinced.

"We could start with the black tar bust," I said. "We know Tommy was behind that, because we've got a connection between him and Luz Maria. We also know somebody tipped off Luz Maria at the last minute. That could have come from a leak."

I finally got Akoni to nod. "All right. Let's look at who knew about that bust."

The station returned to its normal buzz, voices on phones and radio traffic and the occasional siren passing outside. Sunlight came in the big window facing Diamond Head and played on my desk, illuminating the dust motes in the air. The list took a while to put together. It had been an interagency cooperation, after all, with information going up and down the chain of command in two different departments.

One name jumped out at me. Evan Gonsalves, Terri's husband. I'd known him for years and never doubted his integrity, but I remembered what Terri had said when I'd gone out to her house. How there was something wrong with Evan. I didn't want to tell Akoni until I had time to think about it, though. We divided up the list and spent the rest of the afternoon working on it, trying to connect anyone on that list to any other investigation concerning Tommy Pang. When I couldn't find anything that linked him to Evan, I still didn't feel as relieved as I wished I did. Was Evan really clean, or just smart enough to cover his tracks?

We had a list of about twenty Chinese cops, and two dozen haole cops with Portuguese names, who had all crossed paths with Tommy Pang at some point. Evan's was there, halfway down, but I still didn't tell Akoni about Terri's suspicions. Somehow I just couldn't break that confidence yet.

I looked out through the big glass window that faces Kalākaua Avenue. Two teenage surfers with Clairol-blond streaks and pants down below their hips jaywalked diagonally across the street and I shook my head, hoping a beat cop was out front but knowing there probably wasn't.

"Now that we have this list, I'm damned if I know what we should do with it," Akoni asked. "I hate like hell the idea of turning it over to Internal Affairs without any real evidence."

"We're not giving that list to anybody yet," I said. "We're going to wait for a break. In the meantime, we go back to Tommy's tong connections. Maybe there's something there we missed. And I'd really like to know what Derek and Wayne were putting in those boxes at the pack and ship."

"I think it's time to see those assholes again," Akoni said.

"Not yet. I want to wait until I've got something to hit them with." I had to admit, too, I wasn't too eager to see Wayne Gallagher again, his casually open robe, or his beefy thigh. Or maybe I was eager to see him again, and that's what worried me.

We did paperwork for a couple of hours, clearing up old cases, until it was time to go home. Part of me wanted to go back to the beach to see if Tim was there again, and part of me was scared to. Once I realized I was scared, though, I knew I had to go through with it. I stood in front of the mirror fussing, thinking I needed a haircut, checking my teeth, flexing my arms once or twice. Finally I said, "The hell with it. I am who I am," and walked out the door in my Speedo, carrying my towel.

It was almost seven and still a lot of light, but I didn't see Tim. I dropped my towel and went in for a swim, out beyond the waves and then parallel to shore, like I usually do. Coming back past the breakwater, I recognized his head and stopped, treading water. "Hey, Tim."

"Hey, Kimo. Good to see you." We shook wet hands. "You swimming?"

"Toward the stadium."

"Come on." We matched strokes down toward the stadium, then turned and swam back. By the time we got out, the sun was on its way down and the sunset sails were just leaving Waikīkī. I shivered a bit in the light breeze as we got out of the water. "Are you nervous?" Tim asked.

"Just a little cold," I said, but we made eye contact.

"I don't know," he said. "You seem like a pretty hot guy to me."

I grabbed my towel to keep from showing just how hot I was, but I had a feeling he already knew. "You want to get something to eat?" I asked. "I could start telling you a little about surfing."

"I'd like that." We walked back together down Lili'uokalani, talking easily about nothing much in particular. I pointed out my apartment to him, and he agreed to stop in forty-five minutes and pick me up.

When I got inside, I noticed my hands were shaking. I felt like some teenager who'd just made his first date. It was silly. I was thirty-two years old. I took a shower and then couldn't decide what to wear. I have a good body—flat stomach, strong biceps, good lines in my face. You could see every one of my ancestors there—Hawai'ian roundness, almond eyes from my Japanese grandfather, tempered by the influences of my haole grandmother. Girls always found me just exotic enough to be appealing, but not so foreign as to be dangerous.

I finally decided on a very fancy silk aloha shirt my sister-in-law Tatiana had picked out for me. She'd said that the green in it reflected my eyes, and that the gold in it made my black hair glow. I was sure at the time it was all bullshit. A pair of white pants and deck shoes. My good gold watch.

Jesus, I couldn't stop fussing. Tim was right—I was nervous. I thought for a minute about Peggy, and realized that I was making a decision. It was one I'd have to tell he about, and soon. She wasn't going to like it.

I'd always thought it would be harder, something I'd have to agonize over, debate the pros and cons in my mind. But instead it seemed so simple, the only real choice I had.

I heard a knock on the door and looked at my watch. Tim was right on time.

Show time, I thought to myself. I took a deep breath and opened the door.

Chapter 18

I ALWAYS FIND twilight magical. The sky shades from the orange of sunset through to a deep, dark blue, and you can see the first stars. Drivers are just beginning to put on their headlights, and the neon on storefronts still looks clean and inviting. The streets of Waikīkī are filled with well-dressed tourists on their way to dinner, as the last surfers wash up on the beach and drag their boards home through the growing darkness. The evening is still full of possibility.

As Tim and I drove out toward Diamond Head, the electric current running between us made me excited and nervous. I kept up a steady patter about the fancy residential neighborhoods, things Harry and I had done as kids, crimes I'd investigated, landmarks along the way.

We stopped for dinner at a little restaurant on a bluff overlooking the ocean. We caught the last glimpse of the sunset, and then a tangible darkness settled over the water, broken only by the running lights of a small cruise ship heading toward Moloka'i.

"So what brought you to Hawai'i?" I asked, after we'd ordered, when we were sitting back with beers against the walls of the booth.

"It's about as far away from my family as I can get," he said, smiling a little. "I come from a pretty severe Irish Catholic family in western Massachusetts. College at Amherst, law school at UMass. Then I got a job with a firm in Boston, and after a couple of trips to the Combat Zone I realized there was no getting around the fact that I was gay. I mean, I'd done the dating thing, high school, college, the whole nine yards. I didn't really understand what I felt, and I couldn't talk about it with anybody, so I just hoped it would go away."

He took a long draw on his beer. "I have three sisters and two brothers, and they all live somewhere around Boston. My sister-in-law's cousin worked at the same firm I did, and my brother's best friend lived in the same apartment building. I knew that if I wanted any kind of life I'd have to get out."

"You didn't want to come out to them?"

"My brothers make fag jokes," he said. "My mother knows the Bible by heart. I will never come out to them."

I took a deep breath. "Okay," I said.

"Last year I started looking at ads in bar journals. I finagled my way onto an international trade case with a Japanese client and did a Berlitz class in Japanese. I thought about San Francisco, but it's too much of a cliché. I had a couple of nibbles from firms in LA, but the market there is so cutthroat. Then I saw an ad from Hollings and Arakawa, that they needed an attorney with international background, trial experience, and some Japanese, and faxed my résumé within half an hour. They had me come out for an interview, they liked me, and voila, I'm here."

"I'm glad," I said, and we smiled at each other.

He took another sip of beer and said, "How about you? You always lived here?"

"College on the mainland," I said. "UC San Diego. Two years on the north shore, trying to be surfing champion of the world. Then back here."

"What made you give up trying to be the world champion?"

I thought about it. I could give him the speech I knew by heart, about realizing I didn't want it hard enough. But for the first time, I felt like I could be honest, that I could tell Tim anything. "A guy sucked my dick, and I found I liked it. It scared the hell out of me, and I ran."

When I went to pick up my beer glass, my hand was shaking. "It's all right," Tim said. "You want to tell me about it?"

I wanted to. I started with surfing with Harry in high school and went on, as our salads arrived, to tell him about college in San Diego, and then living on the north shore. By the time the waiter took the salad plates away, I had told him about Dario and his little shack on the beach.

"Must have hurt like hell," Tim said. "Giving up all that stuff. Your dreams."

"It did. And I could never tell anyone my real reason."

It was easy to talk to him. I had been pretty honest in every facet of my life, except when it came to my sexuality, and I found that when I finally could talk about it, the honesty came easily.

Over dessert and coffee we laid out our love lives for each other. He'd done a couple of foolish things in Boston, bookstore blow jobs and such, but he'd been lucky. He hadn't caught anything, and he'd been careful for the last two years or so. One very discreet affair with a guy he'd met at the health club, just before he left Boston. "It wasn't really what you'd call a relationship," he said. "I mean, we never dated or anything. It's just sometimes after we worked out we'd go over to his place and have sex. Safe sex, you know, no exchange of bodily fluids. But we never went to dinner or the movies or held hands walking down the street."

I told him about the string of short-term flings I'd had, picking up tourist women at beachfront bars, romancing and bedding them, always hoping the next one would be the one who could change me. "I was as safe as I could be," I said. "Always condoms, and I get tested every six months."

"Are you out to your family?"

"Not yet. But I think I will be eventually. In a way, that's what's scariest to me. I mean, I'm the kind of person who's like a dog with a bone. I can't stop worrying it. That's the kind of detective I am— I can't give up on a case until I finish it. I still have open cases from years ago, and every now and then when things get slow I go back to them. There's one missing girl, a teenager. She disappeared two years ago, right after I became a detective. I still have her picture in my wallet, and I take it around sometimes, to shelters for runaways and out on the street. I know she didn't get off the island, so she's got to be here somewhere. I can't stop looking for her. It's the same way with this, with coming out. Once I'm started, I know I can't stop until I see it through."

"You can stop," he said. "It's allowed. You can come to a place you feel comfortable, and then just stop."

"Maybe you can," I said. "Maybe lots of people can. I can't." I paused. "Unfortunately, it seems to be the way I'm made. I can't stop something once I start it."

"We'll see about that later," Tim said, smiling.

After a long romantic walk on the beach, I drove us back to Waikīkī. "You want me to drop you off?" I asked. "Or you want to come up to my place—I don't know, maybe have a nightcap or something?"

"Let's take it slow, okay? I can walk home from your place."

I pulled into a space in the lot behind my building and killed the engine. "So tell me," I said, struggling to keep the tremor out of my voice. "How do you feel about kissing on the first date?"

In response he simply turned to me, and we kissed. Plumeria scented the air, a distant whir of traffic in the background. We kissed a couple of times, and he reached inside my shirt and played with my nipples, which hardened at his touch. I kissed his chin and his cheek and blew in his ear, and he shivered. "You like that," I said.

He put his hand on my crotch, where I was hard, and said, "You seem to like it, too," and laughed.

We kissed again, and I ran my fingers through his hair. It was so short and wiry. I had to laugh.

"What's so funny?"

"I've never kissed anyone with such short hair." I kissed him again. "Or with a mustache, either."

He leaned over and kissed me, deep, tongue to tongue. "So how is it, kissing a man?" he asked.

I didn't know what else to say besides, "I like it."

We made out for a while longer. One part of me couldn't believe what I was doing, and another part didn't want to stop. Finally he pulled back and said, "Let's save some mystery for a second date, okay?"

"So there's going to be a second date?"

"I'd say we could do that. And actually you promised me a surfing lesson."

He had business dinners scheduled for Thursday and Friday, so we agreed to meet at my apartment Saturday around three and go surfing. Though we didn't say anything about the evening, I assumed we'd spend it together.

He got out of the truck then. " 'Til Saturday," he said. "Aloha."

"Aloha." I sat there for a few minutes, watching him walk through the parking lot and turn onto Lili'uokalani. Then I got out and went upstairs to bed.

Chapter 19

THURSDAY MORNING, Akoni and I had to put aside the investigation into Tommy Pang's murder because we caught another homicide in Waikīkī. This one was fairly straightforward, though; a young Filipina was found in her car in the parking garage at a hotel downtown. She was an assistant in the hotel's marketing department, and her co-workers told us that she'd recently broken up with an abusive boyfriend.

Looking at her cell phone, we found she'd received a call from the boyfriend's number shortly before the garage ticket indicated she'd entered. It took us only an hour to track the boyfriend down and haul him into the station for an interrogation, where he confessed to shooting her.

Even so, it took us most of the day to collect evidence, take statements, and handle the paperwork. It was almost the end of our shift before we could get back to Tommy's murder. The organized crime division had passed on some information about tong rivalries, but after a dozen phone calls, neither of us could find anyone who would say that Tommy Pang had been involved on either side. Lieutenant Yumuri was pleased we'd closed the girl's murder so quickly, but he was losing patience with our lack of progress on Tommy's murder, and neither of us wanted it to go unsolved. When our shift ended, I decided to do something I'd been holding off, to stop on my way home and see Uncle Chin. It was possible he could tell me something about Tommy Pang that the computers couldn't.

"Good afternoon, Aunt Mei-Mei," I said, when Uncle Chin's wife answered the door of their home in St. Louis Heights, not far from my parent's.

She peered at me for a moment, looking up with eyes that fought against cataracts. "Kimo!" she said. "Come in! Uncle Chin will be so happy to see you." I followed her inside, down a long hallway toward the back of the house. "He doesn't get many visitors these days."

Uncle Chin was sitting in a bamboo lounge chair on their screened porch, looking down the hillside into the ravine. The porch was jammed with flowering plants—jasmine, hibiscus, and dozens of trailing orchids in hanging baskets. There were also a half-dozen bird cages, covered at the moment, that I knew contained exotic parrots. Next to the chair was a bamboo table with glass top. Uncle Chin's wire-rimmed glasses sat on top of a hard-bound copy of Jane Austen's *Pride and Prejudice*.

"Uncle Chin, look who has come to see you," Aunt Mei-Mei said. Uncle Chin woke out of his light sleep and seemed instantly alert. He must have been in his late seventies, but his eyes were still keen, and his smile was broad.

"I will bring tea," Aunt Mei-Mei said. "You sit."

I sat. We talked first about my parents, my father's heart troubles, my mother's garden club successes. I heard about his plants and his parrots, and we discussed my brothers, especially Haoa and Tatiana's new baby. Keikis always seemed to make Uncle Chin a little sad; I guess he remembered his own son, whose difficult birth had somehow prevented Aunt Mei-Mei from being able to have any more children.

His name was Robert, I knew, and he was a few years older than my brother Lui, so always a remote presence to me. He died when he was twenty-one, a drug overdose of some kind, and according to my father Uncle Chin had never been the same since.

But Uncle Chin had enjoyed the luau and was glad to see us all at a happy occasion. "And what about you? No wife yet?"

I shook my head. "Not yet."

He wagged a finger at me. "You not young forever," he said. "Must make choices for life. Soon!"

"Yes, Uncle. I know." Aunt Mei-Mei brought cups of sweet-smelling Chinese tea and then disappeared again.

Finally Uncle Chin said, "Your work. It goes well?"

"Interesting cases," I said. "Always interesting." I paused. "A man killed behind the bar he owned in Waikīkī. Maybe you know him. A man named Tommy Pang."

For a moment, the light seemed to go out of Uncle Chin's eyes. Then he seemed to return, and consider, massaging the paralyzed nerve in his face with the fingers of his left hand. "I know him, but not well," he said, finally. "Not important man."

"No, it doesn't seem so. Yet someone found him important enough to kill."

"Ah, importance relative, no?" he said. He thought for a while. "I no can help you, Kimo. I not know who could have found this man important in way you suggest." For the first time since I had known him, Uncle Chin looked old. He was older than my father, though I remembered him best when I was a child and he was tall and imposing and yet somehow not frightening at all. Now he had become an old man, retired among his flowers and his birds.

We finished our tea and Aunt Mei-Mei came back in. "You will go to see your parents now," she said. "You are so close to them."

"I don't think so," I said. "I'm tired. It's been a long day." I looked at my watch. It was nearly seven o'clock. Not enough daylight left by the time I got back to Waikīkī for surfing or even swimming. A quick dinner, and then maybe a book. A quiet evening.

"Oh, no, your mother will be so disappointed. She has already put out a place for you at the dinner table."

Of course, I thought. While Uncle Chin and I talked on the porch, Aunt Mei-Mei had been on the phone to my mother, announcing my presence in St. Louis Heights. There was no way out now.

The streets in St. Louis Heights are steep and narrow, and all the houses are very close to each other. We were lucky that my father had decided early he wanted to live in the neighborhood and had built a simple 1960s-style ranch on a lot that backed onto Waahila Ridge State Recreation Area. As a consequence, our backyard is several thousand steeply pitched acres of pine and ravine, and on an island where real estate prices are high, such a huge empty space is now nearly priceless. Though both my brothers have beautiful homes, I know they covet my parents' property.

My parents had the main level of the house, street level. The master bedroom suite, the kitchen, living room, and dining room were all there. My brothers and I shared the basement, three bedrooms, one bathroom, and a big playroom that spilled out to a patio my father had built into the hillside. It was a wonderful place to grow up—when my brothers picked on me, as big brothers always do, I could sneak out into the underbrush, climb the hill, and set my sights on the ocean. The other wonderful thing about our house's situation was that if you climbed to the roof, as I did sometimes, you could see all the way from Diamond Head to downtown Honolulu, and the vast ocean between them. Sometimes my father would disappear for a few hours at a time, usually after a fight with my mother or after the three of us boys were making too much trouble. I knew he went up to the roof, but I never told.

I wondered if my parents would ask, like Aunt Mei-Mei, when I was going to settle down, add to their brood of grandchildren. They were baffled by my frenzied dating, the endless parade of one-night stands and tourist wahines that their friends saw me with all around Waikīkī. My new situation would probably confuse them even more. That is, if I ever told them. I sat in Uncle Chin's driveway for a while, thinking, before I turned the key in the ignition.

Chapter 20

I PULLED MY TRUCK into the driveway, right behind my father's. He could afford a Mercedes if he wanted. Instead he bought new trucks every few years and handed down the old ones to his sons. The four Kanapaʻaka boys, driving around Honolulu in Ford pickups in various states of disrepair. Oh, and then there's my mother, who drives a maroon Lexus with gold trim, and her two daughters-in-law, who are much the same.

My brothers and I are alike in many ways, and then of course very different too. From our father, we inherited a love of the outdoors, the land and the sea, of working with our hands, stubbornness, and a tendency to laugh easily. From our mother, who was born poor on a plantation on Kauaʻi, the daughter of a Japanese workman and a young Hawaiʻian girl, we seem to have inherited a certain kind of strength that my father is missing. He has always been successful, but my mother is the one who pushed. It is because of her that we all went to Punahou, and on to college.

Until 1962 it was actually illegal to give a kid a Hawaiʻian first name. My father has always gone by Al, though his actual first name is Alexander, and my mother's first name is actually Reiko, though she has always been known by her middle name, Lokelani, which means Heavenly Rose in Hawaiʻian. Our names are Louis John, called Lui; Howard Frederick, called Haoa; and James Kimo. In my case, Kimo is simply the Hawaiʻian pronunciation of James, which was the name of my Montana great-grandfather. I always wanted to know why I didn't have two English names, why my first and middle names were essentially the same. It was one of those things the youngest always picks out, to wonder why he is different from his brothers.

I was different. I used to hide from Lui and Haoa, taking books and scrambling away into the woods, where I'd find a quiet safe place and lose myself in the pages of another world. Because they were so much older than I was, I was spoiled sometimes, often treated like the baby, and then from the time I was nine and Haoa left for college, I was the only child.

Of course I was different in other ways too. My big brothers would come home from college, or from their lives as young studs on Waikīkī, and talk about their girls, and I would wonder if I'd ever feel the way they did. It wasn't until I was sixteen that I realized I probably never would.

I was browsing in a used bookstore off Fort Street on a rainy afternoon when I found a stack of all-male porno magazines. I had never known such magazines existed. My heart sped up and my arms and legs began to feel like jelly as I flipped through the pages. I particularly remember a naked guy walking out of the ocean, on a beach somewhere in California. I got so hard it hurt. There were stories as well as pictures, and ads for talk lines and dirty books. I had to buy at least one of those magazines.

I picked the one that had the tamest cover and casually walked up to the register, carrying a paperback I wanted as well. I was glad I didn't have to speak, because my throat was dry and hoarse. The proprietor, an old man, merely looked at the prices and rang them up on his register. I handed him the money, and he put the book and magazine in a brown paper bag and handed them to me.

It was one of those moments after which your life is never the same. I finally understood what I had been feeling in gym class, and not feeling on dates with smart girls from Punahou who wore wire-rimmed glasses and serious expressions. Imagine, it only took me sixteen years to get from that bookstore to the food court at Ala Moana Mall where I bared my soul to Akoni.

I let myself in the front door with my key. "Hey, Mom, you here?" I called as I closed the door behind me.

Surprisingly, it was my father who appeared first. Usually, like Uncle Chin, he holds court from his recliner in the living room. "Hello, Keechee," he said. It's always been his nickname for me, and when Lui or Haoa had tried to tease me with it he'd come down hard on them. He had a nickname for each of us, a special name that was between the two of us alone. Lulu was Lui, of course, and Howgow was Haoa. "Your mother will be pleased to see you."

"And you? Is this torture for you, seeing me?"

"You have always been the wicked son," he said, smiling. My mother came out of the kitchen then and leaned up to kiss my cheek. The Kanapa'aka boys were also lucky to inherit their father's height; my father never quite reached six feet, stopping at five eleven and three-quarters (and he was always so precise in his measurements that he could never give himself the extra quarter of an inch) but the three of us all hover between six feet and six two. Me, I'm six feet and a half inch, and the difference between me and my father is that I tell people I'm six one.

My mother is barely five six, though, and already she has started to shrink. She's sixty-five, my father sixty-eight, though he swears he will never retire. He has been working a lot with Haoa lately, though, joint construction and landscaping projects, and I can tell he wants my brother to take over more of the business. He even wanted me to take over for a long time, and tolerated my years of surfing because he believed I would come back and build with him, eventually. I think one of the biggest disappointments of his life, though I was totally unaware of it at the time, was when I came back from the north shore and announced I was entering the police academy. Like my moment at the bookstore, he must have lost some illusions then, and saw the future in a clearer light, though he was probably unwilling to admit it.

We went immediately to the dinner table. "You went to see

Uncle Chin," my father said, as my mother passed a platter of roasted chicken toward me. "Tell us about your case."

Uncle Chin's associations have always been an unspoken matter between my father and me. When I was a child, I didn't know what tongs were, and thought criminals were those guys on TV with bad hair and guns. After I became a cop, and I started seeing Uncle Chin's name on the police computer system, I never actually confronted my father. Uncle Chin had always been a nice man to me, with crack seed or some other treat for me as a kid, and I wasn't about to change my opinion of him because he had a record. But I think my father is a little afraid of my disapproval of his friend, which is an interesting position to be in with your father.

"A homicide," I said, taking chicken and passing the plate to my father. "We can't seem to get a handle on it. A Chinese guy, owned a bar on Kuhio Avenue. The body was found in an alley behind the bar last Tuesday night."

"What bar?" my father asked.

I took a forkful of roasted potato to my mouth and said, "The Rod and Reel Club."

"I know that place. Māhā club," my father said, using the Hawai'ian for homosexual. "I did renovation there a couple months ago."

I put my fork down. "You know Tommy Pang?"

"A little. A friend of Uncle Chin. A referral." He looked at me, and I could see the wheels working behind his head. "Tommy Pang dead?"

"That's him. Interesting, isn't it? Uncle Chin said he hardly knew the man."

"No more work talk at the table," my mother said. "So, Kimo, who you dating this week?"

"After dinner," I said to my father, "you and I are going to have a talk. All right? Maybe we'll even go back and visit Uncle Chin."

"My association with Tommy Pang was entirely honorable."

"Have you been surfing a lot?" my mother asked.

I looked at my father. "I've never had a reason to doubt your honor," I said. "You're entitled to have your own friends and conduct your business as you see fit. I've never said anything to you, have I?"

"Your Uncle Chin is a good man."

"I know."

My mother was starting to sound desperate. "How is Harry?" she asked. "Does he like teaching at the university?"

I turned to her. "He seems to like it well enough. It's going to take him a while to become Hawai'ian again." I made a face. "A little too much Boston in him now, not enough Waikīkī. But I'm working on him."

We talked about my brothers and their wives and my nephews and nieces. "They all come here much more often than you do, Kimo," my mother said. "What's the matter? You don't like your old mother and father anymore?"

I pushed my plate away and wiped my mouth with my napkin. "When I come here you try to make me fat. What kind of surfer will I be, fat?"

"Oh," my mother said, getting up to clear the table. "You fat? That would be a sight."

She took a stack of dishes to the kitchen and my father said, "It's a difficult time for the contracting business now. Hard to get work. Take business where you find it."

"Did he ask you to do anything illegal?"

My father looked horrified. Even in an aloha shirt, his hair graying at the sides and receding at the top, he looked like a proper businessman. "Of course not."

"Did you have any reason to believe he was going to use the premises for illegal purposes, or that his money came from some illegal source?"

"No. Not at all."

"Then you've got nothing to worry about. Just tell me, from the start, what you know about Tommy Pang."

"Let's go into the living room," he said, standing.

My mother hovered in the doorway of the kitchen. "No dessert?"

"Maybe later," my father said.

He sat on his recliner and I sat on the sofa. "About six months ago," he began, "February, March. I was finishing a big job with Haoa, beach cabanas at that resort in Hawai'i Kai. We had nothing new lined up together; he was starting that contract with the Mandarin Oriental. Uncle Chin sent this man, Tommy Pang, to talk to me."

"Where did you meet, your office?" My father has a small office in an industrial building on the ewa side of downtown Honolulu, near Salt Lake.

"Yes, he came to my office. He wanted to change the image of the club, make it more like a real fishing lodge. Your cousin Mark did the drawings and I pulled the permit. We started work about four months ago and finished the punch list in July."

I got a pad and pen and came back to the couch. "Did you meet anyone else who worked for Tommy Pang?"

My father thought. "I met his son. Nice boy. Dick? Danny?"

"Derek."

"Derek." He frowned and sighed a little. "It's very difficult to be a father. You know that, Kimo?"

"What do you mean?"

"Some fathers, it seems like their sons can never please them. Work hard, bow low, no matter. Fathers never satisfied."

"Tommy Pang was like that?"

He nodded. "You could see, all he wanted was his father's approval, but Tommy could never give that to him." He shook his head again. "Unhappy people. Now his father is dead, and they can never make up."

He looked up at me. "I'm not like that with my boys, am I, Kimo? You boys know I love you. I accept each of you for what you are." He sat up a little straighter. "I wanted one of you to work with me. To pass my business on to you. But more than that, I want you to be happy. You, and Lui, and Haoa."

"I know, Dad." I wondered how well he knew each of us, if he knew our secrets or suspected them, and if his love was strong enough to overcome them. I once saw Lui at a Waikīkī nightclub, right after his first child was born, kissing a young Chinese prostitute in a tight cheongsam. I worked with Haoa one summer and knew he padded invoices he was supposed to pass along to clients at cost. None of us was perfect, not even my father, though I still retained an image of him as an honorable man, the kind I would like to grow up to be. Someday.

He knew nothing else of Tommy Pang's business and had been paid in full. The checks had been drawn on Hui 812, the same business that owned the club.

My mother tried to get us to eat dessert or have coffee. "I must call Uncle Chin," my father said. I didn't want to overhear him, so I went into the kitchen with my mother.

"It's good that you come to see your father," she said, sitting at the kitchen table with a deck of cards in front of her. She held them up to me. "You want to play?"

I shook my head. She shuffled and began to deal herself a complicated solitaire game. "He misses his boys. He's starting to retire, you know. Smaller jobs, more time between them."

"How is that for you?"

She didn't look at me as she played. "Your father and I married for love. Not like some women I know, married only for money or power. I still love your father. Sometimes I can't stand him, but I still love him. So we're all right."

My father came into the kitchen. "You should go past Uncle Chin's again on your way home."

I kissed my mother's cheek and said good-bye. My father walked me to the door.

"You want to come?"

"Some things it's better friends not know." He watched me walk down the driveway. "Come home more," he called, as I opened the truck door. "We miss you."

My eyes stung as I swung up into the cab.

Uncle Chin was still out on the porch with the birds and the flowers, though it was dark all around him and there was only a small light on by the doorway. I sat down across from him in the semidarkness. "I apologize, Kimo," he said, as my eyes adjusted to the gloom. "Should have been more honest with you." He spread his hands. "Sometimes know too much, just as bad as know nothing. Have nothing to say."

"You knew Tommy Pang. Tell me about him."

"He wore diamonds. Diamond pinkie ring, gold bracelet with diamonds. He said he was hard, like diamond. He was."

I waited. "There is a way to do even dishonorable business with honor," Uncle Chin said finally. "Tommy not like that. Everything his way, no changes. Hard, like diamond. Don't want to cross Tommy. Three men, I know he killed. I didn't see, no, don't know for sure one hundred percent, but I know. The world not miss Tommy Pang."

But his son will, I thought. His son, who wanted only to please his father, but never could.

"Why didn't you tell me this before?" I asked gently. "I know who you are, Uncle. I am a policeman, after all."

"But you only know me as old man," he said. He waved a hand at me. "Yes, you have memories, when you were boy. But before, even, when I still lived China, I was young man once. Wild, disrespectful, concerned only with myself. I did many bad things. Stole money, hurt people, went with many women. One woman had child, she said was mine. I left, go Hong Kong, met Aunt Mei-Mei. We come here."

A parrot squawked in the darkness and I shifted on my chair.

"Aunt Mei-Mei no can have more children, after Robert. You remember Robert?" I nodded, and he smiled. "After Robert die, I think of my child in China. When he is young man, I get him Hong Kong. Then Hawai'i. I think, he my son. I give him what I have." He shook his head. "He no want. I tell you, Tommy Pang, he hard man." He looked straight at me. "Like his father when young."

The shock knocked me back a little in my seat. A dozen ideas suddenly ricocheted around in my brain. I'd always had this image of Uncle Chin as basically harmless, an old friend of my father's who'd always been kind to me, even when my own father raged. When I was a kid and my father was angry, yelling and chasing one of us around with his belt, only Uncle Chin could calm him down. Now I saw that Uncle Chin was full of his own secrets, his own fury.

On the drive back to Waikīkī, I wondered about my father. When I was a kid, he worked most of the time, often doing the work of his subcontractors on weekends. He would disappear on Sunday mornings, and return in the evening, daubed with paint or Sheetrock dust, and then turn around on Monday and go back to being the general contractor. I only wanted to be with him, to know that he loved me, to seek in his arms protection from my bullying brothers. Too often, though, he brought anger home with him from those construction sites, and he brooded or yelled or disappeared instead of spending time with his boys.

The latest studies say that homosexuality is genetic, that it was imprinted on me at conception. But as I drove under the starlit sky down to Waikīkī, I wondered if I was still looking for my father's love, and I felt sorry for Derek Pang, who had lost the chance to gain his father's love, and for Tommy Pang, who would never know that his father sat among his birds and flowers and cried for him.

Chapter 21

FRIDAY MORNING I told Akoni most of what I had learned the night before. It didn't seem relevant to the case, for example, that my father had recently renovated the Rod and Reel Club. But the rest of it might have a bearing on our case.

I had asked Uncle Chin to see if anyone in a tong had a grudge against Tommy Pang. His parentage, it turned out, was an open secret among the tongs, Tommy's connection to Uncle Chin being his ticket in. "Be careful," I had warned as I left his lanai.

Uncle Chin had smiled. "To be old man in my business must be careful. No worry about me, Kimo." He stood up quickly, and I was surprised at the vigor he could generate when he wanted to. "He was hard man, but he was my son. I find out what I can."

"Great," Akoni said. "First we get your geek friend to help us break into the dead guy's computer. Now we've got some old used-to-be tong guy checking out leads for us. We're a great pair of investigators, you know that?"

Just the fact that Akoni still referred to us as a pair made me feel good. "This is a case that is not getting solved," Akoni said. "These tong guys, they bring in a hit man from Hong Kong to do this kind of thing, and he's already on a plane out of here by now."

Peggy Kaneahe finally returned my call, and I went over to her office to work on a subpoena for Tommy's cell phone records. She was having a bad week, it was clear, and she snapped at me three times during the hour we spent together. Her skin was pale and waxy, like she wasn't getting any sun, and her nails had been bitten down to the quick. She wore a black business suit with a white silk blouse, and no jewelry, not even a ring or earrings. Her watch was a simple Timex, and her hair was almost as short as mine.

"I'm not your punching bag, Peggy," I said after the third snap. "Tell me what's wrong, or I'm going back to the station and we'll finish this when you're in a better mood."

"I feel like I don't know you anymore, Kimo." She got up from behind her desk and walked over to the wall of law books. "When I came back to Honolulu, I wasn't sure I even wanted to see you. I was still mad at you. Then we worked together on the Davis case, and I remembered the things that had made us friends, back at Punahou. But now, I think I'm right back where I started. I just don't know what goes through your head."

"Things have been pretty confusing lately," I said. "Not just this case, but stuff going on in my life. I've had a lot of thinking to do."

She turned to face me. "Is there anything you want to tell me? Have you been thinking about us?"

"I have. But I'm not done thinking yet. I just need a little more time."

"A little," she said. "I can give a little. Do you want to have dinner tomorrow night? Maybe we can both relax."

I waffled. "Let's wait and see how we both feel," I said, knowing I was surfing with Tim at three. I knew Peggy, and knew if she was this stressed on Friday she was likely to cancel on Saturday. We went back to work on the subpoena, and then we went upstairs to Judge Yamanaka's chambers, where she signed it with hardly a glance. I hand-carried it to the phone company office a couple of blocks away, and handed it to the Japanese woman behind the counter. "Do you want to wait for the printout?" she asked. "It'll probably take a half hour or so."

"I'll wait." I sat down in an uncomfortable plastic chair and tried to look through a couple of magazines, but I was too fidgety to concentrate. I felt like our investigation was finally moving forward, and I was antsy to get on with things.

Finally the woman came back, carrying my printout. There were two incoming calls the night Tommy was killed, one right after the other. I didn't recognize the first number, though the second seemed familiar. I ran it through my brain until it came up with a match. Uncle Chin. Of course, Tommy was his son, after all. I pointed to the first call. "This number," I said. "Can you trace it for me?"

She took the printout and walked to a terminal, where she sat down and typed something in. She waited a minute and then looked up at me. "It's a pay phone." She read off the address to me, and I realized it was a couple of blocks from the bar where we'd all gone after the failed black tar bust. I drove past it on my way back to the station, and saw it was a single phone attached to a post on the sidewalk. Anyone could pull up on the street and use it, or walk up after leaving a nearby bar.

I thought of Evan Gonsalves again, and tried to remember what time he'd left the bar. The details of that part of the night were fuzzy, but I thought he must have left around midnight. Just when the call came through to Tommy's cell phone, as he was breaking up with Treasure Chen.

By the time I got back to the station, Akoni had left—he was taking Mealoha up to the north shore for a family reunion weekend. It saved me having to share my suspicions about Evan with him, and let me table the whole investigation until Monday morning.

I passed on dinner with Harry, even though it was Friday night. I picked up a chicken breast at the grocery and left it marinating in a mango sauce while I went for a swim. I felt the heat of the pavement rising up through the cheap plastic of my flip-flops and crossed Lili'uokalani to walk on the shady side of the street. There wasn't a hint of a trade wind, and the palm trees at Kuhio Beach Park stood still. The air was heavy with humidity, sweat, and the smell of seaweed washed up on the shore at high tide.

I jumped in the ocean hoping it would be cool, but it was warm as bathwater until I swam out beyond the shallow breakers. I finally hit a pocket of cold water and it stunned me, raising goose bumps on my arms. It was as if I'd forgotten what cold felt like.

I swam for almost an hour but didn't see Tim, and then went home and grilled the chicken breast on my barbecue, cutting a green pepper into slices and roasting them until their skins charred. I drank a macadamia nut brown ale in a twenty-two-ounce bottle with dinner, turned the ceiling fan on high, and relaxed for what seemed like the first time in days. It was a brief jump back into my old life, the one where I knew what was going on.

I slept late the next morning, a treat I almost never allow myself, and it felt great to be able to look at the clock, smile, and then just roll over. I finally got up around nine-thirty, made myself macadamia nut pancakes, and then got back into bed with a surfing magazine.

The phone rang around eleven, and I half hoped it was Tim Ryan, and then worried he'd be canceling our surfing lesson. It was Terri Gonsalves, and she was crying. "Okay," I said. "It can't be so bad. Just tell me what's wrong."

"This morning I told Evan that I wanted him to take back the bracelet he gave me, that it was too nice a present. He said he couldn't."

"Yeah?"

"He said he'd been doing some private security work, just like you said. A jewelry dealer visiting Honolulu who needed somebody to go along with him. For payment, he gave Evan the bracelet."

"So what's wrong?"

"He's lying, Kimo. I know he is. I didn't believe him, and he got mad, and he walked out." In the background I heard her son come into the room. To him, she said, "It's okay, Danny. Sometimes Daddy and Mommy get mad at each other. Why don't you go to your room and play for a while, and then Mommy will come and get you. Okay?"

She came back on the phone, speaking softly. "I just don't know what to do."

"He can't take back what he's already done, however he got the bracelet. Just tell him not to do any more. Whatever he's into, you have to say it doesn't matter, you just want him to stop. I'd offer to talk to him myself, Terri, but you know we're walking a fine line here. I don't want to find out anything I don't want to know."

"I understand," she said. "All right, I'll tell him."

"Good girl. Call me whenever you need to."

I hung up and then paced around the apartment for a while. I thought about Evan, about the growing list of ways he might be connected to Tommy Pang. Was the bracelet he gave Terri what Derek had seen his father give to the nameless cop? Had Evan been the leak on the black tar bust? I didn't want to call Akoni and ruin his weekend; if indeed Evan was our guy, he would still be around on Monday morning.

It was a gorgeous day, too nice to stay cooped up inside, so I went for a walk, all the way through Waikīkī past Fort DeRussy, to the Ala Moana Center, where I turned around and walked all the way back. It was wonderful to turn my brain off, just concentrate on the walk and the world around me.

When I got back, there was a message on my machine from Peggy Kaneahe. I returned her call, and we talked about a case that was keeping her swamped. A pair of petty thieves had stolen some rare and valuable artifacts from the Bishop Museum but were refusing to name their fence. She was sure they were part of a bigger plan to smuggle Hawai'ian art treasures out of the country and was frustrated because they wouldn't cooperate.

"You sound beat," I said. "Would you rather skip tonight?"

She paused. "You wouldn't mind? I just, I need to, I guess, just relax."

"Sure. Read a book tonight, or watch TV. We'll talk next week."

"You're sweet, Kimo," she said. "Aloha."

I felt lucky and guilty at the same time. I puttered around until just three o'clock, when Tim Ryan rang my bell, and as we walked down Lili'uokalani toward the beach together, I gave him a brief lesson on surfing. "Light winds cause ripples out in deep water. The water molecules travel in stationary circles as these ripples travel over them, gradually getting stronger and becoming waves. As that wave hits the coral reef, its height and speed increase. That's when the surfer jumps on and rides."

"So that's why some beaches are better for surfing than others," Tim said. "Because they have different reef configurations."

"Exactly." We dropped our towels on the beach and swam out beyond the breakers, me dragging one end of my board. "Now we wait," I said, once we were in position. There were more surfers around than I like; that's why I usually surf so early in the morning or late in the day. On a beach like Waikīkī, the waves are insistent, so you don't want to have to compete for them with too many other surfers. I even saw Alvy Greenberg down the beach and waved at him.

"How do you know when the right wave is coming?" Tim asked.

"You can't explain it," I said. "It's very Zen. You just have to feel it. Let's hang out here and just let a bunch of waves wash over us."

So we did. I relaxed, treading water and holding onto one end of my board, Tim on the other. We felt the waves, and watched the other surfers. "That wasn't a good choice for him," I said, pointing to one guy as he fell off his board. "See, the wave petered out." We watched another and I said, "His balance is off. He's going to fall," and sure enough, he did.

"You jinxed him," Tim said, with a smile.

"Surfing is hard. Nobody gets it right the first time." After a while, I saw a good set building outside. "Get on the board," I said, and I held it down a little in the water as he put one leg over. "Now crouch up toward the front." As he did so, I swung myself onto the board, too, just behind him, not crouching but straddling the board with my legs in the water. The board rode lower in the water than usual, because of the extra weight, but if the wave was as strong as I thought, it would carry us.

"Hold on." The wave started to carry us forward, and I paddled fast to help it. When it really had us, I stopped paddling, pulled myself into a quick crouch, and then stood up. Tim was still crouched beneath me, holding the sides of the board. "Stand up," I yelled, over the roar of the water. "Don't worry, I've got you."

I held his shoulders, and then slid my hands down to his waist as he stood. He had good balance, especially with me holding him. "Wow," he yelled, as we knifed through the water, the beach and high-rise hotels rushing toward us, salt spray and sun, and the noise of the water, and the clear exhilaration of it all.

As the wave started to die, I moved back into a crouch, pulling Tim down with me. We lost our balance then and took a spill, but the water was shallow and the coolness felt great. I was surprised to find, as I came up for air, that the ride had given me an erection. Fortunately, it was already subsiding. "So?" I asked, as Tim appeared beside me. "You like?"

"That was amazing. I see why you like it. Can we do it again?"

"Let's get you a board." We headed down the beach toward one of the rental concessions. "The widest, longest boards are best for beginners," I said. "They catch the waves earlier, and you get a chance to get accustomed to the wave before it gets too steep." My custom board is six feet long, made of fiberglass and resin and specially cut, shaved, and sanded by hand to my own instructions. His was a regulation beginner board, dinged up and bruised, and looked like a big fat older brother to mine.

We practiced for an hour or so, spending a lot of time just hanging out beyond the breakers, waiting for the right waves. Every now and then we'd see Alvy but I never did speak to him. By the end of the hour, Tim was starting to get a feel for which wave to choose, and he'd mastered all the beginning steps: getting on the board, paddling fast to catch the wave, standing up. He couldn't ride for very long without taking a tumble, but that would come with time and practice.

Finally we quit and returned his board. "I'll bet you're kind of achy," I said. "Your muscles really take a beating when you first start surfing."

"You're not kidding. I want to go directly home and tumble into the hot tub." He looked over at me. "Want to come?"

"Sure." We stopped at my apartment to drop off my board, and then walked down Lili'uokalani to a low-rise building of six stories clustered around a central pool and patio area. The hot tub was off to one side, shaded that late in the day by a big koa tree.

It felt great to slip into the hot water. We both submerged down to our necks in front of jets, feeling the pulsing water massage our tired muscles. The buoyancy kept pushing us up to the surface, and our legs kept touching. I opened the top of my bathing suit to let a big bubble of air out, and then settled back to the shelf inside the tub. The toes of his right foot grazed my thigh. He sat back against the side of the hot tub and his legs rode up and brushed against mine.

After about twenty minutes, not really talking, just looking at each other goofily and smiling, Tim wiped sweat from his forehead with the back of his arm. "I'm ready to get out. How about you?"

I agreed, and we dragged ourselves out and flopped onto lounge chairs nearby to dry off.

We lay in the sun for a while, but our suits were still wet when Tim said, "My place is just over there. Why don't you come over— I've got fresh towels."

"Sure." We stood and walked across the courtyard to his first-floor apartment. He used his key on the patio door and we stepped inside. I followed him through a simple living room to a vanity area adjacent to the bathroom, where he opened a tall closet and pulled out plush dark green towels from a low shelf.

Standing again, he said, "Ow, that hurt," and put his hand on the small of his back.

"The hot tub doesn't do everything," I said. "Come on, let me rub your back."

He was still hunched over, crablike, as he led me to the bedroom, where he flopped down on the big queen-sized bed in pain. "Shit, that hurts."

I wrapped the towel around my wet bathing suit and sat on the bed next to him. Starting at the shoulders, I worked his muscles, feeling them ease under my touch. At first he twitched with pain when I pulled on sensitive tendons, but gradually he relaxed. "Oh, man, that feels great. Where'd you learn to do that?"

"The north shore," I said. "You really work yourself into the ground when you surf all day, every day. A bunch of us used to help each other out."

"Mmm." To get a better position, I pulled the towel off and straddled his legs, kneading the muscles in his lower back. "Geez, you don't need to be a cop," he said. "You could make a living doing this."

I was hard again in my Speedos. I was confused about what I wanted. I knew that sometime I would go to bed with Tim, but was this the right moment? How would we get there from where we were? I sat back on my haunches for a minute and Tim took that opportunity to twist around onto his back. He looked directly up at me and there was no way to disguise how I felt. He motioned to me with his finger.

"Come down here."

I did. His skin was cool and his touch was slow and gentle, his fingers barely grazing the edge of my jaw, the center of my nipple, the inside of my thigh. I shivered and twitched under him like a rabid dog, unable to stand the teasing yet unwilling for it to stop. He wrapped his arms around my back and we kissed, deeply and hungrily, and then he pulled back. "Slow down," he said. "We're not in any hurry here."

We explored each other's bodies. His was all uncharted territory to me, from a tiny, half-moon-shaped scar on his right shoulder to the discovery that his insteps were sensitive and responded to tickling. He worked my body like he knew what he was doing, licking and sucking me until just that knife-edge before release and then pulling back. Together we charted the regions of armpit and groin, the inner ear and the erotic zone just behind the scrotum.

I had never made love like this before. With women I'd been a tender and attentive lover, a good technician, making sure the patient was satisfied. My own pleasure had come easily and quickly, and had always seemed to me to be a separate part of the process. But with Tim, pleasing him and pleasing myself were part of one organic whole. We lingered so long over foreplay simply because it was fun. I shut off my brain and let my body take over, as I did on my best surfing days, and when we were both spent and exhausted and I looked at the clock, I saw that hours had passed. I lay there under his arm, my hand on his warm thigh and felt, finally, comfortable.

Chapter 22

"YOUR SUIT'S STILL WET," Tim called from the bathroom. "Why don't you borrow something of mine and we'll get some dinner?"

"Better yet, why don't we order in?"

He came out of the bathroom and stood in the bedroom door, naked. "You're a naughty boy. Pizza?"

"Sure."

We ordered a large mushroom pizza, and he said, "I can't answer the door like this. I'm going to put some clothes on. You can do what you want."

What I wanted, I thought, was to stay in bed with Tim all weekend long, practicing, exploring the whole new world that had opened up before me. But instead I went into his closet and pulled on a pair of shorts and a T-shirt. "You don't wear underwear?" he asked.

"I do. I just don't want to wear yours."

He burst out laughing. "You'll suck my dick but you won't wear my shorts? Don't you think that's a little weird?"

I just shrugged. Fortunately then the doorbell rang.

We watched old movies on TV after we finished the pizza, and then made love again before we went to sleep, snuggled next to each other with the window open and the ceiling fan creating a gentle breeze.

I'm an old hand at sleeping in strange beds. I did some counting once and figured I'd slept in rooms in half the hotels in Waikīkī. But I stayed awake for a few minutes, thinking about where I was and what I was doing. Though I tried, I just couldn't feel bad about it. I liked Tim, and I'd had fun with him. There wasn't anything wrong with that.

The next morning I woke up before Tim. We had separated during the night, and he was curled up on the right side of the bed, one arm on top of the damask print sheets. His skin looked even more tanned against the white-on-white pattern.

I wanted to reach out and touch him, stroke his shoulder, curl my fingers into his hair, but I thought it would be a shame to wake him. I did feel a little freaky, a little panicked by the speed with which my new life was moving, but I pushed down those fears and tried to concentrate on enjoying the moment.

He woke then, yawned, and looked at me. He smiled. "Morning. You sleep all right?"

"Great," I said. "You?"

He nodded, then reached out and took my hand. I smiled back at him and snuggled up close to him under the sheets. We fooled around a little and read the Sunday paper. We went to one of those big tourist buffet brunches, and then walked on the beach for a while. "This has been great, Kimo," Tim said eventually, as we were sitting on the sand in front of the Royal Hawai'ian Hotel. "But I've got work I've got to do before tomorrow morning."

It was late afternoon but the sun was still high in the sky, the beach glittering golden around us. I said, "I understand." We walked back to my apartment together, and this time we hugged each other, not caring who was around to see.

Monday morning, I didn't get a chance to tell Akoni any of my suspicions about Evan Gonsalves because he wasn't at the station. He left a message that he'd gone to Honolulu Hale to check out an idea he had.

Around ten, my phone rang, and I thought it was Akoni, but instead it was Lieutenant Yumuri. "I want you and Hapa'ele in my office now."

He hung up before I could tell him Akoni wasn't there, so I went down the hall to his office alone. "Akoni's at Honolulu Hale doing research," I said. "Anything I can do for you?"

The lieutenant had a small office at the back of the station, but its size was made up for by its window on the beach. Through the glass I could see sunshine, surf, sand, and hundreds of tourists turning red. I didn't know if I could ever concentrate on my job if I had that office and that window.

"How close are you to closing that murder case?" he asked. "It's been almost two weeks. Why haven't I seen any progress? I thought this was a simple gay-bashing." He shook his head. "Goddamned faggots. Just what I don't need on my watch."

"That was our first direction," I said. "Because the victim wasn't gay, because he had tong connections, because he was robbed, we've eliminated that as a possibility. But it took us a while. That was just one of the dead ends we ran into." I explained about the information we'd gotten from other divisions that hadn't panned out. Then I hesitated. "The victim's son said he believed his father was paying off a cop," I finally said. "He says the cop was there that night. Akoni and I have been examining the victim's background to see if there's any possible connection to someone on the force."

"That's bullshit and you know it," Yumuri said. "That's the first thing these people do—they blame the cops."

"We've actually been finding some connections," I said. I told him about the black tar bust, and a couple of more tenuous connections we'd found in the past.

"And what are you going to do when you find this cop?"

"We found the murder weapon and the lab is checking it for trace evidence," I said. "We may get a print we can match." I hesitated again. *What the hell,* I thought. I'd been covering it up long enough. "And I actually have some additional evidence we haven't put on paper yet." Deep breath.

"I was out late that night, and I was on my way home past the alley when I saw a man drag the body down the alley, from the office door to the street."

Yumuri laughed. It certainly wasn't what I expected of him. "Good try. But you'll never get the DA to believe that."

"I saw it," I said. "The man left in a black Jeep Cherokee." I closed my eyes for a second and saw again the man dragging Tommy Pang's lifeless body down the alley. I remembered what I had done, and felt the shame again. "I went over to the victim and felt for a pulse, and I was the one who made the call to 911. The coroner lifted my fingerprint from his neck."

"You could have put that print on his neck during the investigation."

I shook my head. "I wasn't present at the scene while the body was still there. By the time I arrived, the body had already been taken to the ME's office. I had no further contact with the victim until I was present at the autopsy, when the fingerprint was lifted from his throat."

While Yumuri digested what I had to say, I looked around at the walls of his office. I'd never really noticed the pictures there— Yumuri with the mayor, Yumuri in a crowd of officers being blessed by the archbishop of Honolulu, though he wasn't Catholic. Every citation he'd ever received had been carefully framed and hung, even the routine commendations for passing a year without discharging his weapon that were sent out by some computer program downtown.

There were three photos of his family on his desk, including one of him, his wife, and his sons in ski parkas and goggles. They looked like large insects from a snowy planet in a distant galaxy.

The impact of what I was saying finally hit Yumuri. "Jesus Christ," he said, and I wondered if that would be considered blasphemy from a nonobservant Buddhist. "This is the sloppiest piece of police work I have ever seen in my career. If you're not lying through your teeth, you're telling me you witnessed a murder and then left the scene?"

"I didn't see the murder, Lieutenant. All I saw was a man drag something down an alley, which I didn't discover was a man's body until after the perp had left the scene. I had to leave the scene to find a phone so I could call 911."

"I saw the report. That was a citizen call, not a cop. A cop would have given his badge number, and a cop would have returned to secure the scene until backup arrived."

"I didn't."

"Why the hell not?"

I was conscious that my life was falling apart while just a few feet away hundreds of people were enjoying the vacation of a lifetime. "I'd been in a bar for a while," I said, looking down at the floor. "I didn't want anyone to know." I looked up. "I know what I did was wrong. But I want to keep investigating this case. I know we can wrap it up."

He shook his head. "You know what your trouble is, Kanapaʻaka? You just don't think half the time. When you think, you're a good detective. But goddamn it, you've screwed this one up royally."

I didn't say anything. Finally he said, "I want to see you and Hapaʻele back here before your shift is over." He looked back down at his desk. "Dismissed."

It was about two o'clock by then. I didn't know when Akoni would be back, but I knew he'd check in by four, the end of our shift. I tried to go back to research, but I couldn't keep my mind on the paper in front of me. I hadn't really spilled my secret yet, just told the lieutenant that I'd been in a bar, but eventually the truth was going to come out. Soon enough I was going to have to confront my homophobic boss, and probably the rest of the world, with the news that I was gay.

Finally the phone rang and I pounced on it. "Kanapaʻaka, Waikīkī station," I said, hoping it would be Akoni.

Instead it was Thanh Nguyen from the special investigations section, with the results on the police lock. It was indeed the murder weapon; traces of blood and hair on it matched the victim. There were no clear prints, though, only smudges.

I had always assumed that once we found a suspect, my evidence would be added to what we had found. I'd be able to show that I was in the alley, that I'd seen the man drop Tommy's body and take off in the Cherokee. But talking to Lieutenant Yumuri, I realized how tenuous my evidence would be, because I had made the 911 call anonymously. Nothing but my fingerprint proved I'd been in the alley at all.

Then I remembered the giraffe. Would he recognize me again? Would I recognize him? He could place me at the club at the right time, and he'd seen me go out the door.

I wasn't sure if I felt better or worse. Each thing I had to do to prove my case was taking me one step farther out of the closet. And it assumed I'd be able to find the giraffe and that he could testify correctly.

The phone rang again. This time I answered, "Akoni?"

It was Uncle Chin. "Sorry, Uncle, I was expecting another call. *Ní hao ma?*" When I was really little, Uncle Chin taught me a couple of Chinese phrases, and now they sprang up every time I talked to him.

"I am well. I ask questions about Tommy. Maybe you want come here sometime, find out answers."

"My shift ends at four. I could come sometime after that."

"Aunt Mei-Mei very happy you stay for dinner. Maybe your parents come too."

How could I tell him my world was about to fall apart? "Sure," I said. "But you and I will talk first."

"Of course."

When I hung up, the phone rang again almost immediately. "Thank God," I said, when I heard Akoni's voice. "The lieutenant wants to see us both before the end of shift."

"What's up?"

I told him. "Shit, Kimo, I told you this was going to happen."

"I'll do what I can to keep you out of it."

"Shit," he said. "I'm on my way back."

I shifted some papers around on my desk. I looked up every time the door opened, then looked back down. Two Japanese tourists came in with a complaint and needed a translator. I volunteered, more to pass the time than anything else, but all they really wanted was directions to the Kodak Hula Show.

While I was up, I looked at the little kiosk full of bus schedules by the front door, but couldn't find one that went anywhere I wanted to go. Then I went back to my desk and stared at a poster announcing Citizen Anti-Crime Week for a while. It was pretty ugly, the HPD shield in a kind of burnt orange with a lot of text around it.

I straightened out a paper clip and then tried to bend it back into its original shape, but it wouldn't go. I couldn't get the same smooth curves, no matter how hard I tried. Finally Akoni got back from Honolulu Hale.

"Did you find anything interesting?" I said, as he put his folder down on his desk.

"Tell me again how this happened," he said. "The lieutenant called you in to ask about our progress."

I nodded. "I wanted it to sound like we were close to an arrest." I told Akoni what Yumuri had said. "When I told him I had personal evidence, that I'd seen the guy dragging Tommy Pang's body down the alley, he laughed."

"He laughed?"

"Yup. He thought I was lying. I finally convinced him, and he wasn't happy."

"Shit," Akoni said. "All right, let's get this over with."

We walked back to the lieutenant's office, and this time he spoke mostly to Akoni. "Do you think you can wrap this up soon?"

"We're making progress," Akoni said.

"Progress!" Yumuri exploded. "Progress is a suspect behind bars! You don't have shit, do you?" He paused, seemed to struggle to maintain his temper. "You have until Wednesday, end of shift," Yumuri said. "I want results on this or I'll have your asses. Is that understood?"

He looked at each of us. "Understood," Akoni said.

"Understood," I said.

"You are history," Akoni said as we walked back to our desks. "Kiss your badge good-bye. Sign up for the private security detail at the Ala Moana Mall."

"Thanks for your support. You find out anything useful downtown?"

He shook his head. "Not a thing. I'm not giving up on the idea that there's a dirty cop in this somewhere, but I still have my doubts about the son and his friend," Akoni said. "We need to know if their story held up."

"All right, so tonight we check out the bar and see if they were really there."

"I really don't want to go to that place. Suppose somebody makes a pass at me? I don't want anybody blowing in my ear."

"Hold on a minute." I picked up the phone and at the same time pulled Tim's card out of my wallet. "Tim Ryan," I said, when the receptionist answered. "Hey, Tim, it's Kimo. Yeah? Good. Listen, I have to go out to a bar by the Aloha Bowl called the Boardwalk tonight, to show some pictures around and check out an alibi." I listened. "Oh it is, is it? You want to go with me?" I laughed. "I promise. All right, I'll pick you up around ten."

"You're off the hook," I said when I hung up. "I've got a friend to go with me."

"You're not wasting any time, are you? That the guy who blew in your ear?"

"He's a lawyer. I met him at Kuhio Beach Park."

Akoni held up his hand. "I don't want to hear about it."

I gathered my stuff from my desk and packed up. "I'm going to see Uncle Chin now. He said he had some information about Tommy Pang."

"We've got to get this solved," Akoni said. "Or it's both our asses."

"I know," I said, as I walked out of the station.

Chapter 23

MY PARENTS were already at Uncle Chin's house by the time I arrived, the four of them sitting out on the lanai chatting, surrounded by birds and flowers. "You know your father built this house," Uncle Chin said, as I settled into a lounge chair across from him.

"I didn't know that," I said. "How long ago?"

"This was my first project on my own," my father said. "Right after you were born, when I left Amfac." In my memory, my father had always had his own business, but I knew that at some time in the past he had worked for Amfac, one of Hawai'i's Big Five companies, as a construction superintendent.

"This was new area back then," Uncle Chin said. "I bought many pieces land. Sold your father one where your house is."

They kept on talking about the old days, when they were young men and the world stretched out before them like a treasure chest of riches waiting to be plundered. It was hard for me to concentrate, because I kept thinking about my own future. What would I do if I left the force? I was too old to be a professional surfer; I had let that chance pass me by when I fled the north shore. As Akoni suggested, I could become a private cop, working security details for fancy condos or Ala Moana Center. I could become a private detective, chasing down errant husbands and bogus slip-and-fall claims.

I looked at my father. He was still a handsome man, graying, distinguished. He had once had many powerful friends and connections, but his friends aged as he did, and consequently the business he had built, which had provided for us all for so many years, was fading away too. Maybe I could work with him, rejuvenate the business, become a minor tycoon like he was.

But would he want me? I'd seen his face when he described Derek Pang as māhū. He didn't want a gay son any more than Tommy Pang had. "Kimo, you gone away somewhere?" my father asked.

I looked up. "Sorry, Dad. It's been a long day."

"Time for dinner," Aunt Mei-Mei said, standing up. "Lokelani and me, we have dinner ready chop chop."

When the women had left the room, Uncle Chin said, "I ask many people about my son. What he do, who hate him."

I looked at my father. He said, "I knew Tommy was Chin's son. I helped him get his papers."

I guessed my father was willing to stay and listen, so I said to Uncle Chin, "What did you find?"

He picked up a silver harmony ball from the table next to him and rolled it in his palm. "He was hard man, like I tell you, but no one know anyone who kill him. He was smart, my son. Not like his father like that."

"You're plenty smart, Chin," my father said.

Uncle Chin smiled. "Good to have friends, no?" Then his smile faded. "My boy not have many friends. Not many enemies either, but not many friends. Many women, lots of money."

"What kind of stuff was he doing, Uncle Chin? I know about the legitimate businesses—the bar, the pack and ship, the lingerie shop. But he must have been doing some illicit stuff too. Smuggling? Gambling? Prostitution? Drugs?"

"Hate drugs," Uncle Chin nearly spit out. I remembered Robert, his death. Uncle Chin had always been adamantly against the drug trade. "Stupid business," I remembered him telling me once. "Get customers, then kill them. How make life like that?"

"Did Tommy deal in drugs?" I asked gently.

Uncle Chin nodded. "Bad business. I told him many times, stop. Drugs kill his brother. He not care. Truth, I think he resent Robert's memory. Robert born here, have advantages he no have. Even though I tried make up to him."

"Was Derek involved in any of Tommy's businesses?" I asked. "I know about the bar. How about the others?"

"Sounds like," Uncle Chin said. "Two boys, Derek and friend. They collect money sometimes, carry messages. Like learning business."

"The drugs, too?"

Uncle Chin shook his head. "No. Tommy said. Derek no in drugs. I make him promise."

"He gets all the businesses now?" I asked. "Derek?"

Uncle Chin looked disturbed, like he was seeing where I was going. "Wife gets, but Derek runs. You think Derek kill Tommy?"

I shrugged. "I don't know. You think Derek could kill his father?"

"I'm a contract builder," my father said unexpectedly. "You hire me, I work for you. There are men like that, who kill."

I wondered again about the relationship between my father and Uncle Chin, how much my father knew about Uncle Chin's business, how closely he was connected. "Could that be?" I asked Uncle Chin. "Could Derek have hired someone to kill Tommy?"

Uncle Chin looked very sad, very old. "Don't know," he said, shaking his head. "Don't know."

Just then my mother came in. "Come for dinner, now," she said. My father stood and offered his arm to Uncle Chin, who struggled up from his chair. He murmured something to my father, who laughed. I wondered if Harry and I would end that way, still friends, helping each other over the rough places in our lives.

We didn't talk any more about Tommy Pang. At dinner, Aunt Mei-Mei and my mother kept a light banter going, my father occasionally making jokes. I was happy they could all be together, support each other. Uncle Chin had aged a lot over the last few days, and it surprised me to consider that he must have loved Tommy

Pang very much, even though he had called him a hard man. I knew that my father loved me and my brothers very deeply, in a way that often could not even be expressed, and I was sure he would be as crushed as Uncle Chin if one of us were to die.

I think your attitude toward your parents changes as you get older. You're more able to see them as human beings who have made choices and handled their lives as best they could. I didn't always agree with the decisions my father had made; I would rather he had worked less when I was a kid and spent more time with us. I thought we could have had a few less toys, eaten more rice and poi and less steak, and in return had more of him, but it was the 1960s and 1970s then, and that's what fathers did. I'm sure my mother, born poor and determined never to be poor again, had a lot to do with that, too, but again, you couldn't fault her for doing what she thought was best for her family.

It was saddening to know that I would never have more family than this, and that I would lose them eventually. I wouldn't have a wife, though I hoped someday I would find a partner. I would never have children and have to make choices on how to raise them; never see their first steps or first day at school, nor their graduations or weddings. I would never have a luau to celebrate the birth of my child, and never have grandchildren to swarm over me the way my nieces and nephews did to my father.

I would always be a part of my brothers' lives, or hoped I would, be Uncle Kimo to Jeffrey and Ashley and their brothers and sisters, and that would have to be enough. Like my parents, I took the hand I was dealt and tried to make the best of it.

I looked at my watch. It was already late; I had to drive back to Waikīkī and pick up Tim, and then go out to the Boardwalk and see if anyone could identify Wayne or Derek. I made my excuses as my mother and Aunt Mei-Mei were clearing the dessert dishes. "So late, you have to work?" my mother asked.

"I have to check out a suspect's alibi. He was there late, so I have to go there late."

She shook her head. My father said, "Be careful, Keechee."

"I will be." To Uncle Chin I said, "I am very sorry for you, about Tommy. I'll do my best to catch whoever killed him."

Uncle Chin smiled at me. "You my son, too, Kimo," he said. "*He kanaka pono 'oe, lokomaika'i 'oe.*"

I looked down. "You flatter me, Uncle Chin." He had told me I was a powerful person and good-hearted as well.

"He says the truth," my father said. "Your mother and I are very proud of you."

How proud would they be, I thought, as I drove back down to Waikīkī, if they knew who I really was?

≈

THE BOARDWALK LOOKED NONDESCRIPT from the outside, stuck near the end of a strip mall, with nothing but a wooden walkway over the concrete sidewalk to distinguish it from the karate school and beeper store on either side. Tim said, "This is it?" when we pulled up in my truck.

"This is it." We walked up to the front door and stepped through a beaded curtain into a dark vestibule. I heard the pounding beat of Bruce Springsteen's "Born in the USA" as we turned right and stepped through another curtain into a pile of sand.

At least that's what it felt like. It was a long, narrow sandbox that I guess those in the know stepped over. As it was we both stepped in it, and then as we stepped out, the sand sifted out of our shoes.

The room was dark, but spotlights washed places on the rough wooden walls. It was as kitschy as the Rod and Reel, but in a different style. This was early beach bum, with fishing nets hung from the ceiling, and tattered pinups of boys in skimpy bathing suits on the walls. The centerpiece was a long bar that ran the length of one wall. Instead of a polished top, its surface was made of rough wood planks, like a beachfront boardwalk, and at about the middle a well-muscled Hawai'ian boy in his early twenties strutted and danced in a jockstrap, reaching in often to fondle himself. At the far end, in his own pool of light, an equally well-muscled, dark-haired haole boy of about the same age practiced his own posturing.

"They have bars like this back in Boston," Tim whispered. "But I never went to one."

"There's a first time for everything," I whispered back.

There was another smaller bar in a back room, through a wide archway, and on the other side of the room were four pool tables, each lit by its own fake stained-glass lamp. Two or three guys were at each of the tables, and maybe a dozen by the bar.

I hadn't changed from the clothes I'd worn all day—a maroon polo shirt and jeans. Tim had taken off the tie I guessed he'd worn to work, but was still wearing a white oxford cloth button-down shirt and a pair of neatly pressed khakis. The guys around us, who ranged in age from what I guessed to be late teens to mid-fifties, were all dressed similarly, though a few were in T-shirts and another couple in leather pants with chains attached to the pockets.

We walked up to the bar and tried very hard to avoid the boy thrusting his crotch toward our heads. I ordered beers for both of us, and then when the bartender, a guy who looked half Hawai'ian and half Chinese, brought them, I showed him my ID. "Yeah?"

I'd deliberately chosen a place where one of the spotlights washed a section of bar. I pulled out a picture of Wayne I'd found on a club page of the Yale Web site, and asked, "Have you seen this guy?"

The bartender looked at it and shrugged. "I think so."

"You remember when?"

He laughed. "You gotta be kidding."

"Think a little harder," I said. "I've got some friends in the department who don't like underage drinking very much. I could send them over here."

He didn't like that. He picked up Wayne's picture, looked at it again, and then closed his eyes. "Not for a couple of weeks," he said when he opened them again. "He's got a friend, doesn't he?"

I showed him a picture of Derek I'd found at the same place. "Yeah, that's him," he said. "They're usually together, though sometimes the haole cruises by himself."

"So they weren't in here a week ago Tuesday, the sixteenth?"

He shook his head. "No. I know that for a fact, because we were closed that night." He looked at me. "Your friends in the department were here the Saturday before. They said they were looking for drugs, but they didn't find anything. And I don't serve anybody under twenty-one. Still they decided they didn't like the idea of a fag bar, so they closed us down. It took us a full week to get it cleared up and reopen."

I nodded. He walked away to serve somebody else down the counter. If the police didn't like fags getting together at a bar on the edge of town, they certainly weren't going to like one on their force.

For an hour or so we stood around and watched the guys playing pool, me leaning back against Tim, feeling the contact my shoulders made against his chest, his arms around my waist. Every time his fingertips grazed my skin I felt shock waves rolling through my chest and down into my groin. I was hard almost the entire time.

We drank our beers and swayed to the rhythm of the music on the jukebox, and every now and then we turned around and kissed. Around us, men moved through the shadows and the light, talking in small groups, flirting, or silently cruising the bar waiting for sparks to fly. A Thai or Vietnamese boy who couldn't have been more than fifteen or sixteen chatted at the bar with a haole man in his fifties, and, as I watched, the man stroked the boy's cheek in a gesture of unexpected tenderness.

Tendrils of smoke drifted through the wash of light near us, and the air smelled of cigarettes, beer, and testosterone. At a table in the back, two men who looked like brothers alternately kissed and sat back and stared at each other with wide smiles. Near the door, three men had a heated discussion, one of them gesturing wildly and repeatedly pointing his finger at his head as if he was shooting himself. A rotating stable of six guys danced on the bar, all of them young, well-muscled, and well-hung.

It was interesting to be out in public with Tim and not care about anybody else. And nobody seemed to care about us. A pool table opened up and we played, and then around midnight both of us started yawning and I drove us back to Waikīkī.

"That was fun," he said as I pulled up in front of his building.

"Yeah, it was, wasn't it? I'll tell you, it was a hell of a lot more fun going there with you than with Akoni."

He laughed. "I doubt you'd kiss Akoni in public."

It was my turn to laugh. "I think if I kissed Akoni, in public or in private, it would take him a minute to collect his wits, and then he'd give me a good roundhouse punch."

"Well, I'll never do that when you kiss me." He leaned across then and we kissed for a long minute, and then he yawned again and said, "Work in the morning. See ya."

Chapter 24

THE NEXT MORNING I went to Kuhio Beach Park for a half hour or so, but the surf was choppy, so I was at my computer a few minutes before eight, trying to organize my thoughts. Akoni came in with a cup of coffee and I said, "You didn't bring one for me?"

"Hey, you were here first. You could have had coffee for me." He sat down in his chair and turned around to face my desk. I told him what I'd discovered at the Boardwalk, that Derek and Wayne couldn't have been there. "That means they were lying," I said.

Akoni sat back in his chair. "What do you think really happened?"

I shrugged. "I don't know that it matters. Derek and Wayne couldn't stay at the Rod and Reel because they didn't want Tommy to know about them. So they left. Tommy must have gone back to the club after his date with Treasure, where he met up with the cop, who was probably there to get a payoff for tipping Tommy about the bust earlier that night."

"They argued?"

"Must have. Maybe Tommy didn't want to pay. They got into a scuffle, and the cop whacked him over the head."

Akoni and I looked at each other for a while. In the background we heard the radio crackle with beat cops checking out license plates and driver records. The 6-1 officer was checking "Golf, Bravo, Golf, three-four-three," and the dispatcher told him it was a 1998 red Mazda Miata and gave him the registration information.

They checked the driver and made sure he had no outstanding warrants.

We worked the phones and the computer all morning, getting nowhere. Finally, the phone rang and I answered. "Really," I said. "Cool. Keep it in the back; we'll be out to see you."

"That was Lucky Lou." He ran a pawnshop out by the Aloha Bowl, and he was responding to a list of Tommy Pang's jewelry we'd circulated around the city. "He thinks he's got Tommy's watch."

"Looks like we get to get out of here." Akoni stood up. "You want some lunch? We could hit Zippy's," he said, and it was almost like having my partner back.

Lucky Lou's pawn shop is located in an industrial neighborhood out by the Aloha Stadium just beyond Pearl Harbor, not far from the Boardwalk. We took the H1 ewa, found ourselves at Zippy's, and ordered our burgers.

"Who do you think pawned the watch?" I asked, when we'd given our orders.

Akoni shrugged. "The murderer?"

"Good a guess as any," I said, as the clerk brought our burgers out to the window. "No way we're going to get prints, but maybe they've got video surveillance."

Akoni laughed. "If the camera works." We ate, Akoni telling me about how Mealoha had dragged him to an outlet mall in Waipahu, about fifteen miles west of Honolulu.

Lucky Lou ran a tourist trap operation out front, catching visitors on their way to Pearl Harbor with counterfeit Guccis and Cartiers, and rows of shiny gold chains that would turn your neck green about a day after you got home from your vacation. Around the back, there's another entrance for the pawn shop, and that's the one we took.

Lucky Lou was about 300 pounds and balding, a crabby New Jersey transplant. "Hey, Lou," I said, making my way past racks of nearly new guitars, stereo equipment that would probably be warm to the touch, and cameras that GIs from Schofield Barracks pawned to pay for cootchie-cootchie girls and their tender ministrations. "Let's see that watch you got."

He pulled out a tray. It was a Rolex like the one Genevieve Pang had described for us, engraved with "Tommy" on the back in fancy script, next to a couple of Chinese characters that I knew meant luck. I guessed Tommy's luck had run out.

"The guy bring anything else in at the same time?" Akoni asked.

Lucky Lou grimaced. "I knew you were going to ask that," he said. He pulled out another tray, and there were the diamond rings and gold and diamond bracelet Tommy'd also been wearing. "You know we're going to have to pull this in," I said.

"This gives me a credit, right?" Lou asked. "I get in any trouble, you vouch for me?"

"That depends," Akoni said. "You murder your wife, we can't do a thing for you. Parking ticket, that's another story."

"You know what I mean," Lou said.

"Yeah, Lou, we'll be a character reference for you." I wrote him up a voucher for the watch, the rings, and the bracelet. After the investigation was over, it would all go back to Genevieve Pang, and she could decide what she wanted to do with it.

"So, Lou," Akoni said. "Your cameras working all right?"

"One step ahead of you," Lou said. "I already checked. The guy was smart, kept his head down the whole time he was here."

"And you didn't suspect a thing," I said.

He shrugged. "I got a lot of customers don't want to get recognized," he said. "You're out pawning your mom's engagement ring so you can buy crack, you really want your picture taken?"

"So what you're saying is you got nothing for us," Akoni said.

"One thing," Lou said. "The guy was packing. He shifted his feet, his jacket came open a little, I saw the holster."

"Don't tell me," I said. "You think the guy might have been a cop."

"You know him?" Lou asked.

I shook my head. "You got a description?"

"Haole guy," he said. "Maybe late twenties, early thirties. Good build, not fat or scrawny. Dark hair, wedding ring. That's about all I noticed."

"You noticed the wedding ring?" Akoni asked. "What, you thinking about asking the guy out?"

"My line of work, I see a lot of guys pawning jewelry, all right?" Lou said. "Lotsa times, it's the wife's. I got in the habit of looking for wedding rings. Sometimes I mention it, the guy's willing to pop it off and add it to the stash, he's desperate enough."

We bagged the jewelry and left the pawn shop. "You want to see if we can connect with Derek Pang?" I asked. "Get him to ID the jewelry, confront him and Wayne about their stories?"

"We could do that," Akoni said.

I checked my notes, dialed up Derek Pang's home number. Surprise, surprise, he answered. He and Wayne were going out soon, but we could stop by on our way back to the station.

The day had not yet cooled down even though a light trade wind was blowing. The mountains around us shone green in the mellow light, and heat seemed to rise up in waves from the steaming black pavement around us. I thought about haole cops who had connections to the case, and my thoughts kept coming back to Evan Gonsalves.

Chapter 25

WAYNE ANSWERED THE DOOR again and showed us into the living room. "Derek'll be right out," he said. "He's just on the phone."

"I went to the Boardwalk last night," I said. "You could have warned me about that sandbox by the front door."

He smiled. "It's a little thing they do to keep track of who's been there before."

"And you've been there. The bartender recognized you. Said you go there sometimes with Derek, sometimes without. Cruising, I think he called it."

"I wouldn't say that. Sometimes I want a beer and Derek doesn't." He picked a paper clip up from the table and started fiddling with it.

"Just to refresh your memory, you told us that the night Tommy was murdered, you and Derek left the Rod and Reel and went to the Boardwalk. That true?"

"Yeah, we needed to chill out."

"When you've been to the Boardwalk in the past, you ever see anybody in there drinking, doesn't look old enough?" I asked.

"There are guys there who like chicken." We must have looked confused, because he added, "Younger guys. Boys, almost. So the chickens come there, and sometimes they drink, I guess. I never paid much attention."

I nodded. "See, the liquor control board, they pay attention. Matter of fact, they closed the place down Saturday, the ninth. They didn't get open again until the following Saturday. So the Boardwalk was closed on Tuesday the sixteenth, the night you said you and Derek went there. You want to rethink that story a little?"

By then he had twisted the paper clip into a tortured shape that resembled the double helix of DNA. "Okay, you got me. I lied," he said. "You've got to understand, I come from an Irish Catholic family. My older brother's a goddamn priest." He shook his head. "I'm accustomed to lying when it comes to my sex life. The fact is, I still don't think it's anybody's business who I get off with and where, but I don't want you guys to think I'm holding out on you."

He looked right at me, smiled, and then licked his lips. I felt he was looking right into my heart and knew that even as I sat there, I was lusting for him. He said, "Derek and I have been together three years now, and sometimes, the sex gets boring, so we try to spice things up a little. The truth is, after we left the Rod and Reel I was horny and I wasn't taking no for an answer."

He licked his lips again, and I shivered. I hoped neither he nor Akoni noticed. "We drove up to Mount Tantalus and I spread Derek against the hood of the car and plowed his ass, howling at the moon like a dog in heat. I was hoping some breeder couple would stumble on us and get the shock of their lives, but no such luck."

"You're a pervert," Akoni said.

"You ever had a piece of ass up against a warm engine, Detective?" he asked. "You ought to try it sometime. Your wife, maybe one of those boys from the Boardwalk. You just might like it."

"You freak," Akoni said, jumping up.

I jumped up, too, holding him back, just as Derek Pang entered the room. If he'd heard anything, he didn't let on. "You have jewelry that belonged to my father?" he asked.

We sat back down, Wayne putting his arm protectively around Derek's back, and I showed them both everything, in plastic bags. Derek nodded. "It was all his." He seemed to swallow hard. "You think the man who pawned this stuff is the one who killed him?"

"We don't know yet, but it's a good chance," I said. "Listen, Derek, there's just one little thing we need to clear up. Would you tell us again what happened after you left the Rod and Reel Club the night your father was murdered?"

He relaxed back into Wayne's embrace. "I know we weren't honest with you before, Detective, but you've got to understand, we're both in the habit of keeping our sex lives out of public view. As soon as we heard than my father had been killed shortly after we left him, we knew we would have to account for our time, and neither of us wanted to come out and say we'd been having sex while he was geting his head bashed in. So we both decided to say we'd gone to the Boardwalk."

"And now you're both saying you had sex at the top of Mount Tantalus," Akoni said. "How convenient."

Do you want me to describe what we did, Detective?" Derek asked. "You could put us in separate rooms, then compare our stories."

"Come on, let's show them," Wayne said, standing up, bringing Derek up with him. "I bet the big one likes to watch."

"Okay," Akoni said. "That's all we need." He stood up. "You'll be able to get this jewelry back after the investigation's over."

I didn't say anything until we were in the elevator. "What was that all about?" I asked. "Derek was in the middle of his statement."

"Yeah, and you know as well as I do the two of them rehearsed the whole thing," he said. "They were baiting us, Kimo. I didn't need to hear the details all over again." He looked over at me, and I was sure he'd seen what was in my heart when I looked at Wayne Gallagher. "And you didn't either," he said.

≈

WE WERE ON OUR WAY back to the station when we got a radio call that a man's body had been found in Kapiolani Park, on the Diamond Head end of Waikīkī. When we arrived, we found Lidia Portuondo keeping traffic away from the spot and Alvy Greenberg standing over a body, which had been discovered by a young haole woman out walking her dog. The body was in an advanced state of decomposition, so much so that we could not even determine, at first glance, whether it belonged to a man or woman.

Apparently the body had been buried, at the far end of the park near the Dillingham Fountain, and recent wind and rain had uncovered it. We waited for the coroner to come out and take the body away, but it was clear we wouldn't have much to investigate until Doc had a chance to do some analysis.

The girl whose dog had discovered the body was pretty upset, and we took a statement from her there, along with all her information, in case we needed to get back to her. "This one not get solved," Akoni said. "Not without a lucky break."

"No argument from me, brah," I said. We couldn't even search missing persons reports back at the station until we found out if the body was male or female and got a race and approximate age. This one certainly wasn't getting solved quickly, probably further adding to Lieutenant Yumuri's unhappiness with us.

Chapter 26

WE DIDN'T EVEN BOTHER to go back to the station, but instead headed over to the DA's office to go over the evidence we had collected on Tommy Pang's murder. When we arrived, the receptionist told us Ms. Kaneahe was waiting for us in her office.

Peggy had met Akoni a couple of times. The three of us shook hands, and then he and I sat down in old-fashioned wooden chairs across from her desk. The room was spare and professional—a bookcase filled with impressive legal volumes took up one whole wall, and the other was decorated only with Peggy's framed diplomas, including one from Punahou. There was nothing personal about the room, no knickknacks or photos on the desk, no attempt made to overcome the institutional sterility of the bland white walls and lay-in acoustic tile ceiling. I wondered how she could spend every day there. I'd have gone crazy before my first coffee break.

"Why don't you tell me about the case in your own words?"

I looked to Akoni, but Peggy said, "No, you first, Kimo. Since you seem to play a larger than usual role in this case."

I took a deep breath. "Okay," I said. "It started the night that black tar bust failed." I told her about drinking with the other cops, and then going to the Rod and Reel.

"So you weren't just in some bar in the neighborhood, you were in that bar," she said. "I don't understand. What were you doing there?"

I should have told her then, but I knew it was something I had to talk to her about in private, as a personal thing, nothing related to work. "You know we've had a number of gay bashings outside that club over the last few months. I guess I had a couple of beers, and I got to thinking of myself as a neighborhood cop. The place is only a few blocks from my apartment, you know. So I decided I would stop by there on my way home, make sure everything was okay. I had another beer, and saw that things were fine."

I looked at Akoni, but he was very carefully staring at the wall of Peggy's diplomas. "I was about to leave when a guy came up to me." I told her about the giraffe, about leaving the club and standing in the alley, seeing the guy drag Tommy's body. How I'd called 911, and then gone home.

It made me feel worse every time I had to tell it. There was no way to explain how desperate I'd been feeling, how every instinct I had said *get out of there*. In retrospect, I wished I'd never touched Tommy Pang's body, never called 911, just run the minute I heard something being dragged down the alley. But that would have been even more wrong.

Peggy didn't say anything, so I continued. I told her about our fruitless attempts to tie in Tommy's tong connections and about retrieving his jewelry from Lucky Lou. "The man Lou described might be a cop," I said. "Derek and Wayne told us that Tommy had a cop on his payroll, that the cop had been there that night."

"You have any ideas who that cop might be?"

"We've been doing some research," I said. "But I don't want to say anything until we have some proof. I'm sure you can understand how damaging it could be to an innocent man's reputation if we're wrong."

"You've got to wrap this one up quickly," Peggy said. "You know your lieutenant isn't happy with your progress, and neither is my boss. But first you've got a problem. If you find a suspect, you're the only one who can tie him to that truck, that alley, that time of night. You're also the investigating detective. Not very convincing."

"How do we make it convincing?" Akoni asked.

Peggy kept looking at me. "We have to independently establish your presence at that bar, that night, at that time. We've got a recording of the 911 call; we'll try to do a voice print and prove you made it. Now go on. What happened the next day?"

I explained about going surfing, and she frowned. I'd broken many dates with her when we were in high school because I was out on the waves and lost track of time. Akoni started talking then, telling her about the crime scene, and then the two of us alternated describing the rest of our progress.

"At least your investigation is well-documented," she said at last, throwing us a little bone. She directed us to go back to the Rod and Reel and see if we could find the giraffe, get him to sign an affidavit that he'd seen me at the club that night. "And I don't want you going alone, or acting like some neighborhood Rambo either," she said. She turned to Akoni. "Detective, I expect that any reports will read you were there, too. You're in this almost as deep as Kimo is."

"Understood," Akoni said.

"I could do it myself easier. We have no idea when this guy will be back at the club, if ever. I live nearby, so I can stop in randomly. That's a big imposition on Akoni."

"It's his job." Peggy gave us a short lecture about minimizing personal connections with cases. "You should have stepped away as soon as you recognized the scene," she said. "That was what, your third or fourth mistake on this case?"

I told her I got the message.

She closed the folder on her desk and put it to the side, in a neat pile of similar ones. I could see that the seeds of her personality had been there even back in high school, when her textbooks were crisply covered in brown paper, her penmanship perfect, and her locker always tidy. We shook hands on the way out, and she said she'd call me.

Akoni waited until we were out of the building to ask, "When you want to go back, look for this guy who blew in your ear?"

"We could try happy hour again."

Akoni shrugged. "You're starting to like this part of the investigation, aren't you?"

"Hey, you got the lingerie shop. I get the gay bar."

At the Rod and Reel Club, Fred the bartender was on duty again. "I'm trying to track a guy I saw here two weeks ago. About six two, really thin, blond hair shaved down to a stubble. You recognize him?"

"Sure, Gunter," he said. "Comes here two or three times a week, usually late, after eleven or so. I think he works a late shift somewhere. What do you want with Gunter?"

"Just want to ask him a question or two," I said. "He didn't do anything. I talked to him two weeks ago, and I just want to see if he remembers."

"Gunter talks to a lot of guys," Fred said, laughing. "Some of them talk back. You didn't talk back, he might not remember you."

"Gee, and I thought I was unforgettable."

Fred said, "Maybe to some," and looked me straight in the eye.

I said, "Mahalo," and took a pair of Big Wave Golden Ales out to Akoni on the patio, flattered and smiling.

"I guess we'll have to come back later," I said, explaining about Gunter.

"Just what I wanted to do," Akoni grumbled. "I better call Mealoha." He stood up. "Don't let anybody take that beer. I'm going to need a few more before this evening's over."

I sat back in my chair and looked around. The Rod and Reel wasn't that scary in the light of day. It was just a bar, after all. There were gay people there and straight people, and nobody seemed to care who was who. That was nice.

Akoni went home for dinner with Mealoha, and I went back to my apartment. I couldn't eat, and I couldn't concentrate on anything. I kept watching the clock, until finally it was ten and Akoni called to say he would be at my apartment in a couple of minutes. He parked out front, and we walked back down Kuhio Avenue toward the Rod and Reel.

From a block away, we could hear the music and noise coming from the club. We walked in together, and for a minute my heart seized up the way it had when I'd gone in there two weeks before. But then I looked around, and I realized it was still just a bar.

We circled slowly around the main room. Akoni was careful not to establish eye contact with anyone. I thought his unease was kind of funny. So what if a guy came up to him and asked him to dance, or blew in his ear? If he wasn't interested, he shouldn't have been threatened. "No" works if you weigh over 230.

Gunter wasn't in the main bar. I headed toward the back bar, wondering what Akoni's reaction would be when he saw the explicit videos being shown there. The one playing was a little wild even for me, a close-up shot of one guy humping another's butt. They'd lit it so that the lube and the sweat glistened in the light, and a thumping beat behind it established a rhythm.

Akoni looked away almost as soon as he saw the screen. Then I saw Gunter sitting at the edge of the bar, nursing a shot glass of something clear.

I showed him my ID and explained. Gunter said, "I don't think I remember you. You said I walked up to you?"

"And blew in my ear."

"That sounds like me," he said, laughing. "But you don't look like my type."

"I'd been working undercover. I was a little grungier, a little more like . . ."

"Rough trade," he said, and I nodded. He stared at me for a minute, and I had the feeling he was trying to envision me without my clothes on. It was a weird feeling. "I remember. You ran away!"

I nodded. "Out toward the alley."

"And I followed you to the door, but then I came back inside." He nodded. "I met the most delightful boy after you left. A fraternity brother from Illinois, I think. He just wanted a beer—he didn't realize what kind of place this was. But he was happy to let me suck his dick."

Akoni winced. "They like it, you know, straight boys," Gunter said to Akoni. "Their girlfriends won't suck their dicks for them. Does yours?"

"My partner's married," I said. "So Gunter, would you come down to the station and give us a statement?"

"A statement? Of what?"

"Of what you just said. That you saw me here, two weeks ago, around three a.m."

"That's all?"

"Just that. I need some proof that I was here then."

"Whatever for?"

"I witnessed a crime, just after I left here. I need to establish I was in the area."

Gunter nodded. "The body they found in the alley. You saw it?"

I nodded.

"I work from three to eleven," he said. "I sleep in the mornings. I like to sleep in, particularly if I have a guest. Can I come in tomorrow afternoon, before work?"

We agreed, but before we let him go I got his full name, home address and phone, and his work address. He was a security guard at a fancy condo tower. He was thin, but wiry, and I could see he was strong. With his evident muscles and his no-nonsense haircut, you wouldn't want to mess with Gunter.

"Hallelujah," Akoni said when Gunter had walked away. "We can go home. And never come back to this place."

"Never say never," I said.

Chapter 27

WE HAD TO table Tommy Pang's murder the next morning, because Akoni and I had to attend a training session at the downtown station. Neither of us wanted to go, but since the case wasn't going anywhere we didn't have much of an excuse. We spent the morning watching videos and hearing speakers about diversity training, sustainability, and community policing. I was interested to note that the diversity training included a section on the rights of gay people.

Akoni called in for messages when we broke at one. "Our buddy Melvin called and said he found a bunch of the receipts from packages Derek and Wayne sent. We ought to swing past his place on our way back and find out what that's all about."

"We've got Gunter coming in this afternoon for a statement," I reminded him.

"Why don't you go back and do that interview yourself," he said. "I'll go to the pack and ship place. We can compare notes later."

I was back at the station by two, and a little later Gunter showed up. I pulled Lidia Portuondo in with me to take his statement, so that somebody else was there. Knowing how Peggy Kaneahe and the lieutenant felt, I wanted to be extra careful. And besides, I thought that since Lidia had her own secrets, namely her relationship with Alvy, she ought to be able to keep mine.

Gunter looked a lot more presentable in his work clothes than he did in the torn T-shirt he'd worn the night before. He wore a pressed white shirt with epaulets and a name tag and khaki slacks, and even his buzz-cut head looked more normal in the light of day.

Lidia and I took him into one of the interview rooms. There was a coffee maker on a table against the far wall. "Coffee?" I asked. I poured one for myself.

"I can't take caffeine," Gunter said. I motioned him to sit down at the table. "What do you want from me?"

"Just what we told you yesterday. Just write down what happened to you at the Rod and Reel Club on the night of Tuesday the sixteenth."

"You want me to write down how I blew in your ear?" He leered at me, and I shivered a little. I thought a night with Gunter was more than I was willing to get into.

"You can leave that part out."

Lidia had just come in from her shift, and her uniform made her look tougher than she did in street clothes, especially with her long brown hair pulled into a bun. She leaned against the wall across from the coffee maker, crossed her arms, and listened.

"I think I cruised you for about an hour before I went up to you," Gunter said, looking up from his writing. "That sound about right to you?"

I held up my hands. "You write it the way you remember it."

He went back to writing. He finished and then pushed the paper over to me. He wrote in a neat, careful script, crossing his sevens and his Z's. I had a momentary flash of Gunter as a small boy with the same haircut, painstakingly practicing his penmanship, and then he didn't seem frightening at all. I picked it up and read through it. It was just as he'd said the night before, and corresponded pretty closely to what I remembered. He wrote that he had first seen me at the bar at about two o'clock or so, and described the couple of times we'd made eye contact. He ended by noting he'd looked out the door of the club and seen me duck into the alley.

I signed the bottom, and then handed it to Lidia for her signature as witness. She read it, and then signed next to my name.

"All right, you can go now," I said. "Thanks for coming in."

He stood up. "So, you hang out at the Rod and Reel a lot?"

"I don't think so."

"Shame," he said. "You're cute." As he walked past me he casually ran a hand over my chest. "I'm there most nights. If you change your mind."

Lidia didn't say anything until Gunter had left the room. "Were you on a stakeout or something? At that club."

I shook my head. "I just wanted to go there. Kind of dipping my foot in the waters, you know?"

She nodded as though she understood and left to sign out. I didn't say anything specific to her, but I was sure she'd respect my privacy and not spread any gossip.

I went back to my desk. It was time to think about Evan Gonsalves, much though I had tried not to. He fit the description Lou had given us. I knew he had money problems, trying to support Terri in the style she was accustomed to, and I remembered Terri's suspicions. And he'd known about the black tar bust and could have tipped off Tommy. The other connections we'd made were fuzzier, but possibilities, too.

Akoni finally got back just before the end of our shift. Apparently Melvin Ah Wong had discovered how his son Jimmy had been doing favors for Derek and Wayne, stamping papers with his father's notary seal and forging his father's signature. "Melvin thinks Jimmy's just gullible," Akoni said. "He doesn't realize there was anything else going on."

"That's good," I said. We started making copies of all the documents Akoni had brought for Peggy; it was more than likely there was a connection to her theft case at the Bishop Museum, to the smuggling of Hawai'ian artifacts that she'd been investigating. While we were standing at the copier, I said, "Listen, I've been thinking about Evan Gonsalves some more. You know I know his wife?"

"Yeah, you went to school with her, didn't you? The Clark girl?"

"That's her. Anyway, she called me a while ago, upset that Evan seemed to have more money than he ought to."

Akoni pulled the last pages from the copier. "How so?"

I shrugged. "Buying her expensive gifts, paying cash for things. He told her he was doing some security work on the side."

"Lots of cops do it." We carried the paperwork back to our desks.

"Yeah, but she was pretty sure he was lying. She asked my advice, and I said I couldn't really get involved."

"So where's this leading? You think he's the one killed Tommy Pang?"

"I wish to hell I didn't. Terri's birthday was last week, and Evan gave her a really nice diamond bracelet. She showed it to me—it came in one of those long, narrow jewelry boxes."

It was as though a lightbulb went on over Akoni's head. "Didn't Derek say he saw Tommy give the cop a box like that?"

"Uh-huh."

Akoni slumped back in his chair. "Man, I hate pulling down cops."

"Me too. And I don't want to do anything until we're sure. I was thinking maybe we could take a picture of Evan out to Wayne and Derek, see if they can ID him."

Akoni nodded. "You got one?"

"At home. I can bring it in tomorrow."

We left the station a little later. I was too tired to make dinner, so I heated up a frozen pizza. When I finished it was about seven, and I felt so beaten down by everything that had happened that I lay down to take a nap.

When I woke, my apartment was hot and sticky, even though the sun had gone down hours before. The fans did nothing but move the hot air around. I got dressed and went out for a walk.

Something magnetic about the Rod and Reel Club, kept drawing me there even though I knew I should stay away. It was almost eleven, and even from a block away I could hear the music coming from the club, the strong bass line reverberating in my stomach.

I stood across the street for ten minutes or so, trying to figure out what I really wanted. I finally decided to settle for a beer and went in. Fred was behind the bar again, and he gave me a smile with my beer. I was just about to look for a quiet piece of wall to lean against when I felt a hand on my ass. "So, you decided to come back after all," a voice said in my ear.

I knew without turning around that it was Gunter. "Just for a beer," I said, turning to face him. He pulled up a stool next to me, and we sat there at the bar and talked for a while. I guess about half an hour passed, until I saw a couple at one of the patio tables get up, and my heart rate sped up about a hundred percent.

It was Derek and Wayne, and I could tell immediately that their path toward the door would take them right past me. I turned my head so that Gunter was between me and them, and kissed him.

He was surprised, but it didn't take him long to rally. We sat there at the bar and kissed deeply, and I felt my dick stiffen even though I was watching Derek and Wayne out of the corner of my eye. When they'd passed, I relaxed and leaned back.

"You sure changed your mind in a hurry," Gunter said, smiling at me. He put his hand on my thigh.

"Sorry. I saw a couple of guys who are involved in a case, and I didn't want them to recognize me."

I thought Gunter could still see them over my shoulder, and I was right. "Not Macho Man and his Chinese love child?" he asked.

"You know them?"

He took a deep draw from his Corona and then wiped his lips. "I tricked with Derek a couple of times, when he first got back from college. He used to come over here for happy hour by himself. Then Wayne showed up and suggested that I stay away from his boyfriend." He opened the top two buttons of his shirt and showed me a half-moon-shaped scar around his left nipple. "Powerful suggestion, don't you think? I took him at his word."

"Wayne cut you? Did you go to the police?"

"Do you really think the police care about two fags squabbling over a boyfriend?" He took another pull on his beer. "You trying to break up their little smuggling ring?"

All my synapses started buzzing, and I didn't feel drunk at all. "Well, the case isn't quite pulled together yet," I said.

"I helped the little shits at first, before Wayne went crazy with his Boy Scout knife. See, Derek made some connections through trying to get his gallery set up, people who'd *find* some precious artifacts and then bring them in for resale. Of course, the background on some of those things was a little dodgy, and they had to be sold to the right kind of buyers. The place where I work, I see everything that goes on. The kind of things people have when they move in. You know who's got taste and who doesn't. I made a couple of introductions, made myself a few bucks on the side."

"And it stopped when Wayne cut you?"

"The bastard has a temper! I was just fooling around with Derek one day, had my hand in his pants, nothing more, and Wayne went ballistic! I pulled out right after that." He smiled. "In more ways than one."

I remembered the case that Peggy had been working on, the missing artifacts from the Bishop Museum, and the beautiful pieces I'd seen in Derek and Wayne's apartment. All the puzzle pieces seemed to be coming together.

"But enough talk," Gunter said. "Kiss me, you fool."

And I *was* a fool, because I did.

Chapter 28

BY THE TIME I stumbled home the next morning, I felt raw in a dozen places. Sex with Gunter was nothing like it had been with Tim. With Tim, it had been slow and easy, building heat between us until it erupted like one of the volcanoes Hawai'i is famous for. With Gunter it was athletic and arduous, sweaty and fast-paced, and ultimately no less volcanic. I could still feel the scrape of his beard against my thighs, strain in unaccustomed muscles, and the deep hunger he had awakened in me.

I crawled into bed at first light but couldn't sleep, so I went out to surf for about half an hour on my short board, catching a couple of good waves that I could slash and rip. It was good for me. I was able to shake out a couple of the cobwebs and forget about my personal troubles and the problems with the case.

I can see why my Hawai'ian ancestors were so attached to nature when I get up that early. It's like you can imagine some god pulling back the night, revealing the day to you. Everything seems new and fresh, and the neon signs on the tourist shops are turned off, and there isn't much traffic on the streets, and you can actually hear birds in the trees and the sound of the waves without the background of horns and screeching brakes and emergency sirens. As it always does, the ocean rejuvenated and refreshed me, and enabled me to go on and face another day.

Before I left for work, I found a picture Terri had sent me from her wedding. It was a good, clear shot of Evan Gonsalves. I took it with me to the station, where I got a cup of coffee and wrote up what I remembered of my conversation with Gunter. I was sure Peggy Kaneahe would want to call him in to talk again about the art and artifact smuggling I was sure could be traced to Derek and Wayne, through U.S. China Ship.

Akoni came in then with a cup of coffee and a couple of malasadas. I took a malasada gratefully and told Akoni what I'd learned.

"The pieces are starting to come together," he said. He finished the last of the malasadas and washed it down with the dregs of his coffee. "Let's get this show on the road. You got the picture of Gonsalves?"

I held it up to him. It was only a five by seven, but it would do. I called Derek Pang and told him I had a photo I wanted him to identify. "I've got to go down to the club," he said. "Can you meet me there?"

"Sure," I said. "How about Wayne? Will he be there too?"

"He has to stay here," Derek said. "We're expecting a delivery, and then he has to take that package out to the airport."

"I'd like to get you both to identify the picture," I said. "Hold on." I put my hand over the phone and explained to Akoni.

"I'll get a color Xerox of the photo and go to the club," he said. "You take that copy and go meet Wayne."

I told Derek what we wanted to do and he agreed. A half hour later I was on my way to their apartment. The door was ajar when I knocked, and a voice from inside called, "Come on in; the door's open."

When I walked in, I found Wayne Gallagher in the living room, wearing the same kimono he'd worn before, only this time he hadn't bothered to tie it. The sides hung open, revealing a swath of hairy blond chest, a patch of groin, and a long leg covered with fine light-colored hairs.

I got hard almost immediately. There was something incredibly sexy about him standing there. My mouth was dry; I had to swallow before I could say, "I'd like you to take a look at this picture and see if you can identify it."

He sat down on the sofa, casually arranging the open robe to cover his groin, and then patted the seat next to him. When I hesitated, he said, "Come on, I won't bite." Then he grinned. "Not unless you want me to."

I was sure he could tell I had an erection—my dick was straining against my pant leg, rubbing against the fabric as I moved across the room. I sat down next to him, not touching him, and I had to reach down and adjust myself. "Let me see," he said.

I handed him the picture. "Hunky. That's him all right. That's the cop Tommy was paying off."

"That's the man who was at the club the night Tommy was killed?"

"That's him."

He adjusted his robe a little so that the head of his penis peeked out the side. "You're very sexy. Do you know that?" He put his hand on my arm and my flesh tingled.

I took the picture from him and put it back in the envelope, gently shrugging his hand off. "Thanks. You've been very helpful." I started to get up.

"Hold on a minute." He pulled on my sleeve and I sat back down next to him. He looked directly at me, and I felt a shiver of sexual tension run through me. I didn't know what to do.

He took my right hand and slid it under his kimono, leaving it to rest on his cock, which began to harden at my touch. My mouth was dry again. I couldn't say anything. He leaned over and kissed me.

I started to stroke his dick, which was fully erect by then. He kissed me harder, pressing his tongue into my mouth, then kissing my upper lip and running his tongue behind it. I kissed him back, though I knew it was wrong.

He pushed me back on the sofa and started unbuttoning my shirt, continuing to kiss me and then, when he could, tweaking my nipples until they were hard and sore. I was totally swept up in the passion of the moment, more passion than I could ever remember feeling, and couldn't resist him at all. Soon my aloha shirt was open and he'd undone my pants. It was an incredible rush when he freed my cock from my shorts and then leaned down and put his mouth on it.

I ran my fingers through his curly blond hair. He teased me with his tongue, bringing me to the point of release, and then pulled back. "You like that, don't you?" he said, bringing his face back up to mine. "Faggot cop," he whispered, running his tongue over my lips. "Cocksucker cop."

I wanted to get away, but I couldn't. He had me totally in his control. Even as he kept calling me names, he licked and squeezed and teased me and I couldn't do anything about it. He went down on me again and this time I thought I'd never felt such exquisite agony. Then there was a heavy knock on the door, which I had closed behind me.

"That's my delivery," Wayne said. "Don't move."

He got up and went to the door. I knew this was my only chance. I stood up, buttoning my pants and shirt hurriedly. My whole groin was wet with his saliva and my sweat. My hair was tousled and I'd missed a button on my shirt.

Wayne came back from the door holding a box the size of a small computer. "You can't leave yet," he said. "We've hardly started."

He put the box down and came toward me, but I ducked around him and headed for the door. "Thanks for your help," I said. I made it out into the hallway and to the elevator, where I pressed the down button.

He came to the door and stood there, his robe hanging open, his large dick hard and standing straight away from his body. "You want it," he said. "Come back, baby. Let me give it to you." He put his hand on his dick.

My mouth was dry again. The elevator came and I got in. As the doors closed I heard the phone ringing in the apartment and I could see Wayne still standing in the doorway, holding his dick and licking his lips. I felt like Little Red Riding Hood escaping from the wolf.

All the way back to Waikīkī I kept thinking about Wayne Gallagher. It wasn't supposed to be like that, was it—one person taking such control? There was a meanness under his sexuality that scared me—those names he called me, the roughness he'd used when he'd tweaked my nipples. It scared me to think that I liked that, that I had responded to that kind of treatment. What if that was really what turned me on—guys in leather harnesses with chains and handcuffs, hurting me in the name of pleasure? I had what I considered an essential belief in human dignity, in the need to treat everyone with respect. It was one of the cornerstones of my life as a cop. What if in my personal life I couldn't hold on to that?

Akoni had gotten a positive ID from Derek, and we met back at the station to complete the paperwork for Evan's arrest. We had gotten a fax of the autopsy for the body found in Kapiolani Park, but we had to shelve it until we finished with Tommy Pang's murder. It took the rest of the morning, and it was almost two o'clock before I called Evan's office to say I needed to meet with him. "He's not in today," the unit secretary told me. "A personal day. His wife had to fly to Maui for the day, so he's home with his son." She paused, and I could hear her sucking on the straw in the giant-sized water bottle I knew she kept by her desk. "He's taking calls out there, though," she continued. "I've already referred a couple of people out to him already."

I relayed the news to Akoni. I didn't want to have to arrest Evan in front of Danny, but once we got to the Gonsalves house in Wailupe, we'd deal with that.

We drove out in Akoni's Taurus, with Saunders and Alvy Greenberg in a black-and-white behind us for backup. We pulled up in the half-round driveway, behind Evan's Saturn, and rang the doorbell.

No one answered. I put my ear up to the door and listened. I heard what sounded like a child crying, though at the time I thought it might have been Evan. "Evan!" I called. "It's Kimo. Let me in."

No answer. I looked at Akoni. Without saying anything, we split up and walked around the house in opposite directions. There was a lot of landscaping and it was hard to get close to the building. We met again in the backyard, where there was a stone lanai with a hibiscus hedge. From there we could see into the living room through sliding glass doors.

Danny Gonsalves was sitting in the middle of the living room floor crying. There was no sign of Evan anywhere. "I've got a screwdriver in the car," Akoni said, and walked toward the driveway. While he was gone I tried to communicate with Danny, to get him to come to the door, but I couldn't reach him. Akoni returned a moment later with the screwdriver, which he used to jimmy the lock on the sliding door.

I stepped in first. "Evan!" I called. There was no answer.

Danny didn't move. He was dead scared, rocking back and forth and crying. I squatted down next to him. "What's the matter, Danny?" I asked. "You remember me, don't you? Kimo? I'm a friend of your mom and dad."

He didn't talk, but he grabbed onto my shirt with his fists and held on fiercely. "Something's wrong here," Akoni said. "I'm gonna take a look."

Greenberg and Saunders stood outside, waiting, in case Evan came back, and I stayed in the living room with Danny while Akoni explored the house. He was gone a few minutes before he came back, a grim look on his face. "He's in the study," he said. "The room just behind here. He's dead."

I looked at him, not really believing. "Evan?"

Akoni nodded. "We got a pile of shit here."

Chapter 29

I DISENGAGED DANNY from my shirt and left him sitting on the sofa, with Akoni watching him. He had stopped crying but he still wasn't talking. We had Alvy Greenberg radio in for a crime scene team, and I walked into the study to see Evan Gonsalves. He was sitting behind a modern computer desk, his five-shot Smith and Wesson .38 Undercover in his right hand. The hand lay on the desk and his body was slumped forward. There was a hole in the side of his head where the bullet had gone in, and a lot of blood around him, on the desk, the chair, his body, and the floor.

I didn't touch him, but I did lean down and see that the powder burns matched what I saw, death at close range. It seemed clearly a suicide, even though there was no note anywhere.

I looked around the room, trying to get some sort of psychic sense of what had happened there. What was Evan doing in his study? Had Danny been napping, maybe, and then walked in to discover his father's body? I'd seen a lot of bodies during my years on the force, but the first couple had wrenched my stomach and torn at the linings of my heart. I wasn't surprised Danny was nearly catatonic.

I looked around. The rest of the room was neatly organized— books on the bookshelves along one wall, the stereo and the TV off, Danny's Nintendo sitting on a shelf with the cords wrapped. I knew Evan had been in trouble, and I hadn't reached out to him— I had been too careful, waited too long, because I thought I was protecting him and his family. Fat lot of good that had done.

There was something in the room, some kind of negative energy, and finally I had to walk back out to the living room. Akoni was sitting on the floor next to Danny, talking to him gently, but Danny was not responding. I watched Akoni reach out to stroke the boy's shoulder, and Danny flinched and moved away. I rarely saw Akoni being gentle, and it was always a surprising sight. For such a big man, he is light on his feet, a great dancer, and he has something sweet and kind inside him that he rarely lets out, usually only around kids and animals.

It was the same with Danny. Akoni responded to whatever was hurt inside him and wanted to make it better. I hoped he and Mealoha would have children soon, though Akoni often poohpoohed the idea. I knew he would make a good father.

I had thought Evan was a good father, too, and I didn't believe he'd kill himself when Danny was around. He'd been a cop long enough to see what death looked like, and how it hurt those who saw it. What if this wasn't suicide at all, but just a carefully constructed replica?

Akoni looked up and saw me, and got up from the floor. "You think he knew we were coming for him?"

"Must have," I said. "Though I didn't say anything to him. Maybe he knew somebody in the DA's office, who tipped him off."

"Damn shame," Akoni said.

We searched the house until we found a list in the kitchen, places Terri was going to be, and their phone numbers, in case anything happened to Danny and Evan needed to reach her. Her flight from Maui was due in at three, so she was probaly on her way home.

The crime scene techs arrived and got to work. We notified District 4 and claimed jurisdiction because of our investigation into Evan, and a couple of the local cops came out to give us a hand too. Even though we thought it was a suicide, it was still a crime scene, and Akoni and I took careful notes regarding the condition of the study and the house itself.

Terri arrived as we were finishing up, and Alvy Greenberg held her outside and called for me. "What is it, Kimo?" she asked. "What happened? Is Danny okay? Where's Evan?"

"Danny's okay," I said. "It's Evan." I paused. "It looks like he killed himself."

She crumpled. I put my arms around her and she cried. Then Akoni brought Danny to the front door, and when he saw his mother he ran for her. She cried even more, kneeling on the ground holding her son. It was a beautiful day in Wailupe, high seventies, mauka trades, a light scent of plumeria on the breeze, but there was something hard in my throat, and all I could think of was Terri on our graduation day from Punahou, how pretty she'd looked holding down her cap as the wind lifted the black gown and her brown hair flew back from her face.

It was a scene that happened all too often in the islands, and I was sure, even more often on the mainland. The lives of ordinary people were touched by tragedy, and they would never be the same again. I felt worse than I ever had before. I didn't kill Evan, and I didn't make him turn bad, but I had put the events in motion that had led us to this point, from the day I first heard about black tar and made arrangements for the bust.

I spent a while with Terri, holding her, letting her cry. While my brain ran forward at a hundred miles an hour, I said I was sorry, and promised her it would be all right, though I knew I was lying. Police and technicians ebbed and flowed around us, Akoni managing them, coordinating with the local cops.

Terri called her parents and her sister Betsy, and there was more crying. Danny sat nearly catatonic next to his mother and screamed if anyone tried to move him away. Eventually Akoni and I left and drove back to Waikīkī. The black-and-whites, ours and the local ones, pulled away and were replaced by the cars of Terri Clark Gonsalves's friends and family. The memory of what he'd seen would stay with Danny Gonsalves for years, no matter how much therapy he had, and those images would probably recur in his dreams and nightmares forever.

We'd done what we were supposed to do. We had closed the case. As we walked into the station, Saunders was standing at the desk talking to the sergeant. "So just be careful," he said loudly, as we walked past. "If you're in the shower with him, don't drop the soap."

They both laughed, and Saunders gave me a particularly piercing look. I stared him back down, and he looked away.

Akoni and I filled out paperwork for the rest of the afternoon, closing out the case on Tommy Pang. I felt bad about what had happened, but at least the case was closed, and I could get on with my life. I called and left a message for Tim, who was in a meeting. Akoni left and I hung around for a couple of minutes, hoping Tim would call back. While I was waiting, Alvy Greenberg came up to my desk.

"Is it true?" he asked.

"I think so. We have witnesses who put Evan together with Tommy Pang."

"I don't mean that. I mean, is it true you're a fag?"

I sat up and looked at him. He looked kind of half angry and half ready to cry. "That's the rumor going around the station, you know. You're a cocksucker. I just want to know, is it true?"

"Does it matter to you?"

"Damn right it does. I looked up to you, Kimo. I thought you were the kind of cop, the kind of detective, I wanted to be. Now I see who you really are."

"I haven't changed," I said. "I'm still a good cop. I'm just not lying to myself anymore. Or anybody else."

"So it's true." He paused, then looked me in the eye. "You make me sick."

He turned and walked away.

I sat back at my desk, reeling. I couldn't believe he'd been so angry at me. I'd never come on to him, never acted like anything more than a friend or a mentor. I thought it was bad when I told Akoni, but his reaction had been easy compared to Alvy's. I wondered if everyone at the Waikīkī station knew, and if that was the way they all felt.

While I wondered about that, my phone buzzed. "Kanapaʻaka," Lieutenant Yumuri's voice sounded out of the speaker. "To my office, now."

Jesus, what next? I thought. I supposed the rumors had traveled up the line of command and reached his ears. I got up immediately and walked down the hall to the lieutenant's office. "Have a seat."

"I'll get right to the point," he said, as I sat down. "Your work on this case was a mess. If you had handled this case better, Evan Gonsalves might still be alive. I'm suspending you, pending an internal investigation."

"There was nothing wrong with our investigation," I said. "We did everything you asked for. It's all spelled out in the files." I paused and suddenly I understood. "Word got out, didn't it?" I asked. "That's what Saunders was talking about, and Alvy Greenberg. You don't want a gay cop on your force, do you?"

"I don't," he said. "Clean out your desk and your locker. You'll be hearing from the department attorney."

I left his office in a daze. It had been a hell of a day. From my encounter with Wayne, through discovering Evan's body and ruining Terri's life, to the failure of my own career. I stumbled through a quick cleanup of my desk and locker, avoiding the stares of the other cops, and walked out onto Kalākaua Avenue, without an idea of what I was supposed to do next.

Chapter 30

I DON'T KNOW how I made it home. I dumped my things in my apartment and curled up on the bed. I knew I ought to get out, go surfing, clear my head, but I couldn't. I didn't sleep much that night, just lay there thinking and worrying. I always think, whenever I have trouble nodding off, that sleep is this kind of magical land far away. Sometimes you just forget how to get there.

I tried to go over everything I had done in the case, remembering each detail, every conversation, every note, every official police document. The guy upstairs was playing Pearl Jam at high volume, blasting the same CD over and over again, but I didn't bother to yell or call him or go upstairs. It just didn't seem to matter.

As the sun was rising I did doze off for a little while, then woke finally at seven-thirty and decided to get up and take a shower. I thought about going to the beach, but I just couldn't seem to get myself together. I scrubbed the kitchen, throwing away anything in the refrigerator that looked suspicious, reorganized the books on my bookshelves. I'd started filing away articles I'd clipped from the paper when the phone rang.

It was nine-thirty. I jumped for the phone, hoping it was Tim, but instead it was Peggy Kaneahe. "We need you down at the main station," she said. "Ten-thirty."

"Why?"

"I can't talk about it with you now. We'll talk then."

"But what's going on?" I asked. The phone went dead in my hand.

I called Akoni at the station and told him what had happened. "I know," he said. "The lieutenant called me in this morning."

I waited, and finally Akoni said, "I told you this was going to happen, Kimo. I tried to stand by you as long as I could, but I just can't anymore."

"I understand," I said, and I did. I hoped that if something happened to a friend of mine, I would have the courage to stand by him, all the way, but I wasn't sure I would, and I wasn't sure courage was really at the heart of it. After all, we are all born alone in this world, and we die alone, and there is a limit to what you can do for anyone else. "You've been a good partner," I said. "I'll try not to let any of this wash off on you."

"I'll take my lumps. You do what you need to do. Don't worry about me."

I wanted to say something more, but I didn't know what to say. "Let me know how it goes," he said finally.

"I will."

I finished getting dressed, pulling on a white oxford cloth shirt and a pair of clean, pressed khakis. I thought about wearing my uniform but figured that was a bit much—and I guess maybe I was afraid they would make me take it off, hand it over to them. I didn't think I could take that.

At a few minutes after ten, I got into my truck for the ride to the main station on South Beretania. The weather seemed restless and quickly changeable, a brisk wind sweeping down from the mountains and bringing heavy gray clouds with it. I signed in with the desk sergeant and he told me to go to a meeting room on the third floor. I took the elevator up and had to walk through a warren of cubicles. Maybe I was being self-conscious, but I couldn't help feeling people were watching me, that the tide of conversation quieted in a wave before me and then rose again as I passed. The cops around me worked in special operations, vice, sexual abuse, school intervention, and the like, and there was a general feeling of despair there, of men and women who worked with the dregs of the population and never saw any hope for the future.

I walked out to the exterior hallway that overlooks the courtyard at the center of the building. The sky was the color of burnished aluminum, a solid layer of cloud, and I could hear distant thunder. The static electricity in the air raised the hairs on the back of my arms.

The meeting room was stuck in a corner of the building, and a big circular concrete column stood like a sentinel along one side. There was a cheap folding table and a handful of old wooden chairs, nothing on the walls, and no window to look out.

Peggy Kaneahe was there, with a leather briefcase by her side and a folder open on the tabletop in front of her. Lieutenant Yumuri sat on one side of her, and on the other side was Hiram Lin, a representative of the police union, a dried-up prune of a man counting the days until his full pension kicked in. He hadn't been on the streets since statehood, I thought, and he hadn't even ridden an active desk for a decade, preferring to hide out in the union office. "Come in," Peggy said. "Sit down."

I sat across from her. The chair was hard and a little too low for the table, so I felt like a misbehaving kid called into the principal's office. "You can look at my files," I started to say.

"You don't have a voice at this time," Peggy said. "There'll be a hearing, and you can have counsel then, if you wish. That's when you can give your side of the story. For right now, you just listen."

I looked at Hiram, and he nodded. The way they sat, three of them on one side of the table and me on the other, I felt like I was all alone in this. "You're being suspended, effective immediately," Peggy said. "Your salary will continue through your suspension period, provided you observe certain conditions."

"They are?"

She held up her hand and ticked them off on her fingers. "No contact with police officers other than those specifically designated to communicate with you. In this case that will be Lieutenant Yumuri. No contact with any of the suspects or witnesses in the case you were handling. No comments to the media about the case or your suspension."

"What about police officers who are my friends?" I asked. "Akoni Hapaʻele, for example."

Peggy looked at Yumuri, who nodded slightly. "As long as you don't talk about this case or other cases pending," she said. "Not without Lieutenant Yumuri present."

"I can do that."

"You're going to have to." She pushed a couple of forms at me across the table. "Sign these and we can get out of here."

I looked at the forms. They seemed to spell out in further detail the conditions she'd set. "Got a pen?" I asked.

She gave me a pitying look and pushed a blue ballpoint over to me. The end had been chewed savagely, and I had a quick memory of her in tenth-grade physics class, chewing her pen and puzzling over problems of velocity and motion. I signed the papers and pushed them and the pen back to her.

"Your badge and your weapon," Lieutenant Yumuri said.

I took my off-duty .38 Special out of my holster and slid it across the table to him. He flipped open the barrel and took the ammunition out, then slapped the barrel closed. I opened my wallet and pulled my detective's shield out. I realized I was doing something that was going to reverberate through every part of my life, but I had no control anymore. I just had to do what I was told. I unpinned the shield and slid it across the table.

"You can go," Peggy said. I wanted to talk to her about what was going on, to explain or apologize, but she was all business. She wouldn't even look me in the eye.

I decided not to wait for the elevator. The service stairs were next to the conference room, and I could avoid walking back through that dismal room, hearing the conversations rise and fall around me. I walked slowly down the stairs, wondering what to do next. I wasn't a cop anymore and probably would never be one again. I couldn't go back to surfing full-time and I didn't think I knew how to do anything else. I worried about how long my savings would last, and how I would identify myself to the outside world, to myself. I was a gay man, a faggot, a cocksucker. I had accepted that, but in the context of who else I was. Now it seemed that was all I was, at least to the Honolulu Police Department.

I came out of the stairwell into the lobby, and maybe it was my imagination again, but I couldn't seem to make eye contact with anyone. It was like they all knew me and wouldn't look at me. Then I said to myself that I was a fool. My imagination was running wild. I took a deep breath and walked outside.

I was expecting clouds, rain, wild thunder. Instead there were flashbulbs and the clamor of newspeople. "Detective Kanapaʻaka," a Chinese reporter said. "Is it true you're being suspended from the police force because of your homosexuality?"

I was stunned. How could they have found out so quickly? I just stared at the guy, my mouth agape. "Detective, have you hired an attorney yet?" a Hawaiʻian guy, who I recognized from my brother's TV station, asked. "Will you be suing the police force for reinstatement?"

"Do you think this is a discrimination case?" asked another.

I just stood there. They called out more questions, but I couldn't answer them and I couldn't seem to move. Finally a desk sergeant came out behind me and propelled me away from them, and another sergeant ordered them to disperse. I got my sense back and found my truck. The Hawaiʻian guy from Lui's station ran beside me as I was driving away, still trying to get a comment, and I wanted to do something, give him the finger or yell something, but I knew it would just end up on the news, so I drove off.

I made it back to my apartment, though I'm not sure how. I think my truck was on autopilot. Seeing the guy from Lui's station reminded me that my brothers would know what happened to me, my parents would know, my friends and my Punahou classmates and the guys I saw when I was surfing. I wanted to go back to that night when I went to the Rod and Reel, stop the movie, rewind, go somewhere else, anywhere else. I wanted to make it stop.

Almost as soon as I walked in the door, the phone rang. It was one of the TV stations again. I unplugged it from the wall and sat down on the bed. I knew I should call my parents and warn them about the newscast, but I just couldn't. I tried to take a nap, but I just tossed and turned on the bed for a while, and then finally I got up.

This is stupid, I thought. *I can't do this. I can't just hang around waiting to see what happens.* I put on my bathing suit and got my short board, figuring I would challenge myself with the small waves off Kuhio Beach Park. If I could get out on the water, force myself to pay attention to the surf, then I could forget all this other stuff and maybe, in the forgetting, find a way to deal with it.

I felt better already. I was still a surfer, no matter what else I was, and surfing was how I was going to get out of this mess. But as soon as I opened my door the reporters were there, taking pictures and calling out questions. I shut the door fast.

I didn't know what to do. I didn't want to call anyone, not even Harry, who was the only person so far who had taken my news well. My head was throbbing and my throat was dry and I wanted to cry but couldn't make the tears come. I took a couple of Tylenol PM and lay back down on the bed, and eventually I dozed off.

I slept fitfully, with half-waking dreams of hounding newsmen and disapproving policemen. I was trying to get to the beach, and they lined Lili'uokalani Avenue like a gauntlet, yelling at me, refusing to make eye contact, saying things like, "You'll never be a cop again, Kimo. Who are you, now that you're not a cop?"

When I woke up, it was dark and I felt woozy. Someone was banging on my door. "Goddamn it, go away!" I yelled and tried to bury my head under the pillows. I knew there had to be a law against the press harassing you. They wouldn't stop, though, and finally I had to get up and go to the door. I didn't even bother to look through the peephole, despite all the times I'd asked crime victims, "How come you didn't look before you opened the door?"

"No comment!" I yelled, opening the door. Staring back at me was my father.

"Finally!" he said. Automatically I stepped back to let him in. My mother was just behind him. She took the door from me and closed it.

I just looked at them. They were the last people I'd expected to see at my doorstep and I didn't know what to say. Then, finally, the tears I'd been trying to cry all day came, and my legs got weak and I had to sit down.

"We saw on the news," my mother said, rubbing her hand across my shoulders.

I was embarrassed and ashamed. I tried to wipe away my tears and succeeded only in dragging wet streaks across my face. My mother gave me a tissue and I blew my nose.

"They are terrible," my father finally said. "Those reporters. I told that one, from Lui's station, 'My son is your boss. Go away.' He wouldn't. I told him I would call Lui and have him fired if he didn't leave us alone, and he laughed."

"I'm so sorry," I said. "I didn't want this to happen."

My father paced back and forth in the single room, and my mother and I squeezed back into the corners to get out of his way. "This cannot be happening," he said. "I did not raise my son to be a māhū. You must go back to the police and tell them they're wrong. We'll call your brother. He can bring a camera crew over to take your statement."

"They aren't wrong," I said. "It's true." I swallowed. "I'm gay. I'm sorry it happened this way, but I can't change who I am."

"How can this be?" my father asked. "We didn't raise you this way. You were a normal boy. A little quiet, sometimes. Maybe we let your brothers tease you a little too much. But you've had girl-friends. Many girlfriends. Why have you changed?"

"I haven't changed. I've always been this way. I just haven't had the courage to face it until now."

"I wish you were still a coward," my father said.

"Al, that's enough," my mother said. "Kimo, you must pack now."

"Pack?"

"We want you to come home with us for a while," she said. "These reporters outside. You're upset. You should come to us."

"I can't. I would just bring more of my troubles down on your heads."

My father walked over and opened my closet door. "Here are some shirts," he said. "Lokelani, find the suitcase."

"No," I said.

I stood up, and my father glared at me. "You don't know what's best for you right now. We do. You're coming home with us."

I felt as if all my willpower had drained from me. Too much had happened to me in too short a time, and I couldn't process it anymore. I said, "My suitcase is on the top shelf, in the back. I'll pack it."

"Good," my father said. "Do you have any brandy?"

I nodded toward the kitchen. "In the cabinet over the sink."

While I packed my suitcase, my father poured brandy into juice glasses for the three of us. When I was finished, we lifted our glasses together and my mother said, "You are our son, and you always will be. We love you."

My father drank his brandy in one shot, and so did I.

Chapter 31

I RANDOMLY PICKED out aloha shirts and polos, shorts and khakis and bathing suits I would probably not get to wear to the beach. I took my uniform and the one suit I owned, a simple navy one that served for funerals and weddings and family command performances.

I scooped a haphazard pile of books I hadn't yet read into a knapsack, and placed it by the door with my short board and my long board. I always carry extra books with me when I travel, afraid of landing in some distant place without something to read. What else to take? My Rollerblades? The half-eaten box of chocolate-covered Oreos from the kitchen? My pocket knife, camera, a deck of playing cards for solitaire? I took them all, without discrimination. By the time I was finished, there were four bags by the door along with a pile of sporting equipment.

"I'm ready," I said finally.

My mother went around the room, turning off lights, checking the windows and the burners on the stove. "The reporters will still be there," she said.

I took a look around my apartment. It was only one big room, with the kitchen off to the side, but it was my home, and I wasn't sure I wanted to leave it, even though I knew it would be easier to stay at my parents' house, where at least I could move from room to room, talk to people when I wanted to, even sneak out into the backyard when I wanted to feel the sun and the wind.

Iacta ilea est, I remembered from some long-ago history class.

The die is cast. I slung my knapsack over my back, put one board under each arm, and slung my Rollerblades around my neck. "I'm ready to go," I said, and walked out into the glare of flashbulbs.

My mother drove us home in her Lexus, and I knew the TV crews would find us soon enough. It was just sunset and the day had turned beautiful, as it often does on this island of microclimates. You can start in Honolulu, head to Diamond Head and beyond, to the windward shore, travel along the coast as far as Laie, land of Mormons, ride along the north shore, then head back through the central valley and pass through a dozen different types of weather along the way. Stay in one place, and the weather changes around you, often gorgeous, but with passing showers, winds, and clouds alternating with brilliant sunshine.

If I hadn't been dogged by reporters, I might have spent the afternoon at the beach. The morning clouds and rain would have brought stronger waves; I remember often waking, when I was surfing in earnest, hoping the morning would bring rough weather and with it rough surf, and being disappointed at another gorgeous day.

The weather seemed to me also to symbolize people's lives. Somewhere on the island people enjoyed the sun, baking away the troubles of the week on the beach or washing them away in the cool Pacific. It happened every day in Hawai'i. And somewhere someone was having a bad day, like me, full of emotional storms and cloudy thoughts. Microclimates, both natural and emotional.

I wondered what kind of day Tim had experienced, if he'd seen my name in the paper, on the radio or the TV. Would he try my phone, not realizing I had unplugged it? When would I find a few private minutes to call him?

Once home, my mother took a casserole out of the oven and we had dinner, all the time not talking about anything that mattered—a job my father was bidding, some antics by Ashley and her sister, even, God help us, the weather forecast. My troubles were like an unwelcome guest at dinner, one we had to feed but tried hard to ignore. There was no word from either of my brothers.

Finally we were finished. I stood up to help clear the table, then paused. "I don't know how this is going to end," I said. "I'm gay. I can't change that. But I don't think I did anything wrong, and I don't deserve to be suspended. I want to fight, but I don't want to do anything that will hurt you."

"I think you should give this up," my father said. "There are other things you can do where they won't care about you. Be a decorator. A hairdresser. Something like that, that māhūs do."

"I don't want to be a decorator. I want to be a cop."

"Well, you can't be," my father yelled. "They don't want you. They can't be any clearer than they have been."

"I won't back down," I yelled back. "What I do on my own time doesn't make a goddamned bit of difference when I'm on the job!"

"Please, no more yelling," my mother said. "Now, Kimo, bring those dishes to the kitchen. Al, go into the living room and sit down."

We watched a couple of silly sitcoms together, the tension between me and my father simmering, my mother always ready to jump into the breach between us. The occasional calls that evening were from family friends, some close, some merely curious. My mother or my father would answer, give a brief explanation, and then beg off.

We watched the eleven o'clock news together in the living room, Lui's station, of course. The reporter who had harassed me did a live shot in front of the Waikīkī station, all professional and businesslike. All he had to say, really, was that the department had uncovered improprieties in my handling of an important case, the murder of a prominent Honolulu businessman. The official department statement said that was the cause of my suspension. "But our own inside sources say Kanapa'aka was suspended because of the discovery of his homosexuality," he said. "Starting Monday, a new series will investigate gay cops, here and on the mainland. Stay tuned!"

My parents and I went to bed soon after the news, still without hearing anything from Lui or Haoa. I thought it was very strange, though I imagined Lui might be working. Haoa ought to be home with Tatiana and the children, and even if he didn't want to call I was sure Tatiana would make him.

I was back in my childhood room, Town and Country Surf posters on the wall, long-forgotten books on the shelves. I picked up a few—a couple of Punahou textbooks, some Ursula K. Le Guin and Ray Bradbury from a brief flirtation with science fiction, two dozen paperback Agatha Christie mysteries, a handful of novels by second-rate writers I'd stumbled on in the course of trying to discover my own literary tastes. Even a half-dozen oversized children's books, bright colors and not too many words. I remembered Babar, King of the Elephants, his monkey friend, and the withered old lady who was his teacher.

I slipped under the covers with Babar, trying to lose myself in the innocence of childhood. I read all the way through the book, smiling at the rhinoceros in his three-pointed hat and the monkey Zephyr dressed up for skiing. When I started yawning, I put the book down, but I still could not fall asleep for a long time. I kept going over what I had done, trying to see if I could have done anything differently, and how that might have affected what happened. No matter what I thought I could do, however, the end was always the same.

My room is right over the front door, and I woke to the ringing of the doorbell, adrenaline coursing through me. I looked at the clock; it was almost three a.m. Who could it be? Surely even the television crews went home to sleep at night.

I put my robe on and walked down the hall to my parents' bedroom, where the light was on. My parents both had their robes on, and my father led the way out into the hallway. "Who do you think it is?" I asked.

"There's only one way to find out," my father said. I followed him down the stairs, my mother behind us. The bell rang again before we could get to it. "All right, all right. Keep your pants on."

He looked through the peephole first, then pulled the door open. It was Haoa, looking tired and disheveled, like he'd been in a fight. There was an ugly red bruise under his left eye, and though the night air had turned chilly, he wore no jacket, just a T-shirt with the name of his landscaping firm on it, and a pair of draw-string pants in a wild zebra pattern.

"What's the matter!" my mother said. "Haoa, come in."

My father stepped aside, and my brother came in, not looking at me. My mother took him by the hand and led him to the kitchen, where he sat in the harsh light of the overhead fluorescents as she started to minister to his bruised face. "What happened to you?" she asked. "Have you been home? Does Tatiana know where you are? You should call her. She's probably worried sick."

"She doesn't care where I am. She told me."

"Did she do this to you?" my father asked. "Tatiana?"

He shook his head. "This is not her fault." He nodded toward me. "It's his."

My parents both looked at me. I held my hands out. "I've been with you."

"You've been with men," Haoa said. "That's your problem. Māhū."

"Haoa," my father said. "This is your brother."

"He can say what he pleases. So who did this to you? Another māhū?" I asked

Haoa sneered, and the act of turning his mouth up caused him to wince with pain. "Hold still," my mother said. She dabbed at his wound with cotton dipped in hydrogen peroxide, and he winced again.

"Tell us what happened," my father said.

"We finished the landscaping around the pool at the Mandarin Oriental," Haoa said. "I took the crew to a bar in Waikīkī to cele-brate." He paused while my mother applied mercurochrome with a Q-Tip. It looked like he was being decorated with war paint, prepar-ing for a big battle. I wondered if she could do the same for me.

"The news came on while we were in the bar, and one of the guys recognized Kimo. 'Hey, Howard, it's your brother,' he said. We all watched. It turned my stomach."

He held my eyes for a long minute and finally he had to look away. I wondered how I could feel so connected to him, through bonds of blood and familial love, when he seemed to hate me so much.

"We had some more to drink," he said. "I got angrier and angrier. The guys teased me. Somehow we got the idea to go out and beat up some fags."

"Jesus," I said.

"We raised you better than that," my father said. "A hooligan. A common criminal."

"It wasn't my fault. It got out of control. We went to this bar, the Rod and Reel Club. We hung around outside and waited to see who went in or came out. This māhū came out and, I don't know, a couple of us must have started to hit him."

"He hit you back," I said.

"Not him. A bunch of them spilled out of the bar. Big guys, mean looking, wearing leather and chains. One of *them* hit me."

"You have more bruises?" my mother asked.

He shook his head. She started to pack up her first aid kit.

"Then?" I asked.

"The police came. They hauled us down to the station. I wanted to stick up for my men. Some of those guys, they don't have much. A couple of them already have records. So I said it was all my doing, that I conned them into joining me."

It was funny, but I believed him. I remembered as a kid how he and Lui used to stick up for each other, even as they picked on me. He was capable of loyalty and of kindness, too. He treated his employees well, giving them bonuses and advancing them wages, and even giving them good recommendations when they quit.

"You came here from the police?" my mother asked.

"I called Lui. He came down and bailed me out, and drove me

back to Waikīkī so I could get my truck. I went home, must have been about midnight."

There had to be more, I thought. "So what are you doing here?"

"Tatiana," he said.

My parents looked at each other, and then at me. Haoa had married for love, this beautiful, exotic, Russian-American hippie who had floated down from Alaska and bonded to my big Hawai'ian-Japanese-haole mixed-up brother. I'd seen them at parties, always gravitating toward each other. He seemed incomplete when he was not around her.

"What did she do?" my mother finally asked.

Haoa looked down at the table. "I told her what happened, basically. She was pretty pissed off, but we were getting past it. I told her I was sorry, that I'd been crazy." He looked up at us. "She's been crazy herself sometimes. You don't know her like I do. I thought she owed it to me to forgive me, and she was going to." He paused. "Then the māhū called her."

"What?" I asked.

"The māhū we beat up." He sighed deeply. "My luck. I take a punch at the first māhū I see, it turns out to be her hairdresser."

I laughed. "You mean that guy—what's his name—your kids call him Uncle something?"

"Uncle Tico. I didn't recognize him. I mean, Christ, it was dark. He was coming out of this faggot bar, giggling or some shit." He looked straight at me. "It was like he was you. I wanted to punch you. Jesus, I wanted to kill you. So I took it out on him."

I closed my eyes. How many more innocent people were going to be dragged into this awful vortex my life had become?

"And?" my mother said finally. "What did Tatiana do?"

"She threw a vase at me. Bounced off the side of my head. Hey, Ma, you got any aspirin? My headache's coming back."

Our mother went to get him a pill. When she came back, he continued. "She said she could almost forgive me if it had been a stranger, but not Tico. I had to have known it was him. I had to have been acting out against her. You believe it? Acting out against her. She reads too many goddamn books."

He took the aspirin with a swig of cold water from the refrigerator door. "Anyway, she kicked me out. I could have gone to Lui's but I didn't want to face Liliha. You know she and Tatiana are like this." He held up two fingers, intertwined. "If I'd known *he* was going to be here, I'd have gone there anyway."

"Such discord in my house," my father said. "Husband against wife, brother against brother, man against strangers." To his credit, Haoa lowered his head again. I thought my father was about to launch into another tirade, but instead he looked at the clock. "It's late," he said. "We all need our sleep. In the morning, we'll see how things look."

My mother hurried upstairs to get out fresh sheets for Haoa's old bed. "All the chickens come home to roost," my father said as he shut off the kitchen light behind us.

I did not talk to Haoa as we climbed the stairs. I went into my room, he to his. All I could think of was Robertico Robles, out for a little fun on a Friday night, running into my brother's wrath. I realized Haoa hadn't even said how the man was.

It was dark in the hallway. The lights were out in my parents' room and in Haoa's. I walked to his door, which was ajar, and pushed it open a little more. "Haoa?"

"What is it?"

"How is he? The man you hurt. Uncle Tico."

In the dim moonlight I could barely see Haoa in bed across from me. "He'll survive," he said, and then softened his tone. "I think he might have a couple of broken ribs. Maybe a slight concussion, too. But he was certainly well enough to call Tatiana and rat on me."

Just who was the rat, I thought, as I pulled the door to behind me, was still open to speculation.

Chapter 32

I SLEPT BETTER THAT NIGHT than I had for the last two and didn't wake until almost eight. I put on an old bathrobe and walked downstairs, where my father was in the kitchen making scrambled eggs and bacon for Haoa.

My father looked unaccountably cheerful for a man with two sons in various degrees of trouble with the law. "Morning, Keechee," he said. "Sit. I'll make you eggs."

"Morning," I said. I nodded at Haoa, who gave me a cursory nod in return.

"It's nice to have two of my boys back home," my father said, emptying Haoa's eggs onto a plate and passing it to him. The bacon was already draining on paper towels. I got up and poured orange juice for all three of us while my father scrambled my eggs. I wondered if he got up this way every morning, made himself a solitary breakfast while my mother slept in.

Haoa buried himself in the *Advertiser*, reading the sports section first. I scanned the front section, then the metro, looking for familiar names. And there they were, surprisingly anglicized, our real birth names, James and Howard Kanapaʻaka, though fortunately the two articles, a page apart, had been written by different writers who hadn't made the connection between us. My story was brief, a simple paragraph about an internal disciplinary action by the Honolulu Police Department. The only person quoted was Hiram Lin, the dried-up prune, who said, "No comment." Right on, Hiram.

Haoa's story was two paragraphs concerning a fight between

several men in front of a Kuhio Avenue bar. The bar wasn't named, and the whole gay-bashing context was missing. Haoa's name was there, along with the names of two of his workmen, as well as Robertico Robles and two other men I assumed were the leather boys who intervened. I wanted to seek them out and congratulate them. Instead I casually mentioned, "You made the paper this morning, Haoa," and passed the section to him.

Our father looked at me, then at Haoa, but didn't say anything. We both finished eating at about the same time. He got up and took his plate to the sink, ignoring mine. As he turned the water on to rinse it, I stood up and carried mine to the sink as well.

He positioned himself to block me and I tried to slip through, but he hip-checked me. I pushed him to the side and put my dish down in the sink. He pushed me back.

"Don't push me." I slapped his chest with the palm of my hand.

"It's your fault. All this trouble." He pushed hard against me with both hands.

"Haoa! Kimo! Stop this right now!" our father said, and we backed away from each other, sullenly.

"Spoiled baby," Haoa said. "Dragging everybody else into his problems."

"You get drunk and beat up a poor helpless hairdresser and blame it on me," I said. "Big brother. Great example."

"I mean it," our father said. "No more fighting."

"You're such a loser even your wife doesn't want you around," I said. "Have to run home to Mommy and Daddy."

"You bastard," he said, and he came at me, swinging.

I lunged at him. All my anger and fear and desperate sadness welled up in me with a terrible strength, and I remembered every time Haoa and Lui had picked on me as a kid, when I hadn't been strong enough to fight back. Now he was forty and fat and even though he often did physical labor, I was strong and I knew I could take him. I got in first with an uppercut to his chin that knocked his head back. He gave me a strong punch to the solar plexus that had me doubled over, and then we were all over each other, grunting and punching and trying to rip each other's heads off.

"Boys! Stop! I'm ordering you!" It did no good. We were beyond paying attention to our father, each of us working out fights that were too strong for reason. Then he waded in, trying to separate us, and he was between us and we both hit him, then realized what we had done and fell back in horror.

"My God! What are you doing!"

The three of us turned at the same time to see Mom in the doorway of the kitchen in her bathrobe, her face aghast. I looked at my father. His glasses hung from one temple, and he looked disoriented. I had opened the wound on Haoa's forehead again and blood dripped down the side of his cheek. My own jaw ached and I felt like Haoa might have cracked one of my ribs.

"Go to your rooms," my mother said to us. She hurried over and sat my father down on his stool "Go on. I'll talk to you later."

Sheepishly we walked up the stairs to our rooms, Haoa leading. I had the urge, which I repressed, to kick him in the ass. We were in enough trouble already.

I took a shower and got dressed. In the mirror I could see the beginning of a black eye. *Great visual for the TV cameras,* I thought grimly.

My father knocked on my bedroom door a little later. He'd repaired his glasses and had a small red dot of Mercurochrome on his right cheekbone, but he'd regained his composure. "I'm sorry, Dad," I said, looking down at the floor. "I shouldn't have gotten into it with Haoa."

"I thought I could avoid the problems," my father said. "I'd make breakfast for my boys, just like when you were little. Everything would be fine again." He shook his head. "I forgot what it was like to have three boys in the house. You were always fighting with each other."

"But we're grown-ups now," I said. "I'm a cop. My job is to stop this kind of thing. You don't know the number of houses I've come into where there's been fighting, and somebody's hurt, or worse, dead. I ought to know better."

"These are difficult times, and we only have each other. I'd like you to apologize to your brother."

"Me! He started it."

He had only to look at me. "All right. If he'll apologize too." He looked at me again and I followed him downstairs.

I took a small amount of pleasure in seeing that Haoa looked worse than I did. Of course, it was his second fight in twelve hours.

Our parents sat on the sofa and Haoa and I sat in big wing chairs across from each other. No one spoke. I looked at my parents. They had made the first move in coming to get me, to bring me home. I owed it to them to make the first move with my brother. "I'm sorry for what has happened," I said to him. "I can't change who I am, but if I could, I'd go back and change the way you all found out. You're my brother, and no matter what you think of me, or what you do, I'll always love you."

Our mother smiled. We all looked to Haoa. Finally he said, "I have a bad temper. I know it's my biggest failing—Tatiana tells me that all the time. I shouldn't have fought with you, and I shouldn't have gotten into the fight yesterday. I'm sorry."

"Good," my mother said. "Now we can go on. Kimo, you can call someone about this business yesterday? Maybe the charges against Haoa can be dropped."

"What?"

"We're family, Kimo. We have to look out for each other. You'll do what you can?"

"I will not do anything. In the first place, I don't exactly have a lot of friends on the police force right now, as you might imagine. Second, as a police officer I'm bound to uphold the law, not flout it. Haoa knows he was wrong. Let him admit it and take his punishment."

"You don't get it, do you?" Haoa asked me. "This is all your fault. You made me do what I did."

"Yeah, right. I stood there and forced you to hit Uncle Tico."

"No arguing," our mother said. "Kimo, will you do this for me?"

I shook my head. "You don't understand. I can't. If Haoa gets away with this, then next week someone else will stand outside that bar and wait for someone to come out. One day it might be me coming out of there, and some other guy there waiting to hurt me, or kill me."

"It's always about you," Haoa said.

"Yes, it is." I turned to him. "These are my troubles, and you only make them worse because you can't control your stupid impulses. Tatiana was right to throw your ass in the street. I hope she never takes you back."

"Kimo!" my mother said.

I stood up. "I've got to get out of here. I'm going to the hospital to see Tico. Maybe I can apologize to him for having an asshole brother. I'm not doing any good here." I looked at my father. "Can I borrow your truck?"

"The keys are by the front door," he said.

"Little faggot wants to run away," Haoa said under his breath.

"I'm not done with you yet," I said to him. "Say anything you want to me. And next time you get the urge to beat up a faggot, you come to me. We'll do it when Dad isn't around to rescue you."

"Rescue me!" Haoa said indignantly, as I walked out the front door.

Reporters rushed me as I hurried to my father's truck. "Kimo, do you think you were framed?" one asked.

"When's your hearing?" a woman asked, thrusting a microphone at me.

"Are your brother's problems related to yours?" another called. "We know he was arrested outside the Rod and Reel last night."

"You'll have to ask him," I said. I got into the truck and gunned the engine, and started backing down the driveway fast, scattering them in my wake. It felt good to see one of them stumble and fall onto the lawn.

By the time I got down to the highway, I was sure none of them were following me. I drove over to the hospital where they had taken Tico and got his room number from the clerk at the front desk. When I walked in, Tatiana was sitting by his bed talking to him in a low voice. When she saw me come in, she got up and hugged me.

"Kimo, I'm so sorry," she said. "Howie's an asshole. I think it's great you are who you want to be."

"Mahalo," I said.

She stepped back and looked at me. "What happened to you?"

"Haoa and I spent the night at our parents' house," I said. "We got into it this morning after breakfast."

She shook her head. "Jesus, the man never stops."

"You should see what we did to our father," I said, and Tatiana gaped, knowing how much we usually respected him.

From the bed, Tico said, "Tatiana, can you give us a couple of minutes?"

"Sure. I need a cup of coffee anyway."

She walked out, and I took her place on the chair by the bed. Tico didn't look too bad, though he winced whenever he moved too fast. He was in his mid-fifties, his thin brown hair cut short. His right wrist was bandaged and he looked pale.

I didn't know Tico well. I'd met him a few times at parties at Haoa's house, when he'd always behaved, well, a little over the top. I didn't like swishy men, but I recognized in him a kinship that was closer to me in some ways than my brothers. "How are you doing?" I asked.

"Mezza-mezza." He shook his good hand from side to side. "How about you?"

I was about to say "Fine" but stopped. "Well, in the last twenty-four hours I lost my job, got outed in the media, and had a fight with my brother where we both ended up punching our father. I'd say on the whole things are not going so well."

"It's a hard thing to go through." Tico struggled to sit up a little higher on the bed, and I adjusted the pillow behind him. "It's why I left Puerto Rico, you know?"

"I didn't know."

"I was working nights in a bar, still living with my parents. My father came home early from work one day and found me in bed with a boy from down the street." He shook his head. "He went crazy. I had to leave. I wandered around for a while, New York, Florida, California. I learned to do hair. I ended up here." He smiled. "Like Tatiana. That's why we get along so well. Both wanderers washed up on the shore here."

"You ever go home?"

He shook his head. "I wish I could, now, but my father died. About five years after I left. We never talked again, never made up. I still have this empty place inside."

"I've been lucky," I said. "My parents have been great."

He nodded. "Good. That's the first step." He looked down at the bed, then back up at me. "I forgive Howard, you know. He was angry. He wasn't in control. He didn't really mean to hurt me."

"He wanted to hurt me," I said. "You were just a convenient stand-in."

"That may be true. But still I forgive him, and you should too."

"I don't think I can. I feel like it would be condoning what he did. I can't do that, not for myself, or for anyone else who wants to be free to go to that bar, or be out in the world, without worrying about assholes like Haoa."

"There's a difference between forgiving and condoning," Tico said. "What you have to do now is educate him. We all have to, you know. One by one, the gays of the world are educating the straights that we're people too. Your job is to go on with your life, living it in a way that makes you comfortable, and by doing that you show your brother that you're still a good person, that you still love him, that what you do in bed or who you do it with doesn't change who you are. Gradually he'll change."

"Do you think he will?"

"I think each of us has the potential to change," he said. "Sometimes it's painful, like what you're going through." He took a sip of water from a foam cup on the bed tray. "You're very lucky to have such a warm and loving family. I look at Tatiana and Howard together and I think, that's what I want, someday. I want someone who will love me the way they love each other. I can't bear to think their love will be lost because of me."

I knew what he meant. I had often seen Haoa and Tatiana together and envied them the kind of visceral connection they had. He loved her fiercely, with more dedication than I had ever seen him apply to anything, even football, and when he was a teenager he lived, breathed, ate, and talked football. It was so much a part of him I couldn't imagine him not playing. Nor could I imagine him without Tatiana. He would die. It was as if she gave him some essential nutrient he couldn't live without.

"And you love him, too," Tico said, looking at me. "You know you do. So you have to forgive him. Because if you don't, you'll have an empty place inside you like I have. Trust me, darling, you don't want that."

I reached out and took his good hand in mine, and squeezed. His grip was surprisingly strong.

Chapter 33

I SAT WITH TICO for a while, and then as I was leaving I met Tatiana in the hallway. "Howie's not a bad person," she said as we leaned up against the antiseptic green wall. "He just doesn't think sometimes."

"I know. And I know some people are going to treat me differently now that I'm out of the closet. But it's hard when the trouble comes from inside your family."

"He doesn't do well with change," Tatiana admitted. "I remember when I found out I was pregnant with Ashley, I went running out to this job he was working on with your father. I was so excited! I jumped out of the car and ran up to him, screaming, 'I'm pregnant! I'm pregnant!'"

She laughed. "He had a cow. He was going, 'Oh, my God, how did this happen!' and I said, 'It's sex, Howie. We had sex,' and all the other guys were laughing, and God, he was mad at me for a month." Her face got somber then. "Then he went on a drinking binge and didn't come home all night. I know he's got problems, Kimo, and he really doesn't drink that much anymore, only when something really upsets him. You know he does love you, and this has all been kind of hard for him to take."

"So you're forgiving him?"

"I have to. I was really mad at him when I found out he beat up Tico. I mean, that man is like my brother. At first I thought he knew it was Tico, that he was mad at me about something and taking it out on him. Tico got me to understand."

"Yeah, that it wasn't your fault, it was mine."

"It's not your fault." She faced me, pushing a big crest of ash-blonde hair from her forehead. "Howie overreacted. That's his problem, not yours."

"But I can't help feeling it is my problem." I started to walk down the corridor and Tatiana came with me. "If I hadn't gone to the Rod and Reel Club, none of this would have happened."

An orderly passed us, wheeling an elderly Chinese woman with a tube coming out of her nostrils, connected to an oxygen tank on the back of the wheelchair. Her clawlike fingers gripped the arms of the chair as though she was holding on and wouldn't let go.

"That man would still be dead," Tatiana said when they had passed. "You'd still be investigating his murder. You'd still be stuck in your closet, and maybe you'd never get the chance for the life you deserve." She took my arm and I stopped walking and turned to face her. "Everything happens for a reason," she said. "I believe that. You have to forgive Howie, and you have to forgive yourself."

I nodded. "I know. It's just hard to do."

We turned around to return to Tico's room. Coming down the hall toward us was my big brother. Tatiana saw him and her face lit up, and I remembered what Tico had said, that he hoped someday he would be part of a love like the one Haoa and Tatiana shared, and I felt sad and angry and jealous and I knew that someday I would have to forgive him, but that I just wasn't strong enough to do it so soon. I nodded to him and walked on past, heading back into the world.

When I got back to my parents' house, Harry was in their living room, chatting. "Hey, brah, how'd you get here?" I asked. "I didn't see your car."

"It's at my folks' house. I came through the woods. We can go out the same way and head up the coast for some surfing. Those newshounds outside will never know."

More than ever before, I was noticing the acts of kindness people do every day. I guess when you stop expecting them, each one comes as a small gift. "He brought his boards with him," my father said to Harry. To me he said, "Go on. Everything will still be here when you get back."

I took my long board and Harry my short one, and we went out the back door, sneaking across the yard to the steep wooded slope. No one saw us go, though I did look back for a minute and see my mother framed in the patio doorway. We climbed a narrow, winding trail that led to a higher street, coming out a few doors down from Harry's house. When I was a teenager we used this path almost daily, and I was surprised at how familiar it remained, twisting past a banyan with hanging tendrils, discovering an orchid flourishing under the shelter of a kiawe tree. It was a road back into the past for me, back to a time when all I worried about was the condition of wind and surf.

At the edge of the street we peered out and saw no one. Harry's BMW was parked at the curb, and we bagged my boards and tied them to the roof rack along with his, and then took off for the north shore.

It wasn't the best time to go north; the winter provides really prime surfing conditions up there. But it was a place we could go to get away from the press, where no one would recognize me, and if they did, it would only be as a fellow surfer, not a media target. We put the windows down under a clear blue sky and cruised north, up into the hills, past Schofield Barracks, descending again past fields of pineapple with the glorious blue sea ahead of us.

We snagged an oceanfront parking space just beyond Haleiwa, stripped down to our suits, and dragged our boards toward the ocean. From then on, all I concentrated on was surfing. I emptied my mind of murders, police, sex, and family troubles, and felt wonderfully free as a result. The waves weren't killer, but then I was accustomed to surfing Waikīkī so it didn't really matter. I practiced slashing and ripping for a while, and then just surfed for fun, catching the waves I liked and running them as long as I could hold on.

Harry had packed a picnic lunch, and after a couple of hours of surfing we collapsed on the beach and ate, then dozed for a bit and surfed some more, until the sun was beginning to sink over the hillsides. "This was great," I said, as we carried our boards back up the beach to the roadside. "Mahalo."

"I had a good time too," Harry said. "I've been wanting to get up here again ever since I got back from Massachusetts, but you've been so busy."

"I'm gonna have a lot of time on my hands now."

On the ride back to the city, I tried to hold onto the good feelings. I turned the radio up and when I couldn't find a good station put in a CD of the Makaha Sons, luxuriating in the rhythms of the slack key guitar, the ipu gourds, and the pahu hula drum. We stopped on the way back at a roadside diner we'd loved as teens and reminisced about high school.

"So you were always keeping this secret," Harry said after the waitress had taken our orders. "All through Punahou, and years after."

"I didn't really understand it for a long time. I mean, I didn't have any role models, and I didn't have anybody I could ask questions of. So it was kind of a gradual thing, an awareness that kept growing."

"Does it color your memories? When you look back, you think, oh, if I'd only known, I would have reacted differently?"

I shook my head. "You can't go back and change things. You learn at a certain pace, and what you know to that point colors what you do." I thought about Haoa. I had to give him a chance to learn, to assimilate what he knew about me in the past with the me I was today.

We slid easily into further reminiscences, and then eventually we were home. He dropped me off at my parents' house, and mercifully, all the reporters and vans had disappeared, off to exploit someone else's misery. I spent an hour or so watching TV with my parents in the living room before I went up to bed.

Sunday morning I woke late and had a bowl of cereal while I

read the newspaper. There was no mention of either me or Haoa, a good sign. Funeral services had been set for Evan Gonsalves, at the Kawaiahao Church downtown, across from Honolulu Hale. The Clarks were descended from early missionaries to the islands and had ancestors buried in the graveyard behind the church. Even though they had sold Clark's to a Canadian with a chain of stores across the States, Terri's family was still very prominent in Honolulu. Because of Evan's connection to them, the funeral would be big and well-publicized, and I knew it wouldn't be possible for me to sneak in the back unseen.

I wanted to go, but I didn't know how Terri felt about my part in his death and I was sure that there would be reporters at the funeral who might come after me. I didn't want to add my troubles to her grief.

I didn't feel like doing anything much, so I sat in front of the TV, watching cable reruns of talk shows, hoping the misery of others would make me feel better about my own. Sally Jessy Raphael had bisexuals who were torn between two lovers; Jenny Jones had surprise makeovers for terminal cancer patients; Gordon Elliott mediated a fight between rival high school gangs; and Rolonda had a panel of gossip columnists dishing dirt on celebrities.

By lunchtime my mother was fed up. "Come with me," she said. "We'll go somewhere for lunch, and then you can come along while I go shopping. I need a present for Ashley's birthday and a pair of blue shoes with a low heel."

"I don't want to go."

"You're coming." When her mind was made up, my mother did not tolerate argument. It was the same thing when I resisted going to Punahou because my brothers went there. It was simply not a matter open to discussion.

"All right," I said. "But no place close to home. I don't want to see anyone you know, or anyone I know, all right?"

"You're going to have to face people eventually."

"Eventually is fine. Just not today."

I made her drive all the way to the Windward Mall in Kāhala instead of going down to Ala Moana. There was a Clark's there, along with a Liberty House and a bunch of standard mall shops, the same kind you find in every shopping center in every corner of the United States. Foot Locker, Banana Republic, The Limited, and all their ilk: the chain shoe stores and chain book stores and chain record stores. Without the occasional crack seed stand or tourist knickknack shop selling plastic leis and chocolate-covered macadamia nuts, you could think you were in Florida or California. If you stayed indoors where it was climate controlled, you could imagine you were anywhere from Oklahoma to Oregon or Maine to Maryland.

I'd brought a book with me, a Florida thriller by James W. Hall, and I tried to sit and read while my mother tried on shoes or picked through dozens of junior dresses. But I couldn't concentrate, and I didn't want to make eye contact with any other shoppers. Instead I roamed the aisles restlessly, looking at the merchandise but not really seeing it. Finally my mother said, "All right, I can't take any more of this. We can go home."

That night at dinner she complained to my father about me. "He needs something to do. Why don't you take him to work with you tomorrow?"

We sat at the dining room table under the glow of the chandelier. Our dining room was the most un-Hawai'ian room in the house, lifted almost intact from a home decorating magazine of twenty years ago. The elegant crystal chandelier had been shipped in from San Francisco, as had the formal mahogany table and chairs. "I don't need a baby-sitter," I said. "I can stay by myself. I can even go home."

Behind us was a tall mahogany cabinet filled with chinoiserie and other knickknacks. Across from us the living room was dark. "Your Uncle Chin called today," my father said. "We had a long talk, and I recognized something. Chin had two sons, and he has lost them both. I don't want to lose any of mine. You are who you are, even if I don't like it. You're still my son and I'll try to accept you."

I didn't know what to say. My father continued, "Uncle Chin would like to see you. I said we would have lunch with him tomorrow."

"Where? I don't want to go anywhere people will recognize me."

My father laid his fork down next to his plate, and then used the napkin from his lap to dab at his mouth. "Places Uncle Chin goes are very discreet," he said. "Why don't you come to the office with me in the morning, and we'll go together to lunch?"

"I don't know."

He leaned forward toward me, and the warm light from the chandelier glinted off his glasses. "I'm preparing a bid on a big job," he said. "You could help me. It gets harder for me to read the tiny details on the plans."

"All right." I looked down at my plate.

A little later, from a phone upstairs, I finally reached Tim. "Hi, it's Kimo. I haven't talked to you for a couple of days."

"It's been really busy." He hesitated. "I saw a piece on the news about you. How have you been holding up?"

"It's been hard," I said, and my voice broke. "I just want to be with somebody who accepts me totally, you know? I want to forget about all this for a while."

"I wish I could be there for you. Things are crazy at my office right now. We're in the middle of discovery for this big case, and there are piles of documents to read. I brought home two full briefcases tonight."

"You have to eat. Maybe we can get together. It doesn't have to be for long."

"Kimo." There was silence. I was afraid the connection had been broken, and then he said, "My private life is my business, and I don't want to see it spill out into the headlines. I just need to back away from you for a while. It's not that I don't like you—I do. I think you're handsome and kind and interesting and I enjoy being with you. But you're public property right now, and I can't be part of that."

"I understand." I wanted to argue with him, to say we could make it work. He could stay in the shadows and I'd carry the weight of the spotlight on me. But I'd already seen what that spotlight had done to my brothers and my parents, and I couldn't blame Tim for wanting to avoid it. After all, he'd run all the way from Boston to Honolulu to keep people from knowing he was gay. It wasn't up to me to drag him out.

"You are very nice," he said. "I hope you come through this all right."

"I hope so too." I paused. "Well, I'd better let you get back to work."

"I guess so," he said.

After I hung up the phone, I flopped back on my bed, surrounded by all those artifacts of my teen years, and felt just as confused and lonely and bad as I had back then, before I could really put a name on my problems. What a long journey I had taken from those high school posters and old books, to wind up at the same place. Well, not necessarily the same, but a place so close to where I had been that it felt no different.

I turned the light off and lay on my bed in my clothes, staring out the window at the crescent moon rising over the Ko'olau Mountains, trying not to think of the brief time I had spent with Tim, trying not to worry if I would ever meet anyone else who could make me feel the same way.

I didn't have much success.

Chapter 34

THE NEXT MORNING, my father and I stopped on the way to his office and got coffee and malasadas from a van in a shopping center parking lot. We sipped and ate in silence, and I wondered if this was what I was going to do with the rest of my life.

There were worse things. My father's business was winding down, but perhaps Haoa and I could revitalize it. With his advice, we could be as successful as he had been, maybe even more. My notoriety might even help. Long-lost classmates would remember who I was from having seen me on the evening news. We could even develop a subspecialty among Honolulu's gay population. Build houses with extra-large closets and dressing areas for the fashion plates, and big, comfortable kitchens for the aspiring caterers. Forget about kids' rooms and play areas. I knew a contractor in California who specialized in kitchens for Orthodox Jews, with extra storage space for their second set of dishes, and separate dishwashers, even separate refrigerators, for keeping milk and meat apart. There had to be a similar subspecialty for the gay population.

We pulled up at my father's office, on the second floor of a strip center he'd built near Salt Lake Park. The ground floor was filled with your usual variety of tenants: dry cleaner, deli, karate dojo, beeper store, and mattress warehouse. But unlike the Kāhala Mall, this center somehow seemed uniquely Hawai'ian. The truth came in the details.

My father was big on details. All the storefronts were set back behind a colonnade that provided shade from the hot tropical sun.

He'd had a template of a palm tree made, and pressed it into the front of each of the supporting columns, so the implication was that the roof was supported by a row of palms, like the caryatids in Greek architecture.

When I was a kid, he'd had fancier offices, always moving around from project to project. When he was building homes, it was important that the style of his office match the kind of construction he was doing, and as he built more expensive and lavish homes, the style of his office improved. Now that he was building malasada stands and small warehouses, he had three simple rooms. His office, a reception area, and a conference room where he could lay plans out on a big table.

In each room there were framed photos, artists' renderings and architects' elevations of homes, offices, stores, and shopping centers he had built. As I walked from room to room I marveled at the range of things he'd built, what he'd done to keep us all in food and clothes and pay our school tuition, take my mother on vacations and buy antique furniture for her in San Francisco and ship it to Hawai'i. Over his desk was a photo of a small bungalow I didn't recognize.

"What's this?"

"The first house I ever built," he said. "Before Uncle Chin's, even. I built it nights and weekends while I was still working for Amfac. I found it two years ago and took the picture. Nice, eh?"

The house was nice, but the photo was even nicer. Richly saturated colors, strong contrasts between light and shadow. It looked as professional as any of the promotional shots on the walls. "You took this?"

"I have five grandchildren," he said shyly. "You take a lot of pictures. You learn a few tricks."

"More than a few," I said.

It was interesting, getting to know my father again. He set me up in the conference room with a set of electrical plans and a list of items, from light fixtures to dimmer switches to outlet face plates. I had to count each one and then multiply by unit costs. "This is the worst part of the job for me," he said. "These details are so tiny, but if you miss a couple of expensive light fixtures, there goes your profit."

I worked diligently all morning, surprised that I could concentrate. It was like going surfing with Harry, getting something into my brain that pushed everything else aside. In the other room, I could hear him on the phone, schmoozing with potential customers, calling suppliers, checking schedules. I wondered if I could do that.

As a police officer and then a detective, I always had a sense that my work mattered. I was protecting the people of Honolulu, the office workers, hotel maids, and visiting tourists, from bad elements of the population. Then as a detective, I was righting wrongs, bringing society back into balance. I supposed that building houses mattered too, though I wasn't sure about strip malls and malasada shops. Then again, maybe part of my problem was looking for meaning in everything. Maybe all that really mattered was supporting your family, living a good life, having a little fun on Saturday nights, and not treating your fellow man in a way you wouldn't want to be treated.

So I thought and counted switch plate covers, and around noon my father got me and we drove into Chinatown to meet Uncle Chin for lunch. We ate in a luncheonette with dingy windows and a long row of booths with peeling vinyl. The food was only mediocre, but they knew Uncle Chin there and we were served without even ordering, steaming platters of chicken and shrimp and sticky white rice in chipped porcelain bowls.

Uncle Chin poured us tea and said, "You know my grandson, yes?" I nodded. "Tell me what he like."

I didn't know what to say at first. Did I say he was learning the family business? That I wasn't sure what role he had played in his father's death? Finally I said, "You read about me in the newspaper?" Uncle Chin nodded. "Derek is like me. He lives in an apartment downtown with a guy he went to Yale with. Derek and his friend will probably take over the Rod and Reel Club."

Uncle Chin cupped his hands around his teacup, and I noticed how old and frail they seemed. He looked down at the table and spoke softly. "Tommy not tell me much about Derek. I knew something between them but I don't know what."

"Derek loved his father. I can tell you that," I said. "Even though I don't think his father ever accepted him." I paused to scoop up some sticky rice with my chopsticks. "I can't tell you much more about Derek, because I didn't talk to him much. I know he's intelligent and well educated. He likes art. He wants to open an art gallery, and his apartment is filled with paintings."

"I want know him," Uncle Chin said. "To become man, boy needs much guidance. Took so long know his father, give him what I could. Maybe I start earlier with Derek."

"I know he met you once. He mentioned you by name. I don't think he knows you're his grandfather."

He nodded. "Sometimes easier learn such information from third party. Easier for me, sure. You make arrangements?"

I wasn't supposed to be involved in Tommy's death anymore. But did that prohibition reach to contact with his son on a family matter? My father and Uncle Chin were both looking at me, and to deny this request would disappoint them both. I decided I had disappointed my father enough. I said, "I will. I'll call him."

Uncle Chin smiled. We cracked our fortune cookies, and they were all lighthearted, promising Uncle Chin a promotion and my father great happiness. My fortune said, "You are loved more than you know," but at that moment I felt that, in spite of my troubles, I knew how deeply those around me cared for me.

We got up to leave. I said, "What about the bill?"

"No bill," Uncle Chin said.

"Uncle Chin owns the restaurant," my father said. On our way out, the waiters and busboys all bowed to Uncle Chin, who bowed slightly back.

"How about a little drive?" my father asked after we said good-bye to Uncle Chin. "I'm bidding on a renovation at the Mandarin Oriental and I want to take a look at the room again."

"Sure." We rolled the windows down on the truck and the warm summer air washed over us. My father even turned the radio on and we listened to Keali'i Reichel and The Pandanus Club and Israel Kamakawiwo'ole as we drove. He wanted to introduce me to the hotel manager, but I didn't think the time was right, so I went wandering in the gardens while he went inside.

Somewhere in the back of my mind I remembered Haoa talking about a job at the Mandarin Oriental, but it was still a surprise to me when I rounded a corner and came face to face with him, supervising the planting of a row of yellow 'ilima plants along a walkway. He was wearing a big chambray shirt with Kanapa'aka Landscaping on it, and a pair of khaki shorts. "Hey, brah," I said.

"Kimo. What brings you out this way?"

I nodded back toward the hotel. "Dad," I said. "Today's his turn to watch me. He wanted to take another look at a remodeling job he's bidding on."

"He finished that ballroom two weeks ago." Haoa looked at me, and then at the work. "Keep going like that all the way down the line," he said. "I'll be back in a few."

He pointed off toward the pool. "Come on. I'll buy you a drink."

It was funny, but I hadn't spent much time alone with my brother for years. We usually saw each other at family parties, luaus and christenings, and such, and Tatiana was always around, or Lui, or some other relative or family friend.

I looked at Haoa as we walked through the manicured grounds toward the pool bar, this stranger who was also my older brother. He's as tall as I am but seems larger, because of his broad shoulders, big belly, and stout legs. Our hair is the same jet black, though his is increasingly shot with gray. In family pictures I could see that we had the same cheekbones, the same eyes. Funny how we almost never talked but I still felt close to him, felt the blood in my veins calling out to his, remembering the time we had both spent in our mother's womb, however many years apart.

He ordered us a couple of beers and we sat on high stools around a table with a mosaic tile top. "I don't know what happened to me," he said, after we had sat together for a few minutes in silence. "I acted like an asshole. Tatiana says it's easier for me to blow off steam than to actually confront my feelings."

He put the bottle down on the table and it made a hard sound. "Here's the thing. I don't like fags. It's as simple as that."

I nodded. "I don't either."

He looked at me curiously. "But you're a fag."

I shook my head. "You don't get it. You don't like effeminate men. Guys who flounce all over the place and call you darling."

"Like Tico."

"Like Tico. But I don't do that, do I?" He hesitated. "Go on, you won't hurt my feelings."

"Once in a while you get like that. I always figured you were acting like the baby."

"Maybe," I said. "Maybe I can be a little faggy sometimes. But it doesn't define my personality, is what I mean. I mean, I'm the same person I was before you knew I liked to sleep with men. Right?"

"I guess."

"So you don't have to put me in that group of people you don't like, if you don't want to."

"I just got so mad," he said. "It was like the fags had come and recruited my little brother. I wanted to go out and bash some heads."

"Nobody recruited me." I took a drink from the bottle. "This is the way I was born, just like you were born big and Lui was born sad-looking."

"Sad-looking," he said, and laughed. "You're right. He always looks like somebody just ran over his dog."

"Remember that dog we had? What was his name, Pua? Mom used to go crazy when he got up on the furniture."

"She tried to keep him out in the yard, but you cried," Haoa said. "You convinced her to bring him back in."

"You guys put me up to that! I never would have cried otherwise."

We laughed and drank our beers. "So do you fool around a lot?" Haoa asked after a while.

"I haven't quite gotten it figured out yet. But I think when I was with women, I was looking for ones that wouldn't tie me down, because I knew deep down it wasn't what I wanted. Now that I can admit it, I just want what you and Tatiana have, and Lui and Liliha. Somebody to love, to hold onto at night."

"I was so jealous of you," he said. "You know I love Tatiana. I can't imagine what my life would be like without her. But man, I used to see you with a different wahine every week, and it was like, I want to be there. Just let me be single one weekend, Lord. Let me have Kimo's life for one weekend."

I laughed. "Guess you don't want it now."

"So maybe I was mad because I was wrong about you, too," he said. "I mean, here you were, living out my fantasy life, and then it turned out it was all a lie. It just kind of made me crazy."

We had almost finished our beers when our father came up. "The landscaping looks good, Haoa," he said. "You should be pau soon."

Haoa nodded. "Yeah, finishing up." He drained the last of his beer and said, "Got to get back." He looked at me. "Take care, little brother."

"You too."

My father and I walked slowly back to his truck. "You saw your brother."

I nodded. "We had a talk."

"Good."

"How about the job you're bidding on?" I asked. "Did you get a look at it?"

"Nice job," he said. "We can talk about it sometime."

It was almost three o'clock by the time we got back to the office. I spent another hour or so on the electrical drawings, and then my father announced it was time to go home. "Benefit of being semiretired," he said. "You can make your own hours." He looked at me. "Of course, if you were running this business for real, the hours are much longer. I wouldn't want you to get the wrong idea."

"I won't," I said.

In the newspaper that evening there was a further article on Evan Gonsalves's death. They had found a fingerprint on the jewelry box that matched Tommy Pang's, making a strong connection between the two of them. There was speculation that, as a cop, Evan couldn't live with the idea that he'd killed Tommy, and killed himself over the guilt. I thought it was rotten that the story had to break the same day as Evan's funeral, and hoped somebody was keeping the papers from Terri.

After dinner I called Akoni at home. Mealoha answered and we talked awkwardly for a minute, her asking how I was and me saying I was doing okay. "Hey, brah, howzit?" I asked when Akoni picked up the receiver.

"Okay," he said. "How're you doing?"

"I'm getting by. Yesterday I went shopping with my mother, and today I went to the office with my dad. I don't know who's going to get me tomorrow."

"You'll get through this."

"I read about the fingerprint match in the *Advertiser*. You really think Evan could have killed himself out of guilt?"

"I don't know. Shit, you were my partner for a long time and I didn't know you. How'm I going to speculate on Evan Gonsalves? Hey, by the way. We got notification that the girl in that drug bust, Luz Maria, she went back to Mexico."

"You ever get to interview her?"

"Nope. Just saw the paperwork. And you know there's no way

we'll talk to her now. If she knew anything about Tommy Pang, she took it back to Mexico with her."

We said our good-byes and hung up. I was edgy, worrying that my case was still going on and I couldn't work on it. What was I going to do? I ought to go home, I supposed. Nobody would be hanging around my doorway, and it was a step toward getting my life back together. It was something. I packed my suitcase and assembled all my equipment—the Rollerblades, surfboards, all the other stuff I'd brought.

I carried it downstairs and walked into the living room, where my parents were watching TV. "I want to go home," I said. "I think it's time."

My mother looked at my father, and he nodded. "Why don't you take my truck?" he said. "Your mother can bring me by to pick it up tomorrow."

"Okay." I started for the door, then stopped and turned back around. "Thanks," I said. "For everything."

Then I turned back to the door and went out into the night.

Chapter 35

I WAS HAPPY to be back in my own apartment. It was the first step toward regaining a life of my own. Before we'd left, my mother had plugged the phone back in and turned on my answering machine, and the red light blinked furiously. I left it for the morning light and went to sleep.

I woke up refreshed and felt even better after a good long morning on the waves. I came back to my apartment around ten and switched the answering machine to play while I fixed breakfast. Eating my father's cooking had awakened in me a desire to return to the comfort foods of my youth, and I watched the eggs carefully to keep them runny, so they would soak into the toast.

Most of the messages were from reporters who wanted to talk to me. A call from Harry was in there, from Friday, I guessed, before he'd figured out I was holed up at my parents' house. The last two calls, unexpectedly, were from Terri Clark Gonsalves, and she sounded upset.

"I need to talk to you, Kimo," she said. "About Evan. Please call me."

The second message was more urgent, and then the answering machine kicked into automatic rewind. *What does Terri want from me?* I wondered, as I ate my soggy toast and eggs. Maybe I should have gone to the funeral after all. Did she think her friends were abandoning her because of the scandal over Evan?

I washed my dishes and called Terri. There was no answer, but

I left a message on her machine, that I was back, that she could call me any time. I left her my cell number, too. I began putting away the things I'd taken to my parents', and then answering the mail, paying the bills, cleaning the apartment again.

There was a knock on the door. I walked up to the peephole and saw Terri.

She looked terrible. Her face was red and puffy, and she'd pulled her hair back into a hasty ponytail. She was wearing a navy T-shirt, white shorts, and espadrilles. More than anything else, she looked sad and beaten down.

I opened the door. She looked at me and started to cry again. "Oh, Kimo," she said, and I took her in my arms and we rocked back and forth.

"I'm sorry, honey. I wish it could have come out any other way." We separated and I led her to the couch. I went to the refrigerator for some juice, but all I had was a pog—a pineapple, orange, and guava mix unique to Hawai'i. The bottle caps lads call pogs got their name from capping this kind of juice when it came in bottles. I opened the pint carton and poured it into a glass for her.

"Have something to drink." I handed her the glass, and she drank it thirstily.

"Remember we used to get these at school when we were kids?" she asked. "Always on field trips, too. Danny drinks them now."

"I remember." I sat on the couch next to her. "How's Danny holding up?"

She looked like she was going to cry again, but she held herself back. "He's not talking," she said. "My mother's with him now. He cries, and he stays in his room, but he doesn't talk. I don't think he's said a word since Evan died."

"Suicide can be pretty traumatic for a kid. You don't know—he might have seen Evan do it, or at least heard the shot and seen the body."

She looked up at me. "I just don't believe Evan killed himself.

I mean, we were getting over our problems. He looked better last week than he had in months. He was home more. He paid more attention to me and Danny."

"I guess he'd been working for Tommy Pang," I said. "When he killed Tommy, it was probably a big relief for him. So he would have felt better for a while. He could have been more relaxed." I took a breath. "But killing somebody is a big deal. I could see how it could get to him after a while."

"I've thought about that. Endless hours, all night long, I've wondered how Evan could have killed him, and I think I understand it." She sat back on my sofa, dried her eyes with a tissue, and said, "I think I pushed him toward it. You know—how I told him he had to stop what he was doing. God knows I didn't mean for him to kill anybody."

I put my arm around her and she leaned her head against my shoulder. I could smell her perfume, something light and floral, and her hair was soft where it touched my bare arm. "You can't think like that," I said. "It wasn't your fault. Evan got involved with Tommy Pang all by himself."

She nodded. "I know. But I should have made it clearer that the money didn't matter to me. He never understood that all I wanted was him. I always had enough money for both of us." She balled the tissue up in her hand and sat up again. "That's something I'll always live with. I know he made the decision to get involved with that man, and then he decided to kill him. But at least part of the blame is mine."

"You have Danny to think about," I said. "You need to go on from here."

"But I can't, not yet. I understand everything up until the minute he pulled the trigger. I knew my husband, Kimo. I knew his moods and his feelings, and I knew when he was doing something wrong. I know he loved Danny more than anything else in the world, and he'd do anything to keep him from being hurt. If he was going to kill himself, he'd never do it in the house, and never when Danny was around." She opened her purse and pulled out an envelope. "He left this note for me. I found it in our safe deposit box this morning."

She handed it to me. On the outside was written, "To be opened in the event of my death." It gave me the shivers to know what Evan had expected had come true.

Dearest Terri,

If you are reading this now, then something bad has happened, and I'm dead. I want you to understand why, and to apologize. I only wanted to give you the best, sweetheart. I know I never should have gotten involved with Tommy Pang, but when I first met him, I wanted to get you a great present for your thirtieth birthday, and between my car payments and the money for the house, I was really strapped. He gave me $5,000 just to warn him when Import-Export Control was going to run those surprise sweeps through the airport.

He always wanted more, though. It was never anything very big, just information. And he always paid me well. Then I had to tell him we were about to intercept a drug deal he was involved in, and I knew I couldn't go on working for him. I went to his office two weeks ago to tell him I quit.

I didn't kill him, though. I left the club after he gave me the bracelet I gave you for your birthday, but I had only gotten as far as the alley when I heard Tommy yelling. Then I heard a crack! like the sound of a bat hitting a ball. I saw somebody— a big guy, I couldn't see anything clearer than that—drag Tommy down the alley. He drove away and I couldn't resist, honey. I saw another guy bend over him then run away. I knew Tommy wore a lot of jewelry and I picked it off his body and took it to a fence out by the Aloha Bowl.

There's one more thing I want to do, and that will give me enough money to put aside so I won't have to deal with scum anymore. If you are reading this, you know that I didn't succeed. Please give this letter to Kimo—maybe it will help him track the bastard down.

I love you and Danny with every ounce of my heart, my dearest Terri. Please don't be angry with me. I only did what I did because I wanted to give you and Danny the world.

The words *Love, Evan* were scrawled at the bottom of the page. I looked up at Terri. "I know something happened at my house on Friday," Terri said. "I think somebody else was there while I was away."

"How do you know?"

"I can't say for sure. I feel like things might have been moved around a little—I know, the police were in the house for a while, but this is different."

She reached out for the glass and I handed it to her, and she finished the juice. "You're the only one I can talk to, Kimo. I can't tell my parents anything. It's already on the tip of my mother's tongue to tell me it was a mistake to marry Evan in the first place."

I remembered the imperious Mrs. Clark. Though I got points for going to Punahou, and even for my haole grandmother, I was still a native boy to her. "Do you think Danny might have seen anything? Maybe I can get him to talk." We agreed that I'd follow her out to Wailupe and see if I could talk to Danny.

She got up from the sofa and started for the door. Then I had an idea. "Actually, you go on. I'll be a couple of minutes behind you."

I scrounged around my apartment looking for pogs—the bottle cap type this time. I could only come up with a handful. I put them in the pocket of my shorts, grabbed my sunglasses, and walked over to my grocery store. "Hey, Kimo," the clerk said. "Been out yet today? The surf is awesome." His hair was just as long and scraggly as usual, and it seemed he was wearing yet another earring, though I couldn't be sure.

It was great. At least somebody didn't see me through the prism of my sexuality or my job troubles. "I surfed for a couple hours this morning," I said. "I caught a killer break off the marine stadium. I actually got a full turn in on it."

We talked waves for a couple more minutes, and then I saw what I wanted—an economy-sized bag of assorted pogs. There weren't going to be any spectacular ones in there, but they'd do for my purposes. I paid for the pogs and walked back to my truck.

On the way out to Wailupe I tried to think of what I could say to Danny. I loved my own father so much, and I was so lucky that he was still around to look out for me when I needed him. How could I help Danny, whose father seemed to have abandoned him in the cruelest way possible?

I finally decided, as I pulled into the Gonsalves's semicircular driveway, that I didn't have to say anything much to Danny. I just had to be there, and eventually he'd be ready to talk. Mrs. Clark came out of the house just as I parked. She looked as I remembered her—tall and proud, wearing a white cotton blouse and black skirt that were vintage Clark's, circa 1965. Her hair was grayer than it had been when I was a teenager, but it was immaculately put together, as usual. "Hello, Kimo," she said.

"I'm sorry," I started to say, just as she said the same thing to me.

"It's been a bad week, hasn't it?" she said, and smiled. "So many things for everyone to be sorry about. Will you tell your mother I sent my regards? Sometimes I long for those days when you and Terri were at Punahou, and your mother and I worked together on the PTA, and everything was so much simpler."

"It just seems like it was because we've gotten past it," I said. "I'm sure we gave you plenty of problems back then."

She nodded. "You're probably right." She took my hand in hers. "Take care of yourself, Kimo. And see if you can help my daughter. She has so much ahead of her."

"I will, Mrs. Clark."

"Well, I must be off. William retired last year, you know, and he's very particular about his lunch. If I'm not there to make sure everything is fine, he gets very upset."

What a luxury, I thought, as I watched her walk to her champagne-colored Mercedes. *To worry about lunch.* Then I went inside.

Terri and Danny were sitting at the kitchen table, and she was trying to get him to eat a grilled cheese sandwich. He didn't speak and he didn't eat either. Terri looked up at me. "I don't know what to do with him."

I walked over to the table and sat down. "Hey, Danny." He looked at me, but didn't say anything. "You know, it's a beautiful day. You want to go hang out with me, outside?" Again, there was no response, so I said, "Come on. Come with me, okay?" I took his hand and he got up from the table. We walked together out to the front half-moon of lawn, between the driveway and the road, and sat down, me talking and him not saying anything.

I lay down on my back and looked up at the sky. Danny sat next to me Indian style. "So what do you think that cloud looks like?" I pointed up to the sky. "A sheep? See, there's its woolly body, and there's even a lump at the top like its woolly head."

I babbled on for a few more minutes about clouds, but I wasn't getting anywhere. There was a cool breeze, so close to the water, and I remembered what it was like being a kid, just smelling the fresh-cut grass, listening to birds, hearing the thump of a basketball on a driveway down the street. So I just lay there, and eventually Danny lay down next to me and rested his head on my arm. We lay like that for a while, and then he started to cry.

I held him close to me and stroked his head. "It's okay, Danny. It's okay to cry. Sometimes bad things happen, and they make us feel like crying. You go ahead and cry."

He cried for a few minutes, and then he was calm for a while. "You know what?" I asked. "I remember you have some really neat pogs. Can I see them?"

He nodded. Well, that was a start, I thought. He got up and ran inside, and I got the bag of pogs from my truck. When he came out again with his, I had mine lined up in neat piles. "You want to flip some?" I asked.

He nodded again and sat down across from me. Out of the corner of my eye I saw Terri standing at the front door, but then she went back inside. "I'm warning you, I haven't flipped pogs for a long time," I said. "I might have forgotten how."

"I'll show you," he said. "You make a stack like this." He piled up ten of his pogs, all face up. "And then I flip my shooter at them, and the ones that stay face up are still mine, and the ones that go the other way are yours."

He flipped, and the pile toppled. Eight of them stayed right side up, and he pushed the other two over to me. "Now you do it," he said.

We flipped back and forth for a long time, and pogs seemed to migrate from my side over to his. I guess you have to be six years old to be a champion pog flipper. Some dark rain clouds blew in off the ocean, blocking the sun. Then Terri came to the door and said, "Who's ready for some supper?"

"Will you play with me again?" Danny asked.

"Of course." We gathered up our pogs and went inside.

"Go put your pogs away and wash your hands," Terri said. Danny went off toward his room. "Any progress?"

"He'll come around," I said. "He did talk a little, but don't say anything to him." Terri had made meat loaf and mashed potatoes. We sat at the kitchen table, under a montage of old hapa haole sheet music covers Terri had collected and framed. In the 1920s and 1930s, hapa haole music, or half-white music, was popular in the islands. It featured the ukulele and the slack key guitar, and often was about romance between a haole and a native, under the Hawai'ian moon.

She cut meat loaf for each of us. "Would you like some potatoes?" she asked Danny.

"Yes, please."

She raised her eyebrows to me and smiled.

After dinner Terri and I sat on the overstuffed couch, her with her feet tucked under her, mine stretched out onto the coffee table. Danny sprawled on the floor and didn't speak again, but this time his silence was calmer, less pained. We didn't make a big deal about it. Terri and I talked easily about old classmates, things we'd done at Punahou, while the big-screen TV played in the background.

When Terri announced it was Danny's bedtime, I asked, "I know tomorrow's only Wednesday, and it's normally a school day, but I was wondering, would you guys like to go on a picnic tomorrow? We could go down to Makapu'u Point. I could bring my board along and give Danny a surfing lesson."

"He already loves his boogie board," Terri said.

"Please, Mom? Please?"

"All right. Now go take a bath and then get into bed. I'll come and tuck you in."

"Can Kimo come too?"

"Sure," I said. I reached out and ruffled his hair. "I wouldn't miss it."

Terri waited until he had left the room to speak. "I don't know what you did, but it worked. I don't know how to thank you."

"This is just a start. Give me a little while, and I'll talk to him about what happened to his dad."

"God, you know, I'd almost forgotten. Just for a minute or two there. It was like we were just sitting around watching TV, and our worlds hadn't fallen apart."

"I'm on the way to picking mine up," I said, reaching out for her hand. "Come on along—we can pick up yours on the way."

Chapter 36

WHILE I WAS GETTING READY for bed, I turned on the TV news, Lui's station. I was just in time to see part three of their series on gay cops. Lucky me.

But as I watched, I got more and more interested. There were police forces around the country that had incorporated gay officers into their regular patrols. They primarily worked neighborhoods with large gay populations, and they were more sensitive to issues like gay bashing and regulating gay clubs than straight officers were.

It was a surprisingly well-balanced piece. I didn't know if that kind of enlightenment would ever come to Honolulu, but seeing such a piece on my brother's normally scandal-packed station was a nice change.

The next morning the phone rang at eight-thirty, just as I was getting ready to go out for a late swim. It was Lieutenant Yumuri. "Can you come over to the station this morning?" he asked.

"Sure. What for?" I thought maybe he wanted to talk about the case, ease up on the pressure. Maybe this was the first step toward getting my badge and my weapon back. I wanted to talk to him about a couple of discrepancies, mostly centered on Evan's suicide, which I was now sure was faked.

To his credit, Lieutenant Yumuri sounded uncomfortable when he spoke. "Officer Greenberg is getting his shield. I want to put him at your desk. I'd appreciate it if you'd come by and pick up the rest of your personal belongings."

I couldn't speak for a moment. It was all over. My career as a cop, as a detective. And this is how it ended. Finally I said, "Sure. I'll be over in a little while."

"Thank you." He hung up his end, and I held my receiver there for a minute, listening to nothing, until a female voice came on the line and said, "If you'd like to make a call, please hang up and dial again."

I pulled on a pair of khakis and an aloha shirt and walked over to the station. As I was about to go in, Lidia Portuondo came out in uniform. "Kimo," she said.

"Lidia."

I started to walk past her. She said, "Look, for what it's worth, I'm sorry. I never should have told anybody what I heard in that interview."

"I guess you shouldn't have. I thought you could keep a secret."

She shook her head. "Couldn't even keep my own. The lieutenant found out about me and Alvy. So he gets a promotion and I get transferred to Pearl City."

"I heard he got his shield," I said. "He's taking over my desk." I hesitated for a minute. "Are you two still . . ."

"For now." She gave me a forced smile. "Who knows I might meet some handsome guy out in Pearl City."

I gave her my hand. "Good luck."

"You, too."

I nodded at the desk sergeant and started to walk back to my old desk. He said, "Sorry, Kimo. I've got to call the lieutenant before I can let you back there."

"I understand."

I cooled my heels in the waiting area for a few minutes until Akoni came up front. "I can take him back," he said to the desk sergeant.

"Hear you've got a new partner," I said as we walked back.

"We're working a new homicide, behind the Royal Hawai'ian Hotel," Akoni said. "He's got a lot to learn."

"Be nice to him, all right?" I asked as we got back to our desks. "What happened to me has nothing to do with him."

I started to pack up my desk. I could see Alvy Greenberg had already been sitting there. "I punched him yesterday," Akoni said. I looked up. "He was talking stink about you. I kept telling him to stop and he wouldn't, so I hit him." He had a kind of sheepish grin on his face, like a kid who knows he's done wrong but can't help bragging about it.

"Don't make a habit of it, all right?" I asked. I smiled at him. "It doesn't make for good relationships between partners."

It didn't take me long to box up the rest of my stuff. A favorite coffee mug, some pictures of my nieces and nephews, a miniature surfboard I won in a contest once and kept around for good luck. It hadn't brought me much luck lately, and I could have just tossed it, but I didn't want to tempt fate any worse.

"See you around," I said, sticking my hand out to Akoni.

"Be careful, Kimo."

"I won't take you down with me," I said. "Anything you say that takes any part of this on you, I'm denying it."

"Just tell the truth. If I've got anything coming to me, I'll take it." He looked at me hard. "I'm serious, Kimo. You lie to the bosses, it makes you no better than the criminals who lie to us. It makes our jobs worth nothing."

"I'll tell the truth. And the truth is, I made all my own trouble."

By the time I got back home, it was time to leave for Terri's house in Wailupe. If the department was giving me an enforced vacation, I might as well enjoy it.

Danny was glad to see me, and the three of us squeezed into my truck for the ride out to Makapuʻu Point instead of taking one of Terri's cars. "Makes it more like an outing," I said. We put the picnic stuff in the back along with my surfboards.

When we arrived, Danny ran down to the shoreline to poke around and I helped Terri lay out lunch for us. "He hardly talked this morning," she said. "I was worried we were going right back where we were."

"Give him time. I'm sure he hurts just as much as you do, but he doesn't know how to channel it. The good thing is, kids heal a lot faster than grown-ups." I spread a big blanket for the three of us and sat down on it. While Terri put out the food, I said, "I had a case last year, multiple homicide in a crack house on a side street off Kuhio Avenue. This woman was dealing, and she had her four little kids in the house with her. These two guys from the mainland came in and shot the woman and the kids and stole the crack."

"How awful," Terri said.

"Long way from Punahou, isn't it? One kid survived, a six-year-old girl. She was smart way beyond her years. I mean, from her hospital bed she told us exactly what happened, described the two guys so that an artist could draw them, everything we needed. She even remembered the street name of one of the guys. We picked them up within hours." I shook my head. "Then it was like she shut down, totally. Went into cardiac arrest, though the doctors couldn't figure out why. They had to shock her twice to bring her back. And you know what? We had a follow-up hearing last month, and I saw her. She's living with foster parents, going to school, and she looks like just the sweetest, happiest little seven-year-old you've ever seen. You'd never know anything happened to her."

I opened the bag of potato chips and took one. "Of course, you don't know what's going on inside her head, how it all marked her, but she's surviving. Danny will survive, too. It just might take a while."

She called Danny back to eat, and he brought with him an assemblage of treasures—an odd-shaped rock, an iridescent shell fragment, and the bleached claw of a sand crab. I admired them each in turn and he sat down next to me to eat, his little foot pressing into the side of my leg, making the physical connection.

I think the hardest thing for me about accepting my sexuality and all its implications was thinking that I would never have children of my own. I know it's theoretically possible, but it wouldn't be the way I'd always imagined it. I really wanted to be a dad, and I thought I'd be a good one. I think my parents did a pretty good job of raising me, though I did feel my father worked too much, that he didn't give enough of his time to me and my brothers. I wanted to make up for that with my own kid, to see a little part of me reflected in him, to marvel at the perfection of his tiny fingers and toes and then watch him grow up in the world.

Akoni doesn't want to have kids. He says he's seen so much horror in the world, so many awful things that people do to each other, that he can't imagine having, as he calls it, "a hostage to fate." I feel just the opposite. Sure, I've seen just as much misery and tragedy, but I always see the way people recover, the way the human species is designed to continue in the face of almost insurmountable odds. It gives me faith that a kid could actually survive.

After we finished eating, we sat around on the beach. Danny and I tried flipping pogs, but the sand was too unsteady a base. Instead we just lay together in a haphazard mass, Terri's feet touching my leg, Danny's head resting on my chest, and dozed. Then the sun passed behind a cloud for a bit and the coolness in the air woke us up.

I carefully shifted Danny's head to the blanket next to me, and stood up and stretched. "I think I'll surf for a bit, if you don't mind," I said to Terri.

"Go ahead. This is nice, just lying here relaxing."

Danny woke up then and said, "Can I go with you, Kimo?"

"Tell you what, Danny. Let me check out the waves, okay? Then I'll come back for you and give you a little lesson."

"Okay." He pulled his legs up close to him, wrapped his arms around them, and sat there watching me as I walked down the beach.

I worked on my kickbacks—wave dismounts—for a while, surfing back and forth along the beach, watching Danny, and then came to pick him up. "You're sure it's okay?" Terri asked anxiously. "The surf looked pretty strong out there."

"I'll take care of him. Come on, Danny." He took my hand, and we walked carefully into the water. The bottom is rough, and the undertow is strong, but he held my hand until we got a few feet out, and then I lifted him and sat him on my board.

We didn't go very far outside, just beyond the first line of shallow breakers. I stood him up on my board, me standing in the water next to him, and held him as the board crested over the light waves. It was just the way I'd been taught to surf when I was a kid, learning to keep my balance on the board. Since he'd boogie boarded before, he understood the waves, and pretty soon all I was doing was acting as his safety, my arms in a broad arc around him in case he fell.

Finally I said, "I think it's time to go in, champ," and picked him up off the board. I carried him in past the rough part, and then swam back out for my board, floating on the tide. "Did you see, Mommy?" he called out as he ran up the beach. "I was surfing!"

"I saw," Terri said.

She started to clean up the picnic things, but Danny was antsy and couldn't sit still. "Tell you what, Terri," I said. "Why don't Danny and I take a little walk while you clean up?" I leaned down to Danny's level. "You want to do that, champ? We can walk along the water line and see what else we can find for your collection."

"Yeah," he said eagerly, and he reached up for my hand. We started down the shore, looking out at Rabbit Island, and Danny pointed and said, "My dad always promised to take me out there." He looked down at the ground. "We never went."

"I can take you out there sometime," I said. He didn't say anything, but held on tight to my hand. "Danny, what happened the day your dad died?"

He was silent.

"It's important," I said. "Knowing would make your mom feel a lot better."

He stopped walking, and I sat down on a piece of rock and made a place next to me for him. He sat close to me and said, "I was taking a nap, and I heard these men yelling."

Shit, I thought. "How many men?"

"Two." He continued, in short phrases, as if he was building up his strength for each new clause. "I was scared . . . and then I heard this really loud noise . . . and, and then . . . I heard the men go out the door." He stopped and took a big gulp of breath. "Then, then I went . . . to the door . . . of my dad's study, and, and I looked in, and there he was."

"So you never saw the men?" I asked. He shook his head. He didn't say anything else for a while, and so we just sat there, me with my arm around him. He started to cry again, slowly and quietly. "It's okay, Danny," I said. "Nobody can hurt you anymore."

He looked up at me. "That's all I remember, until . . . until you came—to . . . to the house."

I used the edge of my shirt to dry his eyes. We sat like that for a while, him against me, until I finally said, "What do you say we head back to your mom?" and he agreed, and I hoisted him up on my shoulders and we walked back to Terri.

It was just twilight when we got back to Wailupe, the sky shading between violet and black. The warm breeze coming through the windows of my truck moved the scent of salt water and coconut tanning oil lazily around us. Terri sent Danny inside and stood outside the truck, leaning in the window. "Thanks for today, Kimo. It was good for both of us."

"Danny told me what happened the day Evan died," I said. "He said two men came to the house and argued with his father. Then he heard a shot, and he heard the men leave."

"So he didn't commit suicide! I knew it!"

"Don't jump ahead," I said. "Evan might still have killed himself. He just might have done it in front of witnesses. Do you have any idea who the two men could be?"

She shook her head. I had an idea myself, but the implications were too scary to think about. Akoni and I had shown the photo of Evan to Derek and Wayne, and they'd indicated he was the cop on Tommy's payroll. Suppose they had tracked him down?

But how could they have found him so quickly? We'd never

identified him by name. I said, "The guy Evan mentioned in his letter, Tommy Pang. Did you ever meet him?"

She shook her head. "No, I don't think so."

"You're sure? His wife's name is Genevieve, and he has a son named Derek."

"Wait a second. Derek Pang. I met him. He went to Punahou, you know, before Yale. When he got back to Honolulu he was looking for a job in a gallery, and he called up some Punahou alumni to see if anybody could help him. I met him for lunch one day and we talked about art and galleries and Punahou, of course. I gave him a couple of names, but I never heard anything else."

"Did he ever come to your house?"

"No."

"Did he ever meet Evan?"

"I only saw him that time." She paused. "I wonder if he knows Evan was my husband."

He knew, I thought, because he'd seen the picture of Evan and Terri's wedding. That was how Derek had been able to identify Evan so fast. While Akoni and I were back at the station getting our warrants in order, he and Wayne had come out to Wailupe and found Evan at home with his son. Their lucky day.

Chapter 37

I WANTED TO DRIVE right to Derek and Wayne's apartment and confront them. I paced around, fuming and raging vendettas of biblical proportions against them. But the truth was, I had no real evidence that they'd had anything to do with Evan's death, which Doc Takayama had ruled a suicide. Unless I could do something, that ruling would stand. Derek and Wayne must have thought Evan killed Tommy, then taken their own biblical-style revenge.

With Gunter's help, I thought I could tie Derek and Wayne to the Bishop Museum thefts that Peggy was investigating, but that wasn't enough. I wanted to nail them. I wanted to prove that they had killed Evan.

There wasn't going to be any physical evidence at the house. It had been a week, and no one had dusted the study or the rest of the house for fingerprints or searched for other evidence. No evidence linked Derek and Wayne to Evan other than the fact that they'd identified his picture.

What could I do to prove they were guilty? I knew in my heart that they were the two men Danny had heard yelling at his father. If I got pictures of them and their cars and canvassed the neighbors, maybe someone would remember seeing either of them around the Gonsalves house.

But that would only be circumstantial. What I really wanted was a confession. I wanted Derek or Wayne to admit they'd shot Evan. That didn't seem likely, though.

Or was it? Maybe I was focusing too much on Derek and Wayne

as a couple. Divide and conquer. I remembered the bartender at the Boardwalk telling me Wayne had a taste for Asian boys, that he trolled there by himself on occasion. Suppose I offered myself up as bait? I already knew he was attracted to me. Of course, I was attracted to him, too, which was a problem. Maybe I could get him in a situation where he had his pants off and his guard down.

The phone rang. It startled me, bringing me back down to earth. "Hey, brah, just checking in," Harry said. "Howzit?"

"I'm glad you called," I said. "I've got a lot to talk to you about."

We met at a pizza place on Kuhio Avenue just after dark. It was just a hole in the wall, a half-dozen linoleum-topped tables and a couple of tattered posters of the Italian Riviera on the walls, but the crust was thick and chewy and they topped it with about a pound of shredded cheese. They did a major takeout business. Sometimes customers lined up out the door waiting patiently for their pies.

By then I had refined my plan. "I want to be wired up when I get together with Wayne, but I can't go to Yumuri for the equipment," I said, when Harry and I were sitting at a two-top in the front window. "You're the electronics wizard. Can you rig something up for me?"

"I can put the stuff together, but you need a lot of equipment," Harry said. The waitress came over and we ordered a large pizza with mushrooms and sausage and a couple of Cokes. "A lot of it's specialized stuff. You can't just walk into a store and buy it. Some things, I might have to mail order from the mainland. I mean, I could have it FedExed, but I still might not get it until the beginning of next week."

"I don't want to wait that long. I mean, I wish I could go over there right now."

I forced myself to calm down and think things through. Okay, we needed electronic equipment. Where else could we get it? We could rent it. There had to be a place on the island that rented that kind of equipment, for movies or TV shows, for example. "Would a TV station have the kind of stuff you need?" I asked.

"Sure. I might have to do some jury-rigging, but they'd have most of the things—you're going to ask your brother, aren't you?"

"He owes me a favor, the asshole. He could have called our parents when he knew there was a story on me, but he wimped out."

"This won't be easy, Kimo. You might get in a lot of trouble."

"I've worn a wire before. I've set up stakeouts. I know, things could get hairy. But I'm prepared to take that risk. I have to. I set all this in motion and I have to bring it to a close."

The waitress brought the pizza, and we ate. I told Harry about the other things I had to do to prove what Derek and Wayne had done. "Poor Terri," Harry said. "She was always a sweetheart. I remember when I had a monster crush on Elise Chung and she gave me lots of advice. She even went with me when I got my hair cut and told the barber just what to do." He sighed. "That was the best haircut I ever had."

"You're a sap," I said. "You got a quarter? I need to make a phone call and I don't want to use my cell in case they have caller ID."

"Sure." He handed me the quarter and I walked to the back of the pizza parlor, where the pay phone was mounted on the wall. I dialed Derek and Wayne's number, and Wayne answered.

"Wayne, it's Kimo Kanapa'aka," I said. "How's it going?"

"Kimo." Even his voice was sexy. For a moment I wasn't sure I could go forward with my plan, but I knew I had to. "Heard about your troubles."

"Yeah, most of the island has by now. It'll get to my auntie on Kaua'i pretty soon."

"Maybe we can get together," Wayne said. "I could give you some advice."

"Who knows? I might see you at the Boardwalk sometime. You do go there, don't you? By yourself?"

"I can." He lowered his voice. "Friday night?"

"I think I can be there then." I cleared my throat. "Can I talk to Derek?"

"Sure, hold on."

"Hey, Wayne," I said. "What kind of underwear do you wear?"

"You'll have to wait and see."

Derek picked up the phone a minute later. "What's up? I thought you were suspended."

"I am. This is more a personal thing. It's about a mutual acquaintance we have, somebody who knows you through your family. I'd rather talk to you about it in person, if that's okay."

"Sure. You want to come by here, or meet at the club, or what?"

"I can come by the club. How about tomorrow, like two o'clock?"

"That'll work." We said our good-byes and hung up. I walked back to the table where Harry was paying the bill.

"Harry, I can pay."

"You don't know where your next paycheck is coming from. I can treat you once in a while."

I shook my head. "Well, I hate to eat and run, but I've established that Wayne and Derek are both home. I'm going to run over there and take pictures of their cars."

"You can't do that by yourself. You need a lookout. What if they see you?"

"I don't want to get you involved. I've gotten too many people in trouble already."

"You're my friend. I'm already involved. Come on. Let's get a move on."

While we drove, I called my brother Lui and made a date with him for lunch the next day. "What's up?" he asked.

"I don't want to talk about it over the phone."

"Are you mad at me?"

"You wouldn't ask the question if you didn't think I had a right to be, but, no, I'm not mad at you. I'm sorry I put you in a bad situation."

"I should have called Mom and Dad. But I figured you'd already talked to them. I didn't know you were holed up in your apartment with the phone off the hook."

"Your reporter could have told you," I said. "But come on, I don't want to argue with you, Lui. Just name the time and place for lunch."

We agreed to meet at noon at a little coffee shop around the corner from his station. "You talk to Mom at all?" he asked before we hung up.

"Last night," I said. "She was all right."

"She laid into me the other day for not calling them. You think you can tell her to lay off?"

"I can try," I said. "See you at noon."

We parked around the corner from the high-rise in Kakaʻako where Derek and Wayne lived and walked over to their building, a luxury condominium with valet parking and an underground garage. While the valet was in the lobby chatting with the security guard, we slipped through a fire door that had been propped open and into a stairwell that led to the garage. "How are you going to tell which ones are theirs?" Harry asked.

"While you were hacking into Tommy's computer, I was chatting with Arleen. She was telling me how egotistical Wayne and Derek both are—they have vanity license plates, DEREKS and WAYNES. If I were still on the job, I could just run a DMV check, but instead we'll just have to find the cars that match those plates.

We looked around. The garage was about half-empty, which was good for us. Even better, the parking bumpers had unit numbers painted on them. It was harder to figure out how the numbers ran. They seemed to go in sequence for a while, then have a break and a bunch of random numbers, then resume again in order, and so on.

"This is the goofiest system," I said. Harry stood there, lost in thought. "Harry? You still with me?"

"It is a system. There's a pattern here. See, wherever the garage is completely sheltered, the numbers run in sequence. Wherever there's a grating, they jump out."

"So?"

"So when they first assigned parking spaces, they must have

given one good space to every unit. Then I'll bet people started wanting second parking spaces, so they got these ones that aren't so good, that were probably intended as guest spaces originally."

"Fascinating," I said dryly. "So find me the spaces for unit 1612."

"You take the sequential ones," he said. "I want to see if I can find a pattern in the nonsequential ones."

I shook my head and walked down the aisle. Once a geek, always a geek. It was a little spooky in the garage, open and brightly lit and echoing, and I wanted to get out as soon as possible. I found the space for number 1612 easily and took a couple of pictures of the big black Jeep Cherokee that was parked there. It had a Yale sticker on the back windshield and the vanity plate I expected, WAYNES.

Alarm bells started going off in my head. A black Jeep Cherokee, just like the one I had seen peeling away from the Rod and Reel Club the night Tommy Pan had been murdered. Was Wayne the guy Evan and I had both seen dragging Tommy's body down the alley? Were Wayne and Derek responsible not just for Evan's murder, but for Tommy's as well? And if they'd killed Tommy, then why had they killed Evan?

All those thoughts were ricocheting around my brain when I saw Harry down the aisle waving toward me. Just then I heard the engine noise of a car coming down the ramp. I waved to Harry and we both ducked behind cars.

The valet squealed around the curve and slid into a space, stomping the brakes at the last minute as the concrete wall loomed ahead of him. *We get our thrills where we can,* I thought. The valet, a cute blond guy in tight white shorts and a white shirt with epaulets, jumped out of the car and jogged back up the ramp.

I hurried down to the white BMW convertible Harry had found. It had a Yale bumper sticker and a vanity plate that read DEREKS. I snapped my pictures and we got out of the garage.

Back at my truck, I showed Harry the Polaroids. They were

pretty standard shots, showing the front and side of each car, along with the license plates. They were both in mint condition, not a ding or a dent, nothing to identify them to witnesses.

It was almost ten by then, and I drove Harry back to his condo and then went home myself. I watched the evening news on Lui's station again and saw a special report on a gay task force in a city on the East Coast. It was a mixture of straight and gay officers and detectives who investigated crimes against gays, patrolled gay neighborhoods, and gave lectures to the community on personal safety and community patrols. The report compared it to other units in communities with language or cultural barriers. "Our officers in Little Saigon speak Vietnamese," one spokesman said. "In the gay community we have officers who are sensitive to residents' concerns. It's the same thing."

It was an interesting idea. I yawned and went to bed. I woke early and went for a brief surf, which refreshed and energized me, and prepared me for all I had to do.

Chapter 38

THE NEXT MORNING, Thursday, I stopped off at Harry's apartment, where he had downloaded new copies of the photos of Derek and Wayne for me from the Yale Web site and printed them on his color printer. He wanted to come to Wailupe with me, but he had a class at UH to teach.

"I have to give a pop quiz this morning, which I already know is a bad idea. Then I'll have twenty-five quizzes to correct."

"What you need to do," I said, "is give multiple-choice tests. Then you just make a guide with the right answers on it, stick it over the papers, and then check, check, check—you're done."

"How'd you know that?"

"Wahine I dated once, teacher from Wisconsin," I said. "She told me."

"You dated a vahine from Visconsin?" he asked, giving both words the Hawai'ian pronunciation.

I laughed and headed out the H1 toward Wailupe with the pictures and the Polaroids I'd taken of Derek's and Wayne's cars. I parked in Terri's driveway and knocked on her door. Though it was still early, the sun shone strongly in a cloudless sky, and it was already getting hot.

Danny answered. "Kimo!" He put his arms around my leg.

Terri came up behind him. "I guess you can see he missed you. He kept asking me when you were coming back." She sighed. "I still can't get him to go back to school. Maybe next week."

I leaned down and picked him up. "You missed me, huh? I wish

I could be here more, pal, but I've got lots of stuff to do. I'll come and see you as often as I can, okay?"

He nodded. I put him down and explained to Terri what I was going to do. "Why don't I come with you?" she asked. "I know the neighbors, and they're more likely to talk to you if I'm around."

"I don't know. They may feel awkward, seeing you, thinking Evan killed himself."

"You're not a cop anymore, Kimo. You don't have any authority to go poking around out here. If I'm with you, nobody will complain."

She made a quick phone call and arranged for Danny to go over to the next-door neighbor's. Unfortunately, the woman had been away the previous week and hadn't seen the cars. Danny argued a little but I promised we would go surfing again, and he relented.

It was a mixed neighborhood, some stay-at-home moms and some working ones, and some older couples as well. We started to the left of Terri's house and worked our way down the street, up and down driveways, past manicured lawns, basketball hoops, and sport fishing boats up on trailers, until we came to the Kalaniana'ole Highway. Then we crossed the street and started working our way back down. We didn't have much luck until we came to an older house across from hers and two down.

An elderly woman answered the door. "Hello, Mrs. Ianello," Terri said. "This is my friend Kimo. I wonder if we could ask you a couple of questions about last Friday?"

"Oh, dear," she said. "I saw all the police cars. I'm so sorry for you, dear."

"Thank you," Terri said, looking at the ground for a minute. She had perfected her response over the last week, driven by necessity and years of training to be a Clark, with all that entailed.

"Were you home that morning, ma'am?" I asked.

"I was," Mrs. Ianello said. "Why don't you come inside. I have some iced tea."

"That would be nice," Terri said. As the sun climbed the day had gotten hotter, and for a change there were no trade winds sweeping down her street from the ocean.

Mrs. Ianello was tiny and mouselike, with short brown hair going gray and quick movements. As we walked into her living room, I saw a comfortable armchair positioned with a nice view of the front window. A good sign. She had a pair of small, expensive binoculars on the table next to the chair. An even better sign.

We sat in the living room and she brought us both tall glasses of iced tea with paper-thin lemon slices and long-handled spoons. Her furniture was very formal, some kind of French style, I think, tassels on the lampshades and fancy handles on drawers. "You mentioned you saw the police cars at the Gonsalves house that morning, ma'am," I said, after taking a long sip of my tea. "Did you see anything happen before that?"

Terri and I sat side by side on the sofa, and Mrs. Ianello faced us from her armchair, sitting forward, her hands on her knees. She thought for a minute. "Let's see. Thursday was garbage day. I always watch to make sure they take everything away." She looked over at Terri. "You know, sometimes they leave a bag behind, or a bag comes open and they don't pick everything up."

Terri nodded encouragingly. "They probably came around seven," Mrs. Ianello said. "Then I watched to make sure all the kids got on the school bus okay." This time she looked at me. "You read about terrible things that happen to little children. I just want to do my part to help."

"It's very good of you," I said.

She nodded approvingly. "I think so." She put her index finger up to her mouth, then took it away. "Mrs. Yamanaka's mother came to baby-sit while she went to the grocery. That was about ten. She came back around eleven-thirty, and I remember she had to drive very slowly down the street because there was a big black car in front of her cruising down the street slow, like they were looking for house numbers."

A big black car, I thought. That sounded promising. "Mrs.

Yamanaka has a tendency to drive a little too fast," Mrs. Ianello said. "After all, this isn't the Indianapolis five hundred around here."

I wanted her to get on with it, but it was clear there was no rushing her. She said, "The big black car stopped down the street, at the corner of Wailupe Circle. I thought it was funny that they parked there and then walked back up to your house, dear. I wondered why they didn't just park in your driveway."

"You said 'they', ma'am," I said. "Could you describe the people who got out of the car?"

"Certainly. A tall, broad-shouldered man wearing shorts, with sandy blond hair, and a shorter man, Asian I think from his build, with black hair. He was dressed very nicely, like for business. I remember thinking maybe the Asian man was the boss and the other man was like a bodyguard."

I could see Terri getting more and more upset. If I'd been her, I'd have wanted to scream something like, "You saw the men who killed my husband and you didn't do anything?" but she seemed to be struggling for control.

"They went up to the front door, and then they went inside," Mrs. Ianello continued. "I saw them leave about half an hour later, and then I went in and fixed myself some lunch, and then the next thing that happened was when several police cars pulled up." She peered at me. "Are you a policeman?"

"I'm a detective, ma'am."

"I thought so," she said, nodding. "I thought I recognized you. I may be getting old but I still have my eyesight."

And high-powered binoculars, I thought. I brought out the pictures of Wayne's car, and of Wayne and Derek. "I don't know much about cars," she said. "I suppose it could have been this one. But I couldn't be sure."

She was even less help with the photos of Wayne and Derek. "I'm sorry, I didn't really see their faces, just their general build. Without seeing them in person, I couldn't really tell." She looked at me eagerly. "Do you want me to come down to your station for a lineup?"

"We probably will, ma'am," I said. "But we have more information to gather. We'll be in touch with you." We thanked Mrs. Ianello for the tea and stood up. It was a good start, I thought, and it placed Derek and Wayne at the scene. It wasn't enough to make the case, but it was the first step.

No one else was home until we came to Mrs. Yamanaka, who was busy with twin girls, two years old. Her house was a dramatic change from Mrs. Ianello's, very spare and Japanese, paper-thin shoji screens and low cushions on the floor. Terri and I slipped off our shoes at the front door and stepped down into a sunken living room.

Terri thankfully sat on the floor and played with the twins then so that Mrs. Yamanaka could concentrate on my questions. She was a Nisei, first-generation American, and she periodically threw Japanese comments at the little girls as they played.

She always shopped on Thursdays, she said, because that was the day her mother could come and stay with the babies. "Do you remember anything unusual when you came home?" I asked. "Strange cars in the neighborhood, strangers walking around?"

"This is a quiet area. Sometimes we get tourists looking for a way to the beach. But usually not." She thought. "I remember I had bought ice cream." she said, "And I was afraid it was going to melt, because it was such a hot day. So I was hurrying to get home, and just when I got here there was a car going so slowly in front of me I nearly hit it. I was annoyed. I almost blew my horn, but I only had a block to go and I was afraid they would go even slower."

"Did you see the car stop anywhere?"

She shook her head. "As soon as I got home I started carrying in the groceries. And you know, the twins, they make a fuss, so I couldn't pay attention to anything else."

"You've been very helpful," I said, only telling a small lie. She had indeed corroborated Mrs. Ianello's story, which was important.

No one else in the neighborhood had seen anything. It was eleven thirty by then, and I had to hurry to meet Lui at noon downtown. "Danny will be disappointed he missed you again," Terri said.

"You tell him we'll have another picnic. Soon."

I had to drive hell-for-leather to make it downtown in time. My brother, the big executive, values his time and refuses to wait more than five minutes for anyone. Anyone, that is, with the exception of his wife and our mother. Once, about six years ago, our parents were supposed to take him out to dinner to celebrate his promotion to assistant station manager. Our father got tied up on a project, and they were about twenty minutes late to meet him. He'd already left and gone on to something else. Between his mother and his wife, I think he got blistered enough to burn off a complete layer of skin. So he's a little more patient with them.

I've seen Lui at the office. He's totally in control, and people literally cower when he yells. He can reduce a secretary or a cameraman to tears or inarticulate rage and then turn on his heel like nothing has happened. Yet his wife Liliha rules their home. To a great degree, Haoa's wife Tatiana is the same way. It made me wonder, as I dodged and darted through downtown traffic, if I would break the pattern. Would I end up with a man like my mother, who would control my life? Or would I choose a man like my father, who would be content to sit back and hand me the reins?

Or—and here was a revolutionary suggestion—maybe I could find a partner, somebody who'd share the duties of the drive through life with me. Unfortunately, I didn't think it was really a matter of conscious choice. We don't have much control over who attracts us. The rules of attraction, it seems, are stacked against individual choice. So I could be attracted to Tim, to Gunter, and to Wayne Gallagher at the same time, for different reasons, and though I could fight against those attractions, I couldn't, fundamentally, do anything to change them.

I made it. Lui and I approached the coffee shop from different directions at just the same time. From a slight distance, I could watch him as he came up to me. He's the shortest of the three of us, the one with the most pronounced Asian features. For this, I think, he was always our maternal grandfather's favorite.

Our mother's father lived out beyond Pearl City in an old shack, and refused to move even when my father could have built him a new house. He was crotchety and strong willed, and Haoa and I were always a little frightened of him. Lui, as the first grandson, had a different relationship with him. They would get together and talk in low tones, and his mutual rejection of us was the only unity I knew with Haoa as a child.

Lui is also an impeccable dresser. Very Brooks Brothers, always perfectly pressed. I don't think I've seen him wear an aloha shirt since his teens. He even wears ties on the weekends, because, as he says, you never know who you might meet and the impression you might need to make.

I knew the impression I would make. I was wearing cargo shorts with big pockets and a purple polo shirt, with black and brown deck shoes and no socks. Usually Lui stops a few feet away from me and shakes his head in disdain at my appearance. Today, though, he surprised me by coming right up to me and hugging me.

I hugged him back. It was strange. He and Haoa were so different from each other, and from me, and yet they were my brothers. I loved them deeply and fiercely, with a love I recognized with surprise.

We ordered *bentos*, Japanese-style box lunches, and chatted about his family, then sat down to eat. "So what can I do for you?" Lui asked. "You need money?" I shook my head. "A lawyer, then? Somebody to represent you?"

"I don't need a lawyer, and I don't need any money. I do need something, though."

I told him what I thought had happened to Evan Gonsalves. "I need a confession out of this. I'm going to try to get one out of Wayne Gallagher tomorrow night. But I need a wire, and I can't go to the police because I'm suspended, and I'm supposed to stay out of this case. Besides, Lieutenant Yumuri would never believe me."

"We might have some of the equipment at the station."

"Here's the list Harry gave me," I said. "He can put it all together."

Lui looked at the list. I expected he'd have to pass it on to one of his technicians, but he said, "We have this, and this, and this, three of these. I can get you the wire okay. We have all of this. But where are you going to put it? You'll need some kind of panel truck." Before I could speak, he said, "I can't lend you one of the station's trucks. They're too visible." He thought for a minute. "You can use one of Haoa's trucks. I'll call him and work it out."

"Haoa may not want to get into this. He doesn't exactly approve of what's going on with me at the moment."

"Haoa will do what I tell him to do," Lui said. I looked at him. "He's your brother, too, Kimo. He'll want to help you."

"If you say so."

"Give me Harry's phone number. I'll call him when I have everything together."

I gave him Harry's phone and cell numbers and then said, "I appreciate this, Lui. I don't quite know how it happened, but all of a sudden I'm dragging more and more people into my problems."

"We're your family," he said. "That's what we're here for."

Chapter 39

WHEN I WALKED up the alley behind the Rod and Reel Club, I saw Wayne's black Jeep Cherokee parked in front of the door. Arleen was sitting at her desk, talking to her mother. In Japanese, she said, "The policeman is back, the cute one."

In Japanese, I said, "Tell your mother I said hello," and she turned red.

"You never said you could speak Japanese!" she said, in English.

"You never asked."

"Mom, I gotta go. I'll call you later," she said into the phone. She looked up again. "So how can I help you, Detective?"

"I'm here to see Derek. But first I wanted to ask you a couple of questions, really just follow-up."

"Okay."

"You may know, we've got a handle on the man we think killed Mr. Pang," I said. "Last Thursday, he killed himself."

"I heard. My mother called in the afternoon to say she saw it on TV."

"I'll bet Derek was happy we found the guy."

"He wasn't even here. He was in Thursday morning, and then your partner came by, and, like, right after he left Derek left, too, and he didn't come back all day." She made a sour face. "He and Wayne are just like Mr. Pang. They come and go and they never tell me if they're coming back or not. I'm accustomed to it, but I guess I thought things were going to change."

Wayne came out of the manager's office then. "I thought I heard your voice. What brings you to our lovely office?"

"I'm here to see Derek."

Arleen stood up. "I'm just running out to get Brandon," she said. "I'll be back in a few minutes." She grabbed her pocketbook and walked out, leaving me alone with Wayne in the reception area. The door to Tommy's office was closed; I assumed Derek was in there.

Wayne stepped up behind me. He put his hand on my ass and I jumped. "You like that?" he whispered wetly into my ear.

I didn't say anything, but I did push back a little against his hand. Then the door to Tommy's office opened, and Wayne faded away behind me.

"Come in," Derek said. I walked into his office and took the seat he motioned to. "Is this about my father?"

"In a way. Did your father ever tell you how it was he came to Hawai'i?"

"I fail to see how this is related to his murder."

"It's not," I said. "This is personal. About him and about you."

He looked confused but decided to go along. "I was born in Hong Kong, but we moved here when I was about three. Later on, when I asked my father, he said someone he knew in China had arranged it all for us."

"Did you ever meet that person, the one who arranged things for you?"

"Once. An old man, Mr. Chin. I think I told you, he's the only one of my father's business associates I ever met."

"Actually, he was more than your father's business associate," I said. "He's your grandfather."

"My what? My father was an orphan, raised by distant cousins. He had no close relatives."

"I can only tell you what I've been told," I said. "Chin Suk is an old friend of my family. He approached me because he knew I had met you, through investigating your father's death." I paused, to let that part sink in. "According to Uncle Chin—at least, that's what I call him—your father was born to a woman he'd had an affair with. He left the town before your father was born and made his way to Hawai'i. He was a young man and the fact that he'd left a child behind didn't much matter to him. As he got older, though, his attitude changed. He had a son here who died, and that's when he tracked your father down and brought him and your family here."

"Why didn't he get in touch with me sooner? Why wait so long?"

"I believe he was actually in contact with your father, at least occasionally. Your mother may be able to verify that, but maybe not. Now that your father is dead, Uncle Chin would like to continue the relationship with you."

"And you're the matchmaker?" he asked.

I nodded. "Like I said, he's an old friend of my family, probably my father's best friend. He was embarrassed to come see you himself."

"He ought to be." Derek thought for a minute. "This old man, is he rich? Powerful?"

"I haven't seen his bankbook. But he seems to live well."

"Other children?"

"None."

He stroked his chin. "So I might stand to inherit something."

I stood up. "I can see I read you wrong. I thought maybe the loss of your father might motivate you to seek a connection with somebody else, with your grandfather. Uncle Chin is a good man, and I don't want to see him hurt."

"Hold on, hold on," Derek said petulantly. "How can you deny an old man's wish to know his grandson? We Chinese value family highly, you know. Why don't you give me his phone number and I'll give him a call?"

I thought that was probably the first time Derek Pang had used "we" and "Chinese" in the same sentence. "I'll tell him about our meeting and he can decide if he wants to contact you," I said.

"Anyway, you know his name. You've met him before. If you really want to talk to him, you can track him down."

I turned and walked out, bumping right into Wayne Gallagher in the reception area. His hand immediately reached for my crotch, and I felt myself stiffen in his grasp. "I know what you like," Wayne whispered into my ear.

I smiled at him and managed to pull away. "See you soon, Detective," he called as I walked back toward the front door.

As I walked back to my apartment, I wondered what I'd expected. I'd already decided Derek was a shit and that he might have murdered Evan Gonsalves; why did I think he'd react differently to news of Uncle Chin?

By the time I got home it was almost four, and I decided to go surfing for a while. After all, I might as well take advantage of this enforced leisure time with pay. After my suspension hearing, I might be just another washed-up cop looking for security work. Maybe I'd stop by the Rod and Reel and see Gunter, see if they needed extra guards at the condo where he worked. There might be fringe benefits, if we worked the same shift.

It was overcast and blustery, but still warm. The palm trees along Kalākaua Avenue bent in the wind, and thick clouds clustered over the tops of the rocky Koʻolau Mountains. A piece of newspaper rolled over and over down the brick pavement, past the games tables, where two elderly Chinese men huddled over a game of chess. The beach was sparsely populated, just the occasional tourist on a hotel towel, struggling to get a tan before going back to the mainland.

I took my board with me and dragged it out into the surf past the orange lifeguard station, where flags were posted warning against the heavy wind. The surf was cresting at four to six feet, high for Waikīkī, and I plunged into the water with enthusiasm. At least, I thought, as I ducked and paddled my way through the breakers to get outside, I was getting some good surfing in, at the north shore, at Makapuʻu Point, and now here.

I forgot everything that waited for me back on shore and concentrated on the waves, and it was, as always, a magnificent release. Every time I thought of Wayne Gallagher's hand on my butt, or Derek's greediness, or all the dead or the living people I'd hurt, I willed myself into focusing on the surf.

The rough water gave me a beating, wiping me out over and over, but the struggle was exhilarating. By the time I was finished I ached in a dozen places, but they were good aches, the result of pushing myself to my limits. I finally gave up and dragged my board through the surf and up over the sand. As I was waiting for the light to change so I could cross Kalākaua, I looked ewa and saw Akoni coming toward me.

"Hey, brah," I said as he approached. "Am I allowed to talk to you in public?"

"It's okay. I'm on a mission from Yumuri. You free for happy hour?"

"Give me a chance to shower and change," I said. "What's up?"

"I'll tell you at the Canoe Club, all right?"

"Sure." He turned back to the station and I crossed Kalākaua. I wondered what was up but couldn't figure it out. I took a quick shower and pulled on a pair of jeans and a polo shirt, and walked over to the Canoe Club, where I found Akoni at the bar, sipping slowly on a draft beer.

I stepped up next to him, ordered a draft for myself, and said, "So what's up?"

He nodded toward the outdoor patio. "We'll get a table."

"Not at happy hour," I said, as the bartender slid my beer across the bar and I dropped a couple of singles on the wood. "Look around."

Inside the bar was crowded, but outside you could hardly move. We struggled through the crowd on the porch and went down the stairs to the beach level. Businessmen in aloha shirts talked in small clusters, some smoking cigarettes, a few with fat cigars. Yuppies in polo shirts cracked wise with each other and made eyes at their female counterparts, sizing up opportunities for later in the evening. Small clusters of office friends sat at the tables comparing war stories or gossiping about absent co-workers.

Akoni led the way down toward the beach, and the farther we got from the lights and music, the less crowded it was. Finally we found a sheltered spot and pulled two lounge chairs together. "So what gives?" I asked as we sat down.

"We had a meeting today," he said. "Preliminary for your hearing. Me, Yumuri, Hiram Lin, and your girlfriend from the DA's office."

"I'm not sure she's exactly my girlfriend anymore."

"We went over every line in the file on Tommy Pang's murder and Evan Gonsalves's suicide." Akoni smiled at me. "They didn't find a single thing wrong beyond your first mistake."

"Not calling the body in under my shield number?"

He nodded. "And even Yumuri had to concede that wasn't a big deal."

"So?"

"So the ADA wouldn't accept it. She kept saying there had to be something else in the file we could hang you on."

"I haven't treated her very well," I said. "I should have called her from the very start and told her what was going on. But I wasn't sure myself for a long time."

"I wouldn't be surprised if she was the one who called the media on you. Just something she said. She mixed it up pretty good with old Hiram, too. I was surprised to see the guy had a backbone. He told her it was his mission to root out bad cops. You believe that, his mission? But he also said it was his mission to protect the good ones. And as far as he could see, you were a good one."

I nodded. "Nice of him."

"You bet. Even Yumuri had to admit we'd done everything by the book, and that the worst he could see doing was placing a mark on your sheet."

"So the hearing's off? I've got my job back?"

Akoni looked down at his glass of beer, which was almost empty. "There's still the gay thing." He looked back up at me. "Yumuri doesn't want you back. He wants you to resign and then you can avoid all the scandal of the hearing. Your record will be clean. You can get a job somewhere else, maybe even join a force on the mainland."

"But you just said they had no grounds to dismiss me. Why should I resign?"

He looked sheepish. "Actually I wasn't supposed to tell you they didn't have grounds," he said. "Yumuri wanted me to come out here, as your friend, and give you some kind of snow job, get you to back off before the hearing. I couldn't do that."

"You just can't keep your ass out of the wringer. They give you a simple job and you screw it up." I smiled. "I appreciate it, brah. But I couldn't quit, even if I knew they had real grounds against me."

He drained the last of his beer. "I ought to get going. Mealoha will be waiting dinner for me." He stood up and put his arm on my shoulder, and I remembered when he'd flinched away from me when he first found out I was gay. I was making progress, I thought. Slowly, one person at a time, but it was progress nonetheless. "Take care, Kimo. Watch out for yourself."

"I will," I said. "And give Mealoha a kiss from me."

He grinned. "I can do that."

After he walked away I stayed in the chair for a while, holding my empty beer glass. I wanted a waitress to come by and get me a refill, because I didn't have the energy to go up to the bar myself. I wasn't sure I could even get up from the chair. All my fatigue kicked in as I thought about what Akoni had said. They had no professional grounds to fire me. They just didn't want me around anymore.

It was a hard realization. Guys I'd thought of like brothers, men, like Yumuri, that I had respected, had made a decision about me based on one fact, and that had turned them against me. I could be the best detective ever, I could outperform anybody on physical tasks and written tests, and they still didn't want me on the force with them.

Darkness fell around me, and the noise of the bar diminished in the background. I leaned back in the chair and looked up at the stars. It was hard to see much right above me, because I was too close to the bright lights of Waikīkī, but out over the ocean I could see stars and patches of clouds. The wind was still strong, though I was sheltered in a grove of trees and didn't feel its effect much. But the clouds moved fast across the sky, covering and then revealing the stars, and I wondered which one would grant my wish, and what that wish should be.

Chapter 40

I WOKE EARLY Friday morning in a fit of nerves, startled out of a dream involving Wayne Gallagher. It began when I was surfing on Waikīkī, holding Danny Gonsalves above my head as my board knifed the water. On the beach, Terri was crying, and Tico Robles there comforting her, promising I would never hurt her son.

Then I was back in my room at my parents' house, making love to Wayne on my narrow twin bed, when my father came into the room. He was disappointed, he said, because he and Uncle Chin were lovers and he wanted me to have picked Derek over Wayne. That's when I woke up.

I looked for the newspaper but it hadn't arrived yet, so I began cleaning my apartment, putting away books, organizing the laundry. I didn't want to think about my hearing, and what I would say. I was entitled to have a lawyer present, but I'd made no moves toward hiring one. I thought idly of asking Tim Ryan to defend me, but I knew that was a bad idea.

Finally I heard the thunk of the paper on the concrete outside, and I brought it in and read it sitting up in bed. I made myself chocolate chip pancakes for breakfast, with coconut macadamia syrup, and then cleaned up all the dishes and pans. I was trying to figure out what to do next when the phone rang.

"Good morning, Kimo," my father said. "I hope I didn't wake you."

"I've been up for hours."

"I remember when you were a boy, you could sleep until noon.

I used to tell your brothers to drag you out of bed, and one would take one leg and the other the other leg." He laughed. "You'd hold onto the sheets, and everything would end up a big mess."

"I remember," I said dryly. "What's up?"

"Did you get a chance to speak to Chin's grandson?"

"I did." I told him about my meeting with Derek the day before. "He acted like a jerk. I don't want to see Uncle Chin get hurt."

"Chin is a grown man. He can take care of himself. Come here for lunch today, and you can tell him."

"I've got a lot to do," I said, even though I couldn't think of one thing I had to do before I showed up at the Boardwalk as a decoy.

"No matter. You'll make the time. Be here noon."

I was annoyed. Usually he lets my mother make such calls, relies on her strength to enforce what he wants. Couldn't they keep their roles straight? "All right."

At least then I only had to kill the morning. I kept walking around my tiny apartment wondering what I could do, and then caught a glimpse of myself in the mirror. I could use a haircut, I thought, so I called Tico Robles, and he said he could squeeze me in if I could get to his salon in half an hour.

The first strip shopping center my father built was on Wai'alae Avenue, at the base of St. Louis Heights, not far from our house. Though he's had many offers to sell it over the years, he has held on to it for what I consider purely sentimental reasons, though I have to admit it's always fully leased and the parking lot there is usually jammed. About three years ago Tatiana, unbeknownst to Haoa, bankrolled Tico in a salon of his own, out of money her parents had left her. She convinced my father to rent him a small space in the Wai'alae Avenue center, at a bargain rate, and he prospered.

The center was so busy that I had to park my truck on a side street and then walk almost the full length of it to the salon, passing a dry cleaner, video rental store, lawyer's office, real estate agency, pack-and-ship place, and greeting card store before I got to Tico's salon, Puerto Peinado. They'd huddled over the name for weeks, finally coming up with a tribute to Tico's homeland of Puerto Rico and the Spanish word for hairdo. They'd hired a young artist Tico was dating to paint tropical murals in bright colors on the walls, exotic visions of a Puerto Rico that looked suspiciously like Oahu, and when I walked in fast Latin music was playing and Tico was doing a merengue with an elderly Chinese woman.

He looked totally recovered, except for a slight bruise on his forehead just below the hairline, almost completely covered by a swoop of brown hair I suspected he had gelled in place. "Kimo! Sweetheart!" he said when I walked in. He dipped the old lady, then expertly swung her into a chair and plopped the old-fashioned hair dryer down over her head. He tripped lightly across the salon floor and gave me a big hug. "I'm so glad you came in! I've been dying to see what I could do with your hair since you came to see me in the hospital."

He ushered me to a chair in front of a basin at the back of the salon, talking the whole time. "Now wasn't that a dismal place?" he said. "I mean, really, who decorates those places? They should be shot! I was so eager to get out of there."

"Maybe that's why they decorate them that way," I said, as he swirled a plastic cape around my shoulders. "So you'll want to get well and leave quickly."

"Lean back," he commanded. He washed my hair quickly and expertly, leaving it smelling faintly of coconut and strawberries, and then led me to his chair, in the front window of the salon. "Now I will work my magic," he said. He leaned down and whispered in my ear, "When I'm finished with you, the boys will fall all over you!"

"Just one boy in particular," I said, thinking of Wayne Gallagher.

"Oh, Kimo has a boyfriend," he said as he started to cut. "Dish, baby. Tell Uncle Tico all about him."

"Not a boyfriend, a suspect. Although he *is* cute, even though I know he's bad all the way through."

"Oh, they're the worst," he said. "My weakness. I love a bad boy."

In the mirror I saw him shake his head. "Except eventually they end up being bad to you. But while it works, it can be so wonderful!"

We went on to talk about Tatiana and Haoa and their children. "They're angels," Tico said. "Every last one of them. Angels from heaven. They all take after Tatiana. You know that."

"I thought you weren't mad at my brother anymore."

"Oh, I forgave him. Do you know, yesterday he came to my house and planted a whole row of hibiscus bushes, just for nothing? I tried to thank him and all he said was, 'You needed a hedge out front to shelter the yard.' I mean, do you believe it? He just can't say he's sorry, but he means it."

"Tell me about it. What he did to you last week, he did to me for at least ten years, until I got big enough to fight back. He and Lui would just whale on me whenever they thought they could get away with it. Even when our parents caught them red-handed, they didn't care. They'd take their punishment, and start right in on me again."

"Poor baby."

"Sometimes I don't understand why I love them so much."

"Your family will always be with you," Tico said. "When you have no one else to turn to, you can always go to them."

I nodded, and he pulled my head back up straight. "I saw that this week, for sure."

He worked for a while longer, then styled and combed and moussed, and by the time he was done even I was surprised at how handsome I was. I've never been that vain about my looks—I figure it's all genetics. I was lucky to get the best features my Irish, Hawai'ian, and Japanese ancestors had, and to have them put together in a way that people found attractive. I keep up my body and I stand up straight, and I don't worry about the rest. But what Tico had done had pulled something out of me I'd never thought I had.

"If I were twenty years younger," Tico said, "you'd have to beat me off with a stick."

"I might still have to. You're not ready for Social Security yet."

Tico laughed. "The man I see is fifty-one. Two years younger than I am. On Saturday nights we go out to the clubs to watch, not to dance. By midnight we're yawning and we go home and go to bed." He grinned. "Though not right to sleep."

I tried to pay for the haircut but he wouldn't let me. "Lock up a bad guy for me," he said. "Then I'll consider us even."

From Tico's I drove up to my parents' house, feeling stronger and readier for action than I had in weeks. When my mother saw my truck pull up in the driveway behind Uncle Chin's Cadillac, she came out to greet me. "*Ai ya!*" she said. "My handsome son! You got a new haircut."

"Yeah, looks good," I said, leaning down to kiss her.

"You make me feel like such a frumpy old lady. My handsome husband, my beautiful sons, and me."

"You'll always be the most beautiful woman in the world to me." I nodded toward my father, who stood in the doorway. "And I know someone else who thinks so."

She blushed. "You boys. How did I raise such boys as you? Come on inside; lunch is almost ready."

My father led me back to the porch, where Uncle Chin and Aunt Mei-Mei sat drinking iced tea, and we made small talk while my mother put the finishing touches on plate lunches, the kind of food her mother had prepared for her father as he worked in the fields. Tender, spicy teriyaki steak and two scoops of rice, and fruit salad with fresh pineapple, mango, papaya, and melon.

At the table we talked lightly, about the project my father was bidding on, a Chinese wedding the Chins had attended the night before, my mother's orchids. "And tonight all my grandchildren come for barbecue," my mother said proudly. "*Ai ya,* all afternoon I have to cook. Each one likes something different, and each one wants his favorite. Tūtū Lokelani, why you no make those sweet potatoes I like? You don't love me anymore? Tūtū Lokelani, you no make mango bread for me? Your mango bread so ono." She shook her head. "It's easier to do the cooking than listen to them complain!"

Uncle Chin and Aunt Mei-Mei nodded in agreement, and I felt sad for them that they had no children of their own, no grandchildren, and all they could have now would be Derek Pang, who would certainly not bring little children of his own into the world. Aunt Mei-Mei helped my mother clear the table, and then they retreated into the kitchen to clean up and cook for dinner.

"Your father tells me you met with my grandson," Uncle Chin said, sitting back in his chair.

I nodded. "I'm sorry to have to say he's not a very nice person. Not really a proper grandson for such a kind grandfather as you."

Uncle Chin smiled. "Many people Chinatown tell you I not so nice, either," he said. "Say apple not fall far from tree."

I said, "You know his name is Derek, and he's twenty-five years old. He and his"—here I hesitated, not sure what term to use—"partner are running the Rod and Reel Club now. I told him about you, and he remembered meeting you, but his father never told him your relationship. He said he's willing to meet with you."

Uncle Chin smiled, and I could see the relief in his face. Derek Pang didn't deserve him as a grandfather. But then again, Derek hadn't gotten much fathering from Tommy, and maybe Uncle Chin might be a good influence on him. And, I had to admit, Uncle Chin was probably a much worse criminal than I knew, and maybe their joint malfeasance would be a place of intersection for them. Derek might end up with a record longer than his father's or his grandfather's.

I passed on Derek's phone number. "Too soon I call him tonight?" Uncle Chin asked. "Give him more time think, maybe?"

The wheels clicked in my brain. Putting Uncle Chin and Derek together tonight would leave Wayne free to meet me at the Boardwalk. "Tonight would be good," I said.

"Everybody's busy tonight," my father said. "You, and Lui, and Haoa are together tonight, aren't you?"

"What do you mean?"

He narrowed his eyes at me. "Liliha and Tatiana are coming here with their kids tonight because Haoa and Lui are having a boys' night out. It must involve you, too."

I didn't say anything. "I want to come with you," my father said. "I know you're all up to something. They're going to help you get your job back, aren't they?"

The last thing I wanted was my father in Haoa's van listening to me and Wayne making out as I tried to get him to confess. "Not at all. We're going out for a few drinks, that's all. Just to make things better between us."

"I could come too. Make sure you don't end up in jail again."

"You have to be here, ready to bail us out." I paused. "Don't worry. I'll keep them in line. You stay here with your grandchildren. Imagine how they would complain if Tūtū Al weren't here."

He wasn't happy, but I had no intention of telling him what we were up to, and I hoped my brothers had as much sense. It was almost three by then, so I begged off and drove back down to Waikīkī, where I went through my wardrobe looking for something to wear. I'm no fool; I know what looks good on me. Pale colors like pink, light blue, and yellow go well with my coloring. I have a narrow waist and broad shoulders, so I like to wear tightly fitted shirts that show off my physique. But nothing I took out of the closet seemed to work. Everything was too baggy, or too faded, or just didn't feel right. My wardrobe needed a major makeover.

So I walked down to the Clark's on Kalākaua Avenue. I tried on a dozen different shirts, finally settling on a pink oxford-cloth button-down that made me look younger and preppier. It was a size too small, and with the top three buttons down and my chest threatening to burst through, it even looked a little sexy. I picked up a pair of white painter's pants that fit snugly, particularly across the crotch, and yet had plenty of pockets in case I wanted to carry anything. I stood in front of the mirror, closed my eyes, and thought about Wayne Gallagher.

It didn't take much for my penis to swell up, and I looked at it in profile, easily outlined against my thigh. That'll do, I thought, though it made me nervous to think how easily I could get excited by a guy who had bad news written all over him. I charged it all on my Clark's revolving charge, and took the shopping bag with me as I walked back out to Kalākaua Avenue, where I nearly ran into Jimmy Ah Wong.

"Detective!" he said, surprised. He looked the same—the coxcomb of bright yellow hair, Smashing Pumpkins T-shirt, and flip-flops.

"Hi, Jimmy. How's it going?"

He nodded. "It's okay." He motioned with his head, off to a more secluded spot away from the street. Though it was bright and sunny, back under the trees on this little plaza it was cooler and shady. We sat down on a concrete bench. "I took your advice. I went to the gay teen center today."

"Good. How'd it go?"

"I liked it. The people there were pretty cool." Then he looked down at the ground and spoke softly. "He came back to the store on Wednesday," he said. "Wayne. He knew I would be there by myself. I told him I didn't want to do anything with him anymore, but then he got down on his knees and he—he sucked me, and it felt so good, I didn't know what to do. I knew I needed help, so I came here."

"Good for you. Don't worry about Wayne. I'm going to take care of him."

"I don't know what you can do." He looked up at me and there were tears in his eyes. "I think I might be in love with him."

I put my arm around him. "I know it's hard at your age," I said, "but try to be careful not to confuse love with lust. Just because you want to be with somebody, because you want to have sex with him, doesn't mean you're in love with him." I pulled back and looked at him. "Can I tell you a secret?"

He nodded. "I think he's pretty sexy myself. I mean, I haven't done anything with him, but I'm not sure I could resist." I pulled a tissue out of my pocket and wiped his eyes. "So don't feel bad about the way you feel, okay?"

"I'll try. Will you let me know if you ever arrest him?"

"You'll hear," I said. "Oh, yeah, you'll hear."

Chapter 41

I GAVE JIMMY AH WONG my home phone number and cell number, and told him to call me if he ran into any trouble with Wayne, or if he just wanted to talk. Heading down Kalākaua, I saw Officer Saunders approaching me with a big grin on his face.

"Well, well, well, if it isn't ex-Detective Dicksucker," he said.

"What's your problem, Saunders?" He was wearing street clothes, and I guessed he was heading to the station for the start of his shift. "I ever do anything to you?"

"Guess I just don't like faggots on the force." He leaned in close to me. "I'm glad they booted your ass out. I hope you end up running security for some shopping mall, a rent-a-cop with a little go-cart. Then you can pull your carpet-muncher buddies over for a quickie in somebody's back seat, out in the mall parking lot."

"You've given this a lot of thought," I said. "Sounds like you're the one with the problem. You having wet dreams about guys sucking your cock?"

"You asshole. You pervert that badge you used to wear."

"You're not on duty yet, are you, Saunders?"

"I was on second watch. I got off duty at three fifteen."

"Good." I punched him in the eye, knowing I could blacken it easily. "Then you can't say I assaulted a police officer," I added, as he went reeling backward. "Unless of course you want to cry about the fairy who gave you the black eye."

My hand started to throb, but I didn't care. I brushed past

Saunders and headed for home. "You haven't heard the last of this, faggot!" he called after me.

I smiled all the way home, despite the pain in my hand, imagining the excuses he would come up with for sporting a shiner. He was more flab than muscle and more bark than bite, and everybody knew it. His tiny Chinese wife was really the one who wore the pants in the family. I figured there'd be a lot of snickering at the station, guys asking if his wife had given him the black eye. Good. He'd been talking stink about me; now he'd be the butt of fun.

I decided to change into my new clothes before going over to Harry's to help set up the equipment. I stripped down to my Gap boxers, printed with tropical fish, then poured myself into the too-tight pants and shirt. When I was finished, I admired the results in the mirror.

It didn't look like me, not the me I usually was. It was like I was getting into costume, preparing for a performance. I combed my hair one last time, and left.

When I got to Harry's parking lot, Haoa's van was nowhere in sight. So I walked across the street to the Ala Wai Canal and sat on the stone wall at the water's edge. From there I could look down toward Diamond Head, looming in the distance, or straight ahead to the Ko'olau Mountains, where the spill of suburbia trailed down its sides.

Clouds were starting to mass over the mountains, and though the sun was behind me it got cooler due to the wind. Traffic buzzed steadily on Ala Wai Boulevard behind me, as I sat there staring at the placid water. The occasional jogger or walker went by, but I hardly noticed them, thinking about what lay ahead.

Based on the note Evan Gonsalves had left for Terri, I was pretty sure that Evan hadn't killed Tommy Pang. That left only Wayne. He wanted to manage the club and he wanted to stay with Derek, and I was sure Tommy wouldn't have liked that.

I was pretty sure that Derek and Wayne had been at Evan's

house, and that it was because of them that he was dead. I just didn't know why.

A black bird landed next to me, pecked at the ground, and flew away. Then I understood. Suppose Wayne had killed Tommy, and somehow Evan had witnessed it? Evan could have been blackmailing Wayne, threatening to tell Derek what had happened.

That would explain the cryptic message Evan had left, that he had one more thing to do before he could go back to being legit. Wayne was probably making a lot of money from the sale of those Hawai'ian artifacts, money Evan thought could pay for his future with Terri.

I wasn't sure how I could get Wayne Gallagher to admit it, though. I hoped that I could get him talking, into a bragging mood, and let nature take its course. I was in a good position for that. As far as Wayne was concerned, he had won, and I'd lost my job, and he had every reason to gloat.

The tougher question was what I'd do if he came on to me. How would I react? It was like he emitted some kind of pheromone that was irresistible to me—a combination of sex and danger, a physical and mental presence that drew me in. I had to remember I wasn't there for fun, that I was playing a part and I had to stay in character. But I knew from my brief experiences with Tim and Gunter that I was hungry for that physical contact, and that it would be a struggle to hold back.

I heard a couple of quick beeps behind me and got up. I saw Haoa's green landscaping van pulling into Harry's parking lot and crossed the street. Haoa straddled two guest parking spaces. As I walked up, Lui was sliding open the side doors to reveal Harry sitting among a jumble of boxes and cables. "Hey, guys," I said.

"We've got our work cut out for us," Harry said from inside the van, as he stood up. "You guys are all going to have to pitch in."

We spent the next couple of hours, as night fell around us, unpacking boxes, connecting cables, and hooking up receivers. By eight o'clock we were running tests, and I was running scared. I pulled off my shirt so that Harry could start taping me up, and saw that my skin was covered with goose bumps.

I'd been through situations like this before, most recently that drug bust in Kapiolani Park that now seemed a lifetime away. I remembered that was the night I'd gone to the Rod and Reel, the night that Tommy Pang had been murdered and my life had started falling apart.

"Hold still," Harry said. "Every time I touch you, you jump a foot."

Before, though, the danger had never seemed so great. It was easy to ignore the possibility I might get killed—the brain loves to shelve that kind of stuff in the back, some primitive form of self-preservation. Besides, in a standard stakeout I'm walking in armed, or at least with a half-dozen armed officers behind me. If anything goes wrong, they're there for me.

In a normal stakeout, you want to make your case and put the bad guy away, but if it doesn't work, if he won't talk or he makes your wire, you can go back to your desk the next day and get on with your life. If I didn't get a confession out of Wayne Gallagher, I didn't know where I was going.

Or, actually, I did. I was going to my disciplinary hearing, and then most likely, despite the fact that Yumuri had no case, I was going off the force. I might be able to hold onto my badge for a while, but I'd probably lose my detective shield and end up on patrol somewhere like Pearl City, living with snickers in the locker room and dying inside.

Harry taped the wire to my chest and back. "Jesus, Harry, you can hardly touch me without feeling a wire," I said. "Can't you make it a little more discreet?"

"Just keep your shirt on."

"Easier said than done." I pulled him close so that my brothers wouldn't have to hear. "You know, he might want to feel me up. As soon as he goes for a tit, he's going to feel a wire. End of story."

He re-routed the wire so that it was taped to my shirt, running up my back and around my collar. It was so thin that if Wayne casually ran his hand over my back, he might think it was an imperfection in the fabric. "Excellent," I said, when he was done.

He stuck the transmitter in the back of my pants. "Jesus, these pants are tight," he said. "I can barely get a wire out of them."

"That's the idea. They show off the merchandise."

"I don't want to get into this," he said. Sitting at a makeshift table inside the van, my brothers snickered.

"No comments from the peanut gallery," I said. Harry took the wire off to play with the acoustics some more, and I went out and got us a couple of pizzas and some half-gallon sodas, though I was ready for a few quick beers by then.

We locked up the van and went upstairs to Harry's apartment to eat. "Okay, I've got a couple of things I want to tell you about tonight," I said as we sat around the kitchen table. "First of all, remember I'm working. A deal like this is kind of like a play, one of those improvisational things where the audience throws out suggestions and the actors have to bounce off them. In this case, I'm the actor and Wayne Gallagher's going to throw me lines. I've got to react."

I took a bite of my pizza and chewed. "So you have to remember this isn't necessarily real. I may have to do some things that will surprise you or bother you, but you've got to remember I'm doing it all for a purpose."

"I think we're all grown-ups," Haoa said. He picked up his glass of soda and took a drink.

"So if I have to suck his dick, you won't flip out," I said, and he spewed out the last of his soda, just as I'd expected.

"You don't have to do that," Lui said.

"I might. If that'll get him to spill the beans, then I will. I'm sure we've all said a few things we didn't mean in the heat of passion."

" 'I love you' for one," Harry said, and we all laughed.

"And he may get a little rough," I said. "He's got a mean mouth on him, and he's called me some names before. You can't react to anything."

"Have you been with this guy before?" Haoa asked.

"He's come on to me," I said. "A couple of times. Once in his apartment and once at his office. I pushed him away both times. But I know how he operates, and I can make it seem like I was just playing hard to get."

"This is a crazy deal," Haoa said, shaking his head.

"One more thing. Remember, I'm the professional. I don't want any cowboy heroics. If I get into trouble, count on me to get out of it. If I'm going to end up in a jail cell, or in the morgue, for that matter, I don't want any of you next to me."

"There is no way we're going to let anything happen to you without doing something about it," Lui said. "You might as well accept that. That's our function tonight—to look out for you."

"No, it's not. Your job is to run the equipment and make sure we get the evidence. Don't do anything that will keep us from frying his ass in court. Even if I can't testify, for whatever reason, if you have the tapes we can still put him away."

"I don't like that," Haoa said.

"I don't either. But that's the way it has to be, or we can't do this." I looked at each of them in turn. "Are we all agreed?" One by one, they nodded. "Good. Then let's finish eating and get out of here."

It was almost ten by the time we pulled up at the Boardwalk. I did a quick scan of the parking lot and didn't see either Wayne's or Derek's car. I said, "Okay, I'm going in." The problem with our setup was that I didn't have any way to know if they'd heard me or not, but even before my haircut my hair had been short enough that my ears were fully exposed and I couldn't have a receiver there without being obvious.

By the time I reached the door of the bar, my stomach was turned upside down and my hands were shaking. *It's just a bar,* I repeated to myself. *It's just a bar. Just go inside and get something to drink, and wait for Wayne to show up.* I came through the door, and just at the last minute remembered the sandbox and stepped over it. I felt an unexpectedly large sense of relief. I'd met the first obstacle and conquered it.

Alanis Morissette was pouring out of speakers mounted around the room, but the volume wasn't too loud. The bar was pretty busy, small groups of guys standing around talking or playing pool or watching the boyish model in his jockstrap slink down the runway. I stepped up to an empty place at the bar just as the model was approaching. He turned his back to me and bent down, sticking his ass in my face.

"I think he wants a tip," the guy next to me said and laughed.

"A tip or a kiss," I said. I hoped I could pull money out of my wallet without dropping it or showing how badly my hands were shaking.

The guy next to me laughed. "You can kiss him—I'll tip him." He rolled up a dollar bill and pulled aside the strap that ran down the model's butt crack, stuck the bill right into his hole, and put the strap back. The model straightened up and did a little curvy dance, then pulled the bill out of his butt and stuck it in his mouth. He made a lewd sucking gesture and smiled at me and the guy, then moved off down the bar.

The bartender came up and I ordered a Coke. I desperately wanted a beer, but I knew I needed all my faculties for dealing with Wayne.

"My name's Jerry," the guy next to me said. He was about forty, thin but not particularly in shape, and nobody must have told him that his mustache was too thin and wispy to look good.

"I'm Kimo," I said and gave him my hand.

"You come here often?"

I shook my head. "Friend recommended it. I might meet him here later tonight."

He nodded. "I wouldn't kick his butt out of bed for eating

crackers," he said, moving his head in the direction of the model, who was now grinding his hips in front of a couple of guys down the bar from us.

"Too much of a twink for me. Though you gotta admire those butt muscles."

We talked, on and off, for the next half hour or so. I tried not to drink my Coke too fast and kept scanning the room for Wayne Gallagher. Finally Jerry got the hint and moved on. I got another Coke and decided to scout the room, to find the quietest corner. I made eye contact a couple of times with guys but then looked away. I was only on the prowl for one guy and I didn't want any complications.

I had to say I liked the men at the Rod and Reel better. They were handsomer, better dressed, and, on the whole, younger. This place seemed to attract a slightly older crowd, though there was a contingent of Chinese, Japanese, and Thai boys who looked barely old enough to drink. That's why Wayne came here, I remembered. The bartender had said he had a taste for Asian boys. I wondered if he'd dump Derek as he aged, keep looking for the boys who attracted him.

I was glad my tastes ran to the more mature, at least. I had no interest in Jimmy Ah Wong or any of his counterparts at the Boardwalk. I liked guys my own age and hoped that would stay the same as I got older. I ended up along a side wall, watching a pool game. The players were good, a Japanese guy in his forties in tight leathers and an Anglo guy in his late twenties in tight jeans and an even tighter black T-shirt.

"You could bounce an egg on that butt," a guy next to me said to his friend as the Anglo leaned in front of us to make a shot.

"That's not all I'd do with it," his friend said.

I smiled and wondered if the boys in the van could pick that one up. I drained the last of my Coke and looked at my watch. It was eleven thirty. I wondered how late Wayne could get away from Derek. Did he have to wait until Derek was asleep? Could he just walk out?

My tension evaporated as I got more comfortable in the bar. My hands weren't shaking anymore, and I'd stopped seeing the guys around me as threats. But my adrenaline was running out, and I was getting tired. The music was on a loop, and I was getting sick of hearing Joan Osborne over and over again.

I decided I'd get one last Coke. I walked over to the back bar, where they were showing the porno videos, and waited until I could catch the bartender's attention. It took a long time, and I was almost ready to pack it in, but I got into watching the video. By the time he brought me my soda, I was sure my hard-on was a beacon visible to anybody who looked, so I slunk over to a dark corner to lean against the wall.

Then I looked toward the door and saw Wayne Gallagher walk in.

Showtime.

Chapter 42

WAYNE GALLAGHER MOVED easily through the crowd toward me, and I was glad I'd decided to wait. He walked right up to me and kissed me, putting his right hand on my butt and grinding his thigh into my hard-on. I felt like I was melting and had to struggle to stand up. He stepped back. "Want a beer?"

"Sure." He went to the back bar and the bartender came over to him immediately. "I don't know if you picked it up," I said, speaking down into my chest, "But Gallagher's in the bar now."

He came back a minute later carrying two beers. I took one and led the way toward a table in a far corner, where I knew the acoustics were good. I hoped he'd be following me.

He did. I sat down and moved the other chair so it was right next to mine, and patted the seat. He sat and immediately stuck his tongue in my ear.

It was like he could read my mind, knew exactly what to do to make me feel like jelly. I had to do whatever I could to retain control. "So where's Derek tonight?"

Wayne sat back in his chair. "Home whining. He met this guy who claims to be his grandfather, and he asked the guy for money and the guy said no. So Derek pulled a hissy fit. But you know," he said, stroking my thigh, "he and I have a very open relationship. He knows I like a little variety in my diet and he doesn't mind."

"Mmm-hmm." I felt the touch of his fingertips on the sensitive inside of my thigh and it was all I could do to keep from squirming. "I know he was pretty broken up when his father died."

"Yeah, Tommy was good to him. But I'm not sorry he got whacked. There was no way he was ever going to make me the manager of the bar."

"But still, it was a point of honor for him, having to do something about the guy who killed his dad."

Wayne gave me a look, and I could see I'd gone too far too fast. "So it was a good thing the guy committed suicide," I said. "Must have made it easier on Derek."

"I don't want to talk about Derek." Wayne's hand crept up to my crotch, where I could feel its warmth against my erection. "Let's talk about you. What do you like?"

"Oh, I like surfing," I said. "And I swim a lot. Read when I can—I like mystery novels. Cooking. I like to barbecue, and help out when we have family luaus." I could sense I was babbling, but didn't know how to stop.

"Not that stuff, silly." Wayne took the hand that had been on my crotch and ran it up my chest slowly. "I mean, what do you like? Are you a top or a bottom? I'll bet you like to get it up the ass, don't you?"

My throat was dry, and I could feel the sweat dripping down my back, even though the bar wasn't hot. I picked up my beer, and my hand shook so much that I spilled a little on the table. "You're so tense," Wayne said. "I know how to relax you."

"Maybe we should just talk for a few minutes. I am kind of nervous."

"We can talk." Wayne pulled his hands back and took a drink of his beer. "How long were you a cop?"

"I was a patrolman for five years and got my detective shield two years ago. I've been stationed in Waikīkī since then."

"So you used to wear a uniform?"

"I still have it. You know, sometimes you have to wear it to department things."

"I like a man in uniform. Maybe you can wear it for me sometime."

"We'll see," I said, and I looked him straight in the eye. He stared back at me, and then licked his lips. I was the one who had to look away.

When I did, I saw Harry Ho come in the door of the bar. *Shit,* I thought. *I told them all to stay in the truck.* He looked directly at me and nodded toward the back of the bar, where the rest rooms were, and I caught on. "I've got to go to the little boys' room," I said, pushing my chair back. "I'll be back in a minute."

"I can go with you. Give you a helping hand."

"You'll get yours," I said, smiling. For good measure, I leaned over and licked around the outside of his ear. "I promise," I whispered. He shivered a little, and I thought, *Good, two can play at this game.*

Harry was just in front of me as we walked into the men's room. Two guys were primping and gossiping at the mirror, so Harry took my hand and led me into an open stall. It was tight in there, but I twisted around and closed the door. As I did, I caught a glimpse of the two queens in the mirror, nodding approvingly. "What's up?" I whispered.

"You stopped transmitting," he whispered back. "Turn around."

I turned and he fiddled with my shirt collar. "Jesus, you're dripping wet. No wonder it shorted." He pulled a long strip of toilet paper off the roll and wrapped it around the wire. It was a little more noticeable now, but he thought it would hold up better. "I won't know if it's working until I get back to the van," he said. "If you don't see me again, you'll know it's fine."

"This is hard, Harry."

"I noticed," he said dryly. "Those pants don't leave much to the imagination."

I couldn't help laughing, and that made me feel a little better. "I mean talking to him. He keeps, you know, fooling with me."

"That's what he thinks you're here for. As long as he keeps it up, and I do mean that both ways, that means he doesn't suspect anything."

"I'll keep that in mind." I gave him the Hawai'ian hand signal we call a shaka. "Wish me luck."

He gave it back to me. "You don't need luck. You know what you're doing. Just do it."

By the time I got back to the table, Wayne had a pair of fresh beers there for us. "You just want to get me drunk so you can have your way with me," I said.

"That thought did cross my mind," he said, smiling.

I wondered if I'd be doing this for real soon. Not with Wayne Gallagher, of course, but with somebody else. Would I be cruising these bars, looking for a little fun? Would I duplicate the same pattern I'd had with women, meeting and mating at random intervals, never able to settle down for a long-term relationship? Thinking of that turned out to be just the tonic I needed, relieving the aching hard-on in my pants and letting me steer the conversation back to safer subjects.

We talked for a while, through another set of beers, and I found myself seeing good things in Wayne besides the dangerous sexuality he oozed. He was smart and witty, knew a lot about books and art and music. I almost found myself hoping he was innocent, that it had been two other guys who'd forced Evan Gonsalves to eat his gun. Then I got over it.

By the third beer Wayne was a little boozy, and I assumed he'd had a few more earlier in the evening. It wasn't that his speech was slurred, but he lost track of sentences, was easily distracted, and was all over me even more. I finally said, "Wayne, we're in public here. Save a little for when we're alone."

He leered at me. "We can be alone right here. They have rooms in the back."

"I didn't know that. You mean like a hotel?"

He laughed. "Not quite so fancy." He stood up. "Come on, I'll show you."

We weren't getting anywhere—no matter how I tried to direct the conversation toward Tommy Pang and Evan Gonsalves, Wayne steered it right back to the meeting of our two bodies. Maybe in a more private place I could get him to boast more.

I followed him through the bar, past the rest rooms to what I'd thought was a fire door to the outside. Instead, it swung open onto a narrow corridor. "Gee, I thought this was an exit," I said. "I mean, being back here at the back of the bar, next to the bathrooms."

I hoped they heard that out in the truck. "It's kind of like a back door," Wayne said. He put his hand on my ass and said, "I like back doors."

"I've never done it like that. Is it fun?"

"Oh, baby, it's the best," he said. "I'll bet you have a tight little ass, too."

There were four small rooms on each side of the corridor. The doors to the first two on either side were closed, and in the third on the right a fat biker dude in leathers lay back on a narrow bed with his pants open and his dick out. The room across from his was open and empty. Wayne pulled me in there and closed the door.

"Alone at last," he murmured. He pulled me close and we kissed, and I was in big-time danger right then of dropping the whole plan, unhooking the wire and making love with Wayne Gallagher until we dropped from exhaustion. It was an effort to pull back.

"You're so sexy," I whispered to him. "So big and powerful. I'll bet you could do anything. You could make anybody do anything."

"You know I can." He chewed on my ear and ground his hard dick into my leg.

"You know how to take charge of a situation. Get things done," I said. "I've seen you with Derek. You're the real man in that relationship."

"Baby, I'm all man, and I'm gonna show you."

"You know what would make me really hot," I said, tonguing his ear. "Tell me how you made the cop do it. How did you get him to kill himself?"

I undid the buttons on his shirt and sucked first on one nipple, then the other. "Use your teeth, man," he said. "Make it hurt."

"Go on," I said, between tiny bites. "Tell me."

"Oh," he sighed. "It was that picture you showed Derek. The asshole had been blackmailing us, but we didn't know his name."

"Blackmailing you?"

"He must have seen Derek whack his old man with the police lock. He threatened to tell the cops."

Wayne giggled and hiccupped some beer. "Good thing you aren't a cop anymore."

"Oh, yeah." I licked a trail down through the blond hairs on his chest. He had a little bit of a belly, but I thought it was sexy. "Derek killed Tommy? I would have thought it was you. You're the big strong one."

He had his hands on my head, massaging it at the same time as he pushed me down toward his dick. "Tommy didn't know Derek and I were lovers until he came back unexpectedly and found us making out on the desk," he said. "He pulled out his gun."

I unzipped Wayne's pants and started feeling up his dick through his white jockey shorts. He squirmed and murmured and breathed heavy. "Go on," I said. "This is getting me so hot. What next?"

"Tommy was standing in the open doorway, pointing his gun right at me. Derek was freaking out. He got around behind Tommy, looking around for something he could use to hit him. He grabbed the police lock and Tommy went down, half in the office and half in the alley. He shifted around to release his hard-on. I remembered how Fred the bartender had compared it to a beer can. "The cop must have been hanging out in the alley and saw what happened."

I pulled his dick out of the slit in his jockeys. I didn't have much experience, but it seemed huge to me, fat and fleshy and uncircumcised. I licked the side of it and Wayne squirmed again. I had to admit I liked having him in my power. It was as if I could make him do anything I wanted. "So the cop tried to blackmail you?"

"We were supposed to give him fifty thousand dollars. But once Derek saw that picture, he realized he knew the guy's name. We went right out to his house after that."

I took his dick in my mouth, sucked it a little, then licked it again. When I looked up at Wayne his eyes were glazed and he was breathing heavy. I pulled off him long enough to say, "But Derek was defending you, wasn't he?"

I took my mouth off his prick and started licking the insides of his thighs. He shivered and I knew he was sweating. "We've been doing some other stuff," Wayne said. "We didn't want to have the police messing around."

He started moaning and squirming. "The guy was a prick," he said. "I got mad at him, and he mouthed off to me. He pulled a gun on us—you believe that?"

"What a jerk," I said.

"So I wrestled him for the gun, and I shot him. Derek blew up at me, called me all kinds of names. I smacked him hard and he calmed down. Then he decided we had to make it look like suicide."

He leaned over me as I sucked him, running his hands over my head and down my shoulders. Then I felt him touch the wire. "Hey!" he said. "What the hell is this?" He pulled back from me. "You fucker! You're wired up!"

He pulled the microphone out of my collar and tackled me. "You fucking asshole!" he said. "You think you can put one over on me!"

We wrestled back and forth, knocking against the walls of the narrow room. He got me down on the bed with his hands around my throat. I was kicking him and trying to get out from under him, but he had a big weight advantage on me. I felt my ability to struggle wane. It seemed easier somehow to just give up. In the distance, I heard somebody banging on doors, heard the sound of wood splintering, but it was all far away.

I think I was just about to black out when the door to the room burst open and suddenly I could breathe again. I looked up from the bed and saw Haoa and Wayne wrestling with each other. At least they were better matched for size than Wayne and I were. And I knew from hard experience my brother's self-defense skills. He got Wayne backed up against the wall.

Then I saw Wayne reach for his jacket pocket and I knew, instinctively, that he had a gun in it. I forced myself up off the bed just as he pulled the gun out and flipped the safety off. Haoa had him pinned against the wall and was taking deep breaths, not paying attention. I jumped at Wayne just as he raised the gun toward my brother.

I went for his gun hand. Wayne kneed Haoa out of the way, catching him at a moment of confusion, and it was him and me again, wrestling for the gun, and then it went off.

I swear that's the way it happened. The report of the gun shocked us all, sounding twice as loud in that tiny room. Then Harry was in the doorway, and so was Lui, and Haoa and Wayne both slumped down to the floor, and all I wanted to do was go home for a nice long sleep.

Chapter 43

"JESUS! GET THIS GUY OFF ME!" Haoa said. There was a gaping hole in Wayne Gallagher's chest, and he was lying on top of my brother and bleeding over everything. From then on, things started happening very fast. Somebody called an ambulance and somebody else called the police, guys whipping out cell phones all over the place. I borrowed Lui's and called Akoni at home.

"I hate to drag you out like this, brah," I said. "But I'm in a little trouble and I need your help."

I gave him the thirty-second version of what had happened and he said, "I'll call Greenberg and be there as soon as I can. Don't tell anybody anything."

I desperately wanted a beer, sedatives, something, but I knew I couldn't have anything. I was so wired I couldn't stand still, and I jumped in to help a drag queen in silvery spandex perform CPR on Wayne. We couldn't do much for him, and by the time the ambulance arrived he was dead, too much blood leaking out of the hole in his heart.

The TV crew from Lui's station arrived right on the heels of the ambulance, and the correspondent taped a segment outside the bar. They got some footage of me and the drag queen, both soaked in Wayne Gallagher's blood.

The uniforms cleared the bar except for a couple of witnesses, the owner and the bartenders grumbling about the lost business, and the place turned into a standard crime scene. The cops kept me and my brothers and Harry separated, at different tables out in the bar, until Akoni came in and took over.

"You wanted that shield. Now you're going to have to work for it," I overheard Akoni say, as he forced Alvy Greenberg to look over Wayne Gallagher's body with Doc Takayama. He looked sleepy and a little lost, and I got a perverse joy out of seeing his visible discomfort.

By 3 a.m. Doc had released the body, and the crime scene techs had finished with the little room. "This place is a mess," the bartender said, surveying the blood and fingerprint powder everywhere. "I'm not cleaning it up. I pour drinks. That's what I do. I pour drinks and I listen to drunks complain. I don't clean up nobody's blood."

They let us go a little while later. "Hell, I know where to find you," Akoni said.

Harry, Lui, and I got into the back of the van, with Haoa driving. "I'm wired," he said. "No way I'm gonna get to sleep tonight. You guys want anything?"

"I could use a cup of coffee," Lui said.

"Iced tea," Harry said.

I said, "The Denny's on Kalākaua is open twenty-four hours."

We made a quick pit stop past my apartment so that Haoa and I could change out of our blood-soaked clothes, and then parked under the Norfolk Island pine trees near the band shell and walked up to the Denny's, on the second floor overlooking the beach. A dozen other night owls were scattered around the restaurant, one tired, middle-aged Chinese waitress in a pink uniform pouring coffee. We sat at a big round table out on the terrace, and Haoa ordered the Grand Slam breakfast. I got a big piece of pie, and Harry and Lui just had drinks.

"It almost goes without saying that I appreciate what you guys did for me tonight," I said after the waitress left. "But I still want to say it. Thanks. I know Terri and Danny Gonsalves will want to thank you too. You're a bunch of heroes, every one of you, and I'm proud to be your brother and your friend."

They all looked down, not sure of what to say. The patio lights, which gave the terrace an otherworldly glow so late at night, made a low humming sound, punctuated by the occasional car passing on Kalākaua. "I never really knew what you did," Haoa said finally. "I mean, I saw the cop shows on TV and I knew your job wasn't really like that. I figured you sat around and ate donuts a lot, pushed paper, that kind of thing." He shook his head. "Man, I'm glad all I do is work with plants."

He looked up at me. "Dad said you might be coming into the business with him. I think that's cool. Maybe the two of us can work together sometime, building and landscaping." He paused. "I'd like that."

I took a big drink of ice water to ease the swelling I felt in my throat. "If that doesn't work out, I might be able to find something for you at the station," Lui said. "You can keep your cool, work under pressure. That's a good thing to have in my business."

I smiled and looked at Harry. "What about you? You got any job offers up your sleeve?"

"The only job description I've got to offer is friend," he said. "And you've been doing that for about twenty years just fine."

The waitress brought our food. Across from us, a solitary guy walked slowly along the beach, stopping to look up at the stars and listen to the waves. I thought about going surfing in a couple of hours. I said, "I appreciate what you want to do, guys, but I think now, more than ever, I just want to be a cop. Maybe it sounds goofy, but there are things wrong with the world, and somebody has to try to fix them. I'm not going to let anybody take that chance away from me, at least not without a fight."

"Think the force will take you back?" Harry asked.

"I don't know. But I'm not just going to walk away."

It's funny, but I hadn't really decided that until just then. I'd been so caught up in the task of seducing Wayne Gallagher, of putting him and Derek away, that I hadn't thought past that night. Once I did, the answer seemed clear. I was still a cop, just as I was still a surfer and I was still a gay man. It was up to me to make a unique individual out of all those identities.

Haoa and Lui made plans to return the equipment to the station the next day, and Harry and I said our good-byes and walked out together into the warm, fragrant night. "You feel good?" he asked.

"I do," I said. "First time in a long time."

"Good." We walked along in silence for a couple of minutes. Somewhere a dog barked, and a cloud passed quickly over the moon. "Your brothers were definitely squirming in the van," he said after a while. "It was kind of funny, or it would have been if we all hadn't been so damned scared. Then when Gallagher found your wire, it was like somebody shocked them with an electric poker. Haoa jumped up, knocked back his chair, and lit out for the bar. Lui and me, it took us a little longer to react." He shook his head. "I was going down that hallway and I heard the shot, and man, it just chilled my bones. I was never so glad to see anybody as I was to see you alive in there."

We stopped at Ohua so he could head mauka toward his apartment. "I'm gonna walk for a while," I said. "I'll talk to you tomorrow."

He gave me a shaka. "Take care."

I gave it right back to him. "I will. Maybe we'll get together sometime this weekend. You have any plans yet?"

"Tomorrow night, I'm having dinner with Arleen. We were going to talk about her taking some courses at UH, sharpen up her skills. Maybe she could jump up to a programming job next time. Now maybe we'll talk about job hunting. Who knows what's going to happen with the Rod and Reel Club?"

I shook my head. Once again, Harry surprised me. "Not tomorrow, then," I said with a smile. I crossed over Kalākaua and walked along the beach, listening to the gentle lap of the waves. Waikīkī almost never sleeps, but this is about as close as it comes, just before dawn, before the surfers and the early shift workers and the second-watch cops come on duty and the city starts to wake up. I hadn't been out this late in a long time, and I liked it. It was as if Waikīkī belonged to me, my private slice of paradise. You don't get many chances to slow down, pay attention to everything around you, and I wanted to take this one. I picked up a piece of crumpled newspaper and put it in the trash, listened to the night birds calling and the sound of a siren somewhere in the distance. It meant that somebody's life was falling apart out there, a fire or a rush to the hospital, an accident or a theft or maybe even a murder. That was bad. But I knew that there were people, like that little seven-year-old who watched her mother and her brothers and sisters murdered, who could find their way back. And now I knew that I could find my way back too.

We told our stories over and over again during the next couple of days, as my brother orchestrated the reports on his TV station, and those that followed on other stations and in the newspapers, to make me into the hero of the hour.

Derek was arrested in the early morning hours on Thursday, and, not surprisingly, Uncle Chin stepped forward to organize his defense. It has made things a little touchy between him and my father, but they both believe in making the necessary sacrifices for your family's sake, so I think they'll come out of it okay.

It was interesting to see how the media treated Tommy Pang and Evan Gonsalves. From "a prominent Honolulu businessman," Tommy became "a local underworld kingpin," a description I'm sure he would have relished.

Evan was officially cleared of Tommy's death, though the department stopped short of calling him a martyr. Even though there was suspicion that he had been both a snitch and a blackmailer, a plaque bearing his name was ordered for the front wall at headquarters, where people often leave memorial leis for officers killed in the line of duty.

I learned that Akoni had passed on to Peggy what Gunter had told me, that Derek and Wayne had been buying stolen Hawai'ian artifacts and shipping them through U.S. China Ship, forcing Jimmy Ah Wong to forge the paperwork. He told me she wasn't very happy that I'd been the one to break the case.

My suspension hearing was held on the Monday morning following Wayne's death. I got up early and surfed for an hour, then went home and showered. I was about to put on my one good suit when I changed my mind and decided to wear my uniform. I was a cop, after all, and if I was going to end my career, I wanted to end it in the uniform that had always made me proud.

Lieutenant Yumuri and Hiram Lin were waiting for me in that same conference room at the main station on South Beretania. Another man was there, too, a lieutenant from the Criminal Investigation Division whom I recognized but had never met.

The DA himself was at the hearing, but Peggy Kaneahe was not. The Honolulu County District Attorney is a half-Chinese man with the unlikely name of Peter Furst, and he began by announcing that because of ADA Kaneahe's personal relationship with me, she had been removed from the case. He went on to apologize to me personally, saying he had been unaware of the relationship, and that he was investigating to make sure that no department policies had been breached.

Hiram Lin beamed as if he was announcing a newborn grandson. Furst continued, "As a result of my office's investigation, I have found that it was appropriate for the department to suspend Detective Kanapa'aka while his personal involvement in the criminal investigation was reviewed." *This is it,* I thought. *The beginning of the end.*

"Further, we find that while he may have exhibited questionable judgment in the initial stages of the investigation, his practices were sound and followed department procedures."

I looked at Yumuri and, to his credit, he held my gaze for a minute before he looked away. Despite his attitudes and problems, I don't bear any grudges against him. He's a good cop and he was a good boss.

"In light of the publicity surrounding this case, and Detective Kanapa'aka's unique qualifications, an administrative decision has been made to reassign him. Lieutenant Sampson?"

He turned to the lieutenant. He was a big man, broad-shouldered, with a salt-and-pepper beard. "I'm aware of your record in Waikīkī, Detective, as well as the good things Lieutenant Yumuri has had to say about you. I've requested that you be transferred to headquarters to work as a detective in my unit."

He stood up and began to walk around the room. "Sometimes I think we're fighting a losing battle out there. The criminals come up with new crimes every day, and it seems that every new crime that passes my desk is bloodier and more violent than the one before it. We need sharp detectives more than ever."

He stopped and leaned against the round concrete column. "More is demanded of us every year. We're not just here to chase the bad guys, but to help the good guys as well. I think your," he paused for a second, "sensitivity, to people who might not get a fair shake otherwise, will be important to us, and valuable."

No one else was saying anything. "It won't be easy," Sampson said. "There'll undoubtedly be units, and individual officers, who won't think you ought to be a cop. That's a battle you've got to be prepared to fight, although I want you to know I'll be in your corner." He paused. "You may not be comfortable continuing on the force given all your recent notoriety. I wouldn't blame you if you decided it was time for a change in your life. I don't expect you to make up your mind immediately, but I'd like a response within forty-eight hours. There has been a lot of pressure to get your situation resolved, and I want to be able to relieve some of that pressure."

It was clearly my turn to talk by then. "I appreciate everything you've said, Lieutenant. You're right, there are some things I need to change in my life. But my career as a detective is not one of them. I'd be honored to work with you, and I'm prepared to return to active duty as soon as you need me."

Sampson smiled. "I needed you last week." Then his smile died. "I've discharged my weapon four times in the line of duty, Detective. I can still remember each one of those times. I was walking past the Iolani Palace two years ago when I saw a man come out of the post office with a sawed-off shotgun in his right hand. His left arm was around a woman's neck. I identified myself as a police officer and told him to drop the weapon and let the woman go." He looked at all of us. "He refused, and fired at me. I shot once and killed him."

No one in the room said anything. Finally Sampson said, "It took me quite a while to get over that, and I don't think I'll ever forget what I felt. You may not know it, Detective, but you need a few more days, especially now that this hearing is over. Think about it, and then call me."

I saluted him, and he saluted me back. I was a cop again.

Afterward, Yumuri came up to me. "I expect we'll continue to work together," he said. "You know how I feel, but I believe there's no discipline in a force unless we all agree to follow our orders. You shouldn't expect anything less than that from me or the men in my command."

"I appreciate that, sir," I said.

After the hearing, I drove up to my parents' house to tell them the news, as I had promised them. My father hadn't gone to the office; he said he'd have been too worried to concentrate on anything. "Good news?" my mother said when she opened the door.

"I got my job back." I leaned down and kissed her cheek. My father came up behind her. "They're reassigning me to downtown. But I'll still be a detective."

"I knew they wouldn't be able to let you go," my father said.

"How about some iced tea?" my mother asked. "I'll get some."

"The lieutenant who would be my new boss told me there's been a lot of pressure to resolve my situation," I said, as my father and I walked into the living room. "You wouldn't happen to know anything about that, would you?"

"Me? How would I know anything?"

I pointed to a framed picture of my father with the former mayor of Honolulu, an old friend from UH. "Just wondering."

"I may have made some calls. Most people I know are old, like me. Not much influence any more."

"Somehow I doubt that." I paused. "I do appreciate it, you know, Dad. You going out on a limb for me with your friends. I know it probably wasn't easy for you."

"I collected a few favors over the years. Once in a while I use them." He held up his hand. "Wait, wait, I know you. You want to complain. You want to do everything on your own, no help from anybody else. Well, you're not the first of my sons I had to ask a favor for."

He sat back in his chair and put his feet up on the coffee table. "Your brother Lui was not a good student, you know. He barely graduated from UH. And then he couldn't find a job. I knew he was a hard worker, just not a student. You remember my friend Milton Gardner?"

I nodded. Gardner had once owned the TV station Lui manages. "I agreed to build a family room on his house, at cost, if he'd give Lui a job. I had to do most of the work myself, nights and weekends." My father smiled. "Lui never knew about it. And if you tell him, I'll deny it."

"I know how to keep a secret."

"Yes, I know." He paused again. "You never knew Haoa was arrested, did you?"

"You mean before last week?"

"When he was seventeen, he and some of his friends from Punahou, from the football team, stole a car and went for a joyride, and crashed it. There was no question Haoa was the ringleader. Even the police could see that, from the way he acted with the other boys."

"I never knew this."

"We didn't tell anyone. I knew old Judge Fong—I used to take care of his yard, when I was a boy. I rounded up the other fathers, and we made a deal. The boys worked that summer, for free, cleaning up the beach, and the other fathers and I chipped in and bought a new car to replace the one that was destroyed." He shook his head. "It all came out all right in the end, but Judge Fong never thought the same of me."

My father smiled. "I have three sons. Each of them so different, yet each of them so much like me. Or like a part of me. You know, when I was younger, before I met your mother, I had a bad temper. Like Haoa. Chin and I used to run together. We'd get in fights, make mischief." He shook his head. "*Ai, ya,* I'm glad I grew out of that. I hope one day your brother will. And then Lui, well, Lui is the businessman in me. I knew some influential people in my time, the men who made things happen in this state. I was privileged to call a few of them my friends. Lui's the same way, with his own generation."

"And me?" I asked. "What part of you is in me?"

He smiled. "You're my dreamer. You know, when I was a boy, I used to climb up to the roof of our house and watch the stars. Just like you. And I loved to be out in nature, swimming and surfing like you."

My mother came back in then, with three glasses of iced tea on a silver tray. My father picked up his glass and raised it to me. "To you, Kimo. Keep dreaming." He and my mother smiled and we all clinked glasses. I knew he would never tell me the deal he had made on my behalf, what it had cost him in money, or work, or the regard of his fellows. The funny thing is that it didn't matter. I understood that he did these things for us as a matter of course, because he was our father, because he was the man he was.

Chapter 44

AFTER I LEFT MY PARENTS, I drove to Lui's office downtown. It was
just after five, but I knew he often stayed around until after the six
o'clock news. I signed in with the guard, who recognized me.
"Your brother's in his office," he said. "You can go right up."

"Thanks."

"Can I tell you something?" He was an older guy, haole, maybe
in his late fifties.

"Sure."

"I've got a nephew that's gay. Sweetest kid you ever want to know.
He worked for this department store on the mainland, and they fired
him when they found out. He sued the bastard, and won. Got enough
money to set up his own little store. He sells used clothes, vintage
stuff." He looked up at me. "You do your job, nobody should be able
to stop you just because of who you are."

"Thanks," I said. "Where's his store, on the mainland?"

"Sausalito. Little town just north of San Francisco."

"I know it. I ever get over there, I'll stop by."

"You do that." He smiled. "You can take the first elevator, goes
direct to the executive floor."

I found Lui in his office with the door open, and knocked on it.
"Kimo," he said. "Come on in."

I stuck out my hand to shake his, and instead he grasped me in a
big hug. I hugged him back, surprised, because it was the second
time in a week he'd hugged me.

I told him about the hearing, and that I thought our father had pulled some strings on my behalf. "I wanted to tell you I appreciate that series you ran," I said. "About gay cops. I didn't catch all of them, but I'm sure that they helped convince HPD that they weren't exactly blazing new trails."

"It wasn't easy to convince the powers that be about that one." He looked a little embarrassed. "We started out with a sensational angle. You know that's the kind of stuff we do around here."

I smiled. "I know."

"But then as the guys did the research, they found all this positive stuff. So we kind of snuck it past, and I think the viewers liked it. We actually did some pretty good numbers because of that series."

My father was right. Lui was definitely the businessman in the family. "You stuck your neck out for me," I said. "I appreciate it. If the numbers had gone the other way, you'd have been in trouble."

"TV news is ephemeral." He snapped his fingers. "You blink and the segment's over. Nobody even remembers it twenty-four hours later."

I looked around his office. One wall was filled with photos of Lui talking, shaking hands, sharing drinks with most of the movers and shakers in Honolulu. "I want you to know I appreciate everything you did for me," I said. "Everything. The series helped, but I know it took more than that for me to keep my job. Dad knows a lot of people, sure, but even he admits you know more of the people who make things happen nowadays. I'm sure you put a word or two in on my behalf." I nodded my head in the general direction of the photos.

"I might have called in a few favors."

"That must have cost you."

"Nothing I can't afford."

That night I called Akoni at home. He'd already heard, from Yumuri, the basic outline of what had happened. "Are you going to take the job?"

"I worked hard to get to homicide. I'm not going to give it up.

There are guys who aren't going to like me, but that's their problem. I've got to be who I've got to be."

"You're the first homosexual I've known." Akoni paused. "It's made me think a lot, you know. Changed my attitudes. I mean, I'm not saying I don't still have a long way to go. But it isn't even a place I ever thought of going until you—came out, I guess."

"So?"

"So I'll bet there's lots of other guys, cops and other people, too, who could start changing the way they think. That's an important job, changing the way people think."

"That's the part of the job I don't like," I said. "I'm not all that comfortable with being gay yet. I want people to think of what I can do, not who I am. I'm worried people are going to see me as the gay cop, and they'll only see the gay part, not the cop part. And that's not who I am."

"I think it is," Akoni said quietly.

"What?"

"You're not just a cop anymore, Kimo. Like it or not, you're a gay cop. True, people are going to see you that way, just like if you went to the mainland they'd see you as a Hawai'ian cop, or some kind of mixed-race cop. You better get accustomed to it."

"Maybe I should just quit the force. I could be a security guard or an insurance agent or something."

"You'd still be a gay security guard or a gay insurance agent. At least as a gay cop, you can do some good. People still like to victimize fa—I mean gays. Look at that guy your brother beat up. Just minding his own business and somebody whales on him. You could do something about that. And that gay teen center in Waikīkī. You could go there, help out. Maybe you can make it so it's not so hard to come out for some kids there."

I thought a lot about what Akoni said after we hung up. I could do good things. I could be an example, raise some consciousness, be a role model for some confused kid. But it would mean sacrificing privacy, letting myself be defined by my sexuality, opening myself up to the kind of conversations I had with the security guard at Lui's station, who wanted to talk to somebody about his gay nephew. For Christ's sake, I didn't want to be gay at all, if I could help it. It made me really uncomfortable to become the poster boy for gay life in Honolulu.

There was just too much to think about, and I had to shut it all off for a while. I surfed, and then I swam until my arms and legs felt like jelly. Then I dragged myself home and read for a couple of hours in the afternoon. Eventually I got into my truck and started to drive.

It was as if the truck was on automatic pilot, finding its way out to Wailupe on its own. I turned the volume up on an Uluwehi Guerrero CD, letting the pounding of the ipu hula take over my brain, keep it from thinking. I played with Danny for a while, hide-and-seek in the backyard, then racing him down the street until he collapsed happily. After he went to bed, Terri poured us a pair of Fire Rock Pale Ales into two tall pilsner glasses, and we sat out in the backyard under the stars.

"We're in the same situation, you know," she said. "We both have to reinvent our lives. I can't just be a housewife and mother anymore. I have to do something."

"If you need some money, I can probably give you a loan."

She laughed. "I don't need the money. My trust fund isn't huge, but I could certainly run the house on it. And my parents have already put away money for Danny's education." She shook her head. "No, I need to do something more with my life. I'm not sure what. Maybe some volunteer work at first. Or else I could go back to the cosmetics counter at Clark's."

A bank of clouds moved in front of the moon and the yard darkened. "You've got options," I said. "Options are good."

"You have them too. If this job makes you uncomfortable, then don't take it."

"Actually I kind of think that's a reason *to* take it," I said. I took a long draw on my beer and thought about what I wanted to say.

"These last couple of weeks have been really awful, you know? But at the same time they've been exciting. I mean, I remember the summer I was thirteen I was miserable, just laying around the house, sleeping like eighteen hours a day, and my whole body ached, because I was having a growth spurt. I was five feet two when school let out and I was five nine when it started again. And it was great. I wasn't the baby anymore. My basketball improved dramatically. My mother started buying my clothes in the men's department."

I had some more beer. "So even though it was miserable, in the end I was better off. Maybe this is just the next step in my growth process."

"It's funny how society labels us. You're a gay man, now, and I'm a widow. And you know, we're not the same people we were a month ago, before we had these labels. So maybe the labels change as we change. Who knows what they'll be calling us a year from now."

"To new labels," I said, clinking my glass against hers. "And to becoming new people."

That's what finally decided me. Just like sharks must keep moving to stay alive, I think we all must keep growing and changing. Sometimes that growth hurts, and sometimes you have to give up things that matter to you. My father had made sacrifices for me and my brothers, and though I'm sure they hurt him, he made it through. They made him the person he is.

My brothers had sacrificed for me, too. They had stood by me, taken chances, and given me, eventually, their unconditional love. Even men like Tico Robles were willing to take the risk that some asshole would beat them up just because they were at a gay bar.

The next morning, Derek was freed on bail and he began to spend most days with his grandfather. Aunt Mei-Mei said that the two of them spent a lot of time together, driving out to Windward Oahu and walking the long stretches of beach there.

Tim Ryan called me at home that night. He congratulated me, and we talked for a couple of minutes about the choice I had to